About the Authors

Susanna Carr has been an avid romance reader since she read her first Mills & Boon at the age of ten. She has written sexy contemporary romances for several publishers and her work has been honoured with awards for contemporary and sensual romance. Susanna Carr lives in the Pacific Northwest with her family. When she isn't writing, Susanna enjoys reading romance and connecting with readers online. Visit her website at susannacarr.com

Maisey Yates is a *New York Times* bestselling author of over one hundred romance novels. Whether she's writing strong, hard-working cowboys, dissolute princes or multigenerational family stories, she loves getting lost in fictional worlds. An avid knitter with a dangerous yarn addiction and an aversion to housework, Maisey lives with her husband and three kids in rural Oregon. Check out her website, maiseyyates.com or find her on Facebook.

A typical Piscean, award-winning *USA Today!* bestselling author, **Yvonne Lindsay**, has always preferred the stories in her head to the real world. Which makes sense since she was born in Middle Earth. Married to her blind date sweetheart and with two adult children, she spends her days crafting the stories of her heart and in her spare time she can be found with her nose firmly in someone else's book.

Dangerous Liaisons

December 2020
Desire

January 2021
Propositions

February 2021
Seduction

March 2021
Innocence

April 2021
Passion

May 2021
Secrets

Dangerous Liaisons: Secrets

SUSANNA CARR

MAISEY YATES

YVONNE LINDSAY

MILLS & BOON

First Published in Great Britain 2021
by Mills & Boon, an imprint of HarperCollins*Publishers* Ltd,
1 London Bridge Street, London, SE1 9GF

www.harpercollins.co.uk

HarperCollins*Publishers*
1st Floor, Watermarque Building,
Ringsend Road, Dublin 4, Ireland

ISBN: 978-0-263-30027-7

MIX
Paper from responsible sources
FSC™ C007454

This book is produced from independently certified FSC™ paper to ensure responsible forest management.

For more information visit: www.harpercollins.co.uk/green

Printed and bound in Spain
by CPI, Barcelona

SECRETS OF A BOLLYWOOD MARRIAGE

SUSANNA CARR

To Sarah Stubbs, with thanks for her editorial insights and support

CHAPTER ONE

TINA SHARMA STOOD at the front door of her home and closed her eyes. She inhaled deeply as she allowed the hot, fragrant breeze to waft along her skin and tug at her thin shirt. She had missed the heat of the night and the familiar scent of tropical flowers. She even longed for the chaotic noise and energy of Mumbai. Once she had thought they were out of her reach forever, but she was back and no one could keep her away.

Not even her husband.

The unexpected tears stung in the back of her eyes as a sob clawed her throat. No, she decided fiercely. She wasn't going to do this. No more crying, especially over him. She had done enough of that to last a lifetime.

Her mouth trembled and her hands shook as the unpredictable emotions balled into a fiery knot in her stomach. Anger. Hate. Fear. She needed to keep it together if she was going to walk alone and unprotected into the lion's den.

Tina's eyelashes fluttered when she heard the door swing open. She had seen the luxury cars parked in the driveway and heard the loud, pulsating *bhangra* music as she had approached the house. Now she saw the men and women dancing to the primitive beat in the main hall. There was obviously a party going on.

Was it to celebrate her absence? Would the party end abruptly once she stepped inside? Perhaps that would be best, Tina decided as she pulled her gaze away from the guests. As much as she would prefer to have witnesses, she knew they would not be on her side.

"Memsahib!" the elderly manservant declared as he stood at the threshold.

Tina flinched. She wasn't used to being greeted as a married woman. But then, she'd been a wife for less than a year. Using all of the acting skills she could muster, Tina carefully smiled and stepped inside before she was denied access. "Hello, Sandeep. You look well." She was pleased that her tone was cool and friendly when she was a jumble of nerves inside.

The old man looked over his shoulder, as if he wanted to hide the signs that a lavish party was going on in her home. "*Sahib* didn't tell me you were returning tonight."

"He doesn't know." She removed the dark blue scarf from her head and let it fall around the collar of her shirt.

"Your hair!" Sandeep exclaimed, his eyes widening in horror. He winced at his unguarded words and abruptly bowed his head.

"Yes, I know," Tina said with a sigh. She wasn't offended. She had the same reaction every time she saw her reflection in the mirror. Tina self-consciously ruffled her fingers through the short tufts. Once she'd had ebony curls cascading down her back and had managed to get an endorsement deal for her crowning glory. Now her hair barely covered her ears. "It was a mistake."

Sandeep cautiously glanced up, his gaze returning to her chopped-off tresses. "And…how was your vacation?"

Tina stilled. Vacation? Was that what Dev was calling it? Did he think she was under his spell and incapable of staying away? The hurt scored through her like a jagged knife, so swift and ferocious that she couldn't move.

Her "vacation" had been more like prison. Like hell. The memory of endless white walls, the acrid smell of disinfectant and the oppressive sense of despair washed over her. She gritted her teeth and struggled to stay in the present. "I'm glad to be back."

The servant took a few shuffling backward steps. "I'll go find *Sahib.*"

"No need." Tina raised her hand to stop him. She had the element of surprise on her side and she wasn't going to waste it. It was time to act like the mistress of the house instead of an intruder. She only needed the role for a moment and then she'd gladly discard it permanently. "I know you're busy with the party. I'll go find him. Where was the last place you saw Dev?"

Sandeep gave a guilty start and looked at his bare feet. "It's hard to say." His mumbling words were barely audible over the dance music.

Was it in the arms of a woman or two? Tina's lips twisted with bitterness. Or was it even worse than she could imagine? She almost wanted a hint of what she would see, but she wasn't going to ask. This was Dev's home and the employees had been with him for years. He had everyone's loyalty and she was the interloper. "Don't worry, I'll find him."

The manservant's shoulders sagged in defeat. He peered outside the door. "I'll have someone take your things up to your room. Where is your luggage?"

"I didn't bring any." She didn't plan to stay long.

Sandeep frowned but didn't voice the questions that were obviously going through his head. He reached out his hand, his fingers lean from decades of work. "Shall I take your purse?"

She instinctively clenched her shoulder bag closer to her body. Tina forced herself to relax. "No, thank you," she said with a smile as she strode away. Sandeep wasn't the enemy, but she wasn't letting her passport or her money out of her sight. They were essential to regain her freedom. She had learned that the hard way when she had walked away from Dev while they were on a movie location in America. Today she wouldn't even let go of the rolled-up tabloid that was stuffed at the bottom of her bag. The one with her husband's picture on the cover. That photo and the accompanying story had lit a fire in her that still burned bright.

Tina walked to the center of the large entryway and stared at the sight before her. As she inhaled the stench of alcohol, sweat and cigarette smoke, she recognized a few of the guests. They were celebrities and actors whose faces graced billboards and movie posters. They still looked gorgeous, their damp hair and clothes plastered to their skin, as they moved feverishly to the heavy beat of the drums.

She narrowed her eyes and watched as two guests competed in a drinking game at the bar. So this was how her husband had spent his days while she was away. After reading the weeks-old tabloid, it shouldn't surprise her.

Tina wondered what the occasion was for the party. It had to be about business. The moment Dev was born he had been destined to reign this world. But it was not enough to take his rightful place at the top. He was driven to succeed, conquer new territories and gain incredible power. Money was secondary to this man yet every moment of Dev's day was consumed with business.

Well, almost every moment. She had been the exception. Once she thought that the aberration meant he loved her. Now she knew differently.

Tina continued to walk through the house. She wondered if he would claim that it was her welcome-back party. He was bold enough to try. And why not? He could lie and break promises without suffering the consequences. Dev was untouchable.

But her return had been impulsive. She hadn't known that she was coming back until yesterday. Now she wondered if that had been the wrong decision. Tina bit the inside of her lip as she walked farther away from the main entrance. Her goal was to show that she was no longer vulnerable. That she was stronger than her husband could imagine.

Tina hesitated before she moved deeper into the house. Once she had felt safe and comfortable here. She had even considered it her home. Now she knew it had been an illusion. Instead of being protected, she had ultimately been stripped of her power and freedom. Her fingers flexed nervously against her purse strap as she looked around, trying to remember where the closest exit was located.

She heard a group of people clapping and chanting loudly in the direction of the billiards room. Tina pivoted and marched to the back of the house, certain that her husband would be there. With his stunning looks, raw masculinity and star power, Dev was always the center of attention.

Tina rolled her eyes when she recognized the song the men were chanting. It had been from Dev's first hit movie. She had seen it countless times but she knew her husband was privately critical of his performance in it. He wouldn't play the song unless it was a special request for someone important.

She suddenly remembered the scene also included an actress. Would he be dancing with a partner? A certain ingenue? Bile burned in her stomach at the thought, but

Tina kept moving. She needed to see this herself and not rely on other sources. She needed to know.

Tina entered the billiards room unnoticed. She was invisible in this brand-name crowd. Her crumpled tunic and baggy jeans didn't cause one head to turn. The only time the Hindi film elite noticed her was when she was on the arm of her husband.

Everyone was facing the center of the room, jumping up and down with their arms outstretched as they sang. She stumbled to a halt when she heard Dev's bold laughter. The sound pierced her heart.

He sounded…carefree. Happy. Tina staggered back as the realization hit her like a fierce blow. How could he be like this after everything that had happened? Didn't he feel anything? Or was it just a relief to him?

Tina hunched her shoulders. Perhaps it was a bad idea to return for one final confrontation. She had always suspected that she had been a burden to Dev. She'd thought they had been desperately in love, but now she realized he had felt obligated to marry her. It hadn't helped that his parents had disapproved of the match. Of her.

Who could blame them? She was not worthy of him. His parents were Bollywood legends and she was from the slums. Dev had given up his parents' grand plans and eventually he'd given up on her.

Everyone had known it was bound to happen, believing she'd tricked him into marriage. They confused her with the bad-girl roles she had in those low-budget *masala* films. Perhaps Dev did, too. It had soon become obvious that she wasn't the brazen and sexy woman of his dreams. Dev had been ready to return to his playboy ways and he wasn't going to let a wife stop him.

And she wasn't going to let him have any more power over her. Determined to get this over with, Tina took a shaky breath and plunged into the crowd. She stopped, her heart lurching when she saw Dev standing alone in the center of the circle. He held the guests captive as he performed the intricate dance step with effortless grace.

Tina's chest squeezed tight. Dev Arjun. Her first love. Her biggest mistake.

She stared breathlessly at her husband, unable to look away. Dev was lean and muscular thanks to years of training for his popular action-adventure movies. Tina shivered as she remembered how his strong and athletic build felt under her fingertips. His golden skin had been warm and rough and she had enjoyed watching his rock-hard abdomen clench as she'd teased him.

She flushed, her skin tingling, as she watched Dev finish the iconic dance, encouraging the others to follow along. Yet no one could match his confident swagger or his bold and precise moves.

As he raised his hands up like a conquering hero, Dev appeared taller than she remembered. Larger than life. Tina noticed how his dark shirt couldn't hide his broad chest and how his jeans encased his powerful thighs.

She wished she wasn't aware of how good he looked, but this was a man in the prime of his life. His strength and vitality came off him in waves. In the past she had yearned to have those powerful arms encircle her. Now she knew to keep her distance.

As his audience roared with their approval, Tina dragged her gaze to Dev's face. Only then did she notice the darker shadows and the deeper lines around his eyes. His angular features were harsh and mesmerizing. He looked older. Harder.

Dev bowed before he accepted a drink from one of his friends. He tilted his head back and her gaze locked with his. Dev froze. He held the glass midway as his eyes widened. Tina felt his shock quiver in the air.

"Tina?"

His husky question scraped at her taut nerves. She wanted to melt back into the protection of the crowd. She wanted to run. She wasn't ready for this. She wasn't ready for *him*. But it was too late.

The room went silent. She couldn't speak, couldn't move, as Dev tossed down his drink and pounced. He moved with a swiftness that stole her breath. Her throat tightened as her heart thumped against her ribs. She suddenly felt cold as her muscles locked violently.

Dev captured her in his arms and gathered her tightly against him. She was trapped. She inhaled his spicy scent and tears sprang in the corner of her eyes as their most intimate memories assailed her.

Tina had imagined how she would act when she was finally in the same room as Dev. This was not part of the plan. She was supposed to be aloof. Icy cold. Untouched. Just like he had been during the last days they were together. This was the moment when she would take back her power and make her demands.

Instead, she remained silent as he slid his large fingers through her short hair. She stared at him as he firmly tilted her head back. Her mouth trembled with anticipation. She knew he was going to claim her with a hard and possessive kiss.

No! Tina reared her head back. What was she thinking? She couldn't lower her guard. This man was dangerous. He had weakened her defenses when they first met. Had turned his back on her when she'd been at her most vulnerable.

Tina felt Dev's arms tense as his eyes flashed. Was that hurt or anger? Suddenly he swept her in his arms.

Tina cried out in alarm as she grabbed the front of his shirt. She felt helpless and off-balance. Too close. "What are you doing?"

"Don't worry, *jaan,*" he said as his crooked smile softened his harsh features. "I got you."

That was the problem! "Put me down," she ordered as she tried to get out of his hold. Dev's arms tightened around her. She was very aware of his heat and his strength.

"Not yet." She saw the gleam in his dark brown eyes as his smile grew wider. He carried her past the cheering crowd and through the door that led to the enclosed courtyard.

She craned her neck, looking around the lush garden. The fountain sprayed cold water and garlands of tiny white lights were draped on the thick bushes and trees. She heard Dev's footsteps on the stone walkway but she didn't see anyone else around.

"Put me down," she said firmly. "I don't know what you're up to, but that display was unnecessary."

Dev tilted his head. "Display? I was welcoming my wife home."

He couldn't be serious! She glanced at the top floor of their home where the bedroom was located. Panic coursed through her veins as the dark excitement curled around her chest. She was ashamed of her body's response. How could she feel this way about Dev? After all he had done to her? It was as if she was conditioned to accept his touch with unbridled enthusiasm.

"Please put me down." She had to stop this before she did something she'd regret. Tina turned and kicked out. Her movements grew wild until Dev halted and carefully set her down. She looked away as her curves grazed his hard body until her feet touched the ground. Tina immediately took a step away.

His eyes narrowed as he watched her create more distance with another cautious step. "I didn't think I would see you again," Dev admitted.

"I know," she whispered. That had been her plan.

"Where have you been?" he asked rawly.

Oh, she wasn't revealing that. That would give him far too much ammunition. "Apparently I've been on vacation for months."

Dev frowned. "What could I say?" He raked his hand through his short black hair. "I didn't know where you were or if you were coming back."

If? "I walked out. I left you. I don't know how I could have made it clearer."

He placed his hands on his hips and glared at her. She knew her words were too abrupt. Too antagonistic, but it was necessary. This wasn't a ploy or a maneuver. She had walked out of her marriage.

"Where did you go?" he said in a low voice that belied his anger.

Tina jutted her chin out with defiance. "That's none of your concern."

"How can you say that?" Dev stared at her with a dark intensity that made her shiver. "You are *my wife*. I've been looking for you."

That didn't make any sense. He had abandoned the marriage long before she'd had the courage to leave. "Why?"

"Why?" His voice cracked like a whip as the tension vibrated in the shadowy garden.

Her heart pounded in her ears but she wouldn't give him the satisfaction of seeing her nervous. Tina gave a careless shrug. "Yes, why? You got what you wanted all along. Or were you concerned that I would pop up at the most inconvenient moment?"

Dev's jaw clenched. "You have no idea what I want."

"You don't want a wife," Tina said as she held her purse tightly against her chest as if it were a shield.

Black fury darkened his eyes. "Tina—"

"And tonight," Tina said, "I'm going to grant you that wish."

CHAPTER TWO

TINA COULDN'T DRAG her gaze away from Dev. She saw the storm in his eyes but he didn't move. The air between them crackled. A tremor swept through Dev's body as he forcibly restrained his anger. "You're not thinking straight," he said hoarsely.

How many times had she heard him say that? "So you're going to do it for me? No thanks." He had tried to take over her life. And for a while he had succeeded. She had been too grief-stricken, in too much in pain, to care.

Dev closed his eyes. "I never should have taken you to Los Angeles."

"Why did you?" She refused to respond to the agony in his voice. Although she had felt too weak to travel, Dev had insisted she accompany him to the United States while he filmed several scenes for his blockbuster movie. She'd like to think Dev had been so in love with her that he couldn't imagine spending a night apart. Instead, she'd barely seen him. She had been alone and isolated. At times she'd felt like she was being punished for some unknown reason.

Dev slowly opened his eyes and glared at her. "You needed someone to look after you. You were not yourself after the miscarriage."

His gaze clashed with hers and Tina's skin went cold.

Miscarriage. He said the word with no problems but it had the power to send her into a tailspin. It still dragged her to those tense moments when the fear choked her. When she was alone, making wishes and prayers that went unanswered. When the doctors told her that she had lost her baby son.

"Not myself? How would you know?" she asked. "You weren't there. You made it very clear that you didn't want to be married anymore. That there was no longer a reason."

His breath hitched audibly in his throat. "Is that how you see it?"

Tina looked away. She didn't want to think about how Dev had no interest in her, especially after she'd lost the baby. Not now, not when the dark and confusing emotions were rolling through her. "You were the first to walk away. What else am I supposed to think?"

Dev sighed heavily and speared both hands through his hair. "I didn't walk away—you *pushed* me away. You wouldn't talk to me or look at me. You moved out of the bedroom and—"

Tina's head snapped back. "Excuse me for grieving!" she hissed. She wasn't going to allow Dev to treat her emotions as weakness. "We all can't shake it off and return to our normal life the day after the loss of our son."

"Don't." Dev took a step forward. "Hate me all you want, Tina, but don't you dare suggest that I wasn't grieving. I didn't have the luxury of hiding away from the world."

His words were like a punch to the chest. Tina flinched as she stared at him with wide eyes. "Luxury?" He made it sound as if she'd had a choice. As if she'd willingly surrendered to the grief that almost suffocated her.

Dev stared at her with a mesmerizing intensity. "You

seem healthier than you did four months ago." He looked deep into her eyes and gave a satisfied nod. "Stronger."

He had no idea, Tina realized. She could stride into the house as if she were a queen and confront her enemy with the daring of a warrior, but it was all an act. Four months ago she had been broken, but Dev's indifference had crushed her. She had tried to put the pieces back together but she didn't think she would feel whole or strong again.

"I know how to take care of myself. I've done it most of my life," Tina said. There had only been one time when she couldn't. After the miscarriage, she had wanted to lean on Dev until she got stronger. Instead, he had taken advantage of her weakness. "But I'm not here about that." She needed to get this over with so she could move on with her life.

"How do you feel now?"

Powerless. Heartbroken. Determined. "I'm ready for the next step of my life."

Dev didn't move but Tina sensed his stillness. His tension. It was as if he could predict what she was about to say.

Tina's heart started to race. It fluttered wildly against her rib cage and it hurt when she took a deep breath. "I want a divorce."

"No."

She blinked at his immediate reply. Unlike her husky words, his refusal was clear and unemotional. "What do you mean, *no?*"

"We are not getting a divorce," he announced as he took another step closer. There was a wintry cold glint in his eyes. "I will fight you every step of the way."

Tina stared at him as her confusion rolled in like dark clouds. That was not the answer she had expected. She had imagined this moment many, many times and assumed Dev would agree with a brisk, almost impatient manner. It was obvious he didn't want her anymore. Why continue this sham of a marriage?

"I'm offering something we both want," she whispered.

"I want an *explanation.* I want to know what was going through your head during those days we were in America. How do you think it made me feel walking into that hotel room and finding that the only thing waiting for me was that note?"

Tina frowned at his tone. Her brief letter had offended him. Angered him. He was lucky she had given him that much. She could have poured out her broken heart, but instead she'd simply stated that she wanted to be left alone.

"Where did you go?" he asked.

"Around. Anywhere quiet where I could think. Where you couldn't make decisions for me," she said. "I needed time to decide what I want to do next."

Dev tossed his hands up in the air as the frustration billowed from him. "You didn't have to leave to do that."

But she had. Dev had too much power. She didn't know why he'd bothered making decisions for her. At times she wondered if he had forgotten her existence. "You took over my life." Her voice trembled as she tried to keep her composure.

"I was taking care of you the best way I knew how," he said through clenched teeth.

"No, you were getting back to your old life with as little inconvenience as possible," she said. "I was no longer pregnant with your child and therefore, no longer necessary in your life."

Dev reached out and grasped her arms with his large hands. "If that's how I'd felt, I wouldn't have married you."

"You *had* to marry me. What would have happened to

your brand if you hadn't?" His family had meticulously created his brand image for years as the romantic hero. The value and power of his brand would have taken a big hit if he had abandoned his pregnant girlfriend. "So you married me to protect your career. The magazines did features about how you had settled into family life but they didn't know how eager you were to return to your bachelor days."

"That is not what happened." His fingers dug into her arms. Tina sensed he wanted to shake her.

"Really? I know what I saw when I arrived here this evening. You were having the time of your life. Tell me, how many parties have you had in the past four months?"

"I wasn't celebrating. It's part of the business. You know that."

She knew that Dev Arjun lived and breathed the mainstream Hindi film industry. It wasn't work or drudgery. He enjoyed every moment of it. Dev was more comfortable on the soundstage than in his home. And from what the gossip magazines suggested, he preferred the company of starlets over his wife. "How many women have there been?"

"I've been faithful." His eyes glittered. "Can you say the same?"

Her eyes widened with surprise. Dev thought she had found someone else? She had never considered it. She had spent the past months fighting for her life, struggling to get through the next day, the next moment. But Dev didn't know that.

Did he think she was capable of gallivanting through the world, hopping from one bed to the next? The idea made her stomach curl. The only man she had ever wanted didn't want her. The man she had fallen in love with had been in her imagination. A man who loved and adored her. A man who would lay down his life to protect his family.

That man no longer existed. She wasn't sure if he ever had. Sometimes she wondered if she fell in love with the fantasy that the Bollywood movie machine created.

Loving that Dev had given her strength but it had also been her blind spot. She had lowered her guard and had tried to lean on him when she had fallen apart. Only he hadn't been there when she'd needed him. He hadn't been there for her during their entire marriage.

She thrust out her chin. "All I'm willing to say is that I want a divorce."

His eyes narrowed as he noticed she didn't answer his question. "And my answer is still and will always be no."

"I'm going to get one," she insisted as she wrenched herself away from his hold. "But first I'm going to get my things and move out."

Tina turned on her heel and marched across the courtyard. She prayed he wouldn't follow. She didn't want to be alone with Dev in their bedroom. She would already be bombarded with too many intimate memories.

That was where Dev held the most power over her. One touch, one kiss and she was his. She squeezed her eyes shut as she tried to forget how wild she had been in their bed. He had always been in control as he guided her to a world of pleasure.

"Tina, wait," he called out to her. "We can't get a divorce…now."

Tina stopped. There was something about his sudden compromise that put her on full alert. She slowly turned around. "What are you talking about?"

He didn't meet her gaze. "I'm negotiating with a few investors. Our film company has taken a financial hit in the past few months."

Few months? It was more like a year, Tina decided. She knew Dev's parents had wanted him to marry Shreya Sen, the daughter of a beloved Bollywood family. Had that arranged marriage happened, Dev would have been the most powerful and influential person in the mainstream Hindi film industry. His legacy would have been guaranteed to last generations. But she had ruined all that.

Dev approached her. "The problem is that they think I'm a lot like the characters I play. A daredevil, reckless…"

"That's what happens when you demand to do your own stunts." She understood his need to take risks. Dev had to push himself to the limit. She knew better than to ask him to stop, even when it tore her up inside as she watched him cheat death.

"But they think being married has changed me. They think I'm more cautious." He shrugged. "If I have a stable family environment, I come across as a better investment."

She did not like where this was heading. "What does this have to do with me?"

"We need to stay married—"

"Forget it."

"—until I get the backing I need."

"I'm not doing it." Dev could find backing elsewhere. There were so many people who wanted to be part of his world and his projects. Why was this deal different?

"Think about it, Tina," he said softly as he stood in front of her. "This means a lot of money. A better divorce settlement for you."

She frowned. Why did Dev always throw money at her? It was as if he knew she was constantly worried about her finances. "I have a career of my own. I can support myself."

Dev raised his hands as if he was trying to calm her down. "You used to, but you've been away from the camera for six months."

"It doesn't matter. Mumbai makes almost a thousand movies a year. I'll find something." She sounded more confident than she felt. Her acting career had been struggling before she met Dev. Her savings were almost depleted and she needed a job as soon as possible.

"You can find a role—a good one, a career-changing one—with the right connections."

"No kidding." It was a well-known fact of the industry. She kept auditioning for roles while the children of Bollywood legends were offered starring roles without trying for them. It didn't matter if they couldn't act, dance or speak Hindi. It wasn't fair, but it was the business. Every Bollywood movie needed a big name.

"I can use my connections for you," Dev said. "If you stay in this marriage."

"No, thank you. I didn't use them while we were together and I'm not using them now." Every reporter had suggested she had married Dev for her career. Those accusations stung, but most of all, she didn't want Dev to think it was true.

"I can find a project for you that Arjun Entertainment is producing."

"So you can control my career the same way you tried to control me?" she shot back.

He gave her a thunderous look. "I can use those very connections against you, *jaan*."

Tina's mouth dropped. "What are you saying? That you will have me blacklisted?" she asked in a horrified whisper as the tears sprang in her eyes. "If I don't agree to this arrangement, you'll ruin my career?"

Dev didn't say anything.

"I need to work." Her mother and sisters relied on her salary. Directors knew she was reliable and hardworking, but none of that would matter if the Arjun family made their wishes known. "You can't do that!"

Her husband was unmoved by her pleas. "Act like a devoted wife for the next two months—until after our wedding anniversary—and I will grant you a divorce."

Dev regretted the moment those words came out of his mouth. He would never destroy the career Tina had spent most of her life building. The only time he had kept her from working was when her health had been at risk. Even then, it had been too late. They had already lost their baby boy. He would do anything to make her dreams come true, but he wasn't going to lose her like they lost their son. She should know that.

But Tina had decided he was the enemy. An obstacle she needed to overcome. Since they had married he had treated her like delicately spun glass. Had been careful not to upset his pregnant bride. Not that it had done any good. They'd still lost the baby and it had created more distance between them. It was time to change tactics.

"Why are you doing this to me?" she asked brokenly. Dev couldn't bear to see her like this, but it was nothing like the deadened look she had given him four months ago. That had scared him in a way that still gave him nightmares. "Is this because your career suffered when you married me? Is this some sort of payback?"

"I need a wife." He needed Tina. His life had always been focused sharply on his career until the moment he had seen Tina Sharma on the stage during a wedding. The woman danced like fire. Her movements were sensual and spellbinding. Fierce and elemental. It was as if she was dancing just for him. He knew he had to claim her.

Their whirlwind affair had showed no signs of slowing down. They were electrifying in bed. It still amazed him that Tina had been a virgin when they met. She knew how to make him hot and rock-hard faster than the most experienced seductress.

He'd always known that she loved him and had never questioned it until the fire inside her had snuffed out. Dev had thought maybe her love wasn't strong enough to last a lifetime. It had begun to fade and nothing he'd done had been able to stop it.

Her love couldn't have been that strong. Couldn't have been real. Perhaps it had been simply desire. Infatuation. Maybe she had been in love with the fantasy hero he had created onscreen.

When he'd seen her standing in the billiards room tonight, his first thought had been that his mind had been playing tricks. He had dreamed of Tina every night and his wishes had spilled into his waking moments. Yet this time her beautiful face was bare and her ebony hair stood up in spikes. Her wrinkled and loose clothes concealed her gentle curves. He hadn't been dreaming. She had finally returned. He'd thought this was a sign that she wanted to save their marriage. Instead she wanted to break the bond between them.

"I don't want to be your wife," Tina said.

Dev braced himself as those words pierced him. He was going to change her mind. All he needed was time and the fire that had slowly extinguished between them would burn hot and strong again. Only this time he wouldn't ignore the signs of trouble. "Play along for the next two months and I will not contest the divorce," he lied.

"Two months?" She shook her head. "That's too long."

It wasn't long *enough*. "Pretend to be a devoted, adoring wife. It shouldn't be a problem for you."

Her eyes narrowed. "What's that supposed to mean?"

He wondered now how much of the love she expressed had been genuine. If it had been real, how could he have lost it so quickly? "You're an actress. You can do it."

Tina cast him a suspicious look. "And what do you mean by devoted and adoring wife?"

"We act like a happily married couple." At this moment, he would accept the fake intimacy and forced smiles. Anything that he could build on. "There are people watching us all the time. Servants, the public, our colleagues. We can't give them any indication that we're going to get a divorce."

"Does this mean you're going to act like a devoted and adoring husband?"

He frowned. "Yes, of course." He didn't need to pretend. His conduct shouldn't be questioned. "We will share this house and a bed."

She held her hands up and took a step back. "I'm not agreeing to that."

Dev gritted his teeth. Where was the newlywed bride who had been so eager to start their married life? Where was the seductive woman who would find him at his desk in the middle of the night and drag him back to bed? "You are in no position to negotiate."

Tina bent her head and curled in her shoulders. She wrung her hands and whispered something to herself. Dev watched as she struggled to make a decision. She acted as if she was making an unpalatable deal with the devil.

She suddenly lifted her head and met his gaze. "I will stay here for two months," she said furiously. "I will act like a devoted wife if I have to, but I am not having sex with you."

"Wait until you get an offer before you reject it," he said coldly. There had been a time when she couldn't keep her hands off him. Did she hate him that much? Was this plan to regain her love impossible? "But we will need to sleep in the same bed."

"Then you'll need to sleep with one eye open," she said with false sweetness.

"Tina, nothing you say or do is going to scare me off." He leaned down until his mouth almost brushed her ear. "Or are you the one who's scared? Worried that you'll reach out for me in the middle of the night."

"No!" She jumped back as if she'd been burned. "That was before I learned that you were not the kind of husband I wanted."

And he had two months to prove to Tina that he was the only man she needed. "We need to return to our guests," he said as he reached for her hand.

She crossed her arms tightly. "I'm in no mood to party."

"I don't care." Dev continued to hold out his hand. She had finally come back into his life and he wanted her at his side. He wasn't going to give her any excuse to create more distance.

She threaded her tense fingers in her short hair and looked down at her jeans. "I need to change first."

"No." She would barricade herself into the room the first chance she got.

Tina's lips flattened into a stern line as she debated her next move. Dev was tempted to grab her hand and gather her close. Hold her tightly against him until their heartbeats were in unison and their movements were one.

"Dev?" A familiar lilting voice carried through the courtyard.

Dev swallowed back an oath when he heard Shreya Sen's voice. He watched as Tina jerked her head up. She took a step back and glared at him. "What is *she* doing here?"

"Careful, *jaan*." Dev grasped her hand. Her fingers were curled into a fist. "You are supposed to be my devoted wife."

"Devoted?" Tina exhaled sharply. "Oh, I'll give you devoted. I'll give you such a performance that you're going to wish you never made this deal."

CHAPTER THREE

"DEV, WHERE ARE YOU?" The click of Shreya's high heels announced her arrival before the woman appeared on the stone path. "I said I would act as the hostess, but that didn't mean—oh, Tina!"

"Hello, Shreya," Tina replied as calmly as she could while the anger swelled against her chest. Hostess? This woman who everyone wanted Dev to marry—his parents, the industry, the movie fans—had been the hostess in her *home?* How often had this occurred?

Tina glanced at Dev for confirmation. An explanation. He didn't look at her, and why would he with the Bollywood goddess around? Her husband had welcomed Shreya with a smile but she couldn't read his expression. Would he really be that blatant? Would he have installed his first choice of a wife in their home?

"I didn't know you were back," Shreya said as she ran her manicured fingers along her long black hair.

Liar, Tina thought with a tight smile. Shreya would have heard that Tina had made an appearance at the party. The woman not only wanted to run interference at any possible reunion, but she also wanted it to be known just how close she had become with Dev for the past few months.

Tina didn't need to hear it from Shreya. She had learned quite a lot in the rolled-up tabloid that was crammed in the bottom of her purse. The cover story had been a mix of fact and speculation, but it was the snapshots around Mumbai that had been like a dagger to the heart. How long have these two been lovers? Dev said that he had been faithful, but Tina wasn't so sure. He shared a past with Shreya and she wondered if they had reunited once he'd got rid of his wife.

Tina glared at the other woman. Shreya Sen had been voted one of the most beautiful women in the world. Tina reluctantly admitted the glamorous actress was stunning. She managed to be sexy and elegant at the same time. Tonight she wore a short and strapless red dress that accentuated her golden skin and feminine curves.

Shreya's gaze swept over Tina's casual clothes and bare face. "Nice haircut," she murmured.

Tina's hands clenched into fists and she refused to touch the short tufts. Instead she flashed a brilliant smile and curled her hand around Dev's arm. It was painful being this close to him. Once she had clung to this man, believing he loved and cherished her. Now she knew he would break her heart without a second thought, that he was doing this for a business deal.

She trembled as she rested her fingers against his muscular arm. Tina gritted her teeth when he covered her hand with his. She knew it was part of the act but she felt trapped.

"Thank you," Tina said hoarsely to Shreya as her pulse kicked hard. "It's a very popular style in America."

She felt Dev's arm tense as he looked down at her. Their gaze held and Tina realized she had just revealed where she'd been for the past few months. She needed to guard her tongue before she confessed everything.

"What do you think of my new look?" Tina prompted Dev.

"I like it," he replied, his eyes darkening as he reached up and tweaked the spiky ends between his fingertips.

He hated it. Tina knew he would but that didn't stop her. It may have been the deciding factor for such a dramatic change. She had wanted a fresh start and was prepared to shed her old self. Cutting her hair had been symbolic of the new and improved Tina Sharma. She'd regretted it the moment she had walked out of the salon.

"America?" Shreya's loud voice jarred Tina out of her daze. "Is that where you've been? People have been treating it like it's a secret."

"I wanted some privacy while I recuperated." Tina said as she rested her head against Dev's shoulder. Her throat tightened as she remembered how easy it had been in the past to make this simple gesture. "I could stay in America and not be noticed."

"Oh, Tina." Shreya clucked her tongue and shook her head. "You didn't need to go that far away. I'm sure you could walk around Mumbai undetected."

Tina took a deep breath as the cutting words found their target, like a stiletto under the ribs. She didn't need the reminder that her career was almost dead and that it had never reached the same heights as the guests at the party. "I wasn't willing to take the chance."

"Shall we go back inside?" Shreya suggested and motioned for everyone to return to the party. She was obviously unwilling to relinquish her role as the hostess.

"Yes," Dev said before Tina could make any response. He held her hand tighter against his arm as he guided her along the path. She was tempted to break free but she refused to show any clues of her crumbling marriage in front of Shreya.

As Dev and Shreya talked about one of the guests, Tina let the words wash over her. She didn't want to return to the party. She wanted to curl up in her bed and block out the world. But she knew that wasn't going to help her situation. She had hidden away for too long and lost everything in the process.

When she stepped inside the billiards room, Tina wobbled as a wave of tiredness crashed through her. She pulled away from Dev and struggled to remain standing when she wanted to rush out of the room, the house, her old life and never return.

"Stay here and I'll get you something to drink," Dev told her.

Tina sighed with frustration as she watched her husband and Shreya get swallowed up in the crowd. She didn't want a drink and she certainly didn't want to see Shreya wrapping her arm around Dev's as if they were more than just friends. She was glad it wasn't Dev who initiated the contact, but she noticed he didn't shake off Shreya's touch.

"Tina Sharma!" someone squealed over the *bhangra* music. "Where have you been?"

Tina stiffly turned around and saw two women approach her. Dread twisted her stomach and she gritted her teeth. Prisha was a choreographer and Khushi was a famous playback singer. Khushi was in high demand and did all the singing for the most popular actresses, and when Prisha was attached to a movie, it guaranteed success. Both of these women had power and influence Tina could only dream of.

"It's been a long time," Tina said as they greeted each

other with air kisses. "You both look wonderful." Once again she wished she'd had the chance to change into a party dress. Then she wouldn't look like the outsider that she was.

"Thank you. By the way," Prisha said as she placed her hand on Tina's shoulder, "I didn't have a chance to give my condolences."

Tina froze as the sudden tears stung her eyes. *No, no, no!* The grief surrounded her suddenly and threatened to pull her down. She wasn't prepared for this.

"It was such a shame," Prisha said, her insincerity shining through her eyes as she moved closer. "I couldn't believe you had miscarried so late in your pregnancy."

"It was a painful time for both of us," Tina said brokenly. She wanted to get away but she couldn't move her feet. She needed to change the subject but fragmented images flickered through her mind.

"Did the doctors figure out what went wrong?" Khushi asked.

Tina closed her eyes. She knew she would have to deal with these questions, but she wasn't prepared to share those dark moments with anyone. "No," she croaked.

Prisha gave a sympathetic pat on her shoulder. "I'm sure next time you'll be more careful."

Tina gasped as the pain radiated through her. She jerked away and glared at Prisha, hating how the other woman's eyes glittered triumphantly. How did she know that the guilt and confusion swirled around her mind at night? That she continued to question what she could have done differently to save her baby?

"She's just offering advice," Khushi said as she held her hands up in surrender. "You'll need to get pregnant again soon if you want to stay married to Dev."

Get pregnant? No, never again. She'd made that decision months ago and it broke her heart to think she wouldn't be a mother. But she refused to take another risk. She couldn't relive the fear and hopelessness. The devastation. It was a matter of survival.

Tina swiped the tip of her tongue over her lips as she struggled to maintain her composure. "What are you trying to say?"

"What everyone else is," Khushi said with a sly smile before she strolled away, arm in arm with Prisha. "That the only reason Dev married you was because you were carrying the Arjun heir."

Tina refused to watch the women leave. She stared straight ahead, the party a blur, as the anger bubbled up inside her. She had no comeback or argument. She had nothing to defend herself with because the women spoke the truth.

Tina remembered the moment she had told Dev she was pregnant. She had been uncertain how he would respond. She'd known the baby was going to change the course of his life but she hadn't expected the excitement to leap in his eyes. His wide smile and fierce embrace had told her everything she'd needed to know. His immediate marriage proposal was more than she could have ever hoped.

He was a better actor than she gave him credit for.

But no one thought she had deserved the marriage proposal. Moviegoers were furious, believing the seductress should never get the hero. Her colleagues didn't think a girl from the slums was worthy of the Arjun name. There was a hierarchy in the Hindi film industry and she had broken the rules when she'd married Dev. Some reporters and bloggers had gone so far as to suggest she'd got what she deserved when she miscarried.

She jumped, her memories scattering, when Dev

thrust a tall glass of mango juice in her hands. "You look pale," he said with a frown.

"It's from the jet lag." She didn't want him to know how fragile she felt. Couldn't, not unless she wanted him to step all over her for the next few months. "If I'd had a chance to put on some makeup and—"

"Tina!" She turned to see Dev's best friend stretch out his arms before he greeted her with a hug. "Where the hell have you been?"

"It's good to see you, too, Nikhil." And she meant it. Ordinarily, she would not have anything in common with a man like Nikhil Khanna. Born into a Bollywood dynasty, Nikhil was rich, educated and had a flair for writing screenplays. Her family had no connections and she had not finished school, yet they had quickly become friends.

"It's been too long." Nikhil held her gaze and she saw the serious glint in his eyes. "Your husband missed you."

Her stomach curled with fear. How much did Nikhil know? Did Dev confide in his friend? "And you didn't?" she asked lightly.

Nikhil gave a dramatic sigh. "You have no idea how much I missed you."

Dev brushed his friend's hand off her. "Watch it, Nikhil."

Tina glanced up at Dev. She hadn't heard her husband use that tone with Nikhil before. She was surprised at the possessiveness etched in Dev's harsh features. Tina gave a cautious look at Nikhil.

The other man didn't seem to mind as he rolled his eyes. "Now you can deal with Dev's bad temper and late-night rants against the world."

"Dev?" That didn't make sense. Her husband was known for his charisma and charm.

"Like I said, your husband missed you." Nikhil reached for her untouched drink and set it down on a nearby table. "Let's dance."

Dance? Horror snaked inside her. "No, no." She took a step away and bumped into Dev's solid body. "Not tonight."

"How can you say that?" Nikhil said over the upbeat music. "You were born to dance."

She had heard that many times throughout the years. Dancing had been her escape and her creative outlet. She was constantly aware of the music around her and had to express it through movement. Dev had once said that he thought she couldn't go through a day without dancing.

And then suddenly her body betrayed her. Failed her. Her senses had shut down. She couldn't move. Didn't feel the music inside her. It was as if her mind blocked it all out. She hadn't danced since the loss of her son.

"The only person she's going to dance with is me," Dev announced as he wrapped his arm around her waist. "But first she needs to greet a few of our guests."

Tina gave an apologetic glance to her friend as Dev dragged her away. Within minutes, her face was stiff from forcing a smile as she met with the guests. They all were part of the Hindi film industry but they were not her colleagues. Once they had been her inspiration as she watched their movies and read about them in the magazines. Now she wished she had never met them in real life. They were nothing like the heroes and heroines they played.

"Why are you friends with these people?" Tina asked as Dev escorted her to another room. She had fielded questions about her absence but no one had really missed her. They were more curious than concerned.

"Only a few of them are friends," Dev admitted, giving a nod of acknowledgment to an actor as they kept walking. "Most of our guests want something from me, and they wouldn't hesitate to stab me in the back the first chance they get."

"Then why invite them into your home?" she muttered.

"Our home, *jaan,*" he gently corrected as his fingers tightened against her waist. "This time it's because we have completed filming."

She frowned. She should've known that Dev would have immediately returned to work as if nothing had happened between them. "What project?"

His grip tightened painfully. Was it her imagination or was there a hunted look in Dev's eyes?

"It was a modern retelling of Majnu and Laila," he said tersely.

She was surprised he had chosen to do a romantic movie, especially one that followed the classic Persian love story. A romance that was more tragic than Romeo and Juliet with a poor man falling in love with a rich girl. They were forbidden to see each other and Majnu was driven mad with love. Driven mad by Laila.

"You should have seen his performance, Tina." One of the inebriated guests interrupted, looping his arms around Dev's shoulders. "It was stunning. It's like nothing you've ever seen. The grief! The pain! You could see him descend into madness."

Madness. Her breath lodged in her throat as she stared at Dev. She jerked out of his hold as if his touch burned her. She knew all about grief and madness. She had been surrounded by it. At times she thought it had engulfed her.

"I'm serious, Tina," the guest said, unaware of the maelstrom of emotions whipping between them. "It was chilling."

"I'm sure it was." She forced the words out as her chest squeezed her lungs. It hurt to breathe. To stand tall when she wanted to fold into a heap. "I'm sorry," Tina said to their guest as she pressed her hand against her head. "But my jet lag is getting worse."

"You should lie down," Dev said. "I'll come with you."

Tina ignored his outstretched hand. She was tempted to wrap her arms tightly around her body to protect herself. She didn't want Dev to touch her or be close to her.

"No need. I'll just get some water. I'll be right back," she lied as she hurried away. "Stay here."

Early next morning Dev glanced up from skimming the newspaper when he heard the chime of Tina's bangles. *Finally.* She had escaped the party last night and he wondered if she was going to hide upstairs all day.

He set down the newspaper as he waited for her to arrive at the breakfast table. Dev grimaced when he heard her hesitant footsteps. Was she considering another escape plan? That was not part of the deal. He wanted—demanded—a devoted wife and he was going to have it even if it meant he had to hunt her down and drag her to the table.

Tina appeared barefoot at the doorway, wearing a pale pink *shalwar kameez.* The tunic and drawstring pants hid her curves. She looked incredibly innocent and feminine, nothing like the seductress roles she played in her movies. But Dev knew Tina was not one or the other. She was an irresistible mix of sweet and spice.

Dev immediately stood up and pulled out a seat for her. "I expected you to sleep all morning."

She gave a little bobble of her head. "I would have but the jet lag has a strange effect on my sleep."

"And on your sense of direction?" Dev asked as he

watched her pass the chair he held out for her. "I found you sleeping in one of the guest rooms."

She dipped her head and hurriedly sat down across the table from him. "I crashed in the first bed I found."

He didn't believe it. Tina was avoiding their marriage bed again. Avoiding him. "That was not our agreement." He had gone so far as to gather her in his arms last night, intent on carrying her back to their bed. He had expected her to kick and lash out. Instead she had snuggled against his chest and given a sigh that had almost brought him to his knees. He had known he wouldn't be able to sleep next to her, not with his willpower in shreds. Dev had reluctantly returned her to her bed, tucked the sheets around her and left her in peace.

Dev sat back down as Tina added vegetables and eggs to her plate. Her eyes lit up at a serving platter that was covered with a towel. "Are those *pooris?*" she said in a whisper.

"The cook made these in honor of your return," Dev said and saw a smile curve on her lips. It was the first time since she'd arrived that he'd seen her happy. It had been even longer since he'd seen her show excitement.

She grabbed for the hot fried bread. "It feels like I haven't had these in forever."

He watched as she reverently broke the *poori* with her fingers. She inhaled the fragrant steam before she scooped up the lightly spiced potatoes with it. She popped the morsel in her mouth and her face softened. Tina closed her eyes and groaned with pleasure.

The sound stabbed at his chest. Dev's body tightened as the desire heated his blood. It took effort for him to lean back in his chair and study his wife instead of reaching for the *pooris* and feeding her. She was a sensual woman who enjoyed her food. She loved to cook as much as she loved to eat. But this was different. He was watching a homecoming.

"You missed *pooris,*" he murmured.

Tina blushed and covered her mouth with her hand. "I missed spicy food. Indian food. Good food."

She missed that more than she had missed him. "Why didn't you make it yourself?"

Tina stilled. "It's better at home."

She wasn't telling him the truth. The woman who found it satisfying to cook, who found pleasure in cooking for her loved ones, hadn't prepared a meal in months. Yet, she hadn't starved. In fact, she had regained the weight she couldn't afford to lose.

But why hadn't she cooked? Or danced? When they had socialized with their guests at the party, he had noticed that her command of the English language had greatly improved. Where had she been all this time? What had she been doing? And with whom?

Tina bent her head as if the food on her plate required all of her concentration. "Why are you at home, Dev? Shouldn't you be at work?"

He glanced at his watch. He needed to go to the Arjun Studios and decided to take Tina with him. It may be too soon to reintroduce her to work, but what if she disappeared while he was away? There had been no hint, no discussion, when she had suddenly left him in Los Angeles. He couldn't shake the feeling that she would do it again.

She wouldn't, Dev decided. Her career was too important to her and dangling his connections was just the right bait to keep her near. "I will this morning and you will come with me." He raised his hand to stop her complaint. "You want my connections? This is the best way for directors and producers to get to know you. And we have special guests waiting for us there."

"Who?" She stopped chewing and glanced up at him. The pleasure fled from her face as resignation set in. "Your parents?"

She didn't know. Dev stared into her eyes and knew she wasn't pretending. How could she not have known? It had been international news months ago. Even if she were in America she would have seen the headlines.

"No," he said gruffly. "Your family will be there."

"My family—my *mother* is at Arjun Studios?" Tina bolted from her seat. "Why? When?"

Dev thought Tina would have been happy with the news. He hadn't expected this level of panic. He had only met her family a handful of times as Tina had made an effort to keep her family away. He hadn't thought much about it until now. "What's wrong?"

She paused and bit her lip. "How did they contact you? Do they know that I'm back?"

"I contacted them. In fact, I've been in touch with them since you were missing."

She winced. "Oh, you have no idea what you've done." Tina clapped her palms against her cheeks as she began to pace. "What did you tell them?"

"What I told everyone. That you were recuperating from your miscarriage. They had no idea where you were. Why couldn't you trust your mother with the truth?" What had she been hiding that was so horrible she couldn't even tell her family?

CHAPTER FOUR

Tina bristled under Dev's question. She saw the disappointment in his eyes. He had no right to judge. She hadn't been selfish or unkind. She needed to protect herself and she wasn't going to feel guilty about her decision.

"My mother would insist that I stay married," she explained as she crossed her arms.

Dev studied her. "So you disappeared?"

Tina felt a sharp twist in her chest. "I did what was best for me." She wasn't going to feel guilty. She had taken care of her family for as long as she could remember and this time she had to protect herself.

"By shutting everyone out," Dev said with bitterness. "It's what you do best. But I didn't think you had it in you to turn your back on your family."

Tina whipped her head around and glared at her husband. "I didn't! You don't know anything about my mother or my sisters." She had made sure of that. She didn't want Dev to see the family dynamics. He would notice how she was treated differently.

"I know your mother is confused and hurt by the silence she's received for four months."

Tina rubbed her hands over her face. The secrecy had been necessary. Her mother wouldn't have been sympathetic. Reema Sharma was not just her mother, she was also her manager. It was not the ideal situation. For a while Tina had recognized that her mother's advice was not based on what was best for Tina, but what was best to support the family.

"I've kept in contact," she muttered.

Dev scoffed at her. "Paying their bills through your accountant is not staying—"

"How do you know about that?" She never discussed her salary and expenditures with Dev and she had been grateful that he had never asked. He was very traditional in his thinking that he would financially support her.

"When you first disappeared, I thought you would have returned to your mother's house," Dev said as he rose from his chair.

Tina groaned and rubbed her forehead. She tried to imagine the rich and sophisticated Dev Arjun visiting her mother's home. She was certain the entire neighborhood would have been there to meet him. And knowing Reema, she had charged for tickets. "How much money did my family get out of you?"

"I was happy to help out," Dev said with a shrug.

"You shouldn't have done it. They are *my* responsibility," Tina said. She hated how much her mother obsessed over money. Tina had been constantly told how much she had cost her mother—the dreams, the security, the husband. She knew she had been a burden on her mother and nothing she did would make up for it.

Dev glanced at his wristwatch. "We should leave for the studios," he said. "I told your mother that we would be there at nine."

Tina recognized the vintage timepiece. She had given it to him early in their affair when she had discovered he appreciated those works of art. Tina looked away as she remembered how she had teased him about his inability to be punctual when he had a collection of high-end and technology-advanced watches.

"My mother is peculiar that way." Tina couldn't shake off the dread that made her sag her shoulders and drag her feet. "When she says she'll be somewhere at nine, she really means nine."

"Let's go meet them," Dev said.

An hour later Tina sat rigidly next to her husband in the back of the luxury car. As the driver turned on a busy street, Tina clenched her hands into fists and bent her head. It had taken longer than usual for her to get ready. She was nervous about her first visit to Arjun Film Studios. He had not invited her before and Tina had been reluctant to drop by unannounced. She had always suspected he kept her away because she didn't meet up to the Arjun high standards. She knew she had to look the part as the boss's wife. Dressed in a bright yellow designer dress, stiletto heels and dark sunglasses, she looked like a Bollywood star. The ensemble was her armor, hiding her tension and uncertainty.

She glanced again at Dev. He was dressed casually in jeans and a black dress shirt. He didn't have to try hard to look like a movie star. "You don't have to be part of the reunion," she muttered.

"Is there something I should know?" Dev asked as he scrolled through the messages on his phone. "Do you not get along with your family?"

"We're fine." The driver took a turn and Tina saw the sign for the Arjun Film Studios. She studied the large modern building. "*This* is your film studio?"

"It was built a couple of years ago to meet international standards," Dev said proudly as Tina stared at the green landscape that surrounded the white building. The entrance was a tower of glass windows. "We have soundstages, recording studios and dance rehearsal halls under one roof."

All the necessities to make a Bollywood hit, Tina thought dazedly as she continued to stare at the building. The music and dancing were required for every *masala* movie. Only when she worked on a movie, her dance rehearsals were done in crowded rooms or outside in the sweltering heat.

Tina noticed the buzz of activity when she walked in the lobby with Dev. Young men and women, dressed casually in a mix of tunic shirts and jeans, were rushing around. They carried papers, cell phones and small glass cups of tea. There was a sense of urgency and creativity in the atmosphere.

Tina spotted her mother sitting on the bright blue chair among the contemporary artwork depicting famous movie scenes. Tina was surprised that tears pricked her eyes when she saw Reema Sharma. Her mother's long black braid was streaked liberally with gray hair and red henna. Her white embroidered *dupatta* slipped over her shoulders and her dark blue *shalwar kameez* strained against her voluptuous curves.

"Amma!" Tina said in greeting as she stood in front of her mother. Inhaling the floral scent that she always associated with the older woman, Tina bowed down and touched her mother's foot with respect.

"I hate your hair," Reema said as she pulled a spiky tuft. "What were you thinking? No one is going to hire you when you look like a boy."

"She could never be confused for a boy," Dev drawled as he greeted her mother.

Tina rose to her full height and glanced at Dev. She felt a pull deep in her belly when she saw the gleam of desire in his eyes. She blushed and hurriedly looked away.

How could he look at her like that, when he had seen her at her very worst? No amount of makeup or gloss could erase those moments when her eyes had been dulled, her hair lank and her face colorless.

What was she thinking? She didn't want Dev to desire her anymore. To look at her with such intensity that her stomach would clutch with anticipation. She needed to keep her distance.

"Would you like a tour?" Dev asked.

"Yes!" Reema said enthusiastically.

"Where are Rani and Meera?" Tina asked as they walked. She was very aware of Dev beside her. Tina didn't like the way he towered over her. It made her feel small and delicate.

"I told your sisters that I needed to speak to you alone," Reema said as she straightened her *dupatta*. "It's a shame that they're missing this. Do you think we'll meet any stars?"

"They will be working," Tina said. She didn't point out that her sisters didn't care about the Hindi film industry. They had other interests and goals, something her starstruck mother couldn't understand.

"Yes, but we will be with the boss," Reema reminded her. She glanced at Dev and then back at Tina. "We can always talk later, when we're alone."

"I'm her husband," he reminded his mother-in-law. "You can say anything in front of me."

That didn't mean a lot to Reema Sharma. She wasn't impressed with Dev's good looks or his male charm. Tina couldn't remember the last time her mother had said anything complimentary about a man. Her mother didn't like, respect or trust men. Not since the day her husband had deserted her with three young daughters.

"Is everything all right?" Tina asked as they walked

through the crowded corridor. When her mother wanted to talk, it was usually about money. Reema was always worried about when Tina was going to get her next role and her next paycheck.

"You tell me." Her mother's voice rose. "Where have you been?"

Tina pressed her lips together. She knew she couldn't tell her mother. Couldn't tell anyone. She glanced at Dev and fear pulsed through her veins in response to his intent look. It was as if he was waiting for her to reveal her deepest, darkest secrets. "I was in California."

"Hollywood?" Reema's eyes lit up. "Did you meet anyone famous? Anyone in the movie business?"

"There was a television director," Tina said, remembering the anxious woman who chain-smoked and drank coffee constantly. "I had lunch with her several times."

"That's good!" her mother said as they walked past several offices. "Did she want to hire you?"

Tina shrugged. "There was some talk about it." She didn't think the director had been serious, which was fine for Tina. She couldn't imagine moving away from Mumbai. It was her home.

"That's it? One director?" Reema asked. "You were gone for so long."

She decided to stick with Dev's vague answer. "I was recuperating," Tina said, ignoring Dev's curious gaze.

"For four months?" Reema shook her head. "That's not recuperating. That's retiring."

"It doesn't matter," she promised with a firm smile. "I'm back."

"It matters," her mother insisted and began to tick off a list with her fingers. "You haven't worked for six months and no one is sending you scripts. Moviegoers have forgotten about you. Your fans turned against you once they decided you were the seductress who tricked Dev into marriage. And your endorsement deals are going to dry up the minute they see your hair."

"I'll find something." Tina tried to sound positive but she was beginning to wonder if she had underestimated the challenges that lay ahead. She couldn't show any concern, especially in front of Dev. If he knew how much she needed his Bollywood contacts, he could dangle the promise in front of her to make her behave for the next few months.

"Here is one of the makeup rooms," Dev said as he guided through an open door. "We have over twenty of them for the main actors."

Tina halted at the threshold while her mother investigated. She had never seen such a luxurious makeup room. It was colorful and cheerful, with red chairs and sofas, small tables and a day bed. This was where the actors went between breaks and it offered everything from a plasma television to a fully stocked refrigerator.

"Look, Tina!" Reema said as she stepped outside of the attached bathroom. "The sinks have hot *and* cold water."

Dev frowned. "What do your makeup rooms usually look like, Tina?"

Tina hesitated to tell her husband. She was a working actress, not a star like him. She wasn't offered these perks.

"Makeup rooms?" her mother said with a laugh. "She's lucky if she gets to share a makeup room with the junior artists and backup dancers. Can we see one of the soundstages?"

"Of course," Dev said as he guided them out. "We also have a gymnasium, lounge and executive dining room for the artists and senior technicians."

"Ooh!" Reema clasped her hands. "Tina, one of these days you'll have to take me into the dining room. I might see a Khan or a Kapoor."

"I don't think I will be allowed in," Tina said. She understood the hierarchy in the Hindi film industry. "They are for the main actors."

"You are married to an Arjun," Dev said. "You will not eat with the production staff in the cafeteria or canteen."

Tina flinched at Dev's tone. It made it sound as if her hasty marriage had been her greatest career achievement. Didn't he notice that she didn't beg to work with him or use his name? She knew a lot of people thought she had trapped him into marriage out of ambition, but she didn't want him to believe it. His opinion meant more than anyone's.

"You need to get back to work right away. I knew getting pregnant was going to ruin your career." Reema gave a huff of exasperation.

Tina squeezed her eyes shut. She remembered the argument she'd had with her mother when she announced she was pregnant. It had brought up some old secrets and fresh wounds. Tina had always known she wasn't the son her father had wished for, but she didn't know that her mother had seriously considered sending her to an orphanage when she was a child.

Her infant son had not been planned, but Tina never thought of it as an inconvenience. "I wanted the baby more than I wanted to be a Bollywood actress." Her voice shook with emotion.

"And what happened? You lost both." Reema tossed her hands up in the air in surrender.

Dev cupped his hand on Tina's shoulder. This time her instinct wasn't to shake him off. Her tense muscles began to relax under the comforting weight.

"You should have gone straight back to work. Dev did." Reema gestured at him with reluctant admiration. "He didn't miss a step. You, however, took a prolonged vacation."

"I insisted that she take some time off," Dev said.

Tina went very still. She wasn't prepared for Dev to take the blame. She didn't need his help. Not anymore.

Reema stopped in the middle of the busy corridor and her eyes widened with horror. "Why would you suggest that? Tina's acting roles were getting smaller and her responsibilities to our family were getting bigger."

"You remember what she was like after the miscarriage." Dev's voice grew colder. "She was grieving."

"She would have snapped out of it sooner if she hadn't taken an extended break from work. The gap between movies isn't going to be easy to overcome," Reema decided. "I knew she shouldn't have married."

Dev's eyebrow rose from that statement. "What do you mean?"

"The moment an actress marries, her career is over. It wasn't too long ago when an actress had to hide the fact that she was married."

"Amma, please," she whispered. She was used to these sweeping statements but she couldn't withstand another fresh wave of guilt. She knew all about how her mother had had to give up her Bollywood dreams because she had gotten pregnant and had to marry.

"You can't just take off work." She turned to Dev and explained. "I have a family to clothe and feed. We need to pay for her sister Rani to complete her education. And her sister Meera is getting married to an engineer with a good family. I don't need to tell you how important her dowry is."

"And you expect Tina to pay for all of this?"

Tina felt Dev's gaze on her and gave a nod. She was the oldest child and the duty to provide had been placed on her at a young age. Once she'd wished she could have gone to school with her sisters, but that had been a luxury she couldn't afford.

"Of course," Reema said. "I always knew Tina was our way of getting out of the slums. Considering all of the beauty pageants, talent shows and modeling assignments we went through, I had expected Tina to earn more by now. I admit she's not a great actress, but plenty of Bollywood stars get by on their looks."

"I will pay for her sister's wedding," Dev announced. "And her dowry."

Dev's words gave Tina a jolt and she stared at him. "What are you doing?" she whispered fiercely. "That's not necessary."

He ignored her as he spoke to her mother. "And if you need anything, anything at all, contact my assistant."

"Why would you do that?" Reema asked as she gave him an assessing look. "This is between Tina and me."

"I don't want Tina under any stress," he explained. "She's recuperating."

"Still?" Reema said in a squawk. She turned and looked at her daughter with disappointment. "Tina, I did not raise you to be so weak."

Tina didn't respond. She knew the hopelessness she had slipped into was not her fault, and yet, she wondered why she broke so easily. She knew how to fight and push through to get what she wanted. Nothing came easy for her. After the miscarriage, she had fought so hard to feel normal but it hadn't worked.

"Tina is not weak," Dev said in a growl. "She won't let me take care of her, but I will take care of this."

Reema pursed her lips as if she was weighing her options. "Thank you, Dev. It's the least you could do since you kept Tina from working. I hope you won't interfere with her career in the future."

"Amma, you and my sisters are a priority," she vowed. Her mother still wanted total control over her career and had been furious when Dev had taken over. But that was going to change. Tina needed to start the process of removing her mother as her manager and taking more responsibility in her career. "I can still take care of everyone."

"From the looks of it, you can't even take care of yourself." Reema sighed. "And you need to do something about your appearance—"

"And here's the soundstage," Dev said as they approached the open elephant door. Tina heard the crew talking over the buzz of electrical tools and the pounding of hammers. She stepped inside and her mouth dropped open. The soundstage was huge but she was even more impressed with the electrical catwalks and lighting grids. Everything was top-of-the-line.

"Tina," Reema said in a hushed whisper. "Do you feel that?"

Tina slowly nodded.

"Feel what?" Dev asked.

"The soundstage is air-conditioned." Reema sighed. "Tina, you need to work for an Arjun Entertainment production."

Never. She couldn't be financially dependent on Dev. He was already too controlling, too powerful. "So I can work in air-conditioning?" she mused.

"Don't forget the executive dining room," Reema said. "And if you're lucky, he might throw in a spot boy."

Tina rolled her eyes. "I don't need one." She didn't have a spot boy to hold an umbrella over her when it was raining or supply her with a steady stream of tea. She could take care of herself.

She glanced at Dev and tensed when she noticed his growing look of outrage. "Are you telling me that while you were pregnant, you didn't have a place to rest, an air-conditioned soundstage or an assistant to look after you?"

"Of course not, Dev." It was only then that she realized Dev had taken many of the perks he received for granted. "My name is not above the title in a movie."

"I will not tolerate this!" Dev said in a growl. "From now on, I will make sure you have all the amenities you need when you are working."

Reema smiled and linked her arm with his. "Now, Dev. This is something we can agree on. Let's talk."

An hour later, Dev sensed Tina leaning back in her seat as she surveyed the atrium of the Arjun Film Studios. She drank her rapidly cooling tea while he sat next to her, checking his emails. The atrium reminded him a lot of their courtyard and it seemed out of place in the modern studio building. It was cool and peaceful, especially now that Tina's mother had left once she realized she wasn't going to see any movie stars.

He knew Tina had been embarrassed when Reema had negotiated to have Dev's driver take her home. She had made a production of how she would take the bus, or splurge and get a rickshaw. Tina had tried to stop it, but neither woman understood that he wouldn't allow a female to travel alone. Tina would soon discover that her mother and sisters would have a full-time driver by the end of the day.

"Why are you playing the attentive brother-in-law all of a sudden?" Tina asked angrily. "What possessed you to offer to pay for my sister's wedding?"

"I will take care of her expenses." He didn't know why this was an issue. He was wealthy and could afford it. "You don't have to worry about it anymore."

Tina crossed her arms and looked away. "Why would you do that? And don't say it's because she's family because we know that's not going to be true in two months," Tina reminded him. "I don't want to be indebted to you."

The anger flared hot in his chest. "It's not like that." Why couldn't she accept his help? What would it take for Tina to trust him again?

The cooing of a baby echoed in the atrium. Dev's heart gave a vicious twist as he felt the color drain from his face. His gaze darted to Tina. The tension pulled at the corner of her mouth and she closed her eyes.

When was it going to stop hurting? Dev wondered. When would he stop bracing himself when he saw a baby on a TV commercial or when a stroller came near him like it was right now?

He saw Shanti, a famous Bollywood legend who had dominated the silver screen a decade ago, walk over to their table holding a bundle in her arms. The baby squealed as the chubby hands pumped with delight. Grief washed over him and he fought to breathe. He barely noticed the nanny following behind with a stroller, as his full attention was on the baby.

Normally he would have risen from his seat when a woman or an elder entered the room, but he couldn't move. He knew Shanti had privately struggled with infertility for years while she played the motherly roles. She'd had her first child a few months ago and she wanted to share her joy with the world.

Dev flinched when he felt Tina's hand on his. She gave his fingers a squeeze before she stood up and fixed a smile on her mouth.

"Shantiji!" Tina greeted the star as she rose from her seat. "Congratulations on your daughter. I'm so happy for you."

Tina was shielding him. Taking charge until he was prepared. He should be the strong one, but this time Tina was looking out for him. It humbled him.

Shanti's smile was radiant. "Thank you. I hope it's all right that I brought Anjali here today," she said as she watched Dev. "I have to go dub some of my dialogue but I couldn't bring myself to leave her alone."

"It's not a problem," he said gruffly as he forced himself to stand. His gaze collided with the baby's big brown eyes. Anjali frowned and stuffed her fingers in her mouth.

"She's beautiful," Tina murmured.

"Would you like to hold her?" Shanti asked.

He felt the wave of tension crash through Tina. It mirrored his own. He knew his wife wanted to decline but she couldn't find the words. Before he knew it, Shanti transferred Anjali into Tina's arms.

Dev's throat tightened as he saw Tina hold Anjali carefully in the crook of her arm. It shouldn't hurt this much to see his wife hold a baby. Watching Tina blink back the tears shouldn't make him feel weak and impotent.

Dev wrapped his arm around her waist as he inhaled the baby's scent. It was agony. He wanted Tina to lean on him but she stood ramrod-straight. Together they could get through this.

Anjali's mouth turned down. Dev had no doubt the baby felt their pain. Sensed the sadness they tried to hide. Suddenly the baby started to cry. The sound pierced through the quiet atrium.

Tina tried to soothe the girl but it only seemed to make the baby cry more. Her movements became more frantic.

Dev rubbed Tina's back, wishing he could stroke the tension from her body. If only he could make a joke or a lighthearted comment, but his mind was blank.

"I think she wants her mother," Tina decided as she handed the infant back to Shanti. The movie star held her baby close and murmured a few words as the baby cried. Shanti reached into the stroller and pulled out a toy rattle.

Dev stiffened as he dropped his hand from Tina's back. The brightly colored rattle was the same as the one he had bought in anticipation for their child. It had been the first toy of many.

The baby's cries faded and Dev thought his knees were going to buckle. Tina reached for Dev's hand and laced her fingers with his. She held on tight as she silently offered her support.

"I'm sorry about this," Shanti said as she waved the rattle to distract her daughter. "Anjali is usually content and happy."

Dev barely heard Tina's response. He fought hard to hold back the dark emotions that threatened to consume him. It felt like an eternity before Shanti carried her baby out of the atrium. His shoulders sagged once the door clanged shut and the infant's cries retreated.

"She shouldn't have made you hold the baby," Dev said in a low rasp as he gripped Tina's hand harder.

"It's all right." Tina's voice was soft as she returned to their table. "She wanted to share her happiness."

Dev shook his head. He couldn't forgive the other woman's thoughtlessness. "Her daughter was due the same time as our son. Shanti knew this. She knew about the miscarriage."

Tina didn't look at him. "Maybe she thought we were over it."

The words were like a punch in the chest. "Over it?" he said in a harsh whisper.

"Look at how our family acts about the miscarriage," Tina pointed out as she sat back down in her chair. "My sisters never offered their condolences or visited me in the hospital. Your parents don't speak about our son. It's as if he has been forgotten."

"I don't want to forget our son." Their son had never gotten a chance to be born but Dev would always love him.

"I'm not going to forget, either." Tina's hands fluttered against her eyes as she brushed away a wayward tear. "I want to honor him in some way."

"*We* will," Dev said hoarsely.

She gave a sharp nod and took a deep breath. Dev knew the signs. Tina didn't want to talk about it anymore. He was tempted to keep talking, consider ways they could honor their son, but he knew he wasn't feeling strong enough for the both of them.

"Until then," she said briskly, "I need to find some work."

Dev rubbed his hands over his face. He wanted to tell her that she didn't have to work, and that she didn't have to take the first role that was offered. But he knew whatever he said would be taken the wrong way.

Now he understood why Tina was driven to work. It wasn't ambition; it was duty. She had taken whatever was offered and made the best out of it. And she would accept any role, any assignment, despite the fact that she wasn't healthy enough to work. He had to keep that from happening since she wouldn't take care of herself.

"You should take your time and consider your options," he told Tina. "The pressure can be intense. I know what it's like. I'm the only child and have to continue the

Arjun dynasty. There was a great deal of pressure from my parents to perform to their expectations. If I had failed…" He shuddered at the thought of it.

"But you didn't," Tina argued. "You exceed expectations every time. Your parents have almost always been proud of you."

Almost. He caught the word. His parents had not been happy with his choice of wife and they didn't hide their opinion. No matter what she did or how she behaved, they disapproved of Tina.

"I'm surprised they weren't at your party," she muttered.

"You really don't know, do you?" he said in a whisper.

Tina stiffened and turned sharply to meet his gaze. "Know what?"

He wasn't sure if he should tell her. He may have decided he wasn't going to treat her like a fading flower, but he wasn't sure how Tina was going to handle the news. "My father died."

Tina's lips parted in shock. "How? When?"

"Four months ago."

She slowly shook her head as if she was trying to make sense of it. "Four…" Tina closed her eyes and swallowed hard. "When?"

"The week after you walked out."

CHAPTER FIVE

"DEV...I'M SO SORRY." She flattened her hand against her chest. Her heart was pounding from the news. She felt shaky and off-balance. "I didn't know."

"It made the international news."

She heard the disbelief in his tone. "I wasn't following the news at that time," Tina explained. She didn't want to tell him that she'd had no access to the television or computer. No magazines or newspapers. The lack of media had been surprisingly helpful.

"The commemorations lasted for weeks. There's going to be another one at an award ceremony soon."

He probably thought she was heartless because she hadn't rushed to his side. She hadn't been there in his time of need. Dev didn't rely on anyone but she knew he'd had a complicated relationship with his father. That would make the loss even harder to bear. "What happened?"

"He had a heart attack and died instantly," Dev said.

Tina closed her eyes as the guilt slammed into her. "How is your mother doing?"

"She's fine and back at work," he said. Tina noticed how he spoke in short, choppy sentences. It was clear he didn't want to talk about it. "She's in London doing a movie."

Tina stared at Dev with incomprehension. What was it with the Arjun family? They didn't grieve or stumble; they kept working. They were like machines.

Or was this how Dev had learned to grieve? She had judged him for returning to work right away. For not showing his grief like she did. She didn't consider that this was how he coped. Dev didn't weep or stay in bed for days. He lost himself in his work. "She couldn't possibly be fine. She was married to your father for over thirty years!"

"Despite the fact that my parents were one of Bollywood's legendary lovers on film, their marriage wasn't a love match. It was a business arrangement. They led separate lives and rarely stayed in the same house together."

"Still..." she protested weakly. Tina had sensed that Gauri and her husband, Vikram, were more of a partnership than a couple. They had worked together to build the Arjun brand instead of the Arjun family. And yet they had managed to stay together. In contrast, Tina had been deeply in love with Dev and their marriage had fallen apart within a year.

"They were indifferent to each other," Dev said. "My mother reacted to my father's death as if he had been a colleague instead of a husband."

Tina shook her head. Dev hadn't been allowed to grieve with his mother. He hadn't been able to turn to his wife in his hour of need. How did he manage to meet every challenge head-on without breaking? "Wait, this means that you're in charge of Arjun Entertainment."

Dev nodded and gave a quick glance at his watch. "And I'm very late for a meeting. I'll have the driver take you home."

"And this is why it's so important to get the investors," she said softly as she rose from her seat. "The industry isn't too sure about having a daredevil in charge of one of the largest media companies."

Dev cast a suspicious glance at her. "They will soon realize that they have no reason to be concerned."

"As long as you can show that you have a stable family life." The deal he had offered her suddenly made sense. "Kind of hard to do that with a missing wife. My sudden appearance has made things very easy for you."

Dev reached out and curled his finger under her chin. Her skin tingled as he guided her to look directly at him. Dev was close—too close—as he leaned forward. His gaze dipped to her mouth and her lips stung with awareness.

"Whatever you're planning," he said softly. His gaze was focused on her mouth. "Don't."

She pursed her lips. "I have no idea what you're talking about."

"Remember the agreement," he said as he dragged his thumb along the curve of her lip. "I want—I expect—a devoted wife."

Tina frowned. Did he think she had the power to hurt him? That was laughable.

Dev's harsh features darkened and he abruptly dropped his hand. "I have several meetings and I'm late. I will see you at home tonight. Be good."

Maybe she was reading the signs incorrectly, Tina thought as she watched him walk away. She could have sworn she had seen the longing in his eyes and felt the tremor in his hand. Dev didn't really want her as a wife, but he still desired her.

And after everything that had happened between them, Tina was ashamed that she still yearned for his touch. She hoped he would never figure that out. If that happened, she would be powerless against him.

* * *

"Dev? What are you doing here?"

Dev glanced up from his computer and saw Nikhil standing in the doorway to his office. He had just noticed that it was dark outside and the office suite was quiet. Everyone had gone home. "What are you talking about? This is my office now."

He glanced around. He had always associated his father with this room. It was ostentatious with the oversize glass desk and the expensive gold conference table. The garish movie posters were splotches of color on the white walls.

"Tina returned home," his friend reminded him as he stepped into the office. "You should be with her."

Dev gestured at his computer screen. "I have work to do." It was where he wanted to be. He was in charge. He knew what he was doing. This was the only place where he felt in control.

He was fighting back some very elemental feelings when he was with Tina. He couldn't stop staring at her, remembering how she tasted and how she felt in his arms. He wanted to drag her to their bed and claim her in the most basic way.

But Tina didn't want him. Didn't want him anywhere near her. He had failed her and their baby and she didn't want to be his wife anymore.

He felt his friend's gaze on him. "What?" Dev asked sharply.

Nikhil hesitated for a moment before he strode to the desk. "I don't know what happened between you and Tina."

Dev tensed. If Nikhil noticed the cracks in his marriage, then the problems were so strong that he couldn't hide it any longer. He was a fool to think he could salvage this marriage, but he wasn't going to give up. Not yet.

"Nothing happened." Dev gave a warning look but Nikhil ignored it.

"That's not true. You've lost a baby. Your father. And pretty soon you're going to lose a wife."

Dev slowly rose from his seat. Nikhil was his friend but he had crossed a line. "You have no right—"

Nikhil crossed his arms. "Where did you and Tina go for your honeymoon?"

Dev frowned from the sudden change of topic. "We didn't. I had to work on a movie." It didn't matter that they didn't take time off to go on a honeymoon. When they were together, their surroundings had faded into the background.

"And where were you when Tina miscarried?" Nikhil asked.

Dev closed his eyes as the guilt swelled inside him. Tina had been alone and she hadn't been able to reach him. She had tried to put on a brave face when he'd finally reached the hospital, but he had seen the tracks of tears on her cheeks and the despair in her eyes. "On the set."

"Of another movie," his friend added. "And where were you when Tina was recuperating?"

In another country. Dev slapped his hands on the desk and leaned forward. "She doesn't need me hovering over her. She's told me that."

"And you agreed? That's not like you, Dev."

It wasn't. Before they got married, he'd wanted to help her in every way he could. She had declined, obviously uncomfortable with his offers. Now he wondered if it had anything to do with him. Tina wasn't used to having someone there for her. Someone who wanted to give without expecting anything in return.

"Nikhil, I don't have time to argue about this. You may think that I'm ignoring Tina but I have been a good husband."

"Seriously?" his friend said with a chuckle. "Dev, you're a great actor. You're a good friend and from what I've seen, a dutiful son. But when it comes to being a husband, you are the worst."

Dev flinched. "That's not true. I give her everything she needs." His friend didn't understand that his home was a battlefield. Tina had pushed him away every time he'd tried to take care of her.

But he hadn't been enough for her. Dev looked down at his hands splayed on the glass desk. When he'd arrived at the hospital and found that Tina had miscarried, Dev had never felt so impotent, so afraid. He had watched Tina fall into a dark place where he had been unable to reach her. He could achieve anything when he set his mind to it, but he hadn't been able to help Tina or save their baby.

Dev bent his head as he remembered one doctor asking about the support system Tina received at home. Dev had assured the doctor that he had provided Tina with everything she needed: the best medical care, a safe environment and servants at her beck and call.

But *he* had not been there. He loved Tina and had been excited about the baby, but he had felt as if nothing more should be expected from him. He had already gone beyond expectations by proposing marriage.

Dev glanced up to see Nikhil watching him with a knowing look. "Don't you have somewhere else you need to be?" Dev asked.

Nikhil tilted his head. "Don't you, *yaar?*"

Tina sat at her makeup table that evening and took another look at her closet. It was filled with her clothes, shoes and accessories. Untouched, as if waiting for her. Just like the small crystal figurine of a dancer she loved so much. It still sat on her bedside table, catching the light.

It was like that throughout the house. Tina had expected Dev would have thrown out her stuff or at least boxed it. She'd thought he would get rid of any reminder of her.

She looked down and stared at the bottles and pots on the makeup table. She reached for her new tube of lotion and dabbed a little on her wrist before smoothing it on her skin. Why had he kept her possessions in the house? Was it to prevent the servants from talking or was it simply that he didn't notice them?

Or was it something much worse? All this time she thought Dev had been indifferent. Had she gotten it all wrong?

Tina jumped when Dev's hand snaked around her as he reached for the tube of lotion.

"Dev!" She glanced at her reflection in the mirror. Dev stood behind her with a stern expression as he read the label on the tube. Her gaze traveled from his hair, damp from a shower, to the dark emotions swirling in his eyes. His golden skin captured her attention. She watched as a few water droplets meandered down his bare chest. Her gaze continued to travel down. Tina shifted in her seat as she noticed the way his blue drawstring pants hung low on his lean hips.

"Please give that back," she said quietly as her cheeks became mottled with red. She couldn't remember what the label explained. She hoped it didn't give too much away.

"What is this for?"

Tina turned around and stood up. She took the lotion

from his hands and set it on her table, desperately controlling the urge to hide it. "Does it matter?"

Dev placed his hands on his lean hips. "It might."

His words set her on full alert and she gave him a cautious look from underneath her lashes. Was he fishing for information or did he know more than she realized? "The less you know about a woman's beauty routine, the better."

He snatched her hand and turned it over before she could protest. Pushing the sleeve of her white *shalwar kameez,* he exposed the slender welts that crisscrossed her wrist.

Tina curled her fingers into her palm but she couldn't hide the marks from Dev. She never wanted him to see the scars. They were a symbol, a reminder, of what she had been capable of when she was at her weakest.

"I noticed the marks last night when you were sleeping." He skimmed his fingertips along the ridges. "I never saw these because you hid them under your bangles."

His gentle touch made her shiver. She stared at his large fingers against her small wrists. Compared to his strength, she seemed fragile. Her marred skin only emphasized his perfection.

She tried to pull away but Dev wouldn't let her go. "I don't…cut anymore," she promised.

"When did you start?" he asked as he continued to caress her wrist. "And why did you do it in the first place?"

"When we were in Los Angeles," she admitted. She wasn't ready to explain why. She didn't quite understand it herself. All she knew was that she had wanted to release the pain that had been howling inside her.

"Why didn't you tell me?"

Because she had been ashamed. Horrified. And yet she hadn't been able to stop. She had felt compelled to hurt herself and watch the blood collect on her skin. "It looks bad now but I was recommended a cream that will make the scars fade."

She felt the sudden, angry tension in his touch. "I'm not worried about the scars," he said in a low hiss. "My concern is that you felt the need to hide this from me."

Tina yanked from his grasp. "I don't cut anymore," she repeated and she heard the defensiveness in her voice. "They are old scars and they didn't get infected."

"The next time you feel like doing this, you tell me," he ordered.

"There won't be a next time," she said as she walked away from him.

"How do you know?" he asked as he followed closely.

"Because I don't feel the need to do it," she explained as she entered the bedroom.

"That's not enough of an answer for me," Dev said. He cupped her shoulders with his large hands and turned her around so she had to face him. "Don't make promises you can't keep."

Tina ignored the way his hands seemed to leave an imprint through her thin tunic. She refused to acknowledge how close he stood. "Don't treat me as if I'm fragile. I can take care of myself and my family."

"You don't need to when I'm around," he announced.

"Is that why you came home so early?"

He gestured at the clock next to the bed. "It's almost midnight."

"I know." This was when the nightlife was starting and the ideal time for Dev as he tried to make deals and bring his colleagues to his club. "Everything okay at work?"

"I dropped out of my next movie," he said, unable to meet her eyes, "and I'm taking a leave of absence."

"*What?*" She snapped her jaw shut. "Why?"

He dropped his hands from her shoulders. "Because my devoted wife has returned home and I want to spend more time with my family."

"That may be your press release," she said as she marched to the side of her bed. "But what's the real reason?"

"You had complained that I was never there in our marriage. Now you're complaining that I'm taking time off to be with you?"

"I want to be left alone!" Tina grabbed her pillow and tossed it on the floor. "You became so overprotective after the miscarriage. I don't want to live like that anymore!"

Dev wasn't listening. "What are you doing?" he asked as he gestured at the floor.

She glanced at the white sheets and pillow on the floor. It wasn't going to be as comfortable as the oversized bed, but she wasn't going to get any rest if she slept next to Dev. "You made it clear that you wanted to sleep in the same room. I'm honoring my side of the bargain."

"What is that?" he asked as he approached her side of the bed.

"Haven't you seen this before? What am I saying?" she muttered. "You led a charmed life. This is a bed pallet."

"No, that is a couple of sheets and a pillow on the floor."

"In my family, it's called a bed," she explained patiently. "This is what I slept on all the time when I was a child."

He swiped up the pillow and threw it back next to his. "This was not our agreement."

She held up her hand to stop him from lecturing her. "You're worried about the servants knowing. They won't because it's so easy to pick this up and—*what is wrong with you?*" she shrieked as he lifted her in his arms and dumped her onto the mattress.

"You will go to great lengths to stay out of my bed." The anger vibrated in his low voice as he crawled onto the mattress and knelt between her sprawled legs. He planted his hands next to her shoulders before she could roll away. "Where was this reluctance when we met?"

She felt the blush crawl up from her chest and neck before it flooded her cheeks. "That was before I knew what kind of man you really are!" She should have known Dev would taunt her with her wanton behavior. Back then, she had been eager to discover a sensual paradise with Dev. She wished it was easier to resist him now, but she knew the pleasure she could find in his arms. It had been unlike anything she'd ever experienced and her body craved for his touch. Craved for him.

"Let me tell you what kind of man I am." Dev's voice was low and raspy as he leaned down until his face was right above hers. "I'm not known for my patience. I expect others to honor their word."

"And yet you can break your promise with no consequences?" Like the pledge he'd made almost a year ago to love her. Be there for her.

"I am also a man who hasn't slept with his wife for over four months."

Her muscles locked and her chest squeezed violently when she saw the hard glint of lust in his eyes. "I'm not having sex with you. We—"

"What are you so afraid of?" he asked.

Her stomach twisted with dark excitement. She knew not to push the issue about sleeping in the same bed and yet she had been reckless. She needed to appear cold and disinterested. This was a man who had never wanted to be her husband. What self-respecting woman would tumble back into bed with a man who had been indifferent to her during their marriage?

"I'm not afraid." Her voice sounded strangled in her tight throat.

"Liar. You're afraid that you'll submit to me. You're afraid it won't be long before you surrender. How little time it will take before I'm buried deep inside you." His voice cracked as lust deepened the lines in his face. "Do you want to find out, *jaan?*"

Tina stared at him as the blood rushed through her veins. He surrounded her and she felt as jittery as a wild bird ready to escape from her cage. Dev always had this effect on her. She hated the power he had over her but at the same time she wanted it.

Her hands itched to explore his bare chest and his masculine scent was distracting. Her *shalwar kameez* offered little protection from his body heat. It suddenly felt scratchy and confining. She wanted it off. She wanted Dev to remove it, slowly, reverently, as he kissed the skin he revealed.

Dev stared into her eyes and his mouth lifted in a crooked smile. "I already know the answer, Tina. Do you?"

CHAPTER SIX

TINA NERVOUSLY LICKED her mouth with the tip of her tongue. Dev watched the movement with an intensity that took her breath away. Stark need pulsed through her veins.

She didn't want to answer Dev. If she lied, he would prove her wrong. If she answered truthfully, he would demonstrate the accuracy of her guess. He needed to learn that she would pretend to be a devoted wife but he could not expect total submission.

But if she got out of bed, would he follow her? Her heart pounded wildly as she imagined his pursuit. She rocked her hips and the ache between her legs intensified. Tina bit her lip and Dev's eyes glittered with knowing.

He knew what she was resisting. He knew exactly how to touch her, how to please her. Dev would ruthlessly use that knowledge and she wouldn't put up much of a fight. He would strip her of her pride well before he stripped off her clothes.

"Yes," she said.

His harsh features sharpened, his skin pulled tight. His carnal look matched the primal need inside her. She sensed the tension coiling inside him as if he was going to pounce.

Tina suddenly realized that her reply sounded like a

request. A whispered plea. As if she wanted him to stay exactly where he was. She cleared her throat. "Yes, the answer is never."

He lowered his head as if he were in a trance.

"Did you hear me, Dev?" Her voice was edged with desperation. "It's not going to happen." She pushed at his shoulders ineffectively, careful not to slide her hand along the sprinkle of curls against his warm and muscular chest. "The only reason I'm in this bed is to fulfill an agreement."

He closed his eyes and she saw the fine tremor sweeping through his body. She felt his struggle before he opened his eyes. His gaze was dull and she wasn't quite sure if he saw her. He was focused on the battle within.

"I heard you," he said gruffly as he rolled onto his back and lay next to her. His movements were stiff and he sounded almost disappointed with her decision.

Tina quickly turned away from Dev and clutched onto the edge of the mattress. She bent her legs and curled into a protective position. She felt hot and her body throbbed for his touch. How was she going to resist him—resist every temptation—like this every night for the next two months?

She couldn't. She would have to play the waiting game. Once Dev fell asleep, she would slide out of bed and make a pallet. She'd remove all evidence that she slept on the floor before anyone woke up. Dev would never know.

The sag of the mattress was Tina's only warning before Dev curled up next to her, his arm lying heavy against her abdomen. Her legs jerked and she was primed to leap out of the bed. It took all of her self-control to remain still.

"What are you doing?" she asked as she felt his erection pressing against her.

"Not having sex."

"I made my choice, Dev." She tried to shove her elbow in his stomach, but he didn't budge. "I'm not about to change my mind."

"About the sex? I believe it," he said drowsily. "About staying in bed? You're going to creep out of it like a thief the minute I fall asleep."

"So you're going to hold on to me all night long?" Tina wasn't sure why she sounded surprised. Dev had always gathered her in his arms while they slept. Back then, the sweet gesture made her feel cherished. Now it felt like imprisonment.

His embrace tightened with warning. "Go to sleep."

"How can I?" she complained.

Dev's large hand slid along the curve of her hip. "I know one technique that always left you soft, warm and sleepy."

She shivered as she remembered how he would drag out the pleasure until her skin was bathed with sweat. Her muscles would be straining, her lungs ready to burst as her heart thumped wildly against her rib cage. She would beg, plead and threaten him if he didn't sink deep into her body. With each measured thrust, he had created a roaring fire that had consumed her.

"Cold?" he taunted, his mouth close to her ear. "Is that why you're wearing this old thing?" Dev pulled at her white cotton tunic.

"No." She had difficulty getting the word out of her mouth.

"Your negligees are still in the closet." Dev crushed the fabric in his fist.

"I know." She had avoided the lace and silk slips on

purpose. She had also tried to ignore another section of her closet. "So are my maternity clothes."

Dev's pause was almost tangible. He seemed momentarily at a loss. As if he hadn't expected her to mention the baby. Tina didn't move when his hand slid along her flat stomach. "I didn't want to get rid of those," he confessed. "Of anything."

Tina felt the tears well up. She blinked rapidly as her nose and throat stung. "Why not?" she whispered.

"Why would I?" He continued to stroke her stomach and the tender caress lulled her. "I knew you would be back."

"All of those clothes hold bad memories." It wasn't quite true. She had been so excited about the baby. Every milestone had been cause for celebration. She'd bought those maternity clothes in anticipation of her ever-changing body. She'd never had a chance to wear some of them.

"There were a few good memories," he said calmly as his hand moved higher. "I remember the silk nightgown you wore on our wedding night."

Tina shook her head. She knew he was trying to distract her from thinking about the unused maternity wear, but that nightgown represented her naïveté. She had carefully chosen the white silk, believing the night represented hope and eternal love.

"I'm never wearing that again," she vowed. "Tomorrow I'm stuffing it in the garbage."

His hand spanned her ribs, just under her breast. "You'll wear it if I ask you."

She scoffed. "In your dreams."

His mouth rested against her ear. "You're not wearing anything in my dreams."

Tina clenched her jaw. "Go to sleep, Dev."

"Good night, *jaan*." She felt him flex his tense fingers

before he reluctantly removed his hand. "Do you want me to keep the light on? Are you still having nightmares?"

"No," she admitted. Those bad dreams after her miscarriage had been so terrifying they had ripped her out of a deep sleep with a scream on her lips. She hated that Dev had witnessed her fears. "I haven't had one for a while."

"Good," he said with satisfaction as he reached for the lamp and turned off the lights. The room was plunged into darkness. "But if you do, don't hesitate to wake me up."

She frowned at his offer. "What good is that going to do?"

He rested his hand on her head. Her scalp tingled and she was very aware of how exposed she felt without her long hair. "I'll chase your demons away, Tina."

She wished that were true, but she'd learned the hard way that he wouldn't be there when she needed him.

Dev watched the sun rising as he held Tina in his arms. It had taken her hours before she had fallen asleep. When her tense muscles had gradually relaxed, it had felt like a hard-won victory.

Tina had always been a restless sleeper but it had never bothered him. It had felt like she was searching for him even in her sleep. Tonight she had reached for him, muttering something indecipherable and quieted down when her hand touched his skin.

Now she was curled up tight against his chest. This was the closest they'd been since they'd lost their son. A sigh shuddered through him. Tina had slowly drifted away and it had gotten worse in the last days before she disappeared.

She was stronger now. He missed her long hair, the way it would fan across the pillow, fall down like a veil when she was on top of him, and how he could wrap it around his hand and hold her still. But he didn't mourn the loss. He wanted to sigh with relief at the sparkle in her eyes and the color in her cheeks. He wanted to swing her in his arms every time she fought back.

It almost hurt holding her like this. It reminded him of how things used to be. Holding Tina, touching her, loving her, had been a privilege he had taken for granted. He missed this intimacy. He missed Tina.

Did she miss him? He didn't think so. The only reason she'd come back was to ask for a divorce. He was surprised she'd asked for it in person. He had expected to get a call from his lawyer as the days dragged on.

But he was going to fight this divorce. Remind her of how good it used to be and that it could be that way again. But first she had to trust him. Forgive him for failing her. He didn't think that was going to happen in the next two months.

Tina stood excitedly at the tiny stall on the corner of the dusty street. The honking horns and the overlapping conversations were the sounds of her childhood. The scent of spices in the air mingling with the odor of garbage was familiar.

She straightened the *dupatta* that covered her short hair and looked around the old neighborhood. The day was wet with humidity and everyone moved slowly. A bright-blue rickshaw kept together with duct tape seemed to shuffle past. The handbag vendor had patches of sweat on his white *kurta shalwar* while haggling with a group of young women in jewel-colored saris.

"I can't believe you chew *paan*." Dev shook his head with disgust as he settled his sunglasses on the bridge of his nose. He leaned against the colorfully painted street cart as small cars and motorcycles drove by. "What would your mother say?"

"That it has no nutritional value and it's going to ruin my teeth." Tina had heard that lecture many times. She glanced up at Dev. "That makes it taste even better."

His slanted smile made her pulse skip hard. She abruptly looked away and watched the *paan walla*'s red-stained hands. The man layered coconut and spices on a bright green betel leaf before he wrapped it into a tight bundle. "My mouth is watering," she confessed to Dev.

"Want to know what whets my appetite?"

She blushed at the heavy innuendo in his tone. "You should keep your voice down," Tina said in English, casting a quick look at the *walla*'s face. He didn't seem to recognize what she said or who she was. "It was named one of the most recognizable voices in Bollywood."

"I believe it was the sexiest voice in Bollywood," he replied in English.

"My mistake." He had also been named sexiest actor every year, which wasn't hard to believe. Dev Arjun was charming, athletic and possessed a sex appeal that wasn't manufactured. He was gorgeous without even trying.

She gave a quick glance at him. For the past two weeks, Dev had stopped shaving. The dark stubble didn't soften his chiseled jawline or diminish his masculine beauty. If anything, it gave a reckless edge to his dark looks. The indigo-blue *kurta shalwar* he wore skimmed his athletic body. She tried not to notice. Dev Arjun looked debonair in a tuxedo and sexy in jeans and a T-shirt, but Tina always thought her husband was stunning when he wore the long tunic and drawstring pants.

"I thought we were in this neighborhood because you wanted to get *chaat*," Dev said.

"I want that, too." For months she'd eaten only for

sustenance, for fuel. Nothing had tasted good and it had been a chore at every meal to spoon the food into her mouth. Yet it was different since she had returned to Mumbai. She noticed the toasted warmth of cumin or the bite of cayenne wafting in the air and needed to taste it. Experience it.

"Are you sure you don't want to go to a restaurant?" Dev said as he placed a protective arm on the small of her back as a barefoot child with spindly arms and legs ran past them. "There's a really good one on the other side of Mumbai."

Other side. She knew he really meant to say *the good side*. The glittery and elite world where he ruled. The exclusive neighborhoods that she still couldn't enter if she didn't have the Arjun name and clout behind her.

"Those restaurants are not authentic. They make appetizers and snacks that are inspired by *chaat,*" she declared with her nose in the air. "You have to get *chaat* from the streets. Tell me you've eaten something from these *wallas* at some point in your life."

He shook his head. "My family considered it unhygienic."

"That just adds to the taste," she teased him. "I can't believe you haven't been to a bazaar or eaten street food. You need to see more of Mumbai."

"I was born and raised here," he reminded her.

"Not *my* Mumbai." She flashed a smile of thanks to the *paan walla* as she accepted the stuffed beetle leaf that lay on a small square of tin foil. As Dev paid with rupees, Tina tucked the treat in her mouth, resting it between her teeth and the inside of her cheek. She tilted her head back and moaned. "Ah, now that tastes like home."

Dev looked away abruptly. As if he couldn't stand the sight of her. Her stomach twisted and suddenly she wanted to spit out the *paan*. "Are you sure you don't want to get one of your own?" she asked.

"I'm sure." His words were clipped with anger. "Let's go find some *chaat*."

Tina hated his mercurial mood. He had never acted like that before and yet it was happening constantly in the past two weeks. Just when she thought they had found a truce, it slipped away. It was like dark storm clouds rolling in suddenly and blocking out the sun.

She also noticed that he hadn't touched her in two weeks. The briefest touch and flirty banter teased her, had her waiting for his next move, but nothing happened. He didn't hold her through the night or swoop in for a kiss.

She was glad about that. Just thrilled. Tina always knew that this day would come, when he no longer found her attractive. It was bound to happen. She may not have a hold on his senses, but he would never know how weak she was for him.

"*Aloo tikki* sounds good, doesn't it?" she asked with determined brightness. "I've always had a weakness for potatoes. Ooh, no. Forget that. What about *panipuri?*" Her hands fluttered in front of her mouth as she thought about the crispy treat that was filled with spicy water. "I haven't had that for ages."

"You could have had that months ago if you had returned home with me."

Tina decided to ignore that comment. "We should move faster before someone recognizes us. And unless you want to start a mob, stop giving money to the beggars."

"I don't know what you're talking about." Dev's attention was straight ahead as they navigated the busy sidewalk.

"You keep slipping rupees to anyone who asks," she said. "They're going to follow and ask for more. And the other beggars will see that you're a soft touch and it's going to get out of hand."

"It's okay, Tina. I can always get more. I just..." He snapped his mouth shut and gave a shrug. "I can't help it."

"I know." Dev didn't know what it was like to go hungry or worry about money, but she could tell how much it upset him to see the suffering. He had always refrained from asking her what it had been like to live in extreme poverty. Tina was grateful for that. She wanted to protect him from the ugly truth.

"Oh, look." She grabbed his arm and pointed at the magazine racks in front of a DVD store. "Movie magazines!"

"I know you love reading these rags, but you can't believe everything they say," he warned.

"I read these all the time when I was trying to break into the business." She turned the carousel until she found the weekly magazine she had always enjoyed. She gasped when she saw an old picture of herself on the cover. "Bollywood's Bad Girl?" she read the headline.

"That reminds me," Dev said as he watched her flip through the magazine to find the story, "how did your meetings go with your agent?"

She winced. "I don't want to talk about it." If there had been any good or promising news, Tina would have immediately shared the information with Dev. It was difficult to share the disappointing news with someone who had the Midas touch.

"It couldn't be that bad."

"Yes, it could." Tina paused and glanced up at Dev.

"The shampoo company dropped me from my endorsement deal because of my haircut."

He nodded as if he wasn't surprised. "I'm sure they had a clause about you changing your appearance without their permission."

"And I lost out on a role," she admitted as her shoulders slumped. "One of the Kapoors got it. I should have known. The director is a cousin."

Dev hesitated. "You know, Arjun Entertainment…"

She immediately straightened her shoulders back and continuing flipping through the magazine pages. "Thank you, Dev, but I can't work for you."

"But you can work for my competitors?"

His sharp tone compelled her to look up. Dev's frustration poured from him like billowing heat. "I hadn't thought of it that way."

"Actresses marry producers and media moguls all the time in Mumbai," Dev continued. "And when it happens, the actress only works for her husband's film company."

"Which is usually what the actress is hoping for all along. I didn't marry you for my career." He didn't understand. She couldn't—wouldn't—be financially dependent on him. He had displayed enough power over her life.

An emotion chased across Dev's face that Tina couldn't define. "Why—"

"Oh, here's the article!" she said, desperate to change the topic before another argument began. "*Huh.* Apparently, I have risen from the dead."

Dev scowled. "You don't want to read that. Nothing good comes from hearing the gossip about yourself."

"It says here that Bollywood's Bad Girl went wild in America. Drinking, drugs and dating countless men."

She made a face. "I'm surprised they didn't add an arrest record or a homemade sex video to the lies."

"That's not funny." His fierce expression sent a shiver down her spine.

She reached out and patted his arm. "According to this, one insider source thought you got the Bollywood mafia to whack me. There's something here about numerous sources suggesting that Shreya Sen was behind my disappearance." She frowned. "And how she got the last laugh because..."

Dev snatched the magazine from her hand. "These magazines are full of lies," he declared as he stuffed it back into the rack.

She stared at him. She wanted to grab the magazine and read the last paragraph again. There was no way that could be true. Dev wouldn't do that to her. Would he?

"Shreya Sen was the leading lady in your film?" She stumbled over the words as the anger and hurt shredded through her. "You are playing star-crossed lovers with the woman you were supposed to marry?"

"Calm down, Tina."

The fury built up inside her with ferocious speed. For one scary moment she thought that she was really on the brink of losing total control. "You know what, Dev? Forget our agreement," she said in a deceptively cool tone.

"Your career—"

"Is dead. Just like this marriage." The hurt swelled inside her like gaping wound. "But I might garner some interest with my dead career. Give that magazine a tell-all story."

Dev watched her cautiously, as if he was trying to determine her mood. "You wouldn't do that."

"I'll let them know just how the most popular action hero—the favorite romantic hero—tried to blacklist me in Bollywood. I can't wait to see how your investors will respond to that cover story!"

Dev's eyes held an unholy glow. "Be very careful, Tina. I'm about to call your bluff."

"This is no bluff." She took a step forward. "I've seen your worst and I survived it. You haven't seen what I'm capable of doing."

CHAPTER SEVEN

DEV WATCHED AS Tina stormed into the house and marched up the stairs. Her anger had not waned since they'd left the bazaar. Nothing he said on the way back home had seemed to pierce the cloud of fury that had surrounded her.

How could she think he preferred Shreya? Wasn't it obvious that Tina held him spellbound? It had been torment the past two weeks to refrain from touching her. Kissing her. He couldn't stop staring at her lips, remembering how they felt and tasted. He didn't want any other woman. He wanted his wife.

"Do you need anything, *Sahib?*" Sandeep asked as he closed the door.

Patience, Dev decided. Because he had officially run out of it.

He shook his head. "No, thank you, Sandeep. Any calls?" He hoped there was urgent business back at the office. Something that would require him to leave. Distract him.

Dev frowned. How often had he done that? Gone to work instead of confronting a problem head-on at home? Work came easily to him but relationships were a minefield he had yet to master. Maybe Nikhil was right. He wasn't a good husband.

"Yes, one message," Sandeep said. He glanced upstairs and lowered his voice. "Shreya Sen called."

Dev exhaled slowly. Even the old manservant knew how Tina felt about Shreya. Everyone had noticed but him. He should have picked up on the clues. He hadn't considered Shreya a threat to his marriage until now.

She had been a colleague and a family friend. She often called for advice. Two years ago his family had started discussions with hers about an arranged marriage. Dev hadn't been enthusiastic about the idea but the union made sense. And then he had met Tina.

The marriage talks had stalled and then broken down completely. His parents thought he was rebelling. Shreya had thought they both needed one last fling before they settled down. But he had found something with Tina that he hadn't thought existed. He had found love that didn't hinge on his box office success. He had a private life. A world that wasn't designed by publicity or the film industry.

He had allowed the fantasy of a family life to slip through his fingers. Now he had a chance to get it back and he was going to hold on tighter. Somehow he was going to get Tina to love him again. Only this time, the love would be stronger and wouldn't shatter at the first sign of trouble.

"Sahib?" Sandeep said. "Would you like for me to get Miss Sen on the phone?"

"No, that won't be necessary." Dev raked his fingers through his hair. "From now on, if Shreya calls, I'm not here."

Sandeep smiled with approval and bobbed his head side to side. "Yes, *Sahib*."

Dev strode up the stairs and went straight to the bedroom. He was going to convince Tina once and for all that he hadn't slept with Shreya.

He paused when he looked around the bedroom. She wasn't there. He heard the scrape of the clothes hangers and immediately went to her walk-in closet. He followed the trail of her sandals that looked like they had been kicked off violently. Her *dupatta* was balled up in the corner.

He stood at the threshold, his heart stopping for one aching moment, when he saw Tina scooping up her clothes and throwing them into a suitcase. She was leaving. Again. She didn't believe him. Didn't trust him. Why did he think he could regain that trust?

"Don't you think you're overreacting?" Dev drawled as he held back the rising panic.

Tina didn't look at him. She didn't answer. She acted as if he wasn't there.

"I will not accept the silent treatment, *jaan,*" he warned. He'd had enough of being shut out. "I'd rather have you shout at me and tell me what's on your mind than ignore me."

"Fine," she said. "When I got married to you, I was seen as the obstacle that kept you and Shreya apart. I was the villainess in the story. The seductress that stole you from everyone's favorite heroine," Tina said as she tossed a shoe in the suitcase. "While I was gone, you take the role of a man who goes mad because he can't have the woman he loves. That woman being Shreya." She threw the other shoe with more force. "You want me to ignore the gossip, but it's a little hard when everyone knows you handpicked Shreya to play Laila!"

"Those were creative and marketing decisions. It wasn't personal." People thought it was his finest performance as he played a man who was heartbroken and descending into madness because he couldn't be with the woman he loved. He hadn't been thinking about Shreya when he played the role. He had been thinking of Tina, who had spurned him and had disappeared from his life.

"Really? It wasn't personal." She walked to her makeup table and yanked open a drawer. She pulled out a rolled-up magazine and tossed it at him. He caught it by reflex. "Then how do you explain this?"

He unrolled the magazine. The headline read Dev and Shreya: Together at Last! and promised pictures of their rekindled romance. "Where did you get this?"

"In America. I had found an Indian grocery market and went in there to get snacks. I found that instead." She picked up the hairbrush from the table and threw it savagely into the suitcase. "Those pictures are not of two colleagues at work. That was in front of our home during the night."

"I did not have an affair with her. I have never had sex with Shreya and I have no interest in her. I was faithful to you." But the pictures were damning. He wasn't sure when they had been taken. Shreya had used one of the guest rooms on one occasion as they worked together on their roles. "You got this in America?"

She placed her hands on her hips. "Yes, why?"

"That's why you came home." Would she have returned if she'd thought he had been pining away for her? Would she have felt the need for one final confrontation if she hadn't seen this tabloid?

He threw the magazine on the floor and approached her. She took a step back and bumped against the wall. Dev grabbed her wrists and held her arms above her head. "Not because I was worried sick about you. Not because your family missed you. It's because of those lies!"

"I'm just supposed to believe you?" Tina thrust out

her chin as her eyes glittered with defiance. "Shreya wants you."

"No, she doesn't. Shreya is secretly dating a married director." Dev had to wonder if Shreya had encouraged the stories about a possible love affair to keep the reporters off the scent of the real story.

"You tried to hide the fact that she was your leading lady," Tina pointed out. "Anything else you're not telling me?"

"No," he said as he leaned into her. His muscles clenched as her soft body cradled him. "Shreya is no threat to this marriage. I have nothing to hide. I haven't done anything wrong."

"Nothing to hide? Then tell me, was Shreya your first pick as a wife?"

"Yes, but—"

"Then you met me and got me pregnant," she said harshly. "I put an end to those plans. Or at least a temporary hold."

And marrying her had been the best thing that had ever happened to him. "So you're going to walk now? Sabotage your future because you believe a tabloid story over your husband's words?"

"It took me by surprise." Her voice rose. "I'm not jealous or anything."

Dev hadn't seen her like this. She had dealt with overly familiar starlets at parties and zealous fans who wanted to sleep with him. His wife had always handled these situations with a sophisticated ease. Tina must know he was under her sensual spell. He didn't want anyone but her and he thought he had proved it every day.

"Fine, Dev. You win," she said in a growl. "I will stay for the remaining six weeks, but I have a few demands."

He slowly let go of her wrists and watched her intently.

What was she up to now? "You are in no position to make demands."

"When we are in public, you need to make it very clear that you are besotted with me." She glared at him. "Why are you smiling?"

"Am I?" He set his mouth in a firm line. Tina was staking her claim. He liked it. He liked knowing that she was protecting what she felt was hers. She hadn't done it that boldly before. Had he mistaken her silence for confidence instead of uncertainty? Did she think she didn't have a right to make a claim? That he would have rejected it?

"I'm serious, Dev." She crossed her arms and leaned forward. "You want to prove to your investors that you have a stable family life? Don't let them think you're having an extramarital affair."

Dev rubbed his hand over his chin, hiding the smile that wanted to break through. Tina was going to be so angry when she discovered that there were no investors. That he had foreign investor groups who were clamoring to work with him since they had discovered Bollywood made billions.

"Do you think I'm going to respond to threats?" he asked silkily.

She rested her head on the wall and sighed as if the fight was leaving her. "Can you at least act like I was your one and only choice for a wife?"

"Yeah, I can do that," he said in a husky whisper. He wished he had shown it earlier and more often. If he had, maybe he wouldn't have made Tina feel unwanted. "But I want something else in return."

She looked at him with suspicion. "What?"

"Tell me where you went after you left me in Los Angeles." He needed to know. He was sure he wasn't going to like the answer, but the not knowing was killing him. "And who replaced me during those months?"

Tina hesitated. She didn't have to tell him. She knew that Shreya wasn't a threat to her marriage. That she never had been. It seemed incredible that the ingenue would choose another man over Dev.

Tina wanted to keep her secret. She was afraid to tell her husband where she had been. It could be used as ammunition.

"Why are you so quick to assume that I was with another man?" she asked. His accusation bothered her. Did he think she was like the bad girls she played on screen?

"Why were you so quick to think I've been with Shreya all this time?" he countered.

Tina flattened her hand against her chest. "I'm not the one with the playboy reputation. I'm not the one who's been caught with photographic evidence. And I was a virgin when I met you."

She saw the possessive gleam in his eye and it made her skin flush. He loved the fact that he was her first and made no secret about it. But now the idea that he may not be her only lover had shaken him.

"You may have been a virgin, but you were not innocent." His gaze drifted to her mouth. He leaned forward and then stopped, catching himself before he kissed her. "You knew how to drive me wild that first time. And once you had a taste of pleasure, you were insatiable."

She blushed. "So what?" She couldn't let him know just how much his touch affected her. How she became almost obsessed with him and his body.

He clenched his jaw and a muscle bunched in his cheek. "There is no way you would have been celibate while we were apart," he decided. "You are too sensual and too passionate to have slept alone."

"That's your evidence? You are using the way I respond to you as proof that I can't be faithful? Where is the logic in that?" she asked angrily. She had given herself freely to him and he was using it against her.

Dev's eyes darkened. "How do I know you wouldn't respond like that to all your lovers?"

All? "Did you ever think that I'm only that way with you?" she said in a hiss. "That I don't feel that way about another man? Why would I take another lover to my bed when I could have you?"

His lips tilted into a slow, sexy smile. Dev's eyes glowed with interest as he flattened his hands on the wall above her head, caging her in. "Tell me more."

"Shut up." She shouldn't have revealed that. He was already arrogant and cocky. Now he knew just how much she wanted him. How much she had always wanted him.

"You walked out on me," Dev said and closed his eyes. "What better way to get back at me than to sleep with another man? Any man would do."

She had walked away because she loved a man who saw her as an obligation. She had felt betrayed and discarded. She had thought the man she trusted didn't care about her at all. Yet the idea of getting back at him by sleeping around had never occurred to her.

"I wasn't thinking of revenge. I was in survival mode."

Dev raised an eyebrow. "Are you telling me you weren't tempted at all?"

"I wasn't looking! And even if I was, there wasn't a great pool of candidates where I was staying."

"And where was that?"

Tina covered her face with her hands before she blurted out the truth. "At a treatment center. For the past four months I've been staying in a psychiatric facility for depression."

The beat of silence stretched until her nerves twanged. She didn't want to see Dev's expression. The judgment in his eyes. The triumph that he could use this against her.

"Why didn't you tell me?" he asked, his voice laced with anger. "Why did you feel the need to hide that?"

"Because I didn't know if you would help me or use the information against me."

"I had been trying to help you."

She wanted to believe that but he had taken some actions that she couldn't understand. She dragged her hands down her face and caught his gaze. "You made decisions about my career and my finances without discussing it with me. You sent me to doctors who wanted to drug me."

Dev dipped his head. "I was taking any advice I could get. I had been concerned about you and I wanted immediate results. Any time I tried to discuss a problem with you, you shut me out. It was as if you didn't know what was going on around you. When you disappeared, I was out of my mind with worry."

"I'm sorry I worried you. I admit that part of it was to punish you. Part of it was to get away." She had been angry and hurt, striking out the only way she could. "I'm sorry for everything. I'm sorry you had to marry me because of the baby. I'm sorry that my body couldn't protect our baby."

"It's not your fault," he said. "We don't know why it happened."

She scoffed and looked away. "I feel like I failed. That my body failed."

"No, Tina. I am the one who failed," he admitted. "I should have been there for you and the baby. I wasn't because I didn't…I focused on the wrong thing. I was too busy providing for you and creating an empire for my son."

"You had to work," she said. "I know how competitive this business is—"

"That is no excuse," he insisted. "And after the miscarriage, I overcompensated."

"There was nothing you could do to intervene," Tina said. "Nothing could have saved our son."

"I couldn't save the baby, but I could have saved you. You were so frail and lost. But you made it clear that it was too little, too late."

"I needed you," she insisted. "I just wanted you there. That's all you had to do." She still needed him. She was always going to have that shadow of fear, wondering if the depression would return. Wondering if she would have to go through hell like she had for the past four months. She had already made the decision that she wouldn't have children to avoid it happening again, but what if that wasn't enough?

Dev curled his finger under her chin and made her look at him. "Tina, you are not weak. You are a strong woman who struggled with depression. The struggle is part of who you are now, but the depression will never define you."

She wanted to believe that. She wanted to believe that Dev could look at her and not see the torment that had overwhelmed her. She didn't want Dev to remember how she had been at her worst.

Tina pulled her chin from his hold and bent her head. "I'm sorry I've been a burden. I know I'm not the wife you wanted. You should have someone who will improve your life and be a business asset."

"You are not a burden." He sounded surprised that

she would suggest it. "I know that if the roles had been reversed, you would have done the same."

She couldn't imagine Dev sick or struggling. He could conquer anything. He had the inner strength that helped him meet challenges head-on.

But she would have looked after him if needed. She would second-guess herself, but she would have done what was best for him. She also wouldn't have walked away from him unless it was the only way he could be happy.

He wasn't happy now and he wasn't going to be for the next six weeks. He was miserable and moody. She was, too. It was painful being next to Dev without touching him. Without connecting. "We should end this now."

"Enough," he said gruffly. "Stop talking or I will make you shut up."

"We can divorce quietly and—"

Dev bent his head and claimed her mouth with his. Her knees buckled as she clung onto his shoulders. His fierce kiss lit something deep inside her. A dangerous fire that she had tried so hard to ignore. It roared through her veins as she returned his kiss.

Tina whimpered when Dev pulled away. Her stomach clenched with anticipation when she saw the lust flaring in his eyes. She didn't protest when he lifted her up. Instead, she wrapped her legs around his waist and grabbed the back of his head. She kissed him hard as he carried her to the bed.

CHAPTER EIGHT

TINA TIGHTENED HER hold on Dev as he laid her down on the bed. She didn't want to let go. She yearned for the feel of him under her hands. She skimmed her fingers down his strong back and bunched his tunic in her fist. She didn't want anything to stand in the way of her skin touching his.

She pulled his shirt off his head, barely taking a moment to break the hungry kiss. Clinging to his strong shoulders, Tina opened her mouth wide as she drew Dev's tongue deep inside.

Tina had missed this fierce touch. The ferocious longing. Her blood was pumping hard through her veins as Dev shoved her drawstring pants down her thighs. His large hand slipped under her tunic and he captured her breast.

Dev pushed aside her flimsy bra and she groaned with approval when he squeezed her breast hard. Her nipple tightened as it rasped against his rough hand. Tina arched her spine so she could thrust against his palm.

When he pinched her nipple, Tina began to rock her pelvis against his. Heat washed over her as a delicious ache centered in her core. She grabbed the hem of her tunic and tore it off over her head. Her bra followed.

Tina reached for Dev but he caught her wrists and

held them against the mattress beside her head. His hips pinned hers but she didn't feel trapped. The dark excitement pulsed through her body as Dev bent his head and took the tip of her breast in his mouth.

Tina tilted her head back and moaned as the fire crackled inside her. She curled her fingers into fists as the edge of his teeth scraped her nipple. Rocking her hips, Tina urged for more. She wanted it harder. Faster. She wanted it all and she wanted it right now.

When Dev let go of her wrists to cup her breasts, Tina reached for him and dug her fingers into his hair. She wanted to guide Dev but he already knew what she craved.

He drew his hands down her body, his touch untamed and possessive. He grabbed the hem of her panties and stripped them off. Dev drew back into a kneeling position and pushed her legs wider apart.

She stared at Dev as her raspy, choppy breaths filled the air. Her heart lurched when she caught his primal expression. For a moment she felt vulnerable as he rubbed his fingers along the folds of her sex. A wicked smile slashed through his harsh features when he discovered she was ready for him.

Dev's gaze clashed with hers. Slowly his eyes narrowed and she looked away. She wasn't sure what had displeased him. Did he see her uncertainty? Feel her hesitation? She parted her lips to say something—anything—just to break the tension that coiled around them. But Dev grabbed her hips and turned her over.

Tina gasped when she was suddenly on her hands and knees facing away from Dev. His fingers tightened against her hips as she felt his tip pressing against her. Dev entered her with one long thrust. Tina shuddered as her slick flesh held him tight, drawing him deeper, as she rocked against him.

Dev's guttural groan echoed in the room as he began a fast and furious rhythm. Tina matched him stroke for stroke, determined to capture the wildness that he sparked inside her. His hands were everywhere, caressing her breast, sliding along the curve of her spine, and dipping under her hips. His finger glided along her swollen folds as he drove into her.

The fire inside burned white-hot. Tina stiffened as the climax ripped through her. She cried out, her flesh clenching his. Dev clamped his hand on her hips with one final thrust, growling low when he found his release.

Tina's arms and legs threatened to collapse but Dev's hands held her up. Her body throbbed with pleasure as he withdrew and laid her down carefully. Tina slowly turned on her back, stunned and shaky, as Dev toppled next to her.

Tina lay sprawled on the bed and closed her eyes. The only sound she heard was her heart pounding in her ears, her rough gulps of air, and the quiet buzz of the ceiling fan.

What had she done? What was she thinking? One moment she was offering a quiet divorce and the next she was tearing her husband's clothes off. It had always been this way with them. The time away had done nothing to diminish the passion they shared.

It was more than passion for her. She didn't know if it was because Dev was her first lover and the only man she had loved. All she knew was that she wanted this skin-on-skin connection. She needed to be part of him. Even now she was tempted to turn toward Dev and curl into his body.

"This changes nothing," she murmured as the panic began to surface.

"It changes everything," Dev replied softly.

She clenched her jaw when she heard the low rumble of satisfaction in Dev's voice. "No, it doesn't. This was a one-off thing."

"I plan to make it an everyday thing," he said as he yawned and stretched. "Every hour. Every moment."

She tried to stop the shiver of anticipation. "It was just sex." For him. She needed to remember that.

He lazily stroked her wrist with the curl of his finger. "Mind-blowing, life-changing sex."

"It was a lapse of judgment," she argued.

The sound of his chuckle skated along her nerves. "It was the best decision we've made in a long time."

"There was no decision." That was what made it so humiliating. He kissed her and she went wild. It was like a spark that suddenly exploded. "It just happened."

"Because we held back until we couldn't," he said with disinterest as he laced his large, dark fingers with hers. "Why fight it anymore?"

"I didn't want this!" She winced at how her voice rose.

Dev's grip tightened and he slowly turned on his side. Tina wanted to leap out of the bed. He moved with lethal grace yet she didn't move a muscle. She knew danger was approaching but she was mesmerized by his hot, masculine scent. Tina bent her legs and crossed her arms against her breasts but she knew that wasn't enough protection.

"Are you saying I forced you?" he asked huskily.

She recognized the growing anger lurking in his voice. She had to be careful or he would prove once again just how easily she would surrender to him. "No," she said, refusing to look at him. "We just got swept up in the moment. I didn't mean to have sex with you."

"You had sex with me by accident?" Dev drawled. "How does one do that? Because it felt very purposeful to me. You knew exactly what you wanted and how. You were very specific—"

"You don't seem to get it," she interrupted as a blush scorched her skin. She blindly searched for the bed sheet and drew it over her. "We are ending this marriage in six weeks. I am not sleeping with a man when the relationship already has an expiration date."

"Yes, you are." He gave a fierce tug on the bedsheet, ripping it out of her clenched hands. "We are still married and we will live as husband and wife for the remaining six weeks."

She sharply turned her head and met his gaze. Her pulse skipped hard as she saw the determined glitter in his brown eyes. "And what if I get pregnant?"

He froze. Tina watched his skin pale as his mouth parted open in shock.

"We didn't use protection," she whispered.

Dev closed his eyes but not fast enough. Was that regret she had seen? Or fear? She couldn't tell but it didn't give her the comfort she desperately sought. "Tina—"

"This is a problem," she said in a hiss as the panic threatened to bubble and overflow. "I am never, ever getting pregnant again."

His jaw snapped shut. "When did you decide this? You loved being pregnant and you couldn't wait to meet our baby. You always wanted to be a mother. Remember how you wanted to have at least half a dozen?"

That was when she'd thought she was strong and healthy. When they first married, Tina had felt protected and invincible. Now she felt broken and weary. "I said that before I miscarried."

Dev reached for her. "Next time—"

She jerked into a sitting position. "There will be no next time! I'm not going to go through that again." Tina propped her forehead against the palm of her hand. "The loss, the pain…"

He sat up and cupped her shoulder with his large hand. "Just because you had a miscarriage, it doesn't mean it will happen every time you get pregnant."

But there were no guarantees. In fact, she was at a higher risk. She didn't feel like she would be whole again and another loss would break her completely. "I'm not willing to take that chance."

"If you're pregnant, I will give you all the support you need," Dev vowed. His voice was clear and confident. "This time I'll put everything on hold so I can be with you every step of the way."

"Be with me?" Her voice cracked. "How is that going to happen? We will be divorced by then."

His harsh features darkened as he frowned. "Do you think I'm going to walk away from my child?" Dev asked coldly. "Our deal is off if you're pregnant. If we have a baby, we are married forever."

He wouldn't grant her the divorce? *No, no, no!* She couldn't stay married to him. He would take over her life again. She couldn't let that happen. "No, that was never part of the agreement."

"Circumstances change," he said as he got out of bed. "It's our agreement now."

"I'm not staying with you, do you hear me?" Tina punched the mattress with her fist as the fear coiled tightly around her chest. "I can't be married to a man who tries to control every aspect of my life because he thinks I'm incapable."

"I thought you understood." He rubbed his hands over

his face and exhaled sharply. "I was trying to help you. And you can't accept that I went through hell, too."

"Hell? You want to talk about hell?"

Dev dropped his hands and she saw the pain etched into his face. Tina bit her lip and watched with fascination as he hooded his eyes. Had he kept it hidden from her all this time, or had she been so wrapped up in her own misery that she hadn't noticed?

"When I say that I will be there for you and that I will care for you," he said slowly, "it does not mean that I'm going to hold your hand and say all the right words. It means making tough decisions when you can't make them for yourself. It means doing what is best for you even if it gives you the right to hate me."

She went still. "What are you saying?"

"If you're pregnant, I will do everything in my power to keep you here." He placed his hands on his hips as he made his vow. "I will give you and the baby the best possible care. You will not work, leave this house or even leave this bed."

She drew her head back as she watched him with extreme caution. She misunderstood. She had to. "You would treat me like a prisoner?"

"I will keep you safe," he said gruffly.

"Wait a second. Do you think I somehow caused the miscarriage?" she asked huskily as her throat tightened with emotions. "I did everything the doctor prescribed. I didn't take any unnecessary risks."

"No, you are not to blame," he said. "I let you continue filming even though it meant long hours and hard physical work."

"You *let* me?" She hated how the tears stung her eyes.

"I didn't know that the soundstages you worked on were so unsafe. No pregnant woman—especially not my wife—should have been working in those conditions. I should have made you stop."

"You just told me earlier that I'm not to blame. Now you think my career harmed our baby."

He scowled. "I don't think that, but I'm not willing to take that risk. I will make sure you will not work in Bollywood while you're carrying my child."

"Don't threaten me!"

The anger crackled in the air as Dev strode to the bathroom. "These are not threats. I am outlining possible events. If you are carrying my child, this time I'm not letting you out of my sight," he said as he slammed the door behind him.

Dev was not going to get away with this, Tina decided days later as she searched for her cell phone in her handbag. She heard the screech of tires and the immediate cry of the car horns as her driver navigated the luxury sedan through traffic.

Tina punched in the numbers on her cell phone and settled back in her seat. Dev seemed to think he could get away with anything. He thought all he had to do was smile and he could get his way.

She noticed he'd changed tactics after they slept together. Instead of confrontation, he courted her. For the past week Dev had treated her as if she was a queen during the day and his courtesan at night. Tina shifted in her seat as she recalled how Dev had brought her to climax the night before. She wasn't armed for that kind of battle.

Dev answered on the first ring. "Miss me already, *jaan?*"

Tina pressed her lips together as her heart leaped from the sound of his voice. "Don't push your luck with me," she said sweetly in English as she glanced at the driver.

"I'm sorry I wasn't able to visit your mother," he said. "I had to go to the office for an important meeting."

She pressed the phone closer to her ear when she heard the shuffle of papers and the clink of glasses in the background. "You're still in the meeting? Why did you pick up?"

"Because you called. What can I do for you, Tina? Name it and it's yours."

Was he acting that way because he had an audience? Tina dismissed that idea. Dev liked buying gifts but it was nothing like the joy he received when he helped her. He liked turning a problem over in his mind and finding a solution for her. There were times when Tina thought she had embarrassed him with her gratitude. Those were the only moments when she had seen his shy smile and the red streak highlighting his cheekbones.

"I just came back from my mother's house where I heard all about the wedding preparations," Tina said. "You are being far too generous."

Dev scoffed at the idea. "Impossible."

"You're giving Meera and my mother everything they want!"

"Not everything. I can't give the bride the sports car she wanted to arrive in at the wedding. I tried, but there are none available."

Tina groaned. She didn't know about the car. Did he know they were planning to cover the car with garlands and roses? "You need to learn to say no. You have no problems doing that with me."

"Did I say no to you at all last night?" Dev's voice rumbled. "Or this morning?"

Tina tried to shut down the memory but she clearly recalled every angle and plane of his gloriously masculine body. Her mouth watered as she remembered how Dev's warm skin tasted when she pleasured him awake.

"Why are you doing this?" She dropped her tone and gave another glance at the front of the car. The driver didn't know English but she wasn't taking any chances. "We will be divorced before Meera has her wedding."

"It's the least I can do," he said seriously, the flirtatious tone disappearing in an instant. "I didn't give you the wedding you deserved."

She pulled the phone away and looked at it before she placed it against her ear again. "What are you talking about?"

"We eloped when I should have given you the wedding of your dreams."

"I liked our wedding." The words tumbled from her mouth. She didn't want to discuss that happy day with the man she was planning to divorce.

"You deserved more." The way he said those words made Tina's heart squeeze. "I see that now. I thought..."

"Thought what?" she prompted when his voice trailed off.

"That I had done my part by offering marriage," he said softly, regretfully. "That I had exceeded expectations."

"I know." Everyone thought he had gone beyond the call of duty and she should be grateful. "Why are you telling me this now?"

"I'm trying to make amends. I can't go back and fix that wedding."

"So you're going to make it up to me by giving my sister the wedding of her dreams? Taking care of it so I don't have to?"

"Something like that," he muttered.

"Dev, I liked our wedding. It was intimate and personal and most important, it wasn't a spectacle." She shuddered as she imagined what the wedding would have been like if they had invited the Bollywood royalty. "It could have easily been a circus, which was the last thing I wanted. I wanted it to be about us and that is what I got."

As the silence pulsed between them, Tina realized how much she had revealed. Her marriage, her growing family, was all that had mattered to her. Now she was on the brink of losing everything.

"I have to go," Tina said briskly. She was flustered and knew it came through in her voice. "I have a stylist and a makeup artist coming over to prepare for the award ceremony."

"I'll be home soon," Dev said.

"I made the mistake of telling my mother about the award ceremony," Tina said, wincing at how she continued to babble on when she should end the phone call. "She watches all of them and she's so excited. She thinks I need to make a good impression and wear a sari and hair extensions."

"Forget the hair extensions," Dev advised. "I'm beginning to like your short hair. You can't hide behind it. But a sari..."

She groaned at how his voice deepened with pleasure. Tina made a face. "I hate wearing saris. You know that. I feel clumsy and swaddled in those things."

"But you like it when I unwrap the sari and—"

Tina held her hand up as if she could stop him. "Enough!"

"Wear the sari."

His gravelly voice made her skin tingle. "Goodbye, Dev." She shut the phone off as the car pulled into her driveway.

She didn't know what to do with this flirtatious Dev.

He had been like that when they first met. He knew how to make her blush and how to coax a smile. And she remembered the gleam in his eyes when she flirted back. It had given her the courage to act a little bolder, knowing that it pleased him.

How could he tease her when the possibility of a baby was there? Tina's mood darkened and she looked blankly out the window. How could he find happiness when the cycle of loss and devastation threatened to continue?

But then, how could she have sex with him every night? Dev made sure they used protection every time but that wasn't the only thing she was worried about. The pull she had with Dev was getting stronger. How was she going to break that bond in five weeks if she kept making love with him?

An explosion of camera lights blinded Tina the moment Dev stepped out of the limousine and onto the red carpet. She heard the reporters yelling questions over the cheering crowd. Tina firmly held on to her smile as Dev reached out his hand. She grabbed on tight and stepped out of the car, praying her strapless pink evening gown stayed in place.

Dev released her hand and curved his arm around her waist as he waved to his fans. She wanted to curl into his body, rest her head against his tuxedo jacket and enjoy the possessive touch. She was proud to be at his side and for a moment, she felt he was just as proud to be with her.

"Dev! Dev!" A reporter with a microphone hurried to them. Tina had not been at an award ceremony before. She had never been nominated and she hadn't been famous enough for invitation until she married. Unfortunately, Dev rarely attended these events because he was always on location. But Tina knew enough about red-carpet etiquette after watching countless award shows on television. Since it was her husband's big night, she didn't wear anything that would detract attention from him. She also knew to step away and let him conduct the interviews. As the supportive wife, she wasn't there to share the spotlight.

She stepped out of his hold so he could do his job, but Dev had other ideas. He snagged her hand and laced his fingers with hers. He wasn't going to let her out of his sight.

"Are those the Arjun jewels?"

Tina turned to see a television reporter standing close. The woman thrust a microphone in her face as she stared at the yellow gold necklace that spanned past Tina's collarbone. The matching drop earrings were heavy and swayed with every move.

"Yes," Tina said as she pressed her fingertips on the necklace, revealing the ornate ring that went with the set. "Dev asked me to wear them tonight."

She had been stunned when Dev had presented the wide, flat jewelry box. She had heard about the Arjun jewels but never thought he would want her to wear them. Tina had been flustered and awkward when he helped her with the necklace. The gesture had almost felt like a sacred ritual. As if he was declaring to the whole world that she was his. His woman, his wife.

"And are you excited about tonight? This is your first award ceremony," the reporter said in a clipped, almost rushed tone. "You missed quite a few in the last few months."

Tina gritted her teeth. Now she understood why this woman had approached her instead of the big names. She was looking for a bigger story. An exclusive.

She wasn't going to get one. The media worked hard

to give the actors and actresses an image and then spent the rest of the time trying to tear it down. She was supposed to be beautiful and sexy, but chaste. Tina had broken that rule when she got pregnant before marrying Dev. She was supposed to be from the high echelons of society and hold on to Indian values. It didn't help that she was from the slums.

It was expected that she showed no cracks in her marriage even though reporters were eager to point out any tension. When she miscarried, she hadn't been able to show her distress or depression. Reality wasn't allowed to touch Bollywood stars. Her world had crumbled but she'd had to act as if everything was fine.

"You weren't even at your father-in-law's funeral," the reporter said.

"I look forward to the tribute for Dev's father," Tina said as she tightened her hold on Dev's hand. "He had an amazing career and influenced the film industry for decades."

"Were you close to your father-in-law?"

"Of course," Tina lied. Vikram Arjun hadn't wanted to have anything to do with her. Their relationship had been cold and distant. He'd offered no condolences or even acknowledgment when she had miscarried.

She would never reveal the truth. No one wanted to hear it and she didn't want to share how unwelcome she was in the Arjun family. The Bollywood fans watched the movies because they wanted to be swept away in the fantasy. They wanted the heroes, stories about star-crossed lovers, and the exotic and luxurious settings. Anything that didn't remind them of their reality.

She felt Dev tugging her hand and she excused herself from the ambush interview. Dev held on to her hand as they slowly made their way down the red carpet. Every reporter wanted to talk to her husband, who was up for several awards. Working the red carpet was nothing new for Dev while she just tried not to look out of place.

When they finally made it into the auditorium, Tina took a moment to look around. The enormous stage was big enough for an entire cast to perform dance numbers. The audience was filled with the most beautiful actors and actresses. As Dev guided her to the front row, there was a ripple of awareness. She heard the whispers and felt the stares but she ignored them. As they reached their seats, Tina saw her mother-in-law was already there.

Tina took a deep breath. It was going to take all of her acting abilities to remain cool and in control. She didn't falter when Dev approached the legendary actress.

Gauri Arjun didn't look like her son. Her delicate and feminine features were framed by waves of dark brown hair. The woman was petite and slender while her son was tall and muscular. Dev favored jeans yet his mother only wore traditional clothes. Expensive ones, Tina noted, to go with her designer shoes.

"*Maaji,*" she greeted in the manner Dev's mother had insisted on. She bent down to touch Gauri's feet. She felt clumsy as everyone in the auditorium watched her. "It's been too long."

"Yes, it has."

Tina knew she was probably being sensitive, but the woman could make any word or phrase sound like a reprimand. "I want to say how sorry I am for the loss of your husband. He—"

Gauri swept away her condolences with the wave of her hand. "Thank you. I see that you are wearing the Arjun jewels."

"She is an Arjun," Dev reminded his mother as he gestured for Tina to sit down next to his mother.

"Before you sit down, Dev, you need to find Rajinder," Gauri said, referring to a legend who only needed to go by one name. "He has to speak to you before the show starts."

Dev sighed and glanced at Tina. "I'll be fine," she said and gave a small bobble of her head. She knew that Gauri would either ignore her or unsheathe her claws the moment Dev left. It was nothing she hadn't dealt with before.

As she watched Dev walk away, Gauri immediately turned to Tina. "I feel the need to be honest," the older woman declared.

Tina's muscles locked as she braced herself. It was never good when someone warned they were going to be honest. She wanted to hunch her shoulders and bend her head. Instead she straightened her spine and thrust her chin out.

"You should not wear those jewels," Gauri said as she flicked her gaze over Tina's throat. "You don't have the pedigree or the right to wear them!"

Tina bit her tongue as she held her hands tightly in her lap. She wanted to answer back. Stand up for herself, but she didn't say anything. The Hindi film industry thought she wasn't worthy of her husband. Sometimes she sensed that her husband had felt that way, too.

"Everyone knows that Dev only married you because you were carrying the heir to the Arjun dynasty," Gauri said.

"You mean your grandchild," she murmured. She would have shielded her baby from the pressure of the Arjun legacy and the expectations of becoming the next

Bollywood megastar. She knew Dev would have felt the same way.

"We could have started grooming this baby for greatness," Gauri said and then gave a shrug, "as long as it inherited your looks and not your acting abilities."

Tina let the backhanded compliment slide. She knew she got most of her roles because of her appearance and dancing skills. Her achievements were small compared to the rest of the audience at this ceremony, but she'd worked hard and made a career.

"Now you're back and Dev has taken time off from work? He backed out on a movie that was a surefire hit?" The anger vibrated in Gauri's voice. "And at the worst time. I can't tolerate this any longer."

"I think this is a conversation you should have with your son," Tina murmured. She gave a sidelong glance and noticed other guests were trying to listen into their conversation.

"Nonsense. You tricked Dev into marrying you in order to help your career." The older woman's voice sharpened with impatience. "That didn't work out. You disappeared and now you have returned. I want to know what you want."

She wanted a fresh start. Before she returned to Mumbai, Tina had thought that meant a life without Dev. Now, she wasn't so sure. There were too many times that she imagined staying with Dev and creating a family.

"What do I want?" she asked as she watched Dev walking back to her. He was sophisticated and gorgeous. A true megastar. But her favorite memories were those quiet moments at home when they'd prepared for the birth of their child. "I want him to be happy."

Gauri rolled her eyes. "The only way that's going to

happen is if you leave him," she said decisively. "For good."

Tina's polite smile dipped. She was often in disagreement with Gauri Arjun, but this time she knew her mother-in-law was right.

CHAPTER NINE

TINA PACED THE courtyard, hoping to find serenity, but nothing relieved her agitation. Her high heels clicked against the stone path and the stack of bangles clattered with every move. The water fountains gurgled loudly and the fragrance of the flowers was overpowering. The morning sun was unbearable. She pulled at the neckline of her designer wrap dress. It felt tight and suffocating.

Why had she ever agreed to this?

"Tina?"

She whirled around at the sound of Dev's voice. Her pulse skipped hard when she saw him walking barefoot down the path. His hair was getting long and a hint of a beard darkened his jaw. Today he wore a long blue tunic and faded jeans but the casual wear didn't hide his powerful and masculine body.

She felt a flutter low in her belly when she saw the lust flare in his dark eyes. She was keenly aware of how the dress clung to her curves. Tina clasped her hands in front of her and remained still as her heart beat fast.

"Sandeep told me you had asked for the car. Where are you going? An audition?"

Tina went still and nervously licked her lips. "I'm going to a charity luncheon."

"Really?" His eyes narrowed on her mouth and he

strolled closer. "You should have told me. I had made plans for us today."

She gave a guilty start. "I'm sorry. I didn't know until the last minute."

He didn't say anything as he watched the blush stain her cheeks. "What charity is it?" he asked silkily.

She gritted her teeth. She was reluctant to share any information and she wasn't sure why. No, that wasn't true. She knew this was going to trigger a discussion she didn't want to have with Dev.

"Tina?" His voice held a steely edge.

She looked away. "It's for mothers who have suffered miscarriages."

The silence pulsed in the courtyard. She gave a cautious glance in Dev's direction. Dread settled in her chest as she watched Dev's harsh features sharpen. She saw the way he clenched his jaw and the hurt that flashed through his eyes.

"They want to promote the resources they offer to these women and they needed a celebrity to get media coverage," she babbled on. "I volunteered. I thought this would be a good way to honor our son."

"Why didn't you tell me?" he asked coldly. "Afraid that I would want to come along? Steal the spotlight?"

Tina's eyes widened with shock. "No, of course not. It's a women's charity. I didn't think you would be interested."

He flinched. "Right, because I don't know anything about miscarriages. It hasn't touched my life, my marriage or my heart." He turned abruptly and walked back to the house.

"I didn't say that," she called out as she hurried after him.

He didn't look back. "You don't have to. You're shutting

me out like you did when you miscarried. You had to suffer alone. Deal with it alone."

"It's just easier that way!" she declared.

Dev stopped and slowly turned around. "Easier?"

"No, that isn't true. It's not easier." Tina dipped her head and raked her hands through her hair. She was used to carrying the weight of others—her mother, her sisters—but this time she didn't have the strength. She needed to rely on someone else but no one was there to help. Dev's absence had felt like a dismissal. A betrayal. She didn't want to put herself in that position again.

But as she looked at the hurt and disappointment in Dev's eyes, she realized she was guilty of the same thing she had accused him of. How many times had he reached for her, searching for solace, only to be rejected? She didn't know. She had been too focused on her own pain. How often had she believed that her grief was stronger, more powerful, because she was the one who had carried the baby?

"It's my fault we didn't have a chance to grieve together." She knew now that Dev hadn't been indifferent. He mourned differently. Silently. "I wanted to handle it alone and I couldn't."

"You got the help you needed," he reminded her. "I know that was a difficult decision for you, but you did it. You don't need my help anymore."

"That's not true." Her voice wobbled and she swallowed hard. She needed his help and he needed hers. "I want you to come with me to the charity luncheon."

His sigh was low and deep. "Tina…"

She raised a shaky hand to stop him. "I thought I could do this on my own, but I can't. I've been walking in circles trying to gather up enough courage to face this luncheon."

"You won't fall apart, *jaan,*" Dev said softly.

He was refusing her offer. Tina took a shallow breath as her chest ached with disappointment. She shouldn't be surprised. She hadn't been there for him in the beginning and she kept shutting him out.

"You're right. I won't," she said as she walked past him. "But one of these days, I hope we can honor our son together. Maybe it's the wrong charity for you. The wrong venue. The wrong time—"

He grabbed her arm and she lurched to a stop. Tina looked down at his large fingers encircling her wrist. She glanced up and stared at the shadows and deep lines in his face.

"I'm still angry that our son didn't get a chance. So damn angry," Dev admitted. "You may want to share how you feel with a crowd of strangers, but I'm not ready for the world to witness my pain."

Tina pressed her lips together and nodded. She hadn't considered that Dev was at a different stage of grief and loss. While she'd had months to focus on her bereavement, Dev had been struggling on his own.

"But I will go to this charity luncheon with you." His voice was gravelly. "Because you are the only person I want to grieve with. If this is how you want to mourn, I will be there for you."

Tina's lips trembled as her throat ached with emotions. She closed her eyes before the tears started to fall. "And I'll be there for you, Dev." She wrapped her arms around him and leaned her head on his shoulder. "No matter what. I promise."

Late one afternoon, Dev stood at the door of Tina's dance studio. He remained quiet, careful not to disturb Tina as she swayed to *bhangra* music. When he had returned from America without her, he hadn't entered this room. As the days had become weeks, he hadn't approached this wing of the house. He'd known it would be cold and empty. The plain room didn't hold her spirit or reflect her personality.

Her dancing, however, revealed everything about her.

How often had he watched her films late into the night? Dev leaned his head against the door frame. He had to admit, the story lines and dialogues were awful. The editing was usually sloppy and the special effects were antiquated. But when Tina arrived on the scene, he didn't notice anything else. Her presence was electrifying and when she danced, the light inside her shone bright.

He knew how she moved and how she expressed herself through dance. It was sensual. Elemental. She could show restraint in the traditional dance styles and energy in the modern steps. Tina conveyed emotion from the tilt of her head to the point of her toe. Most men didn't notice that. They were mesmerized by the shake of her hips and her mysterious smile.

And he could tell right now that something was off. She was upset. Uncertain. Her movements were sharper and a beat faster than the music.

She stepped out of the spin. Her balance wobbled before she planted both feet firmly on the wood floor. Tina stomped her bare foot and placed her hand on her forehead.

Dev lifted his head as he felt a kick of concern. The clumsy move wasn't like her. She was innately graceful and had done that spin countless times.

The music continued to play. He recognized it from one of her movies. It was her signature song. The lyrics were audacious, saying she was going to steal the groom from the bride. The choreography was just as suggestive.

He moved forward without thinking about it. As he slid his arm on her waist, Tina jumped and turned around. Before she could step away, Dev grasped her hand with his and cradled her close.

Tina glanced at the door and then turned her attention back at him. "How long have you been here? Were you watching me?"

"A few seconds," he admitted as they glided across the floor just like old times. Dancing had been just part of the job until he'd met Tina. He'd wanted to be near her, share the music and move as one. He'd found every opportunity to dance with her at clubs, parties and the random moments in the courtyard.

Tina bent her head. "I can't hit the moves like I used to," she confessed.

"You're putting too much pressure on yourself," Dev declared as his hand flattened against her spine. As his fingers stroked the sweat-slick skin, he was acutely aware that she only wore a sports bra and yoga pants. "Give it some time and it will all come back."

"I don't have time." She looked away. "I heard from my agent today. I've been invited to dance at a wedding next month. A very glamorous one for a millionaire."

His wife should have better assignments. She should star in movies instead of dancing to old songs. "You'll be ready."

"I wasn't their first choice," Tina continued. "A famous actress was supposed to do it but she dropped out. My agent won't tell me who the original dancer was but I have a feeling she's a big name."

"The guests won't know," Dev said in an encouraging tone as they continued to sway to the hypnotic beat of the drums. "And they won't care once you start dancing."

"Thanks, Dev," she said shyly. "I know dancing at

weddings is frowned upon with Bollywood royalty. It's just another way to make money, but I enjoy it."

"More than acting?"

"Dancing is my first love. I got into acting because acting paid more money." She gave a small frown. "What about you? Do you enjoy acting?"

"No one has ever asked me that before." It had always been assumed that he would go into the family business.

"You're very good at it. A natural. But then, you're a natural at most things."

She said it as if it was a character flaw. "I'm more interested in the business behind the camera."

"I know. I've seen how excited you get with the new technology and the new markets. But if you're bored with acting, you should retire and focus on what you love."

"Give up being the king of Bollywood?" he mocked.

"King?" She chuckled. "You are a prince at best. And not the only one."

Dev's smile widened. He could always trust Tina to give her real opinion. She was supportive but she always gave her real opinion. There weren't that many people in his life who would do that.

She glanced at the clock. "I have to get ready for Nikhil's party."

"Need help with the sari?" he teased as Tina walked away.

She glanced over her shoulder and smiled. "I'm not wearing a sari."

"What happened to the devoted and adoring wife I was promised?"

Her smile turned bittersweet. "She's long gone."

The dance club was exactly what she needed. It was dark and crowded with colorful lights flashing on the floor.

She lifted her arms and shouted her approval at the DJ when she heard the first few notes of her favorite song.

Tina felt Dev behind her. She leaned against his solid chest as he wrapped his arms around her waist. She'd forgotten how much fun she used to have dancing with Dev.

Nikhil had a very exclusive guest list but the only person she really noticed was her husband. And he couldn't keep his hands off her. She was secretly pleased at how his eyes had widened when he saw the silver dress she had decided to wear. Tina could tell he approved of her short strapless dress. His gaze would settle on her curves and she noticed he hadn't said a word about changing into a sari.

Did Dev know that she had chosen the dress for him? Tina realized she had to stop thinking like that. She stepped away and twirled out from his embrace. She needed to stop thinking like a wife. A full-time, long-term wife. She needed to start distancing herself.

She stumbled to a halt when Dev grabbed her wrist and drew her close. She gave him a questioning look as he guided her off the crowded dance floor. He was frowning and his mouth was a straight line.

"What's wrong?" she asked over the music.

"You were wobbling again," he said with a grim expression as he escorted her to a small table in the very back of the club. "Sit down and I'll get you something to drink."

"I'm okay, Dev." She reached for his hand and held him still. "I want to go back in and dance."

"No, it's not like you to lose your balance," he said. "I want you to rest."

"There is nothing wrong with my stamina or my strength," she insisted.

"I'll decide that."

She tossed her hands in the air and sat down next to the table. "Why are you being overprotective?"

"Why can't I look after you?" he said in a growl.

"Why can't I look after you?" she shot back.

Dev jerked his head back in surprise. "I don't need looking after."

"But I do?" This was the problem of being married to a traditional man.

He leaned forward, his hand on the back of her chair. "You've had a rough year."

"So have you." And she hadn't been there for him when he needed her the most.

"Why won't you let me take care of you?" Dev's eyes flashed with anger. "Why does this always have to be an argument?"

"You help more than enough." He helped her so much that she felt like she couldn't reciprocate. "I live in your house, I spend your money and I don't contribute anything."

"Contribute? You do more than you realize. When we were preparing for our son, it was the first time I felt like I belonged to a family."

The familiar ache settled in her chest when he mentioned their son. "Anyone can give you that."

"You'd be surprised," he whispered in her ear. "Anyone would take what I have to offer. But you reject everything I do for you."

Her shoulders stiffened and she turned her head sharply to stare at Dev's dark brown eyes. "I don't reject you."

"Yes, you do." This time Dev looked away. "You reject every gift I give you, every gesture, every act I make outside the bedroom."

Was that true? Tina nervously licked her lips as she

tried to remember. She had felt uncomfortable when he lavished her with gifts and she couldn't give him anything in return. He could make her life easier with just one phone call and all she seemed to do was make his life a living hell. "I don't mean to. It's just that…"

He turned quickly, his gaze holding hers. "What?"

Tina gestured between them. "We're unequal. You have all the power and I have none."

She saw the shock tighten Dev's harsh features. "That's how you see it?"

"That's how it is!" she insisted and leaned closer. "How can I accept help from you when I can't give anything back?"

"You help your family," Dev pointed out. "Your mother and sisters. You don't expect anything in return."

"Well, that's different because—"

"Because in your family, you're still trying to make up for the fact that you were a financial burden to your mother."

Tina bit her lip as her skin flushed. She felt exposed. She hated feeling that way, but most of all, she hated that Dev knew.

"And you'll keep working every job you're offered," he continued, "and you pay for everything your family needs because you feel like you have to pay a debt."

Tina wanted to look away. How did he see all this? What else did he notice? "My mother could have gotten rid of me once my father left. She had considered taking me to an orphanage," she said as her voice cracked. "Instead she kept me."

"And you're a financial burden to me?" he asked. Dev slowly shook his head. "Just how much money do you think you spend?"

"It's not how much I spend. It's how much I *cost* you.

You could have ignored me and the baby. You married me because you felt like you should. And what did you get out of it? Your career still took a hit once you got married."

"I don't care about that."

"You will one day." If he didn't care about it now, it was because he didn't know how it felt to be at rock bottom. Soon he was going to resent the trouble she caused. Tina slowly rose from her seat. She couldn't discuss this anymore. Maybe she was as fragile as Dev thought. She felt like she needed a few minutes alone.

"Excuse me, I need to find the restroom. No, no." She held out her hand as he rose to escort her. "Don't worry, I can find my way there myself."

"I'll get you a drink while you're gone."

"Thank you." As she walked to the restroom she admitted to herself that she did feel a little wobbly. It might be the stiletto heels or that she needed to drink some water.

Stepping into the dark room with black sinks and counters, Tina glimpsed her reflection in the mirror. Just as she suspected, she looked like a wreck. With a heavy sigh, she combed down her spiky hair with her fingers and readjusted her dress. She stepped into one of the stalls and closed the door. Once she locked it, she rested her head against the cool metal and gave a deep sigh.

Tina frowned when she heard a group of women enter the restroom. She just wanted some peace. Wait until the ache eased in her chest and Dev's words stopped swirling in her head. All she needed was a few moments to regroup before she returned to the party.

"Did you see Dev and Tina?"

Tina lifted her head. The unmistakable voice of

Khushi, the playback singer, was coming from the direction of the mirrors.

"You'd think they were on their honeymoon," Prisha complained. "I mean, come on. Get a room."

Tina rolled her eyes at the choreographer's comment. She was never demonstrative with Dev in public. The reason had more to do with a code of conduct for Bollywood stars than her private nature. One didn't embrace, kiss or show any overt affection. She didn't even graze lips with her costar on-screen because it would offend many moviegoers.

"From what I understand, the honeymoon will end in five weeks," Khushi drawled. "And then they are getting a divorce."

Tina skin went cold as the blood roared in her ears. Had she heard Khushi correctly? How had she known about the secret agreement she had with Dev?

"What?" Prisha screeched. "Where did you hear this?"

"Shreya."

Tina exhaled as her hands began to shake. How did Shreya know? She must have heard a rumor, but there was only one source she could have got it from.

"What else did she tell you?" Prisha asked excitedly.

"Tina agreed to stay for two months and she will get to use Dev's connections in return. I knew that woman had married him for her career. Didn't I tell you?"

Tina closed her eyes as her stomach gave a violent twist. They knew everything. And there was only one way Shreya would have gotten this information. Dev had told Shreya everything.

CHAPTER TEN

TINA STOOD VERY still as the realization hit her hard. She couldn't breathe. Couldn't think. She felt sick. Dizzy. She pressed her hands on the metal door as if it could hold her upright. It seemed like ages before Khushi and Prisha finished repairing their makeup. Once they left the restroom, Tina took several moments before she exited the stall.

Tina glanced at her reflection in her mirror. She looked pale and wounded. She wanted to believe Dev hadn't betrayed her, but she couldn't think of any other explanation. She tried to think of how Shreya could have got this information but the images of the tabloid pictures flickered in her mind.

She slowly walked to the door, her movements awkward and choppy. Her stiletto heels skidded against the floor and she righted herself abruptly. She really didn't think Dev would have shared that information with anyone.

Tina squeezed her eyes shut before the burning tears spilled from her lashes. She had believed Dev when he said he had been faithful. He had been hurt that the only reason she returned was because of the pictures. She had heard it in his voice and had felt it in his touch when they had fallen into bed.

But if he had not been sleeping with Shreya, how did the other woman know all the details?

Tina walked out of the restroom and she cringed at the loud music bombarding her sensitive nerves. The frenetic lights and the wild dance movements were suddenly too much for her. She had to get out of there. She needed to think. Run. Hide.

"Tina?" She heard Dev's voice right behind her. "Where are you going?"

She kept moving, staring at the exit with laser focus as if her life depended on it. "I have to get out of here."

"Why? What's wrong?" Dev was suddenly in front of her, forcing her to stop. She was tempted to push him away but he was stronger than she.

She didn't want to tell him. She wasn't ready for this confrontation. The tears were shimmering in her eyes and the pain was howling through her, threatening to break free. If he had betrayed her confidence like this, she didn't know how she was going to survive.

Every instinct told her to protect herself. If she told him what she knew, he would come up with an excuse. And she would believe him because she wanted to. She needed to get away before he could totally destroy her. But she had to see his face. If she surprised him with what she knew, he wouldn't be able to hide his guilt.

"There were some women in the restroom who were sharing some juicy gossip," Tina said weakly, her throat aching as the emotions clawed at her. "They knew about our agreement. Every last detail."

Dev grabbed her shoulders and bent his head so he could look directly into her eyes. "What are you talking about?"

"Shreya told others about our agreement. She knows that this marriage is going to end in five weeks."

Dev's dark brown eyes narrowed into slits. "That's impossible," he said in a growl.

Was it? Dev said he hadn't had an affair with Shreya, but what if he had shared his thoughts, dreams and problems with the other woman? What if he had talked to her about things he hid from his wife? "I don't know what she's going to do with the information." Tina's voice shook.

"What are you trying to say?" His fingers tightened against her bare arms. "Do you still think I'm having an affair with Shreya?"

"No, but I think you confided in another woman about something private, something just between us."

Tina couldn't take it anymore. She leaned forward and rested her head against his shoulder. She felt Dev's muscles tense with surprise before he gathered her in his arms and held her close. She sighed when he cupped the back of her head with his large hand. For a moment, she felt safe.

"Let's go home, Dev," she pleaded softly.

"Not yet," he said as she stroked her hair. "I need to do something first. *We* do."

She lifted her head. "What are you planning?"

"Follow my lead." He encircled his fingers around her wrist and guided her to the dance floor.

Tina didn't trust the urgency in his tone. "No, no, no." She dragged her heels. "Not until you tell me what you want to do."

He looked over his shoulder. "For once, we are going to face this as a team. A united front. That was our mistake in the past."

United. They hadn't been partners, hadn't shared a life together, since they got married. "What are you talking about?"

"We are husband and wife but we lead separate lives. We didn't grieve together and we didn't help each other after the miscarriage. That stops now. We are going to start by attacking these rumors together." He squeezed her hand. "Are you with me?"

It meant giving him total control and allowing him to lead. It meant trusting him. Believing he wouldn't throw her to the wolves. It meant taking a leap of faith and ignoring every instinct that screamed for her to run and hide.

Tina gave a sharp nod. "Let's do this," she said and was rewarded with Dev's bold smile.

Dev led her through the dance floor. She watched as the crowd parted for him. Tina's shoulders tightened as her husband approached the DJ's platform. She couldn't predict what he was going to do. Call out Shreya and her friends? Tina clenched Dev's hand in warning. She felt too vulnerable.

Her heart banged against her ribs when Dev held out his hand to the DJ and silently motioned for the microphone. The DJ didn't question the request and immediately handed it to him. Tina knew nothing good could come out of this. She wanted to drift into the crowd but she had promised Dev that she would follow his lead. She had no idea it would be this difficult.

"DJ, I would like to dedicate a song to my wife."

Tina went very still as the crowd roared their approval for the romantic gesture. If only it were genuine, Tina thought. She tried to relax under the spotlight as Dev gathered her close. He gave her a look of pure adoration that took her breath away.

"This woman said yes to me almost a year ago. She gave me the pleasure—no, the *honor*—of becoming her husband. I don't know what I would have done without her."

Tina ducked her head as a blush crawled up her neck and flooded her face. Did Dev know that this counterattack was the most precious gift he had given her? Wearing the Arjun jewels had been a stroke of genius. It gave the illusion that he considered her worthy of the family name. But this…this declaration from a Bollywood megastar meant something more. Dev was demanding high society respect his wife, making them believe she had power and influence over the mighty megastar. That he was wonder-struck by her.

"I realized I haven't said it enough. I didn't show this special woman how I feel about her every day." His voice was rough with regret and sincerity. "But I'm going to correct that mistake now."

Tina heard a few women in the crowd sigh at his words. She would have sighed, too, but this was pretend. Part of the fantasy. A ruse to stop the rumors.

"My wife is everything I want. Everything I need. I'm grateful that Tina is willing to share her life with me. So, DJ, I feel like celebrating. Play us a slow song."

The guests clapped and whistled as Dev returned the microphone. The lights in the nightclub dimmed as the first notes of a saxophone played. Dev drew her to the middle of the dance floor and gathered her gently in his arms.

She sensed the other guests finding dance partners and swaying to the music, but she was only aware of Dev. How her soft breasts pressed against his hard chest and how his large hands spanned across her hips. They moved in unison effortlessly.

Tina couldn't look at Dev. He was a good actor. Better than her. If he captured her gaze, he would see how much she wanted those words to be true. How much she wished he had included words like *love* in his speech.

Tina pressed her head against his chest and closed her eyes. A sigh shuddered through her body when Dev cupped her head with his hand. The tenderness made her weak in the knees. When he placed a kiss against her hair, Tina wanted to hold on to this moment. Make believe it was real, just a little while longer.

When the music stopped, Tina reluctantly pulled away. She was an emotional wreck. She felt raw and exposed. "Let's go home now," she suggested.

Dev wrapped his arm around her as he guided her off the dance floor and through the club. He didn't say a word as they exited the lobby. He cradled her close while he called for the car and fell silent again. Was he regretting his speech?

She didn't object as he bundled her into the backseat as if she was a delicate treasure. She didn't say anything until she noticed he wasn't getting into the car with her. "What's going on?" Her eyes widened as she realized he was staying at the party. "You're not coming with me?"

"I saw Shreya at the party and I'm going to find out how she got this information," he said. His voice was calm but she saw the anger in his eyes. "She needs to learn that you are my wife and I will protect your reputation."

"But—"

"Take her straight home," he told the driver before he closed the door.

"Damn it, Dev," she said through the thick glass. But he had already turned away and entered the nightclub like a warrior heading in for battle.

When was he going to realize that the rumors would persist, Tina wondered as the car pulled away from the curb. Nothing they said or did would change that. Their hasty marriage and her brand image made her a burden.

The only way to minimize the damage was if Dev distanced himself from her. He needed to cut her loose.

He needed a drink.

He needed more than that, Dev decided as he swung open the front door of his home and headed straight to his bedroom. What he really needed was Tina. He needed her to believe—really believe—that he wouldn't do this to her.

The house was dark and quiet. Empty. The silence tore at him. It was the last thing he wanted to feel as the fury still rushed through his blood. He had walked into an eerily quiet house like this for the past four months and he wasn't willing to do it again.

He climbed up the steps two at a time. Dev was going to make Tina listen to him. He was going to convince her once and for all that he didn't want Shreya. He didn't want anyone but his wife.

Dev strode into the bedroom and stopped abruptly when he discovered Tina wasn't there. His anger flashed white-hot at the thought that she had moved into one of the guest rooms. He swung around and marched to the nearest guest room. If Tina was trying to make a statement by leaving his bed, she had picked the wrong night.

The bedroom was undisturbed. Something close to panic mixed with his anger and it was a volatile combination. He slammed open the door to the next guest room and he found it empty. He systematically checked every room on the top floor as the urgency pulsed through his veins.

Had she left? Fear, cold and hard, twisted in his stomach as he hurried down the stairs. Was this one truth too hard for her to swallow? He had to admit that the evidence was building up against him.

As he hurried through the drawing room and the massive dining room that had held so many parties, he heard a strain of music. Dev lurched to a stop, listening. The song was familiar. It was from one of Tina's favorite romantic movies.

He pivoted on his heel and walked straight to the kitchen. He faltered to a stop when he saw Tina. The relief crashed through him so hard that he slumped against the door frame.

She was barefoot but still wearing her silver beaded dress. She leaned against the granite counter as she watched *Dilwale Dulhania Le Jayenge* on the TV mounted on the other side of the wall. Shahrukh Khan and Kajol were embracing while standing in a field of yellow flowers. It took him a moment to notice the small coral-colored pot on the stove. He inhaled the scent of *khichri,* the simple comfort food of rice and legumes.

Tina had cooked? This was the first time he had seen her cook since she had returned. It had been something she had enjoyed but she'd lost interest after the miscarriage. He wasn't sure what it meant now. He wanted to see it as a positive sign but he knew to tread lightly.

"You're still here." His voice came out rough and low.

She jerked and looked around. The small plate in her hand held a mound of *khichri* tinged yellow with turmeric. She scooped up the rice and legumes with her fingers and carried it to her mouth. "Where else would I be?"

Her mother's house. A hotel. Another country. Anywhere but here. He slowly approached Tina, unable to read her mood. Uncertain about his welcome.

"You want some?" she asked, holding the thick rice with the tips of her fingers.

He shook his head. That wasn't the question he had expected to tumble from her lips. What was going on?

"I didn't tell Shreya about our agreement," he said. "She had overheard us in the courtyard the night you returned."

Tina slowly lowered her hand and placed the rice back on the plate. She stood still for a brief moment. "I should have known."

Dev reared his head back. "You believe me?" He had thought he was going to have to convince her. Get on his knees and beg for her to listen.

"Yes," she said as she reached for a cloth napkin and briskly cleaned her hands. "I'm not going to lie. I first believed you told her. I almost didn't discuss it with you."

"I'm glad you did." Tina trusted him enough to confront him with the information. She had stayed and waited for his return. That had to mean something. "Shreya has also learned her lesson."

Tina lifted her chin and watched him carefully. "What do you mean?"

"She is no longer working under the banner of Arjun Entertainment," he said grimly.

"You canceled her contract?" Tina eyes widened. "Why would you do that? She is a bankable star."

"She needed my studio more than we needed her."

"Her family is powerful and influential. This is going to cause you so many problems."

"You seem to forget, Tina. Shreya spread gossip about you. About my *wife*. About an *Arjun*. I will not tolerate that. Soon everyone will know that there will be consequences if they disrespect you."

Tina tossed down the napkin and braced the edge of

the counter. "I think your display of adoration fixed everything."

"I hope so." It wasn't a display. He had meant every word.

Tina frowned as she warily studied his face. "It was convincing. Maybe too convincing."

"What do you mean?" he asked. Did she have a problem with his words? With the idea that he adored her?

"It's going to bring up more questions when we divorce in a few weeks," she said, looking away. "Who's going to believe what you say after that?"

"I'm not worried." If all goes to plan, they would still be together.

Tina pressed her lips and gave a shake to her head. "Thank you, Dev. I liked having you rush to my side."

He gave a slow, shy smile. "You're welcome."

"Next time, give me more of a heads-up on what you plan to do."

"I will." He took a step closer until he caught a hint of her perfume.

Tina nervously licked her lips. "We make a good team. I think we should keep doing that. Show that we are partners in every way."

He narrowed his eyes at her matter-of-fact tone. "What are you talking about?"

"It's not enough for your investors to hear that you have a stable family life. We have to demonstrate it. Show the world that our…marriage is an unbreakable force."

Dev wasn't sure if he should trust this offer. Not too long ago she'd seen him as the enemy. "Why would you want to help me?"

"Because it will make you happy." She darted her gaze away.

She wanted to help him. Make him happy. There was

only one thing that would make him happy but he didn't think she would agree to forever. But did this mean that she no longer saw him as the enemy? "Everything has changed."

Dev was right. Tina curled her toes against the cold linoleum as she considered what he had said. Everything had changed between them. He had made it clear that he demanded everyone respect her. He protected her. Protected *them*. That's all she needed to know to stay until their agreement ended.

"We should still sleep in the same room." She was trying to sound blasé but her voice was high and rushed. "Servants talk, you know."

"That Sandeep is a chatty one."

She pursed her lips to prevent a smile. "So we should remain in the same bed."

"If you think that's best," Dev drawled.

"I do," Tina said. She glided her hands over her hips and allowed her fingertips to brush against the short skirt of her dress. She was so nervous. She wasn't sure what words were coming out of her mouth. All she knew was that she wanted to take her husband to bed. But would it feel too much like a reunion? A fresh start?

Dev gave her a speculative look and she felt the thrill of exhilaration.

What were the consequences of seducing your husband? She didn't know. Dev had been the enemy for so long. For months she'd felt like she had to hide from him. Protect herself from her husband. But now she knew the truth. He didn't take control over her life to punish her. He cared about her. At one time he may have loved her.

But he was still dangerous. He made her want things that weren't good for her. He clouded her mind with desire and made her believe in love and forever. She wanted to stay with him, stay as his wife, even if it meant giving up everything. Her freedom. Her peace of mind.

"I want to help you," Tina told him. And it was the truth. She wanted him to have everything he desired. She moved to set the plate in the sink, her body straining, and she felt Dev's gaze linger on her high, full breasts.

Tina slowly straightened as the sexual power pulsed through her. She gently swayed her hips to the music playing on the TV. Dev seemed mesmerized. She knew she had him caught and a dangerous thrill zipped through her veins.

Dev was very still. Her stomach clenched when she saw the glint in his dark eyes. She shouldn't tease a man like this.

"I have the power to make your dreams come true. If you let me." Her words were rushed as excitement coiled tightly around her chest.

She saw his harsh features tighten with desire. The air between them crackled. Now it was time to make her move.

"It's been a long night. I'm going to bed. Are you going to join me?" she asked innocently. Her legs shook slightly as she took a step closer. She forced herself to remain still as her leg bumped against his.

He leaned forward and she found it hard to breathe. Her heart was pounding in her ears and her legs shook. An electric current sparked inside her, pressing just under her skin as he grasped the edge of her short dress.

"Are you inviting me?" he asked. His big hand brushed along her thigh.

"Yes-s-s." Now she was a little afraid that he was going to accept her proposition. Scared, because this night with

Dev would change everything. She was sharing his bed not because she had to, but because she wanted to.

Dev didn't remove his hand. She felt his fingers flex and she knew he wasn't as unaffected as he appeared.

A quivering tension wrapped around them. She knew Dev was tempted to bunch her dress in his fists and strip her bare. And she wanted him to do it.

Dev slowly moved closer, as if waiting for her to change her mind. To run and hide. Tina's anticipation was thick and heavy. She felt as if she would burst out of her skin.

Tina raised her head, jutting her chin as he towered over her. He stood so close that she could feel his body heat and inhale the faint scent of his cologne.

He lowered his head and kissed her. Dev gently explored her lips but she sensed he wanted to claim her mouth. Claim her. He wanted to capture her and press her against him.

She wanted more, too. His soft kisses teased her. Her pulse raced and her skin tingled with need. Tina parted her lips as she stepped closer into his embrace.

Dev gave an appreciative moan as he dipped his tongue past her lips. Her kisses grew urgent as her heart pounded against her chest. Her breath hitched when his large hands skimmed her bare skin.

Tina pulled away. Her lips felt swollen and she wanted to burst out of her tight, hot skin. She looked up at Dev and took a step back.

Dev looked fierce. His touch might have been gentle but he couldn't hide the male aggression that darkened his eyes and pulled at his harsh features. His chest rose and fell with each uneven breath.

And he still didn't grab for her. No matter how much he wanted to. He was allowing her to set the pace.

Her gaze held his. He looked hopeful. Uncertain. Tina reached for his hand. His fingers imprisoned hers. As if he was afraid to let go.

"Come with me," she said in a whisper and guided him out of the kitchen.

CHAPTER ELEVEN

AS SHE FLATTENED her hand against the closed door of the bedroom, Tina paused. Was she ready for this?

Dev pulled his hand away and braced his hands on her hips. She closed her eyes and shivered as his breath warmed her neck. She was unprepared for Dev to span his hands against her waist. Tina gasped as he slid his fingers along her rib cage before cupping her breasts.

She sagged against him as the wicked sensations slammed into her. Her breasts were full and heavy. Her nipples tightened painfully. Tina arched into Dev's hands as he tugged down her strapless dress.

Dev's groan vibrated against her neck as he caressed her bare breasts. Her legs trembled when he pinched her nipples. Pleasure, hot and piercing, forked through her. She let out a high cry as a dew of sweat bathed her skin.

"How do you do this to me?" Dev asked roughly in her ear. "I can't keep my hands off you."

She felt the same way about him. She wanted to beg for more. Plead for Dev to take her breasts in his mouth. She rolled her hips as the lust coiled tight in her belly and she felt his arousal against her.

Tina wrenched open the door and drew Dev into their bedroom. Light from the hallway streamed into the darkness. Once they reached her bed, Tina turned around and clasped her hands on Dev's angular face and blindly sought his mouth with her lips.

Her kisses were wilder and she found it difficult to slow down. She didn't know what made this different than all the other nights. Why the urgency clawed at them. This wasn't their last night together but in some ways it felt like a rebirth.

Dev pulled her short dress down her hips and kicked it away. She was very aware that she was almost naked while he was fully dressed.

"Take off your clothes," she muttered against his lips.

His fingers tightened against her skin. "Take them off for me," he whispered.

She reached for him with barely concealed eagerness and pulled his shirt over his head. While Dev kicked off his shoes, Tina gave a playful push and watched him tumble onto the bed. She squealed with surprise when he grabbed her and took her with him.

His husky chuckle died as she straddled him and explored his solid chest with her hands and mouth. She liked how his muscles bunched under her exploratory touch and how he hissed when she scratched his flat nipple. Tina felt powerful. Desired.

She reached for his belt and suddenly she was underneath Dev. This was where she liked to be. She was surrounded by him and nothing else existed. Nothing else mattered. Tina stopped trying to regain her position as he captured her nipple with his mouth. She went wild as the white-hot pleasure streaked through her.

Tina rolled her hips as Dev dragged her panties down her shaking legs. She couldn't take much more of this. Her sexual hunger was ferocious and the insistent ache in her pelvis made her want to scream.

"Now, Dev."

"Not yet," he said in a steady voice as he rubbed his fingers along the folds of her sex.

His touch wasn't nearly enough. "Please," she said in a broken whisper. "I need you inside me right now."

She nearly sobbed when he withdrew his hands from her. Tina squeezed her eyes closed and heard the rustle of his clothes and then the tear of foil. She opened her eyes and saw him put on protection.

That was a sharp reminder. Tina's breath caught in her throat as she watched him. They weren't starting over. They weren't dreaming of a family anymore. This was the beginning of the end.

Dev settled between her thighs. Her stomach twisted with excitement when she felt the thickness of him against her. He clamped his hands on her hips and he entered her with one long thrust. Tina's gasp echoed in the large room when Dev roughly tilted her hips even more. The most amazing sensations stormed her.

"More," Tina whimpered as she bucked her hips against Dev. He responded with a slow thrust. Tina thought her eyes were going to roll back from the dizzying pleasure.

She wrapped her legs around Dev's waist. He groaned as her tight flesh gripped him like a fist. His pace grew faster, each thrust deeper, as she followed the ancient rhythm.

The pleasure consumed her. She begged for more as she clung to Dev. She wasn't sure what her body was chasing, what it was reaching for until the sensations exploded.

Her mind went blank as she climaxed. Her lungs burned and she forgot to breathe. She held on to Dev as he growled something fierce before he found his release.

It took her a few moments before she realized Dev had

gathered her in his arms. She laid her head on his chest and heard his pounding heartbeat. She stared at him, stunned and shaken.

She was falling for him again. Falling in love with her husband. Had she ever really stopped loving him? The fear threatened to choke her. Tina knew she had to be careful. But how could she when she went wild in his arms every time and then craved his protective embrace?

Tina knew she couldn't get used to this. If she stayed she would lose all her freedom. Dev would have total control of her. Her emotions. Her life.

She couldn't let that happen again.

"Tujhe dekha to yeh janna sanam..." Dev sang softly the next morning as he strode into the bedroom after his shower. One towel was draped low around his hips while he dried his hair with another. He paused when he realized he was singing the romantic song that had been playing in the kitchen the night before.

Damn, what kind of power did Tina have over him? All she had to do was take him to bed and he was breaking out into song. If he wasn't careful, he'd start dancing. But he couldn't hide the satisfaction that poured through his veins or the hope that wanted to burst from his skin. His relationship with Tina had taken a turn and he was so close to his goal. He would keep her as his wife long after their first wedding anniversary.

Dev stopped toweling his hair when he thought he heard a whimper. He glanced at the bed. Tina was huddled in the middle with the twisted bedsheets cocooned around her.

"Tina?" Was she having another nightmare? She'd said she didn't get them anymore. Dev rushed to the bed and saw that she held her hand over her face. It wasn't a bad dream. She would thrash and kick out. Scream. At the moment she didn't seem to have the energy to move. "Tina, what's wrong?"

She grimaced and scrunched her eyes closed. "I don't feel well."

He remembered she'd had a stomachache last night. He'd thought it had been from the stress of dealing with Shreya. Tina was rarely ill and she hadn't shown any signs of pain during the night.

"Was it the *khichri?*"

She opened one eye. "My *khichri* heals stomachaches, it doesn't create them."

He smiled at her offended tone. No one questioned her cooking. "Did you have anything at the party?"

"No."

He tried to remember what she'd had the day before. She had visited her mother but he remembered the number one rule with Reema Sharma's cooking: avoid it at all costs. Tina would know that. She once told him she'd learned how to cook as a matter of survival.

But there was one thing Tina couldn't refuse when she visited that side of Mumbai. "Did you eat street food when you went to your mother's?"

"Of course I did," she said as she wrapped her arms around her stomach. "They have the best *chaat.*"

He placed his hand on her forehead. She looked pale but her skin wasn't warm to the touch. "What did you have to eat?"

"Samosas," Tina said and swallowed hard, as if the thought made her nauseated. "And *channa chaat*. I also had some of Meera's *dahi puri*...."

He shook his head. "And you wonder why you're not feeling well. If they were anything like the *chaat* stalls we've visited, you probably have food poisoning."

She gradually opened her eyes. "I don't think it's the food."

He didn't know what else it could be and he wasn't going to take any chances. Dev knew he was being over-protective but he hated seeing Tina in pain. "Come on," he said as he reached for her hands. "Let's get you to the doctor."

She flinched and jerked back to avoid his touch. "No!"

He stared at Tina as her voice echoed in the large bedroom. He saw the hunted look in her dark eyes and the fear etched across her face. She was shutting him out again.

"I see," Dev said as he slowly straightened to his full height, the pain radiating from his body. The hope shriveled inside once he realized nothing had changed between them.

"I don't want a doctor," she said quietly, unable to meet his gaze. "I hate hospitals."

"No," he corrected her, his voice cold and stiff as the biting hurt slashed his chest, "you don't want *me* to help you."

"That's not it."

"You don't want my name or my protection. My connections? Yes. My concern? No." Dev's tone was harsh. "Now I'm not even allowed to look after you when you're sick?"

Tina weakly closed her eyes. "I don't know why I did that."

"I do." She was rejecting his help again. Rejecting him. "You trust me when I tell you I didn't have an affair with Shreya. You trust me enough to share your bed, your body. But when it comes to taking care of you, you can't trust me at all."

"It was just a reaction," she explained. "I wasn't thinking about it."

That made it worse. Dev clenched his jaw as he fought back the rising tide of anger.

"Go back to sleep, Tina," he said wearily as he took a step away from the bed. "I'll have Sandeep bring something up for you. He'll check up on you throughout the day."

"Where are you going?"

"Out." Any other time, he would have thought she sounded like a wife. But he knew the concern wasn't for him.

"Dev?"

There was something about her tone that pierced through his anger. Dev stopped at the bathroom door and looked over his shoulder. Her back was turned away from him. It was a familiar sight. "What is it, Tina?"

There was a long pause before she spoke. "Would you…stay…with me? Please?" she asked. She said the words slowly, as if they were dragged out from her. "I want you to look after me. No one else."

It wasn't true. She'd rather curl up in a dark corner alone than ask for help. Dev knew she was doing this for him. And yet she acted as if she expected he would reject her. What had he done to make her think that?

"Yes, *jaan,*" he said as he walked to the bed. He didn't feel victorious. He felt as if he was walking on eggshells. One wrong move or wrong word, and he could ruin everything. "I'm here for you."

Hours later Dev set down his laptop computer and leaned back in his chair. He gave Tina an assessing look. "You are a terrible patient."

"So I've been told," Tina said as she flipped through

the movie magazine Dev had asked Sandeep to buy. She sat on the bed and wore her softest, most comfortable *shalwar kameez.* Her stomach didn't hurt as much but her heart was heavy with regret. She couldn't rid the memory of Dev's stricken expression from this morning. She kept pushing him away when she really wanted him near. She didn't know how to stop.

"You don't need to stay, Dev," Tina said with a sigh as she tossed the magazine to the side. "I had some bad *chaat,* that's all."

"You shouldn't try to diagnose yourself," Dev warned her. "You should have a doctor check you out."

"No, that's not necessary." She shivered at the thought. She had grown to hate the sight of surgical scrubs and white coats. "I'm fine. Why don't you go watch cricket or something?"

Dev propped his chin against his hand. He was in no hurry to go anywhere. "Why are you trying to get rid of me?"

Tina leaned her head back against the stack of pillows behind her. "I already feel bad that you're wasting your day in that chair staring at four walls."

"This is where I want to be," he said softly.

"I don't know why," Tina muttered.

"If I was sick, would you look after me?"

She made a face and looked away. "Yes, but that's different."

"Because you never want to rely on anyone," Dev said. "You have to do it all yourself."

It was true. She wasn't comfortable asking for help. Not from anyone, especially her family. She had already been a burden to her mother. A problem for her husband. The last thing she wanted to do was highlight why she was an inconvenience.

"Next time I'm not going to wait for permission to take care of you," Dev said. "I don't mind that you need me. I like it when you depend on me."

Tina frowned. A great many people relied on Dev, from his mother to the people who worked for him. He didn't need another dependent. "You don't want to take on my problems, Dev. You have enough of your own."

"I don't see it that way," Dev said. "When you disappeared, I frequently dropped by your mother's house to check on her and your sisters. You weren't around so I did it for you. Your family is my family."

"Family is important to you." It was a fantasy of his to be part of a big, noisy family. Have the kind he saw in the movies but never had for himself. That was yet another thing she couldn't give him.

"I like being a big brother to Rani and Meera," Dev said with a hint of a smile. "I like helping your mother. She treats me as a son instead of a movie star. I would like to take care of you. You need to stop fighting me every step of the way and just let it happen."

"It's not that easy." She had given him that control, had placed all of her trust in him because she couldn't function. It had been terrifying. And then suddenly he had no longer been there, choosing to be anywhere but at her side. She had felt betrayed.

"Because I wasn't there when you miscarried. I wasn't there afterward."

She raised her gaze to the ceiling. "I didn't ask you to be there."

"I should have been there even if you were trying to kick me out of the room." He paused. "Why didn't you ask for me? Why were you pushing me away? Did you think that I would turn away? Reject you when you needed me the most?"

Tina pressed her lips together as the tears burned in her eyes. "Yes," she said.

The tense silence pulsed in the room. "What did I do to make you think that?"

"It wasn't you. My father ran out when we needed him the most," Tina said softly, lowering her gaze. "When life wasn't turning out the way he thought he deserved it. But he had been absent long before that. I learned not to ask him for anything because it would only lead to disappointment."

"I didn't run out on you. I made sure you had everything you needed." Dev met her gaze. "But it's my deepest regret that I wasn't there when you needed me the most. It wasn't until you disappeared that I realized I was following my parents' footsteps. They were too busy making movies. Sandeep was there for me more than my parents. I don't want to be an absent husband or father. Next time, I'm going to every doctor's appointment and I'm sitting at the table every night for dinner."

Next time. Tina closed her eyes. Next time wouldn't include her. She knew Dev would be a good father. She would've loved to have seen him cradling their baby. He would be a fierce protector, a patient teacher and offer the unconditional love he hadn't got as a child.

She opened her eyes when she heard the beep of his watch. "Time for your medicine and a drink," he announced as he pushed a button on his modern timepiece before rising from his chair.

"No more water." She shook her head. Dev was taking his role as caregiver very seriously.

"You need to keep hydrated," he said as he walked around the bed to the door.

"Be careful, Dev. I might get used to this kind of attention."

He paused and captured her gaze. "That's the plan."

Tina watched wordlessly as he strolled out of the room, whistling a tune from a Salman Khan movie. She stared at the door long after he left. She wasn't sure what he'd meant. Did he want her to stay after the two months were up? No, she shouldn't get her hopes up. His words must have had a simpler meaning. That the next time she was sick, she should turn to him for comfort.

There was probably not going to be a next time. She was usually healthy. She couldn't remember the last time she'd had a cold or the flu. The last time she'd felt nauseous and dizzy was…

Tina's gasp echoed in the bedroom. She flattened her hands against her stomach as the panic raced through her blood. The last time she'd felt like this was in the very early stages of pregnancy.

"No," she whispered as the fear clawed through her. "No, no, no! Not again."

CHAPTER TWELVE

TINA LEANED HER head against the tile wall of her bathroom and closed her eyes. She was sick with nerves. She wanted to double over as the panic threatened to consume her.

Flapping her hands at her sides, Tina tried to gather up the last of her courage. She hadn't been feeling very brave for the past two weeks. Not since she realized her stomachache could mean she was pregnant. Tina had been in denial ever since.

She refused to be pregnant. Refused to go through that nightmare again.

But she couldn't ignore the symptoms anymore. She continued to fight the dizziness. The nausea came in waves. Her appetite increased and her sex drive was out of control.

Dev didn't seem to notice or mind her symptoms. He liked how she reached out for him while they walked side by side. She held on to him, at times clung to him, relying on his strength while her world tilted. He enjoyed sharing his food with her, coaxing her closer as he fed her by hand. Dev never missed the opportunity to stroke her lips with his thumb or capture her chin so he could steal a kiss.

And the sex…Tina's breath hitched in her throat as

her skin tingled. She couldn't get enough of Dev and he reveled in the knowledge. Encouraged it. It was as if he knew the sight of his bare chest and the scent of his skin drove her wild.

Tina rubbed her eyes with the heels of her hands and groaned. She couldn't be pregnant. She and Dev had been careful. It didn't matter if they made love in the courtyard under the stars or indulged in fast and furious sex that took them both by surprise. Dev always used protection. Except for that one time…

She was probably pregnant, Tina admitted to herself. She pressed her trembling lips together as the fear spiked in her chest. She wanted to be a mother, but what if there were complications? What if she miscarried again? The tears trickled down her cheeks. What if she slipped into the darkness, but deeper, and this time never resurfaced?

Dev would take care of her. The thought whispered through her troubled mind. Her eyelashes fluttered as she remembered his promise. He would be there for her this time. He would care for and protect her and the baby. She knew Dev would honor his vow.

And he would insist that they stay married. Tina shook her head and sighed when the hope bubbled and fizzed inside her like champagne. She still loved her husband and wanted to stay with him. But not this way. She wouldn't trap him into marriage again.

Tina wiped the tears from her cheeks with the back of her hands and pushed away from the wall. Perhaps she was borrowing trouble. It was possible that she wasn't pregnant. That her body was still recovering from the stress and changes she had suffered in the past year.

She clung to that belief as she cautiously approached the sink and grabbed the slim pregnancy test stick. Tina braced herself as she glanced at the screen. For a moment her mind didn't register what the two pink lines meant.

Pregnant.

She was pregnant. Tina tossed the stick back on the counter as if it had burned her. A sob erupted from her throat and she clapped her hand over her mouth. It was happening all over again. He legs shook and she slowly slid to the floor. She knelt on the cold linoleum as she cried. What was she going to do? She couldn't lose another baby.

Tina didn't know how long she had been in that position when she heard a hard, authoritative knock on the bathroom door. Her throat was raw and her body ached. Her eyes felt red and swollen. She already felt broken and her journey had barely started.

"Tina?"

She jerked when she heard Dev's voice. She swung her attention to the door as the handle jiggled. He could not come in here. Not when she was vulnerable and needy.

"I'm fine," she lied, her voice wobbling. She forced herself on her feet and glanced at the mirror. She looked horrible. Her skin was tearstained and blotchy. She quickly turned on the faucet and sluiced cold water on her face.

"What's wrong?"

Tina hesitated. A part of her wanted to tell Dev. She was tempted to lean on him and share her deepest fears. But was that wise? Would he take control of her life again?

She had to keep this a secret, Tina decided as she grabbed a towel and patted her face dry. For now. Until she was properly seen by a doctor and understood everything she was facing.

Something heavy slammed against the door and the

solid wood shuddered under the weight. Tina whirled around when she heard Dev's urgent tone from the other side. "Tina, open this door right now."

She looked around the bathroom and found the pregnancy test stick was still on the counter. Her fingers fumbled as she snatched it and threw it in the waste bin. It was blinding pink. She grabbed a few tissues and wadded them as the wall rattled behind her. Tina tossed the bunch of tissues in the waste bin and hurried to unlock the door.

She swung the door open and her gaze clashed with Dev. His dark eyes were wild, his skin stretched taut against his harsh features. He towered over her, the worry and relief pulsating in the air. She noticed he held his shoulder as if it ached.

"Dev—" She faltered into shocked silence as he lowered her arm that blocked his entrance and peered into her bathroom.

"Why didn't you open the door when I asked?" His words were clipped with anger as he grabbed her hands. She instinctively tried to pull away but he was too strong. Dev turned her palms over and checked her wrists.

The old scars on her skin suddenly felt hot and red. "I told you I don't cut anymore," she mumbled. She wished he couldn't see those signs of her weakness.

He glanced up but didn't let go of her hands. "Why were you crying?"

She bit her lip and looked away. "Dev, it's perfectly natural to cry. It's a release from stress and—"

"Not the way you were crying," he said gruffly. "It was as if your whole world was ripped apart."

She swallowed hard. "I'm not going down the rabbit hole again. I promise."

"I think we should stay home."

"Stay home? No, that's not necessary." She blinked

as she suddenly remembered they were supposed to go to a wedding today. The daughter of a business associate was getting married in a huge three-day event. All of Bollywood was attending. Tina wasn't ready to face the pomp and pageantry, but it was better than staying at home and avoiding Dev's probing questions.

She felt Dev watching her intently and the silence was almost unbearable. Tina struggled to meet his gaze. She was taken aback when she saw the pain in his eyes. It was just like when he had told her that he had gone through hell with her. She didn't want him to go through it again. This was her battle.

He didn't need to suffer with her. Because of her.

The *mehndi* celebration was bigger and bolder than Dev had expected. The prewedding ceremony was traditionally to prepare the bride for the wedding. Now it was a huge party that was almost as extravagant as the *walima*.

The ballroom was decorated to give the impression that they were in an ornate tent. Gauzy white curtains and tiny strings of light were draped from the ceiling. The heavy scent of flowers couldn't mask the aroma of the rich, spicy food. He glanced at the circular platform in the middle of the room. The future bride sat next to her groom as they watched a dancing troupe perform.

He noticed that despite the luxurious surroundings, the bride followed tradition and didn't wear makeup or jewelry. Her hands and feet were decorated with intricate henna designs and she wore a simple mustard-yellow gown with a dark green veil over her hair.

The guests were a mix of Bollywood stars and members of the Hindi film industry. They were more interested in the other guests than the proceedings. This was exactly what Tina hated about the wedding extravaganzas of his contemporaries.

Dev looked around the crowd, searching for his wife. He wished she had stayed at his side. He liked linking his hand with hers, but she kept finding an excuse to part.

She was creating a distance between them and he was getting worried. Dev's eyes flicked across the white-and-gold ballroom. Why had she been crying earlier today? It had been more than crying. It had been gut-wrenching sobs that had torn at him.

Instinct had guided him when he'd tried to break down the bathroom door. Dev rotated his shoulder as he felt a twinge of pain. He had panicked but this time he knew not to dismiss the signs.

This time. Dev pulled uncomfortably at his tie. Was she falling into a depression again? Was this arrangement triggering it? No, he decided. He refused to believe that.

Tina might think he had overreacted, but for the past two weeks he had noticed a change in Tina's behavior. She had been listless and staring off into the distance. He had woken her from a bad dream the night before and soothed her back to sleep only for her to talk in her sleep. Why wasn't she telling him what was troubling her?

Dev's heart clenched when he found Tina. She stood among a circle of friends, tilting her head back as she laughed. He yearned to hear that sound more than the chime of her bangles or the faint jingle of her gold anklets.

She didn't wear the sari he had suggested. Dev thought she looked feminine and graceful in a sari but he had to admit she was incredibly sexy in the emerald green *ghagra choli*. The short sleeves emphasized her toned arms and the snug shirt revealed the smooth, golden skin of her midriff. The long beaded skirt flared at the knee, but it wasn't as modest as he had hoped. Instead it clung lovingly to her curves.

Tina looked strong and healthy. Elegant and stunning. He was damn proud to have her at his side. As his wife.

Dev's expression grew fierce as he watched Tina. He was proud of her. She had achieved so much through hard work and perseverance. She didn't seem to be aware of her own strength. Not only had she faced challenges to support her family, but she had also struggled to recover from grief and illness.

He saw Tina's posture stiffen before she raised her head and captured his gaze. She gave him a questioning look and Dev allowed his eyes to linger on her tiny blouse and bare stomach. He dragged his gaze back to her face and watched his wife blush.

Her smile faded as he approached. She quickly said something to the other women and briskly met him in the middle of the ballroom.

"What do you think of the wedding?" Dev asked.

She glanced at the round stage. "I feel sorry for the bride."

Her words pinched his chest. He grabbed at his dark tie and loosened it. Was this her opinion on marriage? Did she feel sorry for all brides and wives? "Why is that?"

Tina gave a small shrug. "It's supposed to be her day but no one is paying attention to her. Not even the groom. They are all too busy trying to do business and make deals."

Dev placed his hand on the small of her back and was rewarded with the touch of her warm, smooth skin. "I paid attention to you at our wedding," he said against her ear.

Tina shivered from his nearness. "Yes, but I made sure there were no other distractions."

Their elopement had been stripped down to the essentials. He had ignored the postwedding rituals that included welcoming Tina into his house and his family. His wife was modern but he should have honored her new role. He should have shown how important she was to him.

"I'm sorry how I acted," he said as they walked outside the ballroom.

"On our wedding day?" Tina frowned. "What are you talking about? You were very solemn during the ceremony."

"I was arrogant when I asked you to marry me," Dev admitted. He stopped on the red carpet and looked at the ropes of lights coiling around the pillars at the entrance of the party. It was quiet and there were only a few servants walking around. "I didn't ask or propose. I told you that we were getting married."

Tina pulled away and stood in front of him. "What's going on? It's not like you to be this…introspective. How many drinks have you had?"

"I'm not drunk. I was thinking about when we first got married. You were my wife but I treated you like a guest in my home, in my life."

Tina gave him a look of concern and rested her hand on his arm. "It's okay, Dev. If I had a problem with that, I would have spoken up."

"No, you wouldn't. You were afraid to make waves. Cause any inconvenience."

She dropped her hand and looked way. "You make me sound like a coward."

"Coward? You?" He scoffed at the idea. "You wanted everything to be perfect even if it required you to make the sacrifices."

Tina crossed her arms. "I'm not a martyr."

"You're too independent," he complained with a growl. "You refuse to ask for help."

"I'm working on that." She took a step back and he followed.

"Why don't you audition for one of my movies?" Dev asked. Her insistence on avoiding Arjun Entertainment was like a thorn in his skin.

"No! You still don't get it, Dev." She thrust her hands in her short hair and gave a harsh sigh. "Everyone wants something from you. If they don't ask for it, you'll offer something. Anything. It's how you work a relationship."

Dev narrowed his eyes. He didn't like where this conversation was going. "What are you talking about?"

"You think you have to do something to earn your way into people's hearts," she said as she gestured wildly with her hands. "You have to be number one in the box office to win approval from your parents. You have to pay everything to gain acceptance with my mother."

Was this how Tina saw him? That he had to buy his way to a person's heart? "I have money and I want to help out."

"At first I thought it was your way of maintaining control in a relationship. Now I realize that you can't just give yourself. You don't think you're enough."

He didn't like this. He jutted out his chin as the dark emotions started to swirl in his chest. "That's not true."

"And you are just as reluctant to ask for help as I am." She placed her hands on her hips. "Do you realize that asking me to stay for two months was the only time you asked for my assistance in anything?"

"You were pregnant and then you were grieving." He had gone out of his way to keep the world at bay. He didn't want her to worry about anything.

"I still wanted to look after you. You were my husband."

"I *am* your husband."

"I ask for your advice all the time," she continued as if he hadn't made that declaration. "But I didn't want you to think I married you because you could help my career. I wanted you, not what you could do for me."

"You didn't need to prove anything," he said. "I know why you married me."

Tina's cheeks went red. "You do?"

"You didn't want to be a single mother."

Tina blinked and gave a slight shake of her head. "Dev, I didn't marry you just because I was having your baby."

Dev clenched his teeth as the curiosity swelled inside him. Why had she married him? He wanted to know but he was afraid the reason no longer applied. What would it take for her to *stay* married?

"This is the problem with attending weddings," Tina said as she cast a look at the entrance. "It makes you think about your own. Your marriage. What you would have done differently."

"You know what I would have done differently?" he asked gruffly.

She gave him a wary look. "No, Dev. What?"

"I wouldn't have gotten you pregnant."

His words were like a punch to the chest. If she hadn't gotten pregnant, he would still be the most eligible bachelor, living a carefree life and driving his career to new heights. "I know," she said softly. "It changed everything, didn't it?"

"No, *jaan*. You misunderstand me." He reached out and gathered her in his arms. She pressed her hands against his muscular chest and felt the solid beat of his heart. "I would have protected you better. I would have looked after you."

"That was my responsibility, not yours." She should have been more careful but apparently she did not learn from her mistakes.

"I disagree." His expression was fierce and she watched the fire in his eyes. "I should never have allowed you to get pregnant. It was an oversight on my part. But I was glad you were carrying my child."

Her heart did a funny, slow flip. She knew he had been excited about the baby but she needed to hear that he didn't regret it. "You always wanted a family."

"And I wanted *you,*" Dev said quietly. "I would have eventually asked you to marry me, but the baby moved up my timetable."

Her heart skipped a beat. "You would have married me even if I wasn't carrying your baby?" That she did not believe. He was idealizing their affair. If she hadn't been pregnant, he would have ended their affair to enter an arranged marriage with Shreya.

"You gave me the one thing I never had," Dev said as she brushed his finger along her cheek. "A home life. A world outside the film industry."

"You could have gotten that on your own," she whispered as her throat tightened with emotion.

His mouth lifted in a lopsided smile. "Not without your insistence."

She rested her forehead against his chest, unable to look at him. She felt shy. Uncertain. She had fought for him to have a life outside the office, but she didn't feel like she had made any significant achievement. "You really don't ask for much," she muttered.

"I asked for everything. And I got it."

And then I lost it.... The words hung above them unspoken. Dev rested his hand against the crown of her head.

"You're the one who didn't ask for anything," he pointed out.

"That's because I would ask for the impossible. What purpose would that serve?"

"I can make anything happen."

She smiled at his arrogant statement. He was confident of his abilities but she knew there were some things even the great Dev Arjun couldn't achieve. She wanted to ask for another chance. Try to save their marriage with no time limit. She wanted to stay but she knew nothing had changed. She couldn't risk her future with a man who would strip her of her voice, her power and her financial independence, believing it was for her own good.

"What do you want right now?" he whispered. "Ask and I will give it to you."

She wasn't going to ask for the moon or the stars. She wasn't going to ask for her heart's desire when she knew it wasn't going to happen. Instead she focused on what she could have for now.

"I've had enough of this wedding." Tina lifted her head, her gaze ensnaring his. "I want to go home and take you to bed."

His smile turned wicked. "I'm all yours."

CHAPTER THIRTEEN

TINA STIRRED IN her sleep, burrowing her head against Dev's shoulder as the blanket slipped down to her waist. She felt as if she should remember something but the memory was just out of reach. She stretched, murmuring with delight when her breasts pressed against Dev's chest as her legs brushed against his.

A small smile formed on her lips as she dragged her foot along his calf. She enjoyed the friction of his rough hair against the side of her toe. Tina felt the solid muscle and strength under his warm skin. She liked waking up next to him this way. Naked with their arms and legs tangled, as if they couldn't stand the idea of letting go in their sleep.

She'd have to get used to waking up alone again. Tina's smile faded as she slid her hand down Dev's rock-hard abdomen. According to their original agreement, she only had a few more days of this—a little more than a week.

Tina didn't want to think about it. She tried to block it from her mind as she brushed her fingertips along Dev's hip, noticing how he didn't stir under her touch. She wanted to wake him up and make love. Lust heated her blood at the thought. She didn't want to waste a minute of the time they had left together.

She was almost embarrassed at how eager she was to

be with her husband. It wasn't too long ago when she had looked for every possible way to stay out of his bed. At the beginning of this deal, she had started a countdown, telling herself that she could get through the two months. Now it was a reminder that this was all going to end and she would have to accept a life without Dev.

She wasn't ready, Tina thought as she wrapped her hand around his erection and sighed. She wanted another chance at her marriage. A do-over.

She could have it if she told Dev about the baby. But she couldn't do that to him again. She couldn't keep him in this marriage because she was pregnant. She couldn't let him take over her life. She knew he was doing it out of a sense of duty, protection instead of punishment, but it was a fate she couldn't accept.

Tina knew she had to tell Dev about her pregnancy. It was the right thing to do and he deserved to know, she decided as she slowly stroked him. Her instincts told her to wait until he no longer had legal power over her. It wouldn't be that many more days before she moved out. Today was the fifteenth and…

The fifteenth. Tina froze, her hand clenched around Dev's velvety soft skin as the shock rippled through her. Today was her wedding anniversary.

Her eyes flew open. Her heart was beating fast, her throat tightening as her gaze collided with Dev's.

She knew. Dev was aware of the moment she realized it was their wedding anniversary. His breath caught in his throat as he watched the myriad emotions flickering in her brown eyes. Not one of them was celebratory.

Did she still think this marriage was a failure? He wasn't ready to give up. Tina was the only woman he wanted and he was going to convince her to stay.

It's a shame she wasn't pregnant, Dev decided. That would give them a bond that could never be broken. Not only would they create the family they wanted, but the nine months would also give him plenty of time to repair their marriage.

Tina looked away. "Why did you stop?" he asked in a husky growl.

She turned. "We should get up."

Dev moved swiftly, covering her body with his, before she could get out of bed. "I was thinking…"

"This early in the morning?" she asked, doing her best not to make eye contact. "That's never a good thing."

"Why don't we take a trip?" he asked as he kissed a trail down her throat.

"A trip?" There wasn't a hint of interest in her voice.

"We could visit the beaches in Goa," he suggested as he brushed his lips along her breastbone. "Or we could visit the foothills."

"Don't you have a few upcoming meetings at the office?" she asked. Her breathing was uneven as she rocked her hips in anticipation.

"I can postpone them," Dev offered absently as he slid his mouth down her stomach. His pulse kicked hard as he hooked Tina's legs over his arms.

"You shouldn't have to," Tina said huskily as she twisted her fingers in his hair. "I know you have a lot riding on these investors. We don't need to go anywhere."

He paused, wondering why she was acting this way. In the past, they had gone on trips together for work. Why would she decline when it was for just the two of them? "We haven't been anywhere since Los Angeles."

Her body jerked. "That was a disaster. Why would you want to try again?"

"Why not? Let's replace a bad memory with a good one."

"I'm sorry I walked out on you," Tina whispered. "Can you forgive me?"

"I already have." And he meant it.

She gave a tight-lipped smile. "You were right. I was so lost in grieving that I pushed you away. I thought you had married me because of the baby. I wasn't sure how you really felt about having me as a wife."

He was also at fault and he was trying to make up for it. Dev wanted to show how much he loved and appreciated her. He wanted to give her the honeymoon she'd never had but he was reluctant to mention that. She was avoiding the topic of their anniversary and now wouldn't be a good time to present her with the jewelry set he had bought that had once belonged to a *maharani*. It was the bridal jewelry she should have had.

"Where would you like to go?" He bent his head and teased her navel with his tongue. "Europe? Australia?"

"I'd like to stay here," she said breathlessly.

He pressed his lips on her inner thigh. "I can take you anywhere in the world and you want to stay here?"

"Why not?" she murmured as she bucked her hips. "Can you think of a better place?"

"No," he said as he pressed his mouth against the slick folds of her sex. The only place he wanted to be was at home with Tina.

"Why don't you wait for your husband in his office, *Tinaji?*" Dev's assistant, dressed in crisply ironed white *kurta shalwar,* escorted her into the garish office. Tina flinched at the sight of the gold-trimmed furniture and campy movie posters. "His meeting should end soon."

Tina gave the older man a knowing smile. Dev was

never on schedule. She was lucky if he showed up within the hour.

"It's a shame he had to work on your wedding anniversary," the assistant said.

"It's not all bad. Dev loves what he does," Tina replied as her courage slowly faded. "But I thought I could steal him away and take him to lunch."

"You should visit more often. He would love that. Can I get you anything to drink?"

She declined, the tension rising in her as she waited in the silent room. She didn't know how Dev could work in this office. It wasn't like him at all. He preferred natural textiles and modern art. Everything here celebrated his family's cinema achievements. It was a constant reminder of his family's legacy.

Tina bit her lip as she looked around. She tried not to compare her modest success to that of the Arjun family. She had made mistakes and taken the wrong advice. While she may never be a Bollywood megastar, she was taking steps to take full control of her career.

And sometimes she needed to take a step away from work. Right now she needed to focus on her family, not her career. *I can do this...I can tell Dev about the baby... This is a good thing...Dev is going to be thrilled, just like last time.*

Only last time, he hadn't thought about what all could go wrong. Neither of them had. Tina slowly sat down on the sofa. Last time he had embraced the news. In his world, everything he touched turned to gold and every choice he made turned out better than expected.

Stop it. You can't hide this anymore. No more excuses. It was time to tell him. Why not now, on their wedding anniversary? Dev cared about her and she had to trust him. Tina knew he would take care of her if anything went wrong and she had nothing to fear.

Tina tugged at her pink sari and made a face. She hated wearing it but she liked how Dev responded when she wore the feminine garment. She needed all the help she could get to place him in a receptive mood.

She looked down at the pile of this week's movie magazines on the coffee table in front of her. A few of them had the Arjun family portrait, commemorating Vikram's long career. Another magazine cover caught her eye. Her stomach clenched when she saw a picture of Dev and Shreya in an embrace.

Why? Why did they have to show these pictures and share these stories on her anniversary? How many "it won't last" or "trouble in paradise" stories must she suffer through?

Tina reached out for it and stopped. She didn't want to know. She wasn't going to read the article or the headline. What purpose would it serve? If she kept reading the gossip it would chip away at the trust she had in Dev. If he said he was not having an affair with Shreya, she would believe him. She wouldn't require proof, just like he trusted her when she swore she hadn't slept with anyone during their separation.

"Tina?"

Tina closed her eyes when she heard the familiar voice. What was her mother-in-law doing here? How could she have forgotten that Gauri Arjun had an office suite in the building?

She reluctantly turned around and saw Dev's mother enter the room. The older woman was stunning in a vibrant green sari. Her hair flowed smoothly against her shoulders and it was all Tina could do not to smooth her own short, spiky hair. What was it about this woman that always made her feel awkward and insignificant?

Tina rose from her seat and adjusted her sari as she politely greeted her mother-in-law. The woman waved away her attempts impatiently.

"What is this about you going to Hollywood?" Gauri asked. "This is unacceptable. The Arjun family is the face of the Hindi film industry. Going to Los Angeles is a betrayal of our heritage and our culture."

Tina's eyes widened as she jerked in surprise. "Who says I'm going to Hollywood?"

"The rumors are everywhere that you are going to star in a television show. An Arjun on American television!" Gauri shuddered. Tina wasn't sure which part of the American television it was that bothered her.

But why did Gauri believe she was… Tina winced as she remembered the tidbit of information she had shared with her mother. The casual remark the television director had said at the treatment center about how they should work together. Nothing was signed or agreed upon, but that didn't matter. Reema was going to make it look like Tina was in high demand. This was yet another indication for Tina that she needed to get another manager.

"Now is not a good time to discuss this, *Maaji,*" Tina muttered as she nervously clasped her fingers in her lap.

"My son isn't going to Hollywood," Gauri said in a hiss. "His destiny is here."

Tina frowned. "Who says he's going to Hollywood?"

"You are his wife. You go where he goes. Unless…" She reared her head back. "What are you saying?"

"I believe she is saying that I'm not invited." Dev drawled. Tina whirled around to see Dev leaning at the door. Her heart stopped for a moment when she saw glittery coldness in his eyes. "Congratulations on the role."

Why would he think she had a role? A role she hadn't even discussed with him. A role that would require leaving Mumbai. Leaving him.

Did he think she would do that without talking to him? Of course he would. She had left him like that in the past. But she was different now. They were different. Why didn't he see that? "Dev, let me explain."

"There's no need," he said as he strode to his desk. He showed no emotions but Tina could tell by his choppy movements and the muscle bunching in his jaw that he was holding back his fury. "You are getting the career that you've longed for, leaving behind the husband you no longer want and settling a few scores before you leave. Am I missing anything?"

CHAPTER FOURTEEN

THE SILENCE PULSED in the office after his mother muttered something and left. Dev felt the tension coiling inside him, so swift and ferocious, that he was surprised his body didn't shatter. She had used their marriage—used him—as leverage to further her career. He never thought Tina would betray him like this.

He rested his fists on the desk and forced himself to look at his wife. "My publicity department is in a panic," Dev said. "It appears that your mother is shopping around a tell-all exposé."

"My mother?"

"Not only will it discuss how horribly I treated you and how amazing I am in bed, but it will also explain your mysterious disappearance."

"This is the first I've heard of it," she blurted out. "You know I would never do something like this."

"Do I?" he asked silkily as the anger ate at him like acid. "And yet you threatened me with this not too long ago. At the time I didn't believe it. I didn't think you had it in you."

"When did I say that?" She tilted her head as it occurred to her. "Wait, do you mean when I found out that Shreya was playing Laila? I said that in anger but I wouldn't do that. That would have hurt me just as much as you."

Dev stared at her. It would have been suicide to her career if she had planned to stay in Mumbai. Now she was ready to throw a grenade on everything they had together and walk away. Tina's action proved only one thing: she didn't want another chance at this marriage.

The blow was staggering. He had done everything he could and she was ready to walk. Why had he thought he could change her mind? She had not mentioned a future together.

"Say something," Tina whispered. She watched him with extreme caution as she wrung her hands together.

"You're a better actress than anyone gives you credit for," he said as he pushed away from his desk. "I believed you."

She frowned as she nervously tugged at her sari. "What are you talking about?"

"You refused to take my name because you didn't want anyone to accuse you of marrying an Arjun for career advancement." He braced his legs and crossed his arms, ready for battle. "You refused to work with me or with Arjun Entertainment. You rejected my help every step of the way because you didn't want to feel obligated to me."

"I was wrong to do that," she said. "I didn't know that my decisions hurt you."

Was that it? Or was she playing the devoted wife for another reason? There had been starlets who had wanted to be part of the Arjun dynasty. They had been traditional with perfect backgrounds, but none of them interested him. Had Tina known how to seduce him? Was she just as devious as the characters she played?

Her career would skyrocket if she didn't play the dutiful wife. Salacious gossip—true or false—would put her in higher demand. But it was a short-term strategy. If she played it right and cashed in quickly, she would have the money and fame she'd always wanted.

"I take it you saw the magazine cover. The one with me and Shreya."

"I don't care about that." She gestured at the magazine on the coffee table.

"Don't lie to me, *jaan*. I know that you saw a divorce lawyer today." He had seen the amateur pictures on a few blogs moments ago in his meeting with the publicity department. The publicist was annoyed that these pictures had been taken on their anniversary. Dev had been stunned. It had been like a sharp dagger to the heart. All this time he had thought they were reconciling but Tina wasn't going to wait one minute longer to start the divorce process.

Tina gasped. "Divorce lawyer? What are you talking about?"

"You must have rushed right over there after seeing the magazine." She'd sworn she would walk out if there was any evidence that he was having an affair. "Or did you make the appointment two months ago when we made our agreement? Or was it longer ago than that? When you walked away? The night after we got married?"

"You've got it all wrong, Dev."

He tried to ignore her stricken expression. "You married me to improve your career in Hindi films. Now you're going to Hollywood and you don't need my help."

Tina took a step forward. "I married you because I loved you."

Dev scoffed at her declaration. "I don't believe that for a second. If you had loved me, it was a very weak love. It broke the moment we faced trouble."

"That's not true. I have always loved you." She squared

back her shoulders and pressed her fists at her sides. "Do you know how demeaning it is to love someone who resents being married to you? Or how much it hurts to love someone who makes you feel unwanted and unworthy of his attention?"

"It wasn't too long ago when you declared that you hated me."

"I hated what you did to me." Her chin wobbled as the tears shone in her eyes. "I hated that you had all the power and I had none. I hated that I could love you even under all the hate."

All the power? He was defenseless when it came to Tina. "Get out." His voice was weak and raspy.

Tina went very still. "What?"

"You heard me. Get out." He pointed at the door. "Get out of this office. Get out of my home. Get out of my life."

She clasped her hands together and gave him a pleading look. "Dev, I didn't go to a divorce lawyer."

"Move out of my house immediately and go to America." He needed her to go across the world. He would breathe easier knowing she couldn't invade his life again.

"But...but..." Tina looked at the door and then at him. "What about your investors?"

He gave a humorless chuckle and rubbed his hand over his face. Once he had felt guilty about lying to her. He knew she would be angry when she found out but he'd thought it was for a good cause. His crumbling marriage. "There are none."

"What? I don't understand. What happened?"

"There never were investors. I lied, Tina." Dev watched the realization dawn on her. "I said that so you would stay. I had this crazy idea that if I could have you back home for a few months, you would fall back in love with me and we could start over."

Tina closed her eyes and pressed her lips together. "Wh-why didn't you tell me that?"

"Right, because you were so receptive to the idea. You would have run as far as you could in the other direction if you'd known what I wanted."

"Dev, you have to believe me. I didn't do anything behind your back. I want to—"

"I've heard enough." That was the problem. He wanted to believe her. He wanted to believe that he misunderstood. That Tina was innocent. And he would keep on believing as she wrung the hope out of him. This time he had to protect himself. "Get out."

She stared at him. He felt the wild energy swirling around her. An urgency. He knew the feeling. It had happened the last time his world fell apart and there was nothing he could do to save his dreams.

"I mean it, Tina." He watched her tremble at the menace in his voice. "If you don't leave right now, I will carry you out myself."

"But…" she gave another quick glance at the door. "What if I'm pregnant?"

Her words stung like the tip of a whip. His anger spiked so hot that it felt incandescent. Dev decided Tina was lucky there was a desk between them. "Don't even joke about it."

"I'm serious. What happens if I'm carrying your baby?"

"Life wouldn't be so cruel."

She gasped and jerked back. He knew his words wounded her. It didn't please him.

"If you're pregnant, I would stay married to you," he said. Only this time, he wouldn't hope for a reconciliation. "We will have separate homes, live on different continents and have separate lives. It worked for my parents. Why should I want anything different?"

"No." She shook her head. "No, you don't want that. I know you, Dev."

But that was before he'd discovered that Tina didn't want a future or a family with him. How long would she have dangled the promise of forever if the American television deal hadn't gone through?

"And the child would stay with me," he said. He couldn't imagine the demands she would have made if she had carried his child. The Arjun heir.

"No court would allow that!"

He didn't know why they were arguing about it. Tina had made it very clear that she didn't want to carry a baby again. Namely, *his* baby. That had hurt him more than he cared to admit. "Do you think you can fight the influence and money I have?"

Tina blinked as she swayed on her feet. She grabbed the back of the chair as her body began to shake. "You wouldn't," she whispered.

He didn't think he would, but he wasn't thinking about what was right or wrong at the moment. He was in pain and he was lashing out. "Don't test me," he warned. "But you're not carrying my baby. This time I walk away. This time *I'm* asking for the divorce. Get out of my life, Tina. I don't want you as my wife anymore."

The drums pounded as Tina spun wildly on the stage. She was giving this performance everything she had. Her lungs burned, her legs shook and she fought the wave of dizziness. She was almost done.... Almost there...

As the music ended with a dramatic flourish, the folds of her tunic still moving, Tina smiled and tossed her hands up in the air to thunderous applause. She wanted to savor this moment, the last time she was going to perform, but the crowd's reaction didn't break through the sadness that had settled around her the past month.

Tina curtseyed to the bridal party and immediately left the stage, ignoring the cries for an encore. She waved to the well-dressed crowd and gave a deep sigh as her lungs threatened to shrivel. She knew this wedding dance was her last performance. She was retiring after tonight.

"I don't think anyone noticed that one mistake." Her mother was at her side wearing her best *shalwar kameez*. The *dupatta* shot with gold thread was barely hanging on to her shoulders. She gave Tina a bottle of water and a hand towel to wipe off the sweat. "And what happened at the end when you stumbled? Are you feeling dizzy again?"

"It'll go away," Tina said. She had overdone it and it was going to take a moment or two to recover.

Reema glanced over Tina's shoulder as if gauging the audience's mood. "After tonight, I'm sure you will get other offers to dance at weddings."

"I'm not interested." Her fingers fumbled as she tried to open the water bottle.

Reema sighed. "You should keep your options open. I understand why you refused the tell-all. It wasn't my best idea."

"That's why you're no longer my manager," Tina reminded her. "You should have told me what you were planning to do before you shopped it around."

"It's easier to ask for forgiveness than permission," Reema said. "And it's a shame the American TV deal didn't go through."

"There was never a deal, Amma."

"No one needs to know that," Reema said. "But that

doesn't mean you have to turn your back on entertaining altogether."

"There's no point in starting up again only to have to stop in the next few months." Her hands brushed against her stomach. "I want to concentrate on getting through this pregnancy."

"Or are you trying to hide your pregnancy from your husband?" Reema asked.

"You know why I have to hide this information," Tina said tightly. When she had moved in with her mother and sisters, Tina told them how she had sought help for her depression. She had hoped to find support but their responses had been awkward and uncomfortable. At times she wished she had kept it a secret.

"I think he should know," Reema said as she hurriedly fixed her *dupatta*. "He should be the one taking care of you."

"I am taking care of myself and I am under the care of the best doctors. Also—" Tina's voice faded as she watched her mother's gaze dart over her shoulder again. "What's going on?"

"Going on?" Her mother's voice was high and screechy. "Nothing."

She sensed a stir of interest in the workers behind her. Dread twisted her stomach as she watched the guilt bloom in her mother's face. "What did you do?"

Reema thrust her chin out defiantly. "I invited him to Meera's wedding. He's still paying for it after everything that happened. And I might have let it slip—"

Tina gasped in horror. Dev had found out about the baby. "No!" She whirled around, her head spinning. It took a moment for her eyes to adjust. She blinked and stared into Dev's dark brown eyes.

Her heart leaped and crashed when she saw his fury.

He towered over her, his hands clenched at his sides. He was an intimidating sight in his dark suit and tie. Her balance weaved as she inhaled a faint whiff of his cologne. She wanted to throw herself in his arms and she wanted to run far, far away.

"It is true?" His voice slashed through the tense atmosphere.

"I…" She frowned as dark spots gathered in the corner of her eyes.

"Just tell me the truth." He reached out and grabbed her upper arms. "Are you carrying my baby?"

The dark spots grew bigger and she suddenly felt very cold. "Dev?" she called out before her head lolled back and she fainted.

Tina didn't want to wake up. For the first time in a month she felt warm and safe. She snuggled deeper into her pillow and sighed. There was something strangely familiar about the bed. It was more luxurious than the one at her mother's house. And the buzz of the ceiling fan reminded her of a different room. A different bed.

She forced her eyes open and looked at the fan whirring above her. Her chest tightened and she decided she wasn't brave enough to look to her side. She remembered fainting at the wedding and waking up in Dev's strong arms. She had struggled to keep her eyes open but lost the battle. When she had opened them again she had been in a car, still surrounded by Dev's arms.

Now she was back in Dev's bed. What was going on?

She jerked when she heard her mother's loud voice down the hall. Reema was complaining and giving orders. Some things were normal.

"I wanted to take you to the hospital."

She froze when she heard Dev's voice. Damn. She

paused to gather all the courage she could muster and turned to see Dev lounging on the chair next to the bed. His jacket had been discarded and his tie was loosened. His hair was mussed as if he had raked his fingers through it continuously. And he still looked incredibly handsome.

"But I know how you feel about those places," he continued. "So I brought you here and we're waiting for the doctor."

"I don't need a doctor." She needed to get out of here. Get out of Dev Arjun's sphere where he ruled all.

Dev's eyes narrowed with impatience. "Don't make me regret this decision, *jaan.* The only reason we are here is because of your fear of hospitals."

"I'm not afraid of hospitals," she insisted. She had been going to doctors and specialists since she left Dev a month ago and the hospital settings didn't bother her. "It just brings back the bad memories."

"You didn't answer my question," he reminded her. "Are you pregnant?"

He knew. She was displaying the same dizziness as the first time she was pregnant. He didn't need confirmation so why did he keep asking? "You don't want the answer."

"You don't know what I want."

"I know that you want me out of your life. You think life couldn't be that cruel to have me carrying your baby. But I don't know why you, who wanted to end this marriage as soon as possible, haven't made a move towards a divorce." His lack of action had surprised her. Confused her. Made her hope for things that weren't possible.

"Because I don't want a divorce. I never did."

She scoffed. "You did when you thought I was giving a tell-all interview. You thought I was betraying you. Hurting you so I could further my career."

He tilted his head in acknowledgment. "I was hurt and I said a few things I shouldn't. What I should have told you, what I should have said a year ago, is that I want you as my wife."

It was too late for her to hear those words and yet they pulled at her. "Don't waste your time revising history," she whispered as her chest ached with regret. "You're only saying this because you think I'm pregnant."

"I want this child, too." He leaned forward and braced his arms on his knees. "I want the family life that I thought only existed in the movies. You made my dream come true and I want to hold on to it forever."

"I want something else," she said, her voice rising. He was saying all the things she wanted to hear and it scared her. Her heart was beating frantically and yet she was settling deeper into the bed when she should be launching out of it and running out the door. "I'm going to Hollywood, remember?"

"No, you're not," he said softly. "I know all about it. When you refused to go to Los Angeles, your mother came to me in a panic. She thought I was trying to control your career again."

Tina wanted to scream with frustration. She didn't think her mother would have said anything to Dev. She wanted him to think she had moved on so she could get through this pregnancy without any interference.

"You didn't think I had an affair with Shreya, did you?"

Tina frowned as she tried to think of an explanation that didn't reveal too much. "I know nothing is going on between you and Shreya." The magazine headlines bothered her because she knew the truth. She didn't like the lies that were said about Dev and wanted people to know that he was a man worthy of her love and respect.

"I was sure you were canceling our agreement on our anniversary," Dev said. "I thought you didn't trust me. It turns out I had jumped to conclusions and ruined everything."

"I trust you, Dev," she whispered.

"If you're pregnant, you can't get rid of me," Dev said as he held her gaze. "I will be there for you whether or not you want me around."

"You don't have to go through this again," Tina said. "Get out now while you can."

"I don't want to get out," Dev said in a growl. "I want to care for you. I protect what is mine."

"I am not yours." It hurt to say that out loud. Tina blinked away the tears that threatened to spill from her lashes. "You threw me out, remember?"

"I felt like I was the only one fighting for us. I wanted you to fight just as hard. Instead, you walked away."

Tina's deep sigh dragged from her throat. "I'm tired of fighting."

"So I'll keep fighting for us," he vowed as he watched her intently. "But if I can't have that, then let me support you. Let me be a part of this."

She wanted Dev to be part of every step in this journey. She needed to rely on him if something went wrong. But if he knew what could happen, why was he volunteering to stay? "You've been through this before. Why would you want to go through it again?"

"Is that why you're not telling me? Is this your way of protecting me? Or were you keeping the baby a secret so I didn't take it away from you?"

"Does it matter?"

"Yes, it matters!" He swore and lowered his voice. "I love you and I want to look after you. Why is it so hard to accept that?"

"You love me?" she repeated in a daze.

"Yes, I have always loved you." He looked away, almost shyly. "I tried to fight it, but it overpowers me. I thought that the love I have was strong enough that it could carry the both of us. I was wrong. I want you to love me. Trust me. Need me."

She hesitated, feeling like she was on the edge of a big cliff and ready to take a leap of faith. "Dev, did you wonder why I went to your office a month ago?"

"I thought you had come back from the lawyers and were going to ask for a divorce."

Her skin felt hot as nervousness raced through her veins. "I was going to ask for you to give our marriage a second chance."

He winced. "You were?"

"I wore a sari, Dev. That should have been your first clue that I was going to ask for something important."

Dev leaned back in his chair and rubbed his hands over his eyes. "You wanted to try again. And I threw you out."

"I want you as my husband," she said, her heart pounding against her ribs. If he rejected her now she wouldn't recover. "But not for a limited time. I'm staying with you through thick and thin. If you don't want this, you need to tell me now."

"Tina, you are what I want, and I will show that to you every day."

EPILOGUE

Four years later

TINA SHARMA ARJUN strode to the front door of her home as the hot, fragrant breeze pulled at her shoulder-length hair. She tilted her head when she heard the loud, pulsating *bhangra* music.

"*Memsahib!*" Sandeep greeted her as he stood at the threshold.

"It sounds like the party has already started," she said with a smile.

"They are in the courtyard," the manservant said as he accepted her bag. "How did the filming go today?"

"It was wonderful," Tina replied. She felt energized even after a full day of shooting an item number. She had always wanted to be an item girl, who made a cameo appearance in a song-and-dance scene. When she casually mentioned it to Dev, he had made sure she got the honor to be featured in the latest installment of his blockbuster movie franchise.

As much as she loved being surrounded by creative people who were excited to work with her, Tina was glad to be home. She walked through the house to get to the enclosed courtyard and noticed the servants were preparing the dining room for the dinner party. Tina was looking forward to celebrating her fifth wedding anniversary with a few close friends.

She stopped when she listened to the music wafting through the windows. It was the song from Dev's first hit movie. He only performed that dance for someone special. Tina hurried outside and along the stone path so she could watch.

She walked past the trees and her heart did a slow flip as she watched her lean and muscular husband holding their son close to his chest as he danced. Her heart did a slow flip as she watched Tanvir's little arms pump to the music as he gave a high-pitched laugh. Dev smiled, his harsh features softening as he completed the dance.

"Again!" Lakshmi, their daughter said, jumping up and down.

She watched Dev patiently teach Lakshmi an intricate step. Tina treasured moments like these. She placed her hand on her stomach, excited that their family continued to grow. She was nervous every time she became pregnant, but she trusted that Dev would be there when she needed him. He would do anything to protect her and their children.

Dev turned his head and captured her gaze. His eyes darkened with love and desire and she blushed when his mouth slanted into a wicked smile. She knew her children spotted her when she heard their squeals of delight. Tina raised her arms as the joy zipped through her veins.

She joined in and danced.

* * * * *

TO DEFY A SHEIKH

MAISEY YATES

To Megan Crane, who said 'obviously you have to write this book' when I told her about my idea. There are few things that are more valuable than the encouragement of friends.

CHAPTER ONE

SHEIKH FERRAN BASHAR, ruler of Khadra, would not survive the night. He didn't know it yet, but it was true.

Killing a man was never going to be easy. But that was why she'd trained, why she'd practiced the moves over and over again. So that they became muscle memory. So that when the time came there would be no hesitation. No regret.

She waited by the door of the sheikh's bedchamber, a cloth soaked in chloroform in one hand, a knife stowed securely in her robe. There could be no noise. And she would have to surprise him.

How could she have regret? When she knew what his legacy had brought onto hers. Tradition as old as their kingdoms demanded this. Demanded that his line end with him.

As hers had ended with her father. With one lone, surviving daughter who could never carry the name. With a kingdom that had lost its crown and suffered years of turmoil as a result.

But now was no time for emotion. No time for anything but action. She'd gotten herself hired on at the palace a month ago for this very purpose. And Ferran had been no wiser. Of course he hadn't. Why would he ever look at her? Why would he ever recognize her?

But she recognized him. And now, she'd observed him. Learned him.

Sheikh Ferran was a large man, tall and lean with hard

muscle and impressive strength. She'd watched him burn off energy in the courtyard, hitting a punching bag over and over again. She knew how he moved. She knew his endurance level.

She would be merciful. He would feel nothing.

He would not know it was coming. He would not beg for his life. He wouldn't wait in a cell for his life to end, as her father had. It would simply end.

Yes, unlike him, she would show mercy in that way at least.

And she knew that tonight, she would win.

Or she would be the one who didn't live to see morning. It was a risk she was willing to take. It was one she had to take.

She waited, her muscles tense, everything in her on high alert. She heard footsteps, heavy and even. It was Ferran, she was almost positive. As sure as she could be with footsteps alone.

She took a deep breath and waited for the door to open. It did, a sliver of light sliding across the high-gloss marble floor. She could see his reflection in it. Broad, tall. Alone.

Perfect.

She just needed to wait for him to close the door.

She held her breath and waited. He closed the door, and she knew she had to move immediately.

Samarah said a prayer just before she moved from the shadow. One for justice. One for forgiveness. And one for death, that it would come swiftly. For Ferran, or for her.

He turned as she was poised to overtake him, and her eyes met his. It stopped her, dead in her tracks, the glittering in those dark depths so alive. So vibrant. He was striking, beautiful even.

So very familiar.

In spite of all the years, she *knew* him. And in that moment, all she could do was stare, motionless. Breathless.

That moment was all it took.

Ferran stepped to the side, reaching out and grabbing her arm. She lifted and twisted her wrist, tugging it through the weak point of his hand where his fingers overlapped, as she crossed one leg behind the other and dipped toward the floor, lowering her profile and moving herself out of harm's way.

She turned and sidestepped, grabbing his shoulder and using his thigh as a step up to his back. She swung herself around, her forearm around his neck, the chloroform soaked rag in her hand.

He grabbed her wrist, a growl on his lips, and she fought to tug out of his grasp, but this time, he held fast. This time, he was expecting her escape.

She growled in return, tightening her hold on his neck with her other arm. He backed them both up against the wall, the impact of the hard stone surface knocking the air from her.

She swore and held fast, her thighs tight around his waist, ankles locked together at his chest. His hand wrapped around her wrist, he took her arm and hit it against the wall. She dropped the rag and swore, fighting against him.

But her surprise was lost, and while she was a skilled fighter, she was outmatched in strength. She'd forfeited her advantage.

She closed her eyes and imagined her home. Not the streets of Jahar, but the palace. One she and her mother had been evicted from after the death of her father. After the sanctioned execution of her father. Sanctioned by Ferran.

Adrenaline shot through her and she twisted to the side, using her body weight to put more pressure on his neck. He stumbled across the room, flipped her over his shoulders. She landed on her back on the floor, the braided rug doing little to cushion her fall, the breath knocked from her body.

She had to get up. This would be the death of her, and

she knew it. Ferran was ruthless, as was his father before him, and the evidence of that was the legacy of her entire life. He would think nothing of breaking her neck, and she well knew it.

He leaned over her and she put her feet up, bracing them on his chest and pushing back, before planting her feet on the floor and leveraging herself into a standing position, her center low, her hands up, ready to block or attack.

He moved and she sidestepped, sweeping her foot across his face. He stumbled and she used the opportunity to her advantage, pushing him to the ground and straddling him, her knees planted on his shoulders, one hand at his throat.

Still, she could see his eyes, glittering in the dark.

She would have to do it while she faced him now. And without the benefit of chloroform either putting him out cold or deadening his senses. She pushed back at the one last stab of doubt as she reached into her robe for her knife.

There was no time to doubt. No time to hesitate. He certainly hadn't done either when he'd passed that judgment on her father. There was no time for humanity when your enemy had none.

She whipped the knife out of her robe and held it up. Ferran grabbed both of her wrists and on a low, intense growl pushed her backward and propelled them both up against the side of the bed. He pushed her hand back, the knife blade flicking her cheek, parting the flesh there. A stream of blood trickled into her mouth.

She fisted his hair and his head fell back. She tried to bring the blade forward, but he grabbed her arm again, reversing their positions. He had her trapped against the bed, her hands flat over the mattress, bent a near-impossible direction. The tendons in her shoulders screamed, the cut on her face burning hot.

"Who sent you?" he asked, his voice a low rasp.

"I sent myself," she said, spitting out the blood that had pooled in her mouth onto the floor beside them.

"And what is it you're here to do?"

"Kill you, obviously."

He growled again and twisted her arm, forcing her to drop the knife. And still he held her fast. "You've failed," he said.

"So far."

"And forever," he said, his tone dripping with disdain. "What I want to know is why a woman is hiding in my bedchamber ready to end my life."

"I would have thought this happened to you quite often."

"Not in my memory."

"A life for a life," she said. "And as you only have the one, I will take it. Though you owe more."

"Is that so?"

"I'm not here to debate with you."

"No, you're here to kill me. But as that isn't going to happen—tonight or any other night—you may perhaps begin to make the case as to why I should not have you executed. For an attempt at assassinating a world leader. For treason. I could. At the very least I can have you thrown in jail right this moment. All it takes is a call."

"Then why haven't you made it?"

"Because I have not stayed sheikh, through changes in the world, civil unrest and assassination attempts, without learning that all things, no matter how bad, can be exploited to my advantage if I know where to look."

"I will not be used to your advantage."

"Then enjoy prison."

Samarah hesitated. Because she wouldn't forge an alliance with Ferran. It was an impossible ask. He had destroyed her life. He had toppled the government in her country. Left the remainder of her family on the run like dogs.

Left her and her mother on the streets to fend for themselves until her mother had died.

He had taken everything. And she had spent her life with one goal in mind. To ensure that he didn't get away with it. To ensure his line wouldn't continue while hers withered.

And she was failing.

Unless she stopped. Unless she listened. Unless she did what Ferran claimed to do. Turn every situation to her advantage.

"And what do I need to give in exchange for my freedom?"

"I haven't decided yet," he said. "I haven't decided if, in fact, your freedom is on the table. But the power is with me, is it not?"

"Isn't it always?" she asked. "You're the sheikh."

"This is true."

"Will you release me?"

He reached behind her, and when he drew his hand back into her line of vision, she saw he was now holding the knife. "I don't trust you, little desert viper."

"So well you shouldn't, Your Highness, as I would cut your throat if given the chance."

"Yet I have your knife. And you're the only one who bled. I will release you for the moment, only if you agree to follow my instructions."

"That depends on what they are."

"I want you to get on the bed, in the center, and stay there."

She stiffened, a new kind of fear entering her body. Death she'd been prepared for. But she had not, even for a moment, given adequate thought and concern to the idea of him putting his hands on her body.

No. Death first. She would fight him at all cost. She would not allow him to further dishonor her and her family. She would die fighting, but she would not allow him inside of her body.

Better a knife blade than him.

Ferran wouldn't...

She shook that thought off quickly. Ferran was capable of anything. And he had no loyalty. It didn't matter what he'd been like in that other life, in that other time. Not when he had proven all of that to be false.

She didn't move, and neither did he.

"Do we have an agreement?" he asked.

"You will not touch me," she said, her voice trembling now.

"I have no desire to touch you," he said. "I simply need you where I can see you. You're small, certainly, and a woman. But you are strong, and you are clearly a better fighter than I am, or I would have had you easily beaten. As it is, I had no choice but to use my size advantage against you. Now I have the size advantage and weapon. However, I still don't trust you. So get on the bed, in the center, hands in your lap. I have no desire to degrade or humiliate you further, neither am I in the mood for sex. On that score, you are safe."

"I would die first."

"And I would kill you first, so there we have an agreement of sorts. Now get up onto the bed and sit for a moment."

He moved away from her, slowly releasing his hold on her, the knife still in his hand. She obeyed his command, climbing up onto the bed and moving to the center of the massive mattress. Beds like this had come from another lifetime. She scarcely remembered them.

Since being exiled from the palace in Jahar she'd slept on raised cots, skins stretched over a wooden frame and one rough blanket. In the backs of shops. In the upstairs room of the martial arts studio she'd trained in. And when she was unlucky, on the dirt in an alley. When she'd arrived in the Khadran palace, as a servant, she'd slept in her first bed since losing her childhood room sixteen years ago.

The bed here, for servants, was much more luxurious than the sleep surfaces she'd been enjoying. Sized for one person, but soft and with two pillows. It was a luxury she'd forgotten. And it had felt wrong to enjoy it. The first week she'd slept on the floor in defiance, though that hadn't lasted.

And now she was on Ferran's bed. It made her skin crawl.

She put her hands in her lap and waited. She had no reason to trust his word, not when his blood had been found so lacking in honor. And not when he'd carried that dishonor to its conclusion himself.

The execution of her father. The order had been his. And no vow of bonds between royal families, or smiles between friends had changed his course.

As a result, she did not trust his vow not to touch her either.

"I'll ask you again," he said. "Who sent you?"

He still thought her a pawn. He still did not realize.

"I am acting of my own accord, as I said before."

"For what purpose?"

"Revenge."

"I see, and what is it I have not done to your liking?"

"You killed my king, Sheikh Ferran, and it was very much not to my liking."

"I do not make a habit of killing people," he said, his tone steel.

"Perhaps not with your hands, but you did set up the trial that ended in the execution of Jahar's sheikh. And it is rumored you had part in the overtaking of the Jahari palace that happened after. So much violence…I remember that day all too well."

He froze, the lines in his body tensing, his fist tightening around the knife. And for the first time, she truly feared. For the first time, she looked at the man and saw the ruthless desert warrior she had long heard spoken of. Thirty days in the palace and she had seen a man much more civilized than she anticipated. But not here. Not now.

"There were no survivors in the raid on the Jahari palace," he said, his voice rough.

"Too bad for you, there were. I see you know from where I come."

"The entire royal family, and all loyal servants were killed," he said, his voice rough. "That was the report that was sent back to me."

"They were wrong. And for my safety it was in my best interest that they continued to think so. But I am alive. If only to ensure that you will not be."

He laughed, but there was no humor to the sound. "You are a reaper come to collect then, are you? My angel of death here to lead me to hell?"

"Yes," she said.

"Very interesting."

"I should think I'm more than interesting."

He stilled. "You made me fear. There are not many on earth who have done so."

"That is a great achievement for me then, and yet, I still find I'm unsatisfied."

"You want blood."

She lifted her chin, defiant. "I require it. For this is my vengeance. And it is all about blood."

"I am sorry that I could not oblige you tonight."

"No more sorry than I."

"Why am I the object of your vengeance?" he asked. "Why not the new regime? Why not the people who stormed the palace and killed the royal family. The sheikha and her daughter."

"You mean the revolutionaries who were aided by your men?"

"They were not. Not I, nor anyone else in Khadra, had part in the overthrowing of the Jahari royal family. I had a country to run. I had no interest in damaging yours."

"You left us unprotected. You left us without a king."

"I did no such thing."

"You had the king of Jahar tried and executed in Khadra," she spat, venom on her tongue. "You left the rest of us to die when he was taken. Forced from our home. Servants, soldiers…everyone who did not turn to the new leader was killed. And those who escaped…only a half life was ever possible. There was no border crossing to be had, unless you just wanted to wander out into the desert and hope to God you found the sea, or the next country." As her mother had done one day. Wandered out into the desert never to return. At least, in recent years it had eased. That was how she'd been able to finally make her way to Khadra.

"I am not responsible for Sheikh Rashad's fate. He paid for sins committed. It was justice. Still, I am regretful of the way things unfolded."

"Are you?" she spat. "I find I am more than regretful, as it cost me everything."

"It has been sixteen years."

"Perhaps the passage of time matters to you, but I find that for me it does not."

"I say again, I did not give the order to have your people killed. It is a small comfort, certainly, as they are gone, but it is not something I did. You aren't the only one who doesn't believe. I am plagued by the ramifications of the past."

She curled her lip. "Plagued by it? I imagine it has been very hard for you. I'm not certain why I'm complaining about the fate of my country. Not when it has been so hard for you. In your palace with all of your power."

"It is hard when your legacy is defined by a human rights violation you did not commit," he bit out. "Make no mistake, I am often blamed for the hostile takeover of your country. But I did not send anyone into the palace to overthrow your government. Where have I benefited? Where is my hand in your country? What happened after was beyond my reach. And yet, I find I am in many ways responsible for it."

"You cannot have it both ways, Sheikh. You did it, or you did not."

"I had choices to make. To stand strong for my people, for my father, for my blood. Had I foreseen the outcome, as I should have done, my choices might have been different."

"Are you God then?"

"I am sheikh. It is very close to being the same."

"Then you are a flawed god indeed."

"And you? Do you aspire to be the goddess?" he asked, moving to the foot of the bed, standing, tall, proud and straight. He was an imposing figure, and in many ways she couldn't believe that she had dared touch him. Not when he so obviously outmatched her in strength and weight. Not when he was so clearly a deadly weapon all on his own.

"Just the angel of death, as you said. I have no higher aspiration than that. It isn't power I seek, but justice."

"And you think justice comes with yet more death?"

"Who sent the king of Jahar to trial, Sheikh? Who left my country without a ruler?" *Who left me without a father?* She didn't voice the last part. It was too weak. And she refused to show weakness.

"I did," he said, his tone hard, firm. "Lest we forget the blood of the king of Khadra was on his hands. And that is not a metaphor."

"At least Khadra had an heir!"

His expression turned to granite. "And lacked an angry,

disillusioned populace. Certainly the loss of the king affected Jahar, but had the people not been suffering…"

"I am not here to debate politics with you."

"No, it is your wish to cut my throat. And I must say, even politics seems preferable to that."

"I am not so certain." She looked away for a moment, just a moment, to try and gather her thoughts. To try and catch her breath. "You left a little girl with no protection. A queen without her husband."

"And was I to let the Jahari king walk after taking the life of my father? The life of my mother."

"He did not…"

"We will not speak of my mother," he said, his tone fierce. "I forbid it."

"And so we find ourselves here," she said, her tone soft.

"So we do indeed."

"Will you have me killed?" she asked. "As I am also an inconvenience?"

"You, little viper, have attempted to murder me. At this point you are much more than an inconvenience."

"As you see it, Sheikh. The only problem I see is that I have failed."

"You do not speak as someone who values their preservation."

"Do I not?"

"No. You ask if I aim to kill you and then you express your desire to see me dead. All things considered, I suppose I should order your lovely head to be separated from your neck."

She put her hand to her throat. A reflex. A cowardly one. She didn't like it.

"However," he said dryly. "I find I have no stomach for killing teenage girls."

"I am not a teenage girl."

"Semantics. You cannot be over twenty."

"Twenty-one," she said, clenching her teeth.

"Fine then. I have no stomach for the murder of a twenty-one-year-old girl. And as such I would much rather find a way for you to be useful to me." He slid his thumb along the flat of her blade. "But where I could keep an eye on you, as I would rather this not end up in my back."

"I make no promises, Sheikh."

"Again, we must work on your self-preservation."

"Forgive me. I don't quite believe I have a chance at it."

Something in his face changed, his eyebrows drawing tightly together. "Samarah. Not a servant girl, or just an angry citizen. You are Samarah."

He'd recognized her. At last. She'd hoped he wouldn't. Not when she was supposed to be dead. Not when he hadn't seen her since she was a child of six.

She met his eyes. "Sheikha Samarah Al-Azem, of Jahar. A princess with no palace. And I am here for what is owed me."

"You think that is blood, little Samarah?"

"You will not call me little. I just kicked you in the head."

"Indeed you did, but to me, you are still little."

"Try such insolence when I have my blade back, and I will cut your throat, Sheikh."

"Noted," he said, regarding her closely. "You have changed."

"I ought to have. I'm no longer six."

"I cannot give you blood," he said. "For I am rather attached to having it in my veins, as you can well imagine."

"Self-preservation is something of an instinct."

"For most," he said, dryly.

"Different when you have nothing to lose."

"And is that the position you're in?"

"Why else would I invade the palace and attempt an assassination? Obviously I have no great attachments to this life."

His eyes flattened, his jaw tightening. "I cannot give you blood, Samarah. But you feel you were robbed of a legacy. Of a palace. And that, I can perhaps see you given."

"Can you?"

"Yes. I have indeed thought of a use for you. By this time next week, I shall present you to the world as my intended bride."

CHAPTER TWO

"No."

Ferran looked down at the woman kneeling in the center of his mattress. The woman was, if she was to be believed, if his own recognition could be believed, Samarah Al-Azem. Come back from the dead.

For surely the princess had been killed. The dark-eyed, smiling child he remembered so well, gone in the flood of violence that had started in the Khadran palace, ending in the death of Jahar's sheikh. What started as a domestic dispute cut a swath across the borders, into Jahar. The brunt of it falling on the Jahari palace.

It was the king of Jahar who had started the violence. Storming the Khadran palace, as punishment for his wife's affair with Ferran's father. An affair that had begun when Samarah was a young child and Ferran was a teenager. When the duty to country was served by both rulers, having supplied their spouses with children. Or so the story went. But it had not ended there. It had burned out of hand.

And countless casualties had been left.

Among them, the world had been led to believe, Samarah.

Was she truly the princess?

A girl he'd thought long dead. A death he had, by extension, caused. Was it possible she lived?

She was small. Dark-haired. At least from what he could

tell. A veil covered her head, her brows the only indicator of hair coloring. It was not required for women in employment of the palace to cover their heads or faces. But he was certain she was an employee here. Though not one who had been working for the palace long. There were many workers in the palace, and he didn't make it his business to memorize their faces.

Though, when one tried to kill him in his own bedchamber, he felt exceptions could be made. And when one was possibly the girl who had never left his mind, not ever, in sixteen years…

He truly had exceptions to make.

He was torn between rage and a vicious kind of amusement. That reckoning had come, and it had come in this form. Lithe, soft and vulnerable. The most innocent victim of all, come to claim his life. It was a testament, in many ways, to just how badly justice had been miscarried on that day.

Though he was not the one to answer for it. His justice had been the key to her demise. And yet, there was nothing he could do to change it. How could he spare the man who had robbed his country of a leader, installed a boy in place of the man.

The man who had killed his family for revenge.

They were two sides to the same coin. And depending upon which side you looked at, you had a different picture entirely.

Also, depending on which version of events you heard…

He shook off the thoughts, focused back on the present. On the woman. Samarah. "No?" he asked.

"You heard me. I will not ally myself with you."

"Then you will ally yourself with whomever you share a cell with. I firmly hope you find it enjoyable."

"You say that like you believe I'm frightened."

"Are you not?"

She raised her head, dark eyes meeting his. "I was prepared for whatever came."

"Obviously not, as you have rejected my offer. You do realize that I am aware you didn't act on your own. And that I will find who put you up to this, one way or the other. Whether you agree to this or not. However, if you do... things could go better for you."

"An alliance with you? That's better?"

"You do remember," he said, speaking the words slowly, softly, and hating himself with each syllable, "how I handle those who threaten the crown."

"I remember well. I remember how you flew the Khadran flag high and celebrated after the execution of my father," she said, her tone ice.

"Necessary," he bit out. "For I could not allow what happened in Jahar to happen here."

"But you see, what happened in Jahar had not happened yet. It wasn't until the sheikh was gone, the army scattered and all of us left without protection that we were taken. That we were slaughtered by revolutionaries who thought nothing of their perceived freedom coming at the price of our lives."

"Thus is war," he said. "And history. Individuals are rarely taken into account. Only result."

"A shame then that we must live our lives as individuals and not causes."

"Do we?" he asked. "It doesn't appear to me that you have. And I certainly don't. That is why I'm proposing marriage to you."

"That's like telling me two plus two equals camel. I have no idea what you're saying."

He laughed, though he still found nothing about the situation overly amusing. "The division between Khadra and Jahar has long been a source of unrest here. Violence at the borders is an issue, as I'm sure you well know. This could change that. Erase it. It's black-and-white. That's how I live my life. In a world of absolutes. There is no room for gray areas."

"To what end for me, Sheikh Ferran? I will never have my rightful position back, not in a meaningful way. The royal family of Jahar will never be restored, not in my lifetime."

"How have you lived since you left the palace?"

"Poorly," she said, dark eyes meeting his.

"This would get you back on the throne."

"I will not marry you."

"Then you will enjoy prison."

The look on her face nearly destroyed what little was left of his humanity. A foolish thing, to pity the woman who'd just tried to kill him. And she could have succeeded. She was not a novice fighter. He had no illusion of her being a joke just because he was a man and she a woman. He had no doubt that the only thing that had kept him from a slit throat was her bare moment of hesitation. Seconds had made the difference between his life and death.

He should not pity her. He should not care that he'd known her since she was a baby. That he could clearly picture her as a bubbly, spoiled little princess who had been beautiful beyond measure. A treasure to her country.

That was not who she was now. As he was not the haughty teenage boy he'd been. Not the entitled prince who thought only of women and what party he might sneak into, what trouble he might find on his father's yachts.

Life had hit them both, harsh and real, at too young an age. He had learned a hard lesson about human weakness. About his own weaknesses. Secrets revealed that had sent her father into the palace in a murderous rage…one that had, in the end, dissolved a lineage, destroyed a nation that was still rebuilding.

She was a product of that, as was he. And her actions

now had nothing to do with that connection from back then. He should throw her in a jail cell and show her no mercy.

And yet he didn't want to.

It made no sense. There was no room for loyalty to a would-be assassin. No room for pity. Putting your faith in the wrong person could have a disastrous end, and he knew it well. If he was wrong now…

No. He would not be wrong.

This was not ordinary compassion leading him. There was potential political gain to be had. Yes, Jahar had suffered the most change during that dark time sixteen years ago, but Khadra had suffered, too. They had lost their sheikh and sheikha, they had been rocked by violence. Their security shaken to its core.

The palace had been breached.

Their centuries-old alliance with their closest neighbors shattered. It had changed everything in a single instance. For him, and for millions of people who called his country home.

He had never taken that lightly. It was why he never faltered. It was why he showed her no mercy.

But this was an opportunity for something else. For healing. One thing he knew. More blood, more arrests, would not fix the hurts from the past.

It had to end. And it had to end with them.

"Can you kill me instead?" she asked.

"You ask for death?"

"Rather than a prison cell?"

"Rather than marriage," he said.

Her nostrils flared, dark eyes intense. "I will not become your property."

"I do not intend to make you my property, but answer me this, Samarah. What will this do to our countries?"

"I almost bet it will do nothing to mine."

"Do you think? Are you a fool? No one will believe one girl was acting alone."

"I am not a girl."

"You are barely more than a child as far as I'm concerned."

"Had I been raised in the palace that might be true, but as it is, I lived on the streets. I slept in doorways and on steps. I holed up in the back rooms of shops when I could. I had to take care of a mother who went slowly mad. I had to endure starvation, dehydration, the constant threat of theft or rape. I am not a child. I am years older than you will ever live to be," she spat.

He hated to imagine her in that position. In the gutter. In danger. But she had clearly survived. Though, he could see it was a survival fueled by anger.

"If you kill me," he said, "make no mistake, Khadra will make Jahar pay. If I imprison you…how long do you suppose it will take for those loyal to the royal family to threaten war on me? But if we are engaged…"

"What will the current regime in Jahar think?"

"I suppose they will simply be happy to have you in my monarchy, rather than establishing a new one there. I suspect it will keep you much safer than a prison cell might. If you are engaged to marry me, your intentions are clear. If you are in jail…who knows what your ultimate plans might have been? To overthrow me and take command of both countries?"

"Don't be silly," she said, her voice deceptively soft. "At best, I'm a lone woman. Just a weak, small ex-royal, who is nothing due to her gender and her gentle upbringing. At worst…well, I'm a ghost. Everyone believes me dead."

"I am holding a knife that says you're far more than that."

"But no one will believe otherwise."

"Perhaps not. But it is a risk."

"What do you have to gain?" she asked.

It was a good question. And the main answer was balm for his guilt, and he had no idea where that answer had come from. The past was the past. And yes, he had regretted her death—a child—when he'd thought she'd been killed. But it had not been at his hand. He would have protected her.

He would protect her now. And in the process, himself, and hopefully aid the healing of a nation too long under a shadow.

"Healing," he said. "What I want is to heal the wounds. Not tear them open again. I will not have more blood running through this palace. I will not have more death. Not even yours," he said, a vow in many ways.

Sheikha Samarah Al-Azem was a part of a past long gone. Tainted with blood and pain. And he wanted to change something about it. He wanted more than to simply cover it, and here she presented the opportunity to fix some of it.

Because it had not been her fault. It had been his. The truth of it, no matter how much he wanted to deny it, was that it was all his fault.

It was logic. It was not emotion, but a burning sense of honor and duty that compelled it. He didn't believe in emotion. Only right and wrong. Only justice.

"What's it to be, Samarah?" he asked, crossing his arms over his chest.

"Prison," she said.

Anger fired through him, stark and hot. Was she a fool? He was offering her a chance to fix some of this, a chance at freedom. And she was opting for jail.

She was not allowing him to make this right. And he found he didn't like it.

"So be it," he growled, throwing the knife to the side

and stalking to the bed, throwing her over his shoulder in one fluid moment.

She shrieked. Then twisted, hissed and spit like a cat. He locked his arms over hers, and her legs, but she still did her best to kick his chest.

"I think, perhaps, *habibti,* a night in the dungeon will cool your temper."

He stalked to the far wall of his room and moved a painting, then keyed in a code. The bookshelf swung open. "We've modernized a bit here in Khadra, as you can see," he bit out, walking through the open doorway and into a narrow passageway. "Though these tunnels are quite new."

"Get your hands off of me!"

"And give you a chance to cut my throat? I highly doubt it. You were given another option and you chose not to take it. No one will hear you scream, by the way. But even if they did…I am the sheikh. And you are an intruder."

He knew every passage that ran through the palace. Knew every secret. A boy up to no good would have to know them, of course, and a sheikh with a well-earned bit of paranoia would, naturally, ensure the passages were always kept up. That he knew the layout of the castle better than anyone, so that the upper hand would always be his in the event of an attack.

He had lived through one, and he was the only member of his family who had. He felt he had earned his feelings on the matter.

In any case, he was well versed on where every dark, nondescript tunnel in the palace led. And he knew how to get down to the dungeon. It wasn't used. Hadn't been in ages, generations. But he would be using it tonight.

Because if he left her free, she would no doubt kill him in his sleep. And that he could not have. Either she formed an alliance with him, or he put her under lock and key. It was very simple. Black-and-white, as the world, when all was in working order, should be.

"I will kill you the moment I get the chance!" she spat, kicking against his chest.

"I know," he said. "I am confident in that fact."

He shifted his hold on her, his hand skimming the rounded curve of her bottom as he tried to get a better grip on her. The contact shot through him like lightning. This was the closest he'd been to a woman in…much too long. He wouldn't count how long.

You know just how long. And if you marry her...

He shut off the thought. He was not a slave to his body. He was not a slave to desire. He was a slave to nothing. He was ice. All the way down.

He took them both down a flight of stone steps that led beneath the palace, and down into the dungeon. Unused and medieval, but still in working order.

"Let me go."

"You just threatened to kill me. I strongly doubt I'm letting you go anytime soon."

He grabbed a key ring from the hooks on the back wall, then kicked the wrought iron door to the nearest cell open. Then he reached down and picked up a leg iron and clamped it around her ankle.

She swore, a violent, loud string of profanity that echoed off the walls.

He ignored her, slung her down onto the bench and moved quickly away from her range of movement before shutting the door behind him.

"You bastard!" she said.

He wrapped his fingers around the bars, his knuckles aching from the tight grip. "No, I am pure royal blood, Sheikha, and you of all people should know it."

"Is the leg shackle necessary?"

"I didn't especially want to find myself overpowered and put in the cell myself."

She closed her mouth, a dark brow raised, her lips pursed. A haughty, mutinous expression that did indeed remind him of Samarah the child.

"You do not deny you would have." He walked to the side of the cell so that he could stand nearer to her. "Do you?"

"Of course not," she said.

"Come to the bars and I will undo the leg shackle. It is unnecessary now that you're secured."

"Do you think so?" she asked.

He stared at her, at those glittering eyes, black as midnight in the dim lighting of the dungeon. "Perhaps I do not now. You truly need to work on your self-preservation. I would have made you more comfortable."

Her lip curled, baring her white teeth, a little growl rumbling in her chest. "I will never be comfortable in your prison."

"Suit yourself. Prison is in your future, but you may choose the cell. A room in the palace, a position as sheikha, or you may rot in here. It is no concern of mine. But you will decide by sunset tomorrow."

"Sunset? What is this, some bad version of *Arabian Nights?*"

"You're the one who turned back the clock. Pursuing vengeance in order to end my bloodline. Don't get angry with me for playing along." He turned away from her, heading back out of the dungeon. "If you want to do it like this, we will. If you want to play with antiquated rules, I am all for that. But I intend for it to go my way. I intend to make you my wife, and I doubt, in the end, you will refuse."

CHAPTER THREE

FERRAN PACED THE length of his room. He hated himself in this moment, with Samarah behind the secret passage doors, down in the dungeon.

She did not deserve such treatment. At least, the little girl he'd known had not.

Of course, if they were all paying for the sins of their fathers, she deserved the dungeon and then some. But he didn't believe in that. Every man paved his own road to hell. And he'd secured his sixteen years ago.

And if he hadn't then, surely now he had.

Marriage. He had no idea what he'd been thinking. On a personal level, anyway. On a political level he'd been thinking quite clearly.

But Samarah Al-Azem, in his life, in his bed, was the last thing he'd been looking for. In part because he'd thought she was dead.

Though he needed a wife, and he knew it. He was long past due. And yet…and yet he'd never even started his search. Because he was too busy. Because he had no time to focus on such matters.

Much easier to marry Samarah. Heal the rift between the countries, ensure she was cared for. His pound of flesh. Because it wasn't as though he wanted this for himself.

But then, it was better that way. He didn't allow himself to want.

This was about atonement. About making things right.

Want didn't come into it. For Ferran, it never had. And it never would.

Samarah woke up. She had no idea what time it was. There was no natural light in the dungeon. If there had been a torch on the wall, she wouldn't have been terribly surprised.

But then, that might have been a kindness too many. Not that Ferran owed her a kindness at this point.

Not all things considered.

But she hadn't been looking to repair bridges. She'd been looking to finish it all.

You can't finish it from in here...

"No," she said out loud. "Fair enough."

But the alternative was to agree to marry him. Or to give the appearance of an alliance.

Anger, revulsion, burned in her blood.

She could not ally herself with him. But…

But every predator knew that in order to catch prey successfully, there was a certain amount of lying in wait involved.

She squeezed her hands into fists, her nails digging into her palms, the manacle heavy on her ankle. Diplomacy was, perhaps not her strongest point. But she knew about lying in wait. As she'd done in his room last night.

This would be an extended version of that. She would have to make him trust her. She would have to play along. And then…then she could have her revenge before the world if she chose.

The idea had appeal. Though, putting herself in proximity with Ferran, pretending to be his fiancée, did not.

She lay back down on the bench, one knee curled into her chest, the chained leg held out straight. She closed her eyes again, and when she opened them, it was to the sound of a door swinging open.

"Have you made up your mind?"

She knew who the voice belonged to. She didn't even have to look.

She sat up, trying to shake out the chill that had settled into her bones. She looked at Ferran's outline in the darkness. "I will marry you," she said.

The room Ferran showed her to after her acceptance was a far cry from the dungeon. But Samarah was very aware of the fact that it was only a sparkling version of a cell. A fact Ferran underlined as he left her.

"You will not escape," he said. "There are guards around the perimeter. And there will be no border crossing possible for you as my patrol will be put on alert. You will be trapped in the country should you decide to try and leave, and from there, I will find you. And you will have lost your reprieve."

He was foolish for worrying, though. She had nothing to go back to. No one waiting for her. And she had arrived at her goal point. Why would she go back to Jahar with nothing accomplished?

It was true that Jahar was not as dangerous for her as it had once been. In the past five years there had been something of an uneasy transition from a totalitarian rule established by the revolutionaries, who had truly only wanted power for themselves, into a democracy. Though it was a young democracy, and as such, there were still many lingering issues.

Still, the deposition of the other leaders had meant that she no longer had a target on her back, at least. But she had no place, either.

That meant she was perfectly happy to stay here, right in Ferran's home, while she thought of her next move.

Well, perhaps perfectly happy was an overstatement,

but it was better than being back in an old room in a shop in Jahar.

She looked around, a strange tightness in her chest. This was so very familiar, this room. She wondered if it was, perhaps, the same room she'd sometimes stayed in when she and her family had come to visit the Bashar family. In happier times. Times that hardly seemed to matter, given how it had all ended.

Lush fabrics were draped over marble walls, the glittering red and jade silks offering a peek at the obsidian and gold beneath. Richness layered over unfathomable richness. The bed was the same. Draped yards of fabric in bold colors, the frame constructed around the bed decorated with yet more.

Divans, pillows, rugs, all of it served to add softness to a room constructed from stone and precious gems.

And the view—a tall, tower room that looked beyond the walls of the palace gardens, beyond the walls of the city and out to the vast dunes. An orange sun casting burning gold onto the sands.

There was a knock on the grand, carved double doors and she turned. "Yes?"

One door opened and a small woman came in. Samarah knew her as Lydia, another woman who worked in the palace, and with whom Samarah had had some interaction over the course of the past month.

"Sheikha," Lydia said, bowing her head.

So it had begun. Samarah couldn't deny the small flash of...pleasure that arched through her when the other woman said her title. Though it had been more years gone than she'd been with it, it was a title that was in her blood.

Still, she was a bit disturbed by the idea of Lydia knowing any details of what had passed between Ferran and herself. More disturbing though was just what she'd been led to believe about their relationship.

The idea of being Ferran's wife…his lover…it was revolting.

She thought of the man he was. Strong, powerful. Broad shoulders, lean waist. Sharp dark eyes, a square jaw. He was clean shaven, unusual for a man in his part of the world, but she couldn't blame him. For he no doubt used his looks to his advantage in all things.

He was extraordinarily handsome, which was not a point in his favor as far as she was concerned. It was merely an observation about her enemy.

Beauty meant little. Beauty was often deceitful.

She knew that she was considered a great beauty, like her mother before her. And men often took that to mean she was soft, easy to manipulate, easy to take advantage of. As a result some men had found themselves with a sword trained at vulnerable parts of their body.

Yes, she knew beauty could be used to hide strength and cunning. She suspected Ferran knew that, as well.

She had spent the past month observing his physical strength, but she feared she may have underestimated the brilliance of her adversary.

"I have brought you clothes," Lydia said, "at the sheikh's instruction. And he says that you are to join him for dinner when the sun sinks below the dunes."

She narrowed her eyes. "Did he really say it like that?"

"He did, my lady."

"Do you not find it odd?"

A small smile tugged at Lydia's lips. "I am not at liberty to say."

"I see," Samarah said, pacing the width of the room. The beautifully appointed room that, like Ferran and herself, was merely using its beauty to cover what it really was.

A cage. For a tigress.

"And what," Samarah continued, "did he say about me and my change in station?"

"Not much, my lady. He simply said we were to address you as sheikha and install you in this wing of the palace. And that you are not to leave."

"Ah yes, that sounds about right." She was relieved, in many ways, that he hadn't divulged many details. "So I am to dress for him and appear at this magical twilit hour?"

"I shall draw you a bath first."

Samarah looked down at herself and put a hand to her cheek, her thumb drifting over the small cut inflicted by her own knife. She imagined she was a bit worse for wear after having spent the night in a dungeon. So a bath was likely in order.

"Thank you. I shall look forward to it."

Minutes later, Samarah was submerged to her chin in a sunken mosaic tub filled with hot water and essential oils. It stretched the length of the bath chamber, larger than many swimming pools. There were pillars interspersed throughout, and carvings of naked women and men, lounging and tangled together.

She looked away from the scenes. She'd never been comfortable with such things. Not after the way her family had dissolved. Not when she'd spent so many years guarding her body from men who sought to use her.

And certainly not when she was in the captivity of her enemy. An enemy who intended to marry her and...beget his heirs on her. In that naked, entwined fashion. It was far too much to bear.

She leaned her head back against the pillow that had been provided for her and closed her eyes. This was, indeed, preferable to the dungeon. Furthermore, it was preferable to every living situation she'd had since leaving her family's palace.

And of course he'd planned it that way. Of course he would know how to appeal to certain weaknesses.

She couldn't forget what he was.

When she was finished, she got out and wrapped herself in a plush robe, wandering back into her room.

"My lady," Lydia said. "I would have helped you."

"I don't need help, Lydia. In fact, and this is no offense meant to you, I would like some time alone before I go and see the sheikh."

Lydia blinked. "Of course, Sheikha." Samarah could tell Lydia was trying to decide whom she should obey.

Ultimately, the other woman inclined her head and walked out of the chamber.

Samarah felt slightly guilty dismissing her, but honestly, the idea of being dressed seemed ridiculous. Palatial surroundings or not. She picked up the dark blue dress that had been laid out on her bed. It was a heavy fabric, with a runner of silver beads down the front, and a scattering of them across. Stars in a night sky. Along with that were some silken under things. A light bra with little padding, and, she imagined, little support, and a pair of panties to match.

She doubted anyone dressed Ferran. He didn't seem the type.

She pondered that while she put the underwear and dress on. He had not turned out the way she might have imagined. First, he hadn't transformed into a monster. She'd imagined that he might have. Since, in her mind, he was the man who killed her father.

He also hadn't become the man she'd imagined he might, based on what she remembered of him when he'd been a teenage boy.

He'd been mouthy, sullen when forced to attend palace dinners and behave. And he'd often pulled practical jokes on palace staff.

He didn't seem like a man who would joke about much now.

Well, except for his ‘when the sun sinks beneath the dune’ humor. She snorted. As if she would be amused.

She considered the light veil that had been included with the dress. She’d chosen to wear one while on staff, but in general she did not. Unless she was headed into the heart of the Jahari capital. Then she often opted to wear one simply to avoid notice.

She would not wear one tonight. Instead, she wandered to the ornate jewelry box that was situated on the vanity and opened it. Inside, she found bangles, earrings and an elaborate head chain with a bright center gem designed to rest against her forehead.

She braided her long dark hair and fastened the chain in place, then put on the rest of the jewelry. Beauty to disguise herself. A metaphor that seemed to be carrying through today.

She found that there was makeup, as well, and she applied it quickly, the foundation doing something to hide the cut on her cheek. It enraged her to see it. Better it was covered. She painted dark liner around her eyes, stained her lips red.

She looked at herself and scarcely knew the woman she saw. Everything she was wearing was heavy, and of a fine quality she could never have afforded in her life on the street. She blinked, then looked away, turning her focus to the window, where she could see the sun sinking below the dunes.

It was time.

She lifted the front of her dress, her bangles clinking together, all of her other jewels moving with each step, giving her a theme song composed in precious metals as she made her way from the room and down the long corridor.

She rounded a corner and went down a sweeping staircase into a sitting area of the palace. There were men there, dressed in crisp, white tunics nearly as ornate as her dress.

"Sheikha," one said, "this way to dinner."

She inclined her head. "Thank you."

She followed him into the next room. The dining area was immaculate, a tall table with a white tablecloth and chairs placed around. It was large enough to seat fifty, but currently only seated Ferran. There were windows behind him that looked out into the gardens, lush, green. A sign of immeasurable wealth. So much water in the desert being given to plants.

"You came," he said, not bothering to stand when she entered.

"Of course. The sun has sunken. Behind the dunes."

"So it has."

"I should not like to disobey a direct order," she said.

"No," he responded, "clearly not. You are so very biddable."

"I find that I am." She walked down the edge of the table, her fingertips brushing the backs of the chairs as she made her way toward him. "Merciful even."

"Merciful?" he asked, raising his brows. "I had not thought that an accurate description. Perhaps…thwarted?"

She stopped moving, her eyes snapping up to his. "Perhaps," she bit out.

"Sit," he commanded.

She continued walking, to the head of the table, around the back of him, lifting her hand the so she was careful to avoid contact with him. She watched his shoulders stiffen, his body, his instincts on high alert.

He knew he had not tamed her. Good.

She took a seat to his left, her eyes on the plate in front of her. "I do hope there will be food soon. I'm starving. It seems I was detained for most of the day."

"Ah yes," he said, "I recall. And don't worry. It's on its way."

As if on cue, six men came in, carrying trays laden

with clay pots, and clear jars full of frosted, brightly colored juice.

All of the trays were laid out before them, the tall lids on the tagines removed with great drama and flair.

Her stomach growled and she really hoped he wasn't planning on poisoning her, because she just wanted to eat some couscous, vegetables and spiced lamb. She'd spent many nights trying to sleep in spite of the aching emptiness in her stomach.

And she didn't have the patience for it, not now.

She needed a full stomach to deal with Ferran.

"We are to serve ourselves," Ferran said, as the staff walked from the room. "I often prefer to eat this way. I find I get everything to my liking when I do it myself." His eyes met hers. "And I find I am much happier when I am in control of a situation."

She arched a brow and reached for a wooden utensil, dipping it into the couscous and serving herself a generous portion. "That could be a problem," she said, going back for some lamb. "As I feel much the same way, and I don't think either of us can have complete control at any given time."

"Do you ever have control, Samarah?"

She paused. "As much as one can have, Sheikh. Of course, the desert is always king, no matter what position in life you hold. No one can stop a drought. Or a monsoon. Or a sandstorm."

"I take it that's your way of excusing your powerlessness."

She took a sharp breath and turned her focus to her dinner. "I am not powerless. No matter the situation, no matter the chains, you can never make me powerless. I will always have choices, and my strength is here." She put her hand on her chest. "Not even you can reach in and take my heart, Sheikh Ferran Bashar. And so, you will never truly have power over me."

"You are perhaps the bravest person I've ever met," he said. "And the most foolish."

She smiled. "I take both as the sincerest of compliments."

"I should like to discuss our plan."

"I should like to eat—this is very good. I don't think the servants eat the same food as you do."

"Do they not? I had not realized. I'll ask the chef if it's too labor intensive or if it's possible everyone eat as I do."

"I imagine it isn't possible, and it would only make more work for the cook. Cooking in mass quantities is a bit different than cooking for one sheikh and his prisoner."

"I've never cooked," he said. "I wouldn't know."

"I haven't often cooked, but I have been in the food lines in Jahar. I know what mass-produced food is."

"Tell me," he said, leaning on one elbow. "How did you survive?"

"After we left the palace—" she would not speak of that night, not to him "—we sought asylum with sympathizers, though they were nearly impossible to find. We went from house to house. We didn't want people to know we'd survived."

"It was reported you were among the dead."

She nodded. "I know. A favor granted to my mother by a servant who wanted to live. She feigned loyalty to the new regime, but she secretly helped my mother and I escape, then told the new *president*—" she said the word with utter disdain "—that we had been killed with the rest."

"After that," she said, "we were often homeless. Sometimes getting work in shops. Then we could sleep on the steps, with minimal shelter provided from the overhang of the roof. Or, if the shopkeeper was truly kind, a small room in the back."

"And then?" he asked.

"My mother died when I was thirteen. At least…I assume she did. She left one day and didn't return. I think… I think she walked out into the desert and simply kept walking. She was never the same after. She never smiled."

"I think that day had that effect on us all. But I'm sorry to hear that."

"You apologize frequently for what happened. Do you mean it?"

"I wouldn't say it if I didn't."

"But do you feel it?" she asked. He was so monotone. Even now, even in this.

"I don't feel anything."

"That's not true," she said, her eyes locked with his. "You felt fear last night. *I* made you fear."

"So you did," he said. "But we are not talking about me. Tell me how you went on after your mother died."

"I continued on the way I always had. But I ended up finding work at a martial arts studio, of all places. Master Ahn was not in Jahar at the time of the unrest, and he had no qualms about taking me in. Part of my payment was training along with my room and board."

"I see now why you had such an easy time ambushing me," he said.

"I have a black belt in Hapkido. Don't be too hard on yourself."

"A Jaharan princess who is a master in martial arts."

She lifted a shoulder. "Strange times we live in."

"I should say. You know someone tried to murder me in my bedchamber last night."

"Is that so?" she asked, taking a bite of lamb.

"I myself spent the ensuing years in the palace. Now that we're caught up, I think we should discuss our engagement."

"Do you really see this working?" she asked.

"I never expected to love my wife, Samarah. I have long expected to marry a woman who would advance me in a political fashion and help my country in some way. That is part of being a ruler, and I know you share that. You are currently a sheikha without a throne or a people, and I aim to give you both. So yes, I do see this working. I don't see why it shouldn't."

"I tried to kill you," she said. "That could possibly be a reason it wouldn't work."

"Don't most wives consider that at some point? I grant you, usually several years of marriage have passed first, but even so, it's hardly that unusual."

"And you think this will…change what happened? You think what happened *can* be changed?" she asked. And she found she was honestly curious. She shouldn't be. She shouldn't really want to hear any of what he had to say.

"Everything can be changed. Enough water can change an entire landscape. It can reshape stone. Why can't we reshape what is left?"

She found that something in her, something traitorous and hopeful, something she'd never imagined would have survived all her years living in the worst parts of Jahar, enduring the worst sorts of fear and starvation and loss, wanted to believe him.

That the pieces of her life could somehow be reshaped. That she could have something more than cold. More than anger and revenge. More than a driving need to inflict pain, as it had been inflicted on her.

"And if not," he said. "I still find the outcome preferable to having my throat cut. And you will have something infinitely nicer than a storeroom to sleep in. That should be enough."

And just like that, the warm hopefulness was extinguished.

Because he was talking as though a soft bed would fix the pain she'd suffered. The loss of her family, the loss of her home.

He didn't know. And she would have to force him to understand. She would make him look at her pain, her suffering. And endure it as she had done.

"Yes," she said, smiling, a careful, practiced smile, "why not indeed?"

CHAPTER FOUR

NOT FOR THE first time since striking the deal with Samarah, Ferran had reservations. Beautiful she was, biddable she would never be.

She was descended from a warrior people, and she had transformed herself into a foot soldier. One he'd rather have on his side than plotting his death.

She'd been a little hermit the past few days. But he was under no illusion. She was just a viper in her burrow, and he would have to reach in and take her out carefully.

Barring that, he would smoke her out. Metaphorically. He wasn't above an ironhanded approach. He supposed, in many ways, he was already implementing one. But the little serpent had tried to kill him.

There was hardly an overreaction to that. Though, there was a foolish reaction. Proposing marriage might be it. And there were the reservations.

He walked up to the entry of her bedchamber and considered entering without knocking. Then he decided he liked his head attached to his shoulders and signaled his intent to enter with a heavy rap on wooden doors.

"Yes?"

"It's Ferran," he said.

He was met with silence.

"If you have forgotten," he said, "I am the sheikh of Khadra and your fiancé. Oh, also your mortal enemy."

The left door opened a crack, and he could see one brown eye glaring at him through it. "I have not forgotten."

"I haven't seen you in days, so I was concerned."

She blinked twice. "I've been ill."

"Have you?"

"Well, I haven't felt very well."

"I see," he said.

"Because we're engaged."

"Did my proposal give you a cold?"

The eye narrowed. "What do you want?"

"I did not propose to you so you could nest in one of the rooms in my palace. We have serious issues to attend to. Namely, announcing our engagement to the world. Which will involve letting the world know that the long-lost, long-mourned sheikha of Jahar lives."

"Can't you write up a press release?"

"Let me in, Samarah, or I will push past you."

"Would you like to try?"

"Let me in," he repeated.

She obeyed this time, the door swinging open. She held it, her arm extended, a dark brow raised. "Enter."

"Why is it you make me feel like I'm a guest in my own palace?"

"These are my quarters. In them, you are a guest."

"This is my country, and in it, you are a prisoner." Her shoulders stiffened, her nostrils flaring. "Such an uncomfortable truth."

"I can think of a few things more uncomfortable."

He arched a brow. "Such as?"

"If I planted my foot between your ribs," she said, practically hissing.

"You and I shall have to spar sometime. When I'm certain you don't want me killed."

"You'll be waiting a long time."

"Careful. Some men might consider this verbal foreplay." He said it to get a reaction. What disturbed him was that it did seem that way. It made his blood run hotter. Made him think of what it had felt like to hold her over his shoulder, all soft curves and deadly rage.

He gritted his teeth. He was not a slave to his body. He was a slave to nothing. He was master. He was sheikh. And with that mastery, he served his people. Not himself. That meant there was no time for this sort of reaction.

Her upper lip curled into a snarl. "You disgust me. Do you think I would sleep with the man who ordered my father killed?"

"For the good of our people? I would sleep with the woman whose father caused the death of my parents." The man who had wrenched the bars open that held Ferran's demons back from the world. The man who revealed what it was Ferran could be with the restraints broken.

He ignored those memories. He ignored the heat that pooled in his gut at the thought of what sleeping with her would mean.

She blinked. "I feel as though we have an impossible legacy to negotiate. I have, in fact, been thinking that for the past few days."

"To what end?"

"To the end that in many ways I understand what you did." Her dark eyes looked wounded, angry. "But I don't have to condone it. Or forgive it."

"Your father killed mine. Face-to-face and in cold blood. My mother…"

"I know," she said. "And…it is a difficult set of circumstances we find ourselves in. I realize that."

"Not so difficult. Marriage is fairly straightforward." It was a contractual agreement, nothing more. And as long as he thought of it in those terms, he could find a place for it in his ordered world.

Both brows shot up. "Is it? As our parents' deaths were

a result of marital infidelity I think it's a bit more complex than you're giving it credit for."

"Passion is more complex than people give it credit for. Passion is dangerous. Marriage on the other hand is a legal agreement, and not dangerous in the least. Not on its own. Add passion and you have fire to your gasoline."

"Okay, I see your point. But are you honestly telling me you act without passion?"

He lifted a shoulder. "Yes. If I acted based on passion I would have had your pretty head for what you tried to do. Lucky for you, I think things through. I never act before considering all possible outcomes." He studied her, her petite frame hinted at by a red, beaded tunic that hung to her knees, her legs covered by matching pants. Her dark hair was pulled back again, the top of her head covered by a golden chain that was laced over her crown. He wondered what her hair might look like loose. Falling in glossy black waves over her shoulders.

And then he stopped wondering. Because it was irrelevant. Because her hair, her beauty, had nothing to do with their arrangement. It had nothing to do with anything.

"Are you passionate?" he asked, instead of contemplating her hair for another moment.

She cocked her head to the side, a frown tugging down the corners of her lips. "About some things," she said. "Survival being chief among them. I don't think I could have lived through what I lived through without a certain measure of passion for breathing. If I hadn't felt burning desire to keep on doing it, I probably would have walked out to the desert, lain down on a dune and stopped. And then there was revenge. I've felt passion for that."

"And that's where we differ. I don't want revenge, because the purpose it serves is small. I want to serve a broader purpose. And that's why thinking is better than passion." Passion was dangerous. Emotion was vulnerability. He believed in neither.

"Until you need passion to keep air in your lungs," she said, so succinct and loud in the stillness of the room. "Then you might rethink your stance on it."

"Perhaps. Until then…in my memory, passion ends in screams, and blood, and the near destruction of a nation. So I find I'm not overly warm to the subject."

"But you don't anticipate us having a marriage with passion?" she asked.

He looked at her again. She was beautiful, there was no question, and now that she didn't have a knife in her hands it was possible to truly appreciate that beauty. She had no makeup on today, but she was as stunning without it as she'd been with her heavily lined eyes and ruby lips.

"Perhaps a physical attraction," he said.

He wasn't sure how he felt about that. The truth of the matter was, he'd given up women and sex that day his family had been killed. That day he'd been handed the responsibility of a nation full of people.

His father had been too busy indulging his sexual desires to guard his family. To guard his palace. And then he had seen what happened when all control gave way. When it shifted into unimaginable violence. When passion became death.

He'd turned away from it for that reason. But he'd known that when he married he wouldn't continue to be celibate. He hadn't given it a lot of thought.

But he was giving it thought now. Far too much.

Those beautiful eyes flew wide. "I hardly think so."

"Why is that?"

"I despise you."

"That has nothing to do with sex, *habibti*. Sex is about bodies. It is black-and-white, like everything else." She looked away from him, her cheeks pink. "You expect a celibate union? Because that will not happen.We need children."

Something changed on her face then. Her expression going from stark terror, to wonder, to disgust so quickly he wondered if he was mistaking them all. Or if he'd simply hallucinated it. "Children?"

"Heirs."

Now her unpainted lips were white. "Your children."

"And yours," he said. "There is no greater bond than that. No greater way to truly unite the nations."

"I…"

Samarah was at a loss for words. She'd been thrown off balance by Ferran's sudden appearance, and then…and then this talk of marriage. Of passion and sex. And then finally…children.

The word hit her square in the chest with the force of a gun blast.

Terror at first, because it was such a foreign idea.

Then…she'd almost, for one moment, wanted to weep with the beauty of it. Of the idea that her love might go on and change. That it might not end in a jail cell of Ferran's making. That she might be a mother.

On the heels of the fantasy, had come the realization that it would mean carrying her enemy's baby. Letting the man who had ordered her father's death touch her, be inside of her. Then producing children that would carry his blood.

Your blood.

You wouldn't be alone.

No. She couldn't. Couldn't fathom it.

And yet, there was one thing that kept her here. That kept her from fashioning a hair pick into a weapon and ending him.

When he'd said, cold, blunt, that her father had killed his, that he had been responsible for the death of his mother as well, she'd realized something for the first time.

She would have done the same thing he had done. Given the chaos her father had caused, were she in Ferran's position, the newly appointed leader of a country…she would have had her father executed, too.

That shouldn't matter. The only thing that should matter was satisfying honor with blood. She could have sympathy for his position without offering him forgiveness or an olive branch of any kind.

But it sat uncomfortably with her. Like a burr beneath her rib cage. And she didn't like it. But then, she liked this whole marriage thing even less than the murder thing.

She was undecided on both issues presently.

And he'd confused her. With his comfy mattresses, delicious food and offers of a life she'd never imagined she could have.

A chance to be a sheikha. To do good in the world. To remember what it was to be poor, starving and homeless, and to have a chance to make it better for those in this country who were currently suffering in poverty.

A chance to be a mother.

A chance to live in a palace with everything that had been stolen from her.

She would not feel guilty for wanting that. Not even a little. Not when she'd spent so many years as she had. She'd been spoiled once, and after all the deprivation, she felt she could use a return to spoiling.

It was all so tempting. Like a poisoned apple.

But she knew it was poisoned. Knew that while it looked sweet it would rot inside of her.

"I can't discuss this just now," she said.

"You've already agreed. It's the only reason I've not had you arrested."

Yes, she had agreed. But inside she didn't feel as if it was a done deal yet. It didn't feel real, this change in her fate. She'd done nothing but focus on her revenge for so many years. Revenge and survival. They'd kept her going. They were her passion. She had nothing else; she cared for nothing else. Food, shelter, safety, sleep, repeat. All in the aim of making it here, and from there? She'd had no plan. She'd imagined...well, she'd hardly imagined she would survive this.

He was offering her something she'd never once imagined for herself: a future. One that consisted of so much more than those basic things. One that gave her the chance to add something to the world instead of simply taking Ferran from it.

He wasn't a monster. And that she'd known since she first came to live at the palace a month ago. It had been uncomfortable to face that. That it was a man she fought against, not a mythical being who was all terror and anguish. Not the specter of death himself, come to destroy her family.

She hated this. She hated it all. She hated how it tempted her.

"I suppose I have," she said, "but I'm still processing what it means."

It was the most honest thing she'd said to him in regards to the marriage. There were implications so far-reaching that it was hard for her to see them all from her room here in the palace.

"As am I. But one thing I do know is that marriage means heirs. I'm a royal, so there is no other aspect of marriage that's more important."

"Certainly not affection," she said.

"Certainly not. I doubt my father had much if any for my mother. If he did, he would not have been with your mother."

"Or perhaps they were simply greedy." She looked down, unsure if she should say the words that were pounding through her head. Because why talk to him at all? Why discuss anything with him? "I think my mother loved them both."

It was a strange thing to say. Especially when love had been utterly lacking in her life. But this was, in part, her theory why.

"What?"

"I think she loved my father and yours. She was devastated to lose them both. That her husband, whom she loved, was killed in the same few days that her lover was killed…I don't think she ever recovered. I don't know that she ever loved anything as much as she loved the two of them." Certainly not her.

He paused for a long moment, his eyes on the back wall. "That's where you're wrong."

"Is it?"

"Yes. I don't think your mother ever loved anyone more than she loved herself."

"You aren't fit to comment on her," she said, but there was something about his words that hit her in a strange way. Something that felt more real than she would like.

"Perhaps not." The light in his eyes changed, and for a moment, she thought she almost saw something soft. "No child should have to see what you did."

She looked away. "I hardly remember it."

Except she had. She and her mother had been staying at the palace. Visiting. Of course, she figured out that meant they'd been sneaking time in for their affair. At the time it had all been so confusing. She'd been a child who hadn't known anything about what had passed between the sheikh and sheikha and why it had caused the fallout that it had.

Honestly, at twenty-one, she was barely wiser about it than she'd been then.

In her mind, male desire wasn't a positive thing. It was something she feared. Deeply. Living unprotected as she had, she'd had to respond with fierce, single-mindedness to any advances.

It didn't take long for the men in the city to learn that she wasn't worth hassling.

And in her life, there had been no place, no time, for sexual feelings.

It made it hard to understand what had driven their parents to such extremes. What had made her mother feel her husband, her only daughter weren't enough for her. What had made her cast off a lifetime of perfect behavior, a marriage to a man she'd seemed to love, and for her father to react with mindless violence. She'd long been afraid that desire like that was some sort of demon that possessed you and left you with little choice in the matter.

But she didn't fear it now. Obviously, it wasn't a concern for her. Particularly not with a man like him.

"I am glad for you," he said. "I remember it with far too much clarity."

"You didn't…you didn't see…"

He swallowed, his eyes still focused on a point behind her. "I saw enough."

All she could remember was being pushed behind a heavy curtain. She'd stayed there. And she'd heard too much.

But she hadn't seen. She'd been spared that much.

"What is your timeline for this marriage?"

"The sooner the better. You're certain no one is going to come for you?"

"You mean am I sure no one will come and save me? Yes, I'm certain. There is no one like that in my life." What a lonely thought. She'd always known it, but saying it out loud made it that much more real, sharpened the contrast between what he offered with marriage, and what she would get if she used him and went ahead with her plan.

It was simple. A chance at a future, or nothing at all.

The offer of a future was so shiny, so tempting, so breathtakingly beautiful….

"That is not what I meant."

"What did you mean?"

"Are any of the old regime, the revolutionaries, still after you in any regard?"

"Not that I'm aware of. The old leader was killed by one of his own, and that ushered in a completely new political era in Jahar. Things are better. But there is still no place for me."

"As a symbol, you would shine beautifully," he said.

The compliment settled strangely in her chest. Lodged between rage and fear. "Thank you." The words nearly choked her.

"It is true. I think people would look at you, at us, and see echoes of a peaceful time. Of a time when our nations were friends. Sure, you won't be sheikha of Jahar, but you will still matter to the people there. They suffered when the royal family was deposed. They will be happy to know that you've risen up from that dark time, as will they. As they have."

"It is an idealistic picture you paint."

"I'm not given to idealism. This is how it will be."

"You seem very sure," she said.

He lifted a shoulder. "I am the sheikh. So let be written, et cetera."

"I didn't imagine you would have a sense of humor."

"I don't have much of one."

"It's dry as the desert, but it's there."

The left side of his mouth curved upward into a smile. "I see, and what did you imagine I would be like?"

"I had imagined you were a *ghul*."

"Did you?"

She shifted uncomfortably. Because sadly, it was true.

In her mind, he'd become a great, shape-shifting creature. A blood-drinking monster.

"Yes."

He reached his hand out, and she swiped it away with a block. He lowered his head, his dark eyes intent. "Permit me," he said, his voice hard.

She froze and he lifted his hand again. She stayed there, watching him. He rested his hand on her cheek, his thumb sliding over her cheekbone, over the cut he'd inflicted on her.

"I suppose," he said. "To a child who saw me as the one who took her father from her, as the one who stole her life, I would seem like a monster."

"Are you not?" she asked, unable to breathe for some reason, heat flooding her face, her limbs shaking.

With one quick movement, she could remove his hand from her face. She could break his thumb in the process. But she didn't. She allowed this, and she wasn't sure why.

Perhaps because it felt like something from another time. When Ferran hadn't been scary at all. When she hadn't hated him. When he'd simply been the handsome, smiling older son of her parents' best friends.

But he isn't that boy. That boy was a lie. And he's now a man who must answer for his sins.

"I suppose it depends," he said. "I am a man with many responsibilities. Millions of them. And I always do what I must to serve my people. From the moment I took power." He lowered his hand, heat leaching from her face, retreating with his touch. "I will always act in the best interest of my people. It depends on which side of me you fall on. If you are my enemy…if you hurt those I am here to protect, then I am most certainly a monster."

"And that," she said, her words clipped, "is something I can respect."

It was true, and it didn't hurt to say. There was honor

in him, and she accepted that. The only problem was, it clashed with the honor in her. With her idea of what honor needed in order to be satisfied.

"Get yourself ready," he said.

"What?"

"I intend to take you out into the city."

"But...no announcements have been made."

"I am well aware of this. But a limo ride with a woman who is hardly recognizable as the child sheikha who disappeared sixteen years ago isn't going to start a riot."

"A limo ride?"

"Yes. A limo."

"I haven't been in a car...well, I rode beneath the tarps in a truck to get across the border into Khadra. Then I got a horse from some bedouins out in the desert and rode here."

"What became of the horse?"

"I sold him. Got a return on the money I spent on him."

"Enterprising."

"I am a woman who's had to create resources, even when there were none. Other than that ride in the truck though, I've not been in a motorized vehicle in years."

"You haven't?"

"I walk in Jahar. I rarely leave the area I live in."

"Then decide what you think would be best for a limo ride. And by all means, Samarah Al-Azem, try to enjoy yourself."

CHAPTER FIVE

SAMARAH MADE HERSELF well beyond beautiful for their outing into Khajem, the city that surrounded the palace. It was hard to believe that the child he had known had grown into the viper that had tried to end him. And harder still to believe that the viper could look so soft and breathtaking when she chose. Hard to believe that if he leaned in to claim her mouth he would probably find himself run through with a hairpin.

Today she was in jade, hair constrained, a silver chain woven through it, and over her head, a matching stone resting in the center of her forehead.

"This is all so different to how I remember it," she said, once they were well away from the palace.

"It is," he said. "Khadra has been blessed with wealth. All I've had to do is…"

"You've been responsible with it. You could have hoarded it. God knows my country had wealth, and it was so badly diminished by the regime that came after my parents. Spent on all manner of things, but none of them ever managing to benefit the people."

"As you can see, we've followed some of what Dubai has done with development. New buildings, a more urban feel."

"But around the palace everything seems so…preserved."

"I wanted to build on our culture, not erase what came

before. But Khadra has become a technology center. Some of the bigger advances are starting to come from here, and no one would have ever thought that possible ten years ago. The amount of Khadrans going to university has increased, and not universities overseas, to takc jobs overseas, but here. Some of the change has been mine, but I can't take credit for that."

"I wish very much Jahar could have benefited from this," she said, her words vacant. As though she had to detach herself in order to speak them. "You have done…well."

"You didn't know about the development happening here, did you?"

"I saw from a distance. From in the palace, but I didn't know the scope of it. I didn't know what these buildings accomplished." She leaned against the window and looked up at a high-rise building they were passing. "How could I have known? We were cut off from the world for years, not just my mother and I, but the entire country. We were behind an iron curtain, as it were. And in the years since it's lifted…well, the rest of the country may have made a return to seeing the world, but mine has stayed very small."

"I think it's time it grew a little, don't you?"

"Why are you doing this?" she asked, turning to look at him.

It was a good question, and he knew she didn't mean why had he improved his country, but why was he showing her. Why was he trying to change her mind about him.

It had less to do with self-preservation than he'd like to believe.

Perhaps it was because he wanted to return something to her that, no matter how justified he thought it might be, he'd taken from her.

Perhaps it was simply a desire to see some of the sparkle return to her dark eyes.

Or maybe it was just that he truly didn't want a wife

who had more fantasies about killing him than she had of him in bed.

Would he truly make her his wife? In every sense of the word?

He looked at the elegant line of her neck, her smooth, golden skin, dark glossy hair. And her lips. Red or plain, they were incredible. Lush and perfectly shaped. He had not looked at a woman in this way in so long. He hadn't allowed himself to remember what desire was. What it was to want.

So dangerous. So very tempting.

If he married her, it would be his duty. His heart rate quickened, breathing becoming more difficult.

Yes, he would make her his wife. In every sense. He was decided.

She would be perfect. Because of who she was. Because she knew. She knew about the danger of passion. She would be the kind of wife he needed. The kind of wife that Khadra needed.

"Have I suitably impressed you?" he asked.

She nodded slowly. "In some ways. It cannot be denied. But I find I'm in need of…something."

"What is that?"

"I've been idle for too many days. You promised me a sparring match. I think I will have it now."

He looked at the lovely, immaculate creature sitting across from him, her elegant fingers clasped in her lap as she asked him to spar with her in much the same tone she might have used to ask him to afternoon tea.

He thought of what she would look like if they sparred. Her hair in disarray, sweat beading on her brow. He gritted his teeth and fought to suppress the rising tide of need that threatened to wash him away.

"If you think you're ready, Sheikha."

"Only if you think you are, Sheikh."

* * *

Samarah was surprised to discover that Ferran had provided her with clothes. Well, he'd already been providing her with clothes, so she didn't mean it that way. But the fact that he'd provided her with clothes for the gym was surprising.

A pair of simple black shorts and a matching tank top. After all the layers she was used to—for protection on the streets, for her disguise in the palace, and then…with all of her beaded gowns now she was in position as Ferran's… whatever—she felt nearly naked in the brief clothing.

She opened the door to her chambers and saw Lydia just outside. "How do I get to the gym?"

"The general facility or Sheikh Ferran's private facility?"

"I…assume the sheikh's private facility."

"Near his quarters. Down this hall, and down the staircase, all the way at the far end. It's the last set of doors."

Dear Lord, he'd put her a league away from him. Probably because he feared for his safety. The thought made her smile as she started the trek down to his quarters. That she had succeeded in unsettling him would do for now. It wasn't revenge, but it was in the right vein.

She moved to the red double doors and pushed them open slowly. And stopped cold when she saw Ferran, his back to her as he punched the large bag hanging from the ceiling.

He wasn't wearing a shirt. The only clothing on his body was a pair of black shorts that looked a lot like hers. Though, they covered more of his legs.

His back was broad. Shockingly so, tapering down to a slim waist. Everything on him was solid. Ridges of muscle shifting beneath skin as gold as desert sand.

She'd known he was strong. She'd come up against him already and seen just what a worthy opponent he was, but seeing him now…she could see why her hesitation had meant the end of her plan.

She could see it in every line of his body as his fist hit the bag and sent it swinging. He was powerful. A weapon. That was the basis upon which she admired him. What warrior, what martial artist, would not appreciate such a finely honed instrument? That was why she stared. It could be the only reason.

Samarah took a breath and assumed her stance, raising her leg high, bringing it down softly between his shoulder blades. A muted outside crescent kick.

He whirled around, reaching out and grabbing her wrist, tugging her forward, her free arm pinned against his solid chest.

"You're here," he said, cocking his head to the side, his eyes glittering.

"You had your back to the door."

"So I did. I suppose I deserved that."

"I could have hurt you," she said. "I didn't skim you on accident."

"I understand that," he said, his breath coming in hard bursts from the exertion, fanning hot across her cheek.

"Are you ready?"

"Just quickly." He released his hold on her and ran his hands over her curves, light and fast. Her heart slammed against her breastbone when his fingertips grazed the sides of her breasts. "I had to check," he said.

Her breath escaped her throat in a rush. "Check what?"

"To see if you had a weapon."

"I have honor," she said. "If I was going to kill you, it wouldn't be during a planned sparring match."

"I see. You'd do it while I slept then."

"Honor," she repeated.

"Clearly. Shall we go to the center of the mats?"

He gestured to the blue-floored open room and turned away from her again, walking to the center of the mats.

She followed and took her position across from him, her hands up, ready to strike or block. "Are you ready?" she asked.

"When you are."

"Are you giving me the handicap because I'm a woman?"

"No, I'm giving you the handicap because you're tiny and I must outweigh you by a hundred pounds."

"I'll make you regret it," she said.

She faked a punch and he blocked high. She used the opportunity to score a point with a side kick to his midsection and a follow-up palm strike to his chin. She wasn't hitting with full force, because she honored the fact that this was for points, not for blood.

He blocked her next hit, gripping her arm and holding it out, miming a blow that would have broken her bones at the elbow if he'd followed through.

One for him, two for her. Her mental score sheet had her in the lead, and she was happy with that, but unhappy that, in reality, that would have been a disabling hit. Points aside, had it been a real battle, she would have crumpled to the ground screaming.

They hit gridlock, throwing hits, blocking them, then one of them would slip a blow through.

He was using a mixed fighting style, while she was true to her discipline. Her training was more refined, but his was deadly.

She was faster.

Only a few minutes in, she had him breathing hard, sweat running down the center of his chest, between hard pectoral muscles. She watched a droplet roll over his abs, and she was rewarded with a swipe of the back of his hand across her face.

She let out a feral growl and turned, treating him to a spinning back kick that connected with the side of his cheek. It wasn't as pulled as she'd meant it to be, and his head jerked to the side, a red mark the lingering evidence of the contact.

He growled in return, gripping her forearm and flipping her over his back. She hit the soft mat and rolled backward, coming to her feet behind him and treating him to a sweep kick under his feet so that he kissed the mat just as she'd done.

He got to his feet more slowly than she had, and she was facing him when he came up, her breathing coming sharp and fast now. She hadn't fought anyone this hard in a long time. Maybe ever. Sparring in the studio had never been quite this intense. There had never been so much on the line.

She wasn't sure exactly what was happening here. Only that it seemed essential she show him who she was. That she was strong. That she wasn't someone he could simply manipulate and domesticate. That no matter that she was, for now, going with his plan, he should never take for granted that she was tame.

It was a warning to him. A reminder to herself. She might have put on some beautiful dresses this week; she might have been impressed with the changes he'd made in the city. She might enjoy the soft bed she had now.

But she could not forget. She was not a princess anymore. Life had hardened her into more. She was a warrior first. And she could never forget that.

She prepared to strike again, and he reached out, his hands lightning fast, his fists curled around her forearms, pushing her arms above her head.

She roared and pulled her hands down, twisting them as she did, but he was expecting it. She'd done this to him once before, and she wasn't able to break through his hold.

She pulled her *kiai* from deep inside her, her voice filling the gym. The sound startled him enough that she was able to pull one hand free, and she used it to land another palm strike against his cheek.

He twisted her captured arm behind her back and propelled her forward so that she hit the thankfully padded wall.

She was pinned.

She twisted, scraped her foot along his instep—somewhat ineffectively since she was barefoot. But she was able to use his surprise again to free herself and reverse the positions. His back was to the wall, his arms in her hold. But that wasn't what kept him still, and she well knew it.

It was her knee. Poised between his thighs, ready to be lifted and to connect hard with a very delicate part of his anatomy.

"I would keep still if I were you," she said.

"We're sparring," he said, his chest rising and falling hard with each breath. "You're not supposed to do full contact hits."

"But I could," she said, smiling.

He leaned forward, angling his head and she stopped breathing for a moment. He was making eye contact with her, and it made something in her feel tight and strange. She looked down, her vision following a drop of sweat again, this time as it rolled from his neck, down his chest.

She found herself fascinated by his chest. By each cut muscle. By the way the hair spread over his skin. So unique to a man's body. These shapes, the hair, the hardness of the muscle.

She looked down farther. At the well-defined abs, the line of hair that disappeared beneath the waistband of his shorts. And she nearly choked.

She'd never been this close to a man. Not for this long. She'd fought them off before, but this was different.

She looked back up at his face, breathing even harder now. Her limbs tingling a bit. From the lack of oxygen, she was certain. Since she was breathing hard. And there was certainly no other explanation.

He leaned forward and bit her neck. It wasn't painful, the sensation of his teeth scraping against her skin. It was something else entirely. Something that made her flail, stumble and fall backward onto the mat.

"I say we call it even, little viper," he said, looking down at her.

Rage filled her and she popped back to her feet. "Of course you'd say that because I won. That was…not a move I recognize."

"You didn't say no biting."

"One shouldn't have to say that!"

"Apparently one did," he said, breathing out hard, the muscles in his stomach rippling.

"I demand a rematch."

"Later," he said, "when I can breathe again. You are a fierce opponent. And considering I do have a major size advantage, I cannot overlook the fact that, were we the same size, you would have destroyed me."

"I very nearly destroyed you as it is," she hissed.

"Very nearly."

"Don't sound so dry. I could have ended you."

"But you will not," he said. "Not now."

"You don't think?"

"No," he said, shaking his head. "Because I can offer you life. Ending me means ending yourself, too."

Her throat tightened, her palms slick. "I was prepared for that."

"I understand," he said, his tone grave. "But I think now that you've been given another opportunity you might see things differently?"

She looked down, hating that the war inside her was

transparent to him. Hating that he could see her weakness. That he could see she *wanted.* That his poisoned apple was indeed shiny and tempting.

A future. One with power. One where she wasn't starving, or freezing or afraid.

One where she lived.

Yes, she was starting to want that. But what it came with…that she wasn't sure of. But the cost would be her honor. The cost would be letting her enemy into her bed.

If it's for the greater good?

That was hard. She'd never much thought of the greater good. Only her own. That was what survival mode did to a person.

But this served the greater good and her personal good.

Weakness. Are you certain this isn't just weakness?

It very likely was. But then, she was tired of being strong. At least in this way. Tired of having to be so strong she didn't care for anything but living to the next sunrise, but living long enough so her life could end in Khadra when she'd ended Khadra's ruler.

Perhaps, in the end, that was the weakness. To aspire to nothing more than revenge, because wanting anything more had always seemed impossible. Too far out of her reach.

She shoved that thought aside.

"Perhaps," she said. "You have to admit, life is a very enticing reward."

"It is," he said. "I was personally prepared to beg for it sixteen years ago."

She blinked. "Were you?"

"It turned out I didn't have to," he said. "I simply hid… and I was able to escape."

She nodded slowly. "That's what I did."

"You were a child."

"You were young."

"I did my best to atone," he said. "Though, in the end it was too late."

"You couldn't have saved them. If your father wasn't strong enough to save them, a boy of fifteen with no fighting skills certainly couldn't have."

It was nothing more than the truth, and she wasn't sure why she was speaking it. Wasn't sure exactly why she wasn't letting him marinate in his guilt. Only that, from a purely logical standpoint, he was wrong. Because, had he not hidden, as she and her mother had done, he would not have lived.

She took a sharp breath and continued. "It would have done your country no good to have you killed that day."

The left corner of his mouth lifted. "Perhaps not. But it would have saved you a trip."

CHAPTER SIX

It was time for him to announce his impending marriage. And Ferran could only hope his viper bride cooperated with him.

She'd been in the palace for nearly a week, and their contact had been minimal since that day in the gym. Partly because he'd found the physical contact a temptation he did not need.

It had put a fire in his blood that he didn't like to remember existed. When he'd been a boy, he'd been all about himself. All about pleasure. Lust, and satisfying that lust.

But then he'd seen the devastation such things could bring. So he'd stopped acting that way. He'd stopped indulging his flesh.

Now Samarah was unearthing feelings, desires, best left buried.

Her father wasn't the only man he'd killed that day. He'd destroyed everything he'd been, everything he'd imagined he could be, in that moment too.

His rage had been regrettable but no matter how things played out, the end would have meant death for her father. But he had never been able to forgive himself for the deaths of Samarah and their mother.

Finding out she was still alive gave him a chance to soothe parts of him he'd thought would never heal.

But attraction, like the kind he'd felt in the gym, sparring with her, biting her…that had no place in this arrangement. They had no place in him.

They would have to consummate, and they would have to have children, but beyond that, Samarah would be free to live as she chose, and to be the symbol he needed.

He hardly needed her in his bed. He ignored the kick of heat that went through his body at the thought. When they'd fought, she'd been passion personified. And it had been beautiful and terrifying in equal measures. Because there was more conviction in her movements than existed in his entire body.

But then, he didn't need conviction. He just needed to do right. He needed to do better than his father. He needed to do better than he'd done at fifteen.

He'd lied to Samarah when he'd spoken of her father's fate. When he'd spoken of simple justice and black and white. So much of that reasoning had come from rage.

Ferran curled his hands into a fist, a spike of anger sending adrenaline through his veins. When he thought of his mother…cold and lifeless… Innocent in every way.

And then he thought of the spare moments before that. When Samarah's father had wrapped his fingers around her throat and Ferran had acted. For his mother. And for him.

But he had been too late. His violent rage utterly useless. In the end, none of his life was the same. Nothing of those whom he loved remained. Not even the good pieces of himself.

That day had destroyed so many things. And it was why he had to guard his emotions, why he must never allow his demons free rein. Ever again.

He rapped on Samarah's door and it opened slowly. Lydia, the maid, peered out. "Sheikh," she said, inclining her head.

"Is the lady ready?" he asked.

"Yes, Sheikh."

"I can speak for myself." Samarah's voice came from beyond the door.

"Leave us please, Lydia," he said.

The other woman nodded and scurried out of Samarah's chamber and down the hall. He walked in, and she looked at him with an expression reminiscent of someone who'd been stunned.

"What?"

"You're in a suit."

"So I am," he said, looking down at his black tie and jacket. "This shocks you?"

"I didn't expect Western attire."

She was elegant, in a long-sleeved black dress with a swath of white silk draped across the skirt and a gold belt around her waist. Matching gold decorated the cuffs of her sleeves, and there was gold chain woven through her hair. Which was still back in a braid.

He felt like making it a personal mission to see her hair loose.

Though, he shouldn't care about her hair. It had nothing at all to do with honor.

"You look perfect in Eastern attire," he said.

She pursed her lips. "I would think you might have liked us to look united."

"Perhaps you wanted it to look as though we got dressed together?"

Her cheeks turned a burnished rose. "That is not what I meant."

"Perhaps one day we will dress together." Though there would be no purpose behind that in their marriage, either. He would go to her at night when it was necessary. They wouldn't share a life. Not in those ways.

"This is not…an appropriate…I don't…"

"Do I fluster you, Samarah?" He did, he could see it. And he had no idea why he enjoyed it. Only that he did.

And he enjoyed so few things, he felt driven to chase it. If only for the moment.

"No," she said, dark eyes locking with his, her expression fierce. "It would take much more than you to fluster me, Ferran Bashar. I remember you as a naughty boy, not simply the man you are now."

"And I remember you as a girl, but I think we're both rather far removed from those days, are we not?"

"Maybe."

"I think we're a whole regime change, an execution and a revenge plot away from who we were."

"And a marriage proposal," she said.

"Yes, there is that. Though you seem to object to all mentions of marital related activities."

"I'm not ready to think about it," she said.

"I see." Heat burned through him, reckless and strange. Nothing like he'd experienced in his memory. Arousal was familiar. But there was a way he handled it now. And that was: alone.

He didn't act on reckless impulse. He didn't try to make the heat burn brighter. He extinguished it as quickly as possible. By working out until he dropped from exhaustion. By submerging himself in cold water.

He'd managed to diminish the desire for release until it was simply a physical need. Like hunger for food, thirst for water. There was no need for fanfare or flirtation. He had successfully managed without another person for years.

But there was a reality before him now. A woman he would marry. A woman who he would share his body with. And he was fascinated by her, by the thought. Now that sex was on the horizon he was finding it a difficult desire to ignore.

Especially with all the questions he had about her hair. How long it was. How it would feel sifting through his fingers.

Yes, he was curious about many things. He looked at her, at the exquisite line of her neck, the curve of her lips. His heart rate sped up. His fingers itching with the need to touch her.

"Tell me, Samarah," he said, ignoring his reservations and chasing the fire, "in all of your time spent on vengeance training and nurturing your rage, did you make time for men?"

She blinked. "No."

"Women?"

She blinked again. "No."

"Have you ever been kissed, Samarah?"

She stepped back as if she'd been shocked, her eyes wide. And he should be thankful she had. Or years of restraint would have been undone. "We're going to be late."

"The press will wait. We're what they're there for."

"I don't like to be late." She strode past him and out the door. "Are you coming?" she asked, out of view.

"Yes," he said, trying to calm the heat that was rioting through him.

They had to present a united front for the nation. He only hoped she didn't decide to attempt to give him a public execution.

Samarah looked out at the sea of reporters and felt the strong desire to scurry off the podium and escape so she could indeed do what Ferran had already accused her of doing. Nesting in the palace. Hiding away from everyone and everything.

She wasn't used to being visible like this. It felt wrong. It felt like an affront to survival.

But then, this pounding, wild fear she was experiencing was much better than the strange, heated fear she'd felt in her bedroom.

Have you ever been kissed, Samarah?

What kind of question was that? And why did it make her feel like this? Edgy and restless, a bit tingly. If this was rage, it was a new kind. One she was unfamiliar with. And she didn't like it one bit.

"It is with great happiness," Ferran said, his tone serious and grave and not reflecting happiness in the least, "that I announce my upcoming marriage. It is happy, not only because marriage is a blessed union—" Samarah nearly choked "—but because I am to marry my childhood friend—" she mentally rolled her eyes at his exaggeration "—who was long thought dead. Sheikha Samarah Al-Azen."

The room erupted into a frenzy, a volley of questions hitting like arrows. Samarah hadn't been the focus of so much attention in her memory. As a child, she'd been shielded from the press, and as an adult, she'd spent her life in hiding.

This wasn't anything she was prepared for. Fear had a limited place in her life. It acted only as a survival aid. To be heeded when she needed to heed it, and ignored when something larger than survival commanded she ignore it.

She never felt as if she was a slave to it.

Until now. Until she found herself doing something that went beyond explanation.

She put her hand on Ferran's arm, her fingers curling into his firm, warm flesh, and she drew nearer to him, concealing part of herself behind his body.

She felt him tense beneath her touch, saw a near-imperceptible shift in the muscles on his face. "I will take no questions now," he said. "I will add only this. I am regretful of the history that has passed between Khadra and Jahar. As are we all. I hope that this ushers in a new time. A new era. We are neighbors. And when children come from this union, blood. And while things will never be as they were, perhaps we can at least forge a truce, if not an alliance."

He put his hand on her back, the touch firm, burning her through her dress. He propelled her from the podium and away from the crowd, who were being managed now by his staff. "I have briefed them on what to say," he said when they were back in the corridor. "They have a nice story about how we reconnected at a small event we both attended in Morocco six months ago."

"That's quite the tale," she said, feeling shivery now, though she wasn't sure why.

"You have not been in front of people in that way before, have you?"

"I'm used to being anonymous," she said. "Actually, I'm used to needing anonymity for survival. This runs…counter to everything that I've learned."

That was a truer statement than she'd realized it was going to be. A far deeper-reaching statement.

Everything she'd been experiencing here this past week countered everything she knew about life. Everything she'd known about Ferran.

And about herself.

It was a lot to take in.

"This is my world," he said. "Everything I do needs a press conference."

"I'm not sure how I feel about that. Well, no, that's not true. I'm certain I don't like it." Because if she was really doing this sheikha thing, she wasn't sure how she would survive something like that all the time. "I feel too exposed."

"You're perfectly safe," he said.

"I'm standing there being useless in formal attire and I'm not at all ready to defend myself if something should happen."

He frowned and took a step toward her, and she took a step back, her bottom hitting the wall behind her. "It's something you'll have to get used to. This is only the beginning. We'll be planning a formal ball after this, to celebrate our upcoming marriage. And then the wedding. I am not going to hurt you," he said. "Stop preparing to collapse my windpipe."

"Should the need arise, I must be prepared."

One dark brow shot up. "The need will not arise."

"Says you."

He planted a hand by her head, leaning in. "I am here to protect you. I swear upon my life. In that room, where the conference is being held, there are always guards. They are ready to defend us should anything happen. And if they should fail, I am there. And I will guard you. I failed you once, Samarah. I let you die, and now that you've come back from the grave I will not allow you to return to it."

She felt the vow coming from his soul, from that place of honor he prized so dearly, and she knew he spoke the truth. So strange to hear this vow when part of her had still been ready to exact the revenge she'd come to deliver from the first.

She looked up and met his gaze. It was granite. And she felt caught there, between the marble wall and the hardness in his eyes. Between the honor he had shown since her return, and the growing respect she felt for that honor, and the years-long desire for a way to repay the devastation he'd been part of wreaking on her life. She couldn't look away, and she didn't know why. She was sent right back to the moment in his room, when she'd been poised, ready to take his life, and she'd seen his eyes.

There was just something about his eyes.

"I have never been able to trust my safety to another person," she said. Even when she'd had her mother with her, she'd often felt like the one doing the protecting. The parenting.

"Entrust it to me," he said. "I've already entrusted mine to you."

She turned that over for a moment. "I suppose that's true. But then, I am a prisoner of sorts."

"Instead of a leg shackle you'll have a ring."

"Sparklier anyway," she said, flexing her fingers, trying hard not to picture what it might feel like to wear a man's ring.

"You don't sound thrilled."

"Jewelry was never an aspiration of mine."

"I dare say it wasn't."

"So you can hardly expect for me to get all girlish over it, now can you?"

"Oh, Samarah, I don't expect that. No matter how much you make yourself glitter, I'm not fooled."

"Good," she said.

"You are a feral creature," he said, leaning in slightly, the motion pulling the breath from her lungs.

"And you think you'll tame me?"

He put his hand on her cheek, his thumb tracing the line of her lower lip. She could do nothing. Nothing but simply let him touch her. Nothing but see what he might do. She was fascinated, in the way one might be of something utterly terrifying. Something hideous and dark that all decent people would turn away from. Her stomach twisted tight, her lungs crushed, unable to expand.

"Have you ever seen exotic animals that were caged?" he asked. She shook her head. "The way they pace back and forth against the bars. It's disturbing. To see all that power, all that wildness, locked away. To see every instinct stolen from them. I do not seek to tame you. For those very reasons. But I do hope we might at least come to exist beside one another."

"We might," she said, the words strangled.

"I will take that as an enthusiastic agreement coming from you. I know this is not ideal but can't you simply..."

"Endure for the greater good?" she asked.

"Yes."

"Is that what you will be doing?"

"It's what I've always done," he said. "It's what I must do. This is the burden of a crown, Samarah. If you do it right, you're under the power of the people, not the other way around."

"Let me ask you this, Ferran," she said. And she didn't know why she was keeping the conversation going. Didn't know why she was standing in the hall with him, backed against a wall, allowing him to keep his hand on her cheek. But she was.

She knew she was extending the moment, extending the contact, but as confused as she was by her motivations, she didn't feel ashamed.

"Ask away," he said.

"You consider me feral."

"I do."

"Does this mean you're domesticated? As you've been brought up in captivity?"

"Of course I am," he said. "I'm the ruler of this country, and I have to be a diplomat. A leader. I have to be a man who acts rationally. With his mind, with his knowledge of right and wrong."

She narrowed her eyes and tilted her head, the motion causing his fingers to drift downward to her jawline. He traced the bone there. Slowly. It felt like the long slow draw of a match. Burning. Sparking.

"That's not what I see," she said.

"Oh no?" he asked. "What is it you see?"

"A tiger pacing the bars."

CHAPTER SEVEN

SAMARAH WAS IN the garden doing martial arts forms when Ferran found her.

"I'm pleased to see you're out enjoying the scorching heat," he said.

She wiped the sweat from her forehead. "It's the desert. There is no other sort of weather to enjoy. It's this or monsoons."

"You don't get so much of the torrential rains here. But if you go west, toward the bedouin camps…there you find your monsoons."

"Then I suppose here at the palace, heat is my only option."

"Mostly."

He watched her for a moment longer. Every graceful movement. Precise and deadly. She was a thing of beauty. A thing of poisoned beauty.

He was much more attracted to her than he'd anticipated. Because he hadn't anticipated it at all. This strange, slow burn that hit him in the gut whenever she was near. He'd never experienced anything like it. He wasn't the kind of man who burned for one woman. For any woman.

He scarcely remembered his past lovers. He'd had one year of his life devoted to the discovery of women. At fifteen, he hadn't been able to get enough. Such a spoiled, stupid boy he'd been. He'd been granted almost his full height then, and he'd had more money and power than a boy his age knew how to wield. That had meant he'd discovered sex earlier than he might have otherwise.

But women had only been a means to him finding release, and nothing more. He'd never wanted one much more than any other.

But here and now, he burned.

It was not at all what he wanted.

Then there was her bit of insight.

A tiger pacing the bars.

When she'd said that, he'd wanted to show her—while he kept himself leashed, he was not in a cage. He could slip it at will, and he'd had the strong desire to make sure she realized that.

To press her head against the wall and let her feel just what he was feeling. To tilt her head back and take her lips with his.

To show her just what manner of man he was.

But that was passion driving that desire. And he didn't bow down to passion. It was too exposing. And he would not open himself up in that way again.

This deadly, encroaching *feeling* had fueled his plan for the day, too. It was time for both of them to get out of this palace, this mausoleum that held so many of their dead.

He would get them both out into an open space for a while.

"I had thought you might like a chance to go out in it for a while."

"Out in it?"

"The heat," he said.

"Oh." She stopped her exercise. "For what purpose?"

"There is a large bedouin tribe that camps a few hours east of the palace at this time of year, and I always like to pay them a visit. See that their needs are being met, what has changed. They have an ambassador, but I like to keep personal touch, as well."

"Oh. And you would…bring me?"

"You're to be my wife. This will be a part of your duties. You will be part of this country."

"It's hard to imagine being a part of Khadra," she said. "Being somehow a part of you."

"And yet, that is to be our future," he said.

"So it appears."

"So it is."

"So let it be written, et cetera."

He smiled. "Yes. I think you just bantered with me."

She frowned in return, the golden skin on her forehead creasing. "I did not banter with you."

"You did. For a moment there, you thought of me as a human being and not a target you'd like to put an arrow through."

"Lies. I am imagining breaking your nose as we speak."

"I don't think you are, princess."

"Don't let my naturally sweet demeanor fool you."

"There is no chance of that," he said.

He didn't know why, but he wanted to tease her. He wanted to make her smile. Because she never did. It was less perturbing than wanting to feel how soft her skin was beneath his fingers, anyway. So perhaps for now he would just focus on the smile.

"How will we get there?" she asked.

"By camel."

An air-conditioned, luxury four-wheel drive SUV was hardly a camel. She realized, the moment the vehicle pulled up to the front of the palace, that Ferran had been…teasing her.

Strange.

He probably wasn't afraid of her anymore, since he

seemed content to poke at her with a stick. Which, all things considered, wasn't the worst thing. That he wasn't afraid of her, not that he felt at liberty to stick-poke her.

Though, she couldn't remember the last time someone had teased her. Maybe no one ever had. Dimly, she recalled a nanny who had been very happy. Smiling and singing a lot. But Samarah couldn't even remember the woman's name. And she was more a misty dream than an actual memory.

Master Ahn had been kind. But he hadn't had much in the way of a sense of humor. He'd been quiet, though, almost serene and it had made a nice counterweight for Samarah's anger. He'd helped her channel it. He'd helped her find some measure of peace. Had helped her put things in their proper compartments.

But he hadn't teased her.

Ferran held the door for her and she got inside, the rush of cold air a nice change from the arid heat. She wasn't used to being able to find this kind of reprieve from the midday sun. It was…luxury.

"This is not a camel," she said.

"Disappointed?" he asked, as he took his place in the driver's seat and turned the engine over.

He maneuvered the car out of the gates and toward and around back behind the palace, where the city thinned out, and there was a gap in the walls. Walls that were left over from medieval times. More of the old mixed with the new.

"I'm not particularly disappointed by the lack of camel, no."

"They aren't so bad once you learn to lean into the gait."

"They are so bad, Ferran. I remember."

"Do you?"

She leaned back against the seat and closed her eyes. "Vaguely. We did a…caravan once. We rode camels. And picnicked out in the sand beneath canopies. It seems like…

like maybe it was a dream. Or another person told me this story. It hardly seems like me. But I remember the rocking motion of the camel so…if I know that, then it had to have been real, right?"

He nodded. "It was real. Your father hosted a picnic like that for visiting dignitaries every year."

"Oh, is that it? I couldn't remember. Weird how you know more about my past than I do. I was so young and my mother never talked about it."

Weird was…too light of a word. It was…everything. Horribly sad. Happy, in a strange way, to hear about her past finally instead of just having vague memories seen through the lens of a child.

But so odd that she was dependent on the man she saw as her enemy to learn the information.

"We used to go to the palace by the seaside," she said.

"My parents' home. Mine now. Ours. Or it will be."

Her stomach tightened. "I'm not sure if I want to go there."

"Why not?"

"I was so happy there," she said, closing her eyes. "It almost hurts to think about it. Like someone scooped out my stomach." She opened her eyes again and looked out at the desert. "I don't think I want to go," she said again.

They were silent for the rest of the drive. Samarah trying to focus on the view and the air-conditioning, rather than the heat the man beside her seemed to radiate. It was stupid. His body temperature should be ninety-eight point six, just like hers. So why did he always feel so damn hot? It was irritating beyond measure.

So were the feelings that he called up out of her. Effortless. Like he was some sort of emotional magician. Creating emotions when there had been none, at least no refined, squishy ones, for years.

"Do you see?" he asked.

She looked up and out the front windshield at the tents in the distance. “Yes.”

“That’s the encampment. And there’s smoke. Likely they’re cooking for us. If not, we’re in trouble because it means they aren’t happy with me.”

“Do they have reason to be unhappy with you?”

“People are unhappy with the leader of their country most of the time for various reasons, are they not?”

“I suppose they are. Though, I’ve had more reason to be unhappy with mine than most.”

“Given the circumstances, yes.”

“They stole my life from me,” she said, looking up and meeting his gaze. “They stole my life.”

“*They* did?”

And not him. She didn’t miss the unspoken part of the sentence.

“Do not read too much into that. It was a complex situation, that’s for sure,” she said. “Many people could be assigned portions of blame. Except for me,” she said, feeling the familiar anger welling up in her. “I was a child. I was six. It wasn’t my fault. And I’ve still had to live it.”

“You have,” he said. “And it is a crime, because you’re right. You had no fault in it. You had no part in the play and yet you were forced to deal with the consequences. So now…accept this. Accept this life. Live something different.”

His words curled around her heart. Sticky, warm tentacles that wrapped her up tight and made her feel secure. And trapped. And she wasn’t sure if she should fight or give in.

“Are you ready?” She knew he was talking about getting out and meeting the people, but it had another meaning for her.

She nodded slowly. “I’m ready.”

She thought, for the first time, she might truly mean it.

* * *

The people did rush to greet them. And there was dinner prepared. They hurried to make a spot at the head of the table not just for Ferran, but for Samarah.

Ferran was pleased that everyone here seemed happy with his choice of bride. Because for the desert people who often traveled near the borders of the neighboring countries, the relations between Khadra and surrounding nations was even more important than to those who lived in the cities.

For them it wasn't about trade. Or import tax. Or the ability to holiday where they pleased. For these people, it was often about survival. To be able to depend on the friendliness of their neighbors for food, shelter, water if there was an emergency. Medical help. It was essential.

For his part, Ferran provided what he could, but if there was ever an emergency on the fringes, then there would be no way for the government to provide aid in time.

He looked at Samarah, who was curled up next to him, her feet tucked beneath her bottom, her hands in her lap. She looked much more at ease in this setting than she had at the press conference, but he still wondered if all of the people looking at her with obvious interest were bothering her.

He didn't like for her to be afraid. That realization hit him hard. But he wasn't sure why it did. Of course he shouldn't want her to be afraid. She was to be his wife, and it was his duty to ensure his wife was protected, regardless of how they'd gotten their start.

Perhaps you find it strange because you know you can't really protect her?

Not from the truth. Not if it ever came out.

He shut down his thoughts and focused on what was happening around them. Most of the tribe was sitting in the mobile courtyard area for dinner. Families in clusters, children talking and laughing, running around on the outskirts of the seating area.

The elders were seated with him and Samarah, on cushions, their food in front of them on a wooden mat that would be easy to roll up and transport. It was nothing like the heavy, grand dining table in the palace that his father had had brought in. So formal. Custom made in Europe.

Ferran found that in many ways, he liked this better. This spoke of Khadra. Of its people. Its history.

"Sheikha."

Ferran watched Samarah's dark head snap up when the tribal elder to his right addressed her. "Yes," she said, seemingly shocked to have been spoken to.

"How do you find the political climate in Jahar at present?"

She blinked rapidly. "I… It has improved," she said. "The sheikhdom is never going to be restored, not as it was. The new way of doing things is imperfect. But since the death of the previous leader, there is something of a more…legitimate democracy in place. All things considered, that is perhaps best for the country."

"And do you think this will unite the countries again?"

Her brow creased. "It's difficult to say. But I do think that the current government won't perceive me as a threat now that I'm marrying into the Bashar family and making my home here. So that is helpful for me. As for everyone else? I think if nothing else it will help old wounds heal."

Ferran nodded slowly. "If she can forgive me, then perhaps Jahar can forgive."

"And," she said, her words slow and steady, "if Ferran can lay aside the pain my family caused him, perhaps Khadra can forgive the pain, too."

"It was a great loss, that of your mother and father," the elder said to Ferran.

"Yes," he said. "It was."

"But you have done well. You've made them proud. You've made us all proud."

Ferran watched Samarah's face. He wondered if she thought he'd done well. Or if she still thought he was the worst sort of man.

The funny thing was, Samarah was more right about him than any of the leaders here. Yes, he'd done some good for his country. That was true. But in many ways he was no less than the murderer Samarah believed him to be.

"You do well in your choice of bride," the man continued. "It is truly a wise choice for us all."

"That," Ferran said, "I will wholeheartedly agree with you on."

And he did. Samarah was a choice he couldn't have foreseen having the chance to make. And she was certainly the best one.

"Well," she said. "Thank you."

"It's the truth," Ferran said.

The other man turned his attention back to the man to his right and Ferran continued to keep his focus on Samarah.

"I'm pleased to be a handy political pawn."

"Better than an instigator of war. You see what might have become of these people if you'd succeeded in executing me? Or if I'd imprisoned you. Marriage is preferable to either of those things."

"Marriage is preferable to death or imprisonment? Someone should embroider than onto a pillow."

"Poetic, I think."

"Very."

"Neither you or I are romantics," he said, watching her very closely, trying to gauge her response. She was so very hard to read. Such a guarded creature. And he shouldn't care about whether or not he was able to break that guard.

It had nothing to do with their arrangement. And neither did his fascination with her. Though, being able to read her might come in handy, just in case she ever got it in her mind to try and kill him again.

"Obviously not," she said, her face remaining impassive.

"Do you ever smile, *habibti*?" he asked.

"That's…an improvement over *little viper,* so I won't push the issue. And no, I don't often smile.

"I think that's too bad."

"Do you ever smile, Ferran?"

"Not often."

"Then don't concern yourself with my smile. I thought you said you weren't a romantic."

"Is smiling a romantic notion now?"

"Maybe just a luxury you and I haven't been able to afford?" she asked, cocking her head to the side.

"Perhaps that. Though, I am a sheikh,"

"As you've reminded me many times."

"It is the most defining part of me."

"Is it?"

"Yes," he said. "If I weren't a sheikh…things would be very different. But I am. And as such I can afford a great many things. Perhaps I should invest in smiling."

"Investing in frivolity? That seems like a recipe for disaster."

"Or at the least a recipe for…shenanigans."

The left side of her mouth twitched. "Shenanigans?"

"Yes."

"You said *shenanigans.*"

"I did," he said.

"Have you ever said that word before in your life?"

"No. I haven't had occasion to."

"It's a good word," she said. "And you got up to a lot of them when you were a teenager. I…I remember."

"I hope you don't remember in very great detail," he said. "I wasn't the best version of myself then."

She frowned. "So…this is the best version of you then?"

"Obviously." Her shoulders shook, her lips turning upward, a choked noise escaping. "Did you just…laugh at me? Is that what that was?"

"I think so," she said.

"You nearly smiled."

"I…did." She looked confused by that.

"I wish for you to do that again," he said. And he meant it. Not because he was being emotional, but because it wasn't fair that a woman like her, one so beautiful, one who should have been happy, had ended up with so few things to smile about.

"Perhaps I shall."

"Consider it at least." The corner of her mouth twitched again. "We will retire to bed soon."

Her eyes flew wide. "We?"

"I have brought my own tent, and it was graciously set up for us. Don't worry, it has rooms. And you will get your own."

"I had better."

"You will have to get over your aversion to sleeping with me." His pulse quickened. He was quickly discovering he had no aversions to sleeping with her. And why should he? Marriage made sex expected. It justified the desire.

As long as desire didn't rule in him, as long as he kept control over his weaknesses, there was no harm in being with his wife.

Her eyebrows lowered. "I am not having this conversation with you," she said, her voice a furious whisper, "sitting next to all these men."

"Your point is taken," he said. "But I come back to the issue of smiling."

She looked hesitant for a moment. As if she was trying to decide if she should say something else to him or bolt off into the desert. "What about it?"

"I should like the chance to try and make you smile tomorrow." Because he wanted to give her something. To give her more than he'd taken away.

"How will you do that?"

"There is an oasis not far from here. It is a place I frequent. I would like to show you."

"I..." He could tell she was considering telling him where to put his offer. But she swallowed her initial response. "All right," she said.

"We will have to ride horses, though, as you cannot drive in with a car."

"Horses?" she asked.

"Yes, horses. Can you ride?"

"I...I don't know."

"Well, you can share mine. I intend to ask for the use of one here."

"All...all right."

"No argument?"

She shook her head. "No. I think...perhaps I might make an attempt to smile."

CHAPTER EIGHT

SAMARAH HESITATED NEXT to the big black horse that was saddled and ready for their ride to the oasis. Ferran was already seated and she was meant to…get on there with him somehow. There was no way to avoid physical contact.

And frankly, physical contact with him was disturbing.

Though, the fact that it was disturbing…disturbed her. Because there was no reason for it to be quite so unsettling.

Sure there is. He ordered your father to his death. He's partly responsible for much of the misery in your life. Of course it's uncomfortable.

Yes, but it wasn't only that.

She wasn't used to touching men. And he was very much a man. So very different from the way she was built. So hard. So…so warm. She always came back to how damn warm he was. Perhaps he had a fever.

He lowered his hand and she stared at it.

"You're meant to take it," he said.

"Take it where?" she asked, crossing her arms beneath her breasts and turning her shoulders in.

"Grasp my hand, Samarah."

She reached out and curled her fingers around his, heat exploding against her palm and streaking up her arm. She didn't even have time to process it before she found herself getting hauled up onto the horse, behind Ferran.

Reflexively, she wrapped her arms around his waist and

leaned into him. Then she started to ponder which was more frightening. The idea of falling onto the sand, or continuing to cling to Ferran and his unnaturally warm back.

His back won. For now.

She should have asked to sit in front. It might have been a bit less disturbing.

But then…then she could have been between his thighs. Though, for the moment, he was between hers. There really was no winning in this situation. At least the current seating arrangement gave her an upper hand of sorts. If she wanted to jump off and run, she could. That was a comforting thought.

"It is not a long ride," he said, "an hour perhaps."

"I'm not concerned," she said, holding her head away from the hollow between his shoulder blades that looked like a very nice place to rest her cheek.

But she would not. She didn't need to use him as a headrest.

"You seem stiff," he said, spurring the horse into a trot.

"I am on a horse. How would you like me to behave?"

"Rest against me."

"I hardly think that's necessary."

"Suit yourself."

"Nothing about this suits me," she said.

"That's not good. Because I'm attempting to make you smile, and if nothing suits you, I won't be able to accomplish that."

"You're making me sound difficult."

"That's not my intent. You are much less difficult than when we first met and you attempted to stab me. That considered, I would hate to get on your bad side again."

"Who said you were off of it?"

Their conversation faded out and she settled into the horse's gait. And eventually, she settled into him. Her neck got stiff, a kink forming in thc sidc, and she looked at the perfect pocket, just there, between his shoulder blades.

It would alleviate the pain. If she could just rest against him for a second.

She lowered her head. He was solid, but it wasn't uncomfortable at all. The fabric of his shirt was damp with sweat, and she didn't find it at all disagreeable.

That only increased her discomfort.

She could hear his heart, thundering in his chest. Could feel the shift of his muscles as he moved with the horse over the desert sand.

She turned her face slightly and caught the scent of his skin. Of the sweat. Really, none of it was disagreeable at all. Which…made it disagreeable in its way.

Samarah shifted and tightened her hold on him, her palms flat against his stomach. He was hard there, too. And she could feel his muscles, the definition of them, even with the fabric of his shirt separating her hands from his flesh.

She'd seen his muscles, so she knew just how very defined they looked. And she also knew about the body hair. Which she found much more fascinating than she should.

She stared at the horizon line after that, trying her best not to think too hard about Ferran's body, and the way it felt beneath her hands. Or the way it looked without his shirt.

It was only because she was trapped against him that she was thinking this way.

The ride stretched on forever. She got hotter, and she got more restless. And her thoughts weren't calming down. Her body wasn't, either. She would have thought you just got used to being pressed against someone eventually, but apparently you didn't.

At least not when that someone was Ferran.

"We're here," Ferran said, his tone hard, tugging back on the horse's reins, bringing his behind pressing hard between her thighs and sending a jolt through her body.

She curled her fingers into his shirt, desperate to hold on to him. And desperate to jump off and run screaming into the desert until she could figure out what the hell was wrong with her.

She looked around his shoulder, and her body slowly released the tension it was holding fast to. The oasis was beautiful. A lush green blot of ink against a dry, pristine background of bone-white sky and pale sand.

"Hang on to the saddle," he said.

She obeyed and he slid down off the horse, then held his hands out.

"Seriously?" she asked.

"What?"

She swung her leg over the side of the horse and slid down onto the sand, landing deftly on her feet. "I'm not a delicate flower, Ferran. Do not treat me like one."

"I wouldn't dream of it."

"You just tried. Now, where is it we're staying?"

"Are you wilting?"

"Be careful, or I will bite you. I believe I owe you on that score."

His expression sharpened, the look in his eyes intensifying. "I can't say I'm entirely opposed to you biting me."

"That makes no sense."

"Perhaps not to you, *habibti*. But if I conduct our marriage in the proper manner, it will make sense to you soon."

"I don't see how it could."

He just looked at her, and he appeared to be amused. And she felt heat—both anger and other sorts of heat, sorts she didn't want to contemplate—rising in her.

"Your imagination is sadly lacking."

"You bit me once already," she said. "I felt nothing."

Her stomach pitched, both because she was lying, and because she was reliving the scrape of his teeth over her skin. It was such an intimate thing. And right then, she started connecting all the dots.

"Surely people don't bite each other when they..." She snapped her mouth shut.

"Not always. And I meant no more than I said."

"I don't believe that," she said. "About there being no hidden meaning, not...not about the biting. I believe that, I just... Where are you going?" He'd taken the horse by the reins and started leading him away.

"I thought you wanted to see where we were sleeping tonight?"

"Fine. Lead the way."

"I am."

They walked farther into the oasis, shielded by a rock formation, and by a thick growth of trees that grew taller as they edged closer to the waterline.

The water was like a sheet of glass. Reflecting the trees, the sky and sun from the still surface.

"This is incredible," she said. "Are there...don't a lot of animals come here?"

"I've never seen many, not when I have a fire going at night. And it's rained recently, so this isn't the only water. Though, you should watch for snakes."

"I don't like snakes," she said, her focus going to the ground as she watched the placement of each of her steps.

"I'm not a huge fan of them, to be honest, but for the most part, you won't be bothered by them."

"Yes, well, sometimes in floods, they would slither into the rooms I was staying in. Fortunately, not usually poisonous ones. But...but sometimes the odd viper would pay me a visit. So, your nickname for me is somewhat fitting."

"You don't have to worry about snakes tonight," he said. "I'll build a fire now."

"It's hot still."

"A precaution. The tent is this way."

She followed him down the well-worn trail that led deeper into the trees, and out to the far side of the small lake. She stopped when she saw it. "It is not exactly a tent."

The "tent" had permanent walls, with windows, and what appeared to be a broad canvas stretched over the roof and anchored into the ground. There was a small deck off the front that went over the water.

"What is this?" she asked.

"My escape, I suppose. Something much simpler than the palace. And quiet. I come out here whenever I visit the tribe. And sometimes for no reason at all."

"Do you bring women here?"

She was curious. Fascinated by who Ferran was as a man. Not as the monster she'd built up in her head, and not even as the man he was around her. But the man he'd been for the past sixteen years. The man who, apparently, had a retreat. And who knew biting was a thing that could be exciting. And who undoubtedly *had* been kissed many times. And had lovers.

Yes, she was very curious all of a sudden, who this man was. Because she had to know her enemy. The enemy she was preparing to ally herself with.

"No," he said. "I don't bring women here."

"Where do you bring women?" she asked.

She was curious now. And she wanted to know the answer. She wanted to know about these women, who knew about how it felt to be pressed up against his back, and to feel his stomach. And…more.

She despised the fascination. It was like giving in to the desire to watch a fight breaking out on the streets. To take in the horror, the anger and blood. To be both drawn to and repulsed by what she was seeing.

"Why do you want to know?" he asked.

"Because I do."

"Why?"

"Because…because I am supposed to be your wife." It was the first time she'd said it. The first time she'd felt like that position might matter. Like it might really be real. Like she was making real steps toward their treaty, rather than just standing in a holding pattern, contemplating the merit of escaping, or exacting revenge of some kind. "It seems like I should know these things about you."

"I don't," he said, his tone hard.

"What?"

"I don't…conduct affairs."

"Never?" she asked.

"No."

"I…I don't…"

He swept past her and into the dwelling.

She looked inside. "This is very much not a tent. Just as your car was not a camel."

Yes, the ceiling was swaths of draped fabric; beneath it stretched canvas that she imagined was completely waterproof, but that did not make it a tent.

There was formal furniture. It was spare, but very expensive looking. Wood and plush fabrics. Nothing as ornate as the palace. This seemed to speak more of Ferran, and not the rulers that had come before him. This was the man, and not the legacy.

At least, it was a piece of him.

She was digging for other pieces.

"I confess, calling it a tent was slightly misleading."

"And the car?"

"Yes, that, too."

"You're telling me you don't conduct relationships with women?" she asked. "I assumed…"

"Why would you assume, Samarah?"

Her cheeks heated. "I would have thought a man such as yourself would have lovers. Several of them. I remember how you were. Though, I suppose being naked with someone makes you very vulnerable to them. Sleeping with someone—they could kill you while you dreamed. I suppose…I suppose that means you have to be selective about lovers."

She wanted to know the answer because if she really was to be married to this man then it seemed like this was important information for her. It seemed she should know how he viewed sex. Why he had no lovers. If he was being truthful. Because if they were going to be married, they would share the marriage bed and all the intimacies that entailed.

Intimacies she was woefully uneducated about.

She'd heard sex spoken of in vile, crude terms. Had heard men make threats that were disgusting. Had heard prostitutes make allusions to things she hadn't fully understood.

She hoped there was more to marital activities than all of that. Really, she knew there had to be, because it was the thing that had driven their families to destruction.

That was the part that scared her. The part of her that feared she would become a slave to it…the part that feared there was a part of herself that was undiscovered that would change completely when she finally found it.

"Being naked with someone does not really make you all that vulnerable to them. And I never slept with any of my lovers."

"You didn't? I was under the impression that…" She trailed off, not liking how innocent she was revealing herself to be.

In so many ways she had no innocence. She'd been in the palace during all that horrible destruction. And then, back at home she'd survived the siege. There had been so much violence on both of those days. She'd survived homelessness, hunger, cold, heat, fear. Grief. So much more grief than one person could be expected to bear.

But she didn't understand the kind of connection that

drove two people to pursue a romantic relationship. She didn't understand sexual desire. Not in a specific way that existed between two lovers.

It was her only piece of innocence really. Her physical innocence. Her emotions were jaded, her mind inundated with the cold ugliness of the world. It was only her body that remained untouched and she had fought fiercely for that. For her body was the one thing she had left that hadn't been violated by the world.

Still, she didn't especially want him to know all of that.

Have you ever been kissed, Samarah?

She had a feeling he might know already. But she didn't need to go revealing herself.

"You do not have to sleep with someone just because you have sex with them. Though, perhaps in your case, since you lacked a steady bed it was easier to stay."

She didn't know what to say to that. She wasn't sure if he was digging for information or not. And she wasn't sure if she wanted to give him any.

"We aren't talking abut me," she said.

"No. We are not. But that should answer your questions."

"It doesn't really."

"Then perhaps you should speak more plainly so I can answer them. I am not playing guessing games with you, Samarah."

"When you say you do not conduct affairs…you are not…I mean, you have been with…"

"I am not a virgin," he said, the word dripping with incredulity. "I slept with enough women that they blurred together during my teenage years, but there was an inciting incident that put me off passion. I had a job to do, and I have not had the time to lose myself in pleasure since I overtook the throne." His expression was hard, a dark, frightening rage filling his eyes. "Do you now feel suitably informed, Samarah?"

No. Now she wanted to ask about the pleasure. The pleasure he was afraid to lose himself in. Wanted to ask what that meant to a man like him. Sixteen years of celibacy. What it would mean when he broke it. And if he really intended to break it with her. For them to… Now she wanted to ask a whole lot of questions, but she was stuck because if she did then she really would give herself away. And then she would be standing in a remote location talking about sex with the man who was caught in a fog in her brain. Somewhere between enemy and ally. Somewhere between monster and fiancé.

It was all too weird.

"I feel more informed. Yes. Are you going to start a fire?"

"Yes," he said. "I'll bring you your things. Why don't you get settled."

"Where is my room?" She wondered for a moment if he would suggest they share. And that terrified her. And made her feel something else that she couldn't quite place.

"Whichever one you choose, I will take the other. Does that suit?"

"As much as anything in this arrangement does."

"You flatter me," he said, his voice clipped.

Now he sounded annoyed with her, and she couldn't for the life of her figure out what she'd done. And she shouldn't care. So she wouldn't.

"All right, I will arrange my things. Enjoy building your fire."

"I'll see you again for dinner," he said. "If it rains, I will cook indoors."

"Do you expect it to rain?"

"I always prepare for a potential catastrophe. Rain, flooding."

"All right," she said, waving her hand, already going off to explore other rooms of the house. She badly needed a reprieve from his presence. He was making her say—and think—crazy things.

She needed to get her head on straight. She needed to remember what it was she was doing here.

That thought deflated her. She sank to the couch. What she was doing here was marrying Ferran Bashar, the man she'd sworn to kill. Because it was the right thing to do. For their countries. It was a greater good she couldn't simply ignore.

This was a true sacrificial act, not just something that would assuage the burning anguish inside of her. She'd talked herself into thinking his murder, and her subsequent death, a death she'd been nearly certain of, would be sacrificial. But perhaps not. Perhaps it had only been an act born of blinding rage and desperation.

The same sort of rage that had driven her father.

The thought hit her hard, a realization she slid sickly through her veins like cold tar. She was not her father. She was not a mindless rage machine who would destroy all simply to get revenge upon his wife and her new lover.

And on the heels of that realization, the other was cemented.

She was going to marry Ferran. She was going to be his wife.

God help her. It was real.

A tear slid down her cheek and dropped onto her hand. And for the first time since her mother wandered into the desert and never returned, Samarah Al-Azem let herself cry.

When she stumbled outside an hour later, she didn't feel any less stunned, but she did feel a renewed sense of purpose. Determination. She felt…she felt as if she was truly on a new path. As if she'd reconciled this change.

At least in part.

She looked up at the sun, which was resting low over the horizon now. A chill spread over the desert sand, along with a hazy blue blanket that seemed to thicken the air. Gnats swarmed over the reeds, and she batted them away from her face as she walked through the tall plants down to the water.

She grabbed a large stick and let it go before her, doing a sweep for snakes as she went along.

Thankfully, none had seen the need to get in her path.

She came to the damp, cold mud and stopped, looking out at the water. The surface rippled, then broke, and Ferran appeared. He stood, his back to her, water droplets rolling through the valleys in his flesh, created by the hard-cut muscles that she'd been enjoying on the ride over.

He took a step up toward the bank that was to the left, and the waterline lowered on his body, so that it revealed two deep grooves in his lower back before showing his…oh.

He took another step and the water slid off his skin. And she could see now that he was naked. And he was…

She'd never really looked at a man's butt before. Not like this. Not one that was bare, and muscular and…well, bare.

More importantly, she'd never been given to the urge to simply stare at a man like this, clothed or not. As a man and not a threat. As a man and not a mere weapon. But flesh and blood. He was fascinating. Especially with their earlier conversation playing through her mind, combined with the close proximity of the horse ride.

And her recent acceptance, full acceptance, of the fact that she was to be his wife.

Yes, it was all that that had her there, staring and unable to stop. Her mouth was agape. Truly. Her face felt like it was on fire and her heart…her heart was beating faster than she'd thought was physically possible.

The only time it had ever come close to this was in moments of sheer, unadulterated terror. Those she'd had.

Those she was familiar with. This? This was something else. Something new. Something that had nothing to do with the past.

He turned to the side and she couldn't breathe. It all just gathered in her chest like a ball and stopped. She was completely frozen, held captive by him. She wanted to see him. All of him. She wanted so badly for the mystery to be solved. To know now what he looked like. All over. Because not knowing…it made her more afraid of the future. She just needed to know.

She tried to swallow, but it got caught with the knot of air.

Then he turned to face her, dark eyes boring into hers. But she only met his gaze for a moment. Then, completely without thought, she was looking down.

She bit her lip, taking the moment to study him in detail. It was her first glimpse of a naked man and she found she could only stare. And that she could not remain wholly detached.

"See something you're interested in."

She wasn't sure *interested* was the word. She forced her gaze back to his. "I'm sorry."

He lifted one shoulder and the muscles in his chest shifted. Fascinating. "No need to apologize. I didn't hang a sign out."

"Do you…do you have a sign?" she asked, feeling slow, her brain processing things at half the speed. The lack of oxygen was probably to blame.

"No, I don't have a sign."

"It would be the best way to warn people."

"I could have sent you a text."

She blinked slowly. "I don't have a phone."

"That will change."

"Will it?"

"Of course," he said, still standing there. Casually naked.

She didn't feel casual at all. There was so much skin on display it made her want to slip out of her own and run away.

"There's no *of course* about any of this. Not to me and I—I can't just stand here and talk to you while you're naked."

"That will change, too."

"I do not think," she said, turning around and heading back up the path, sweeping her stick through the grass and quickly following behind.

She had no desire to run away from a naked man, only to step on a snake. Out of the frying pan and all that.

And it wasn't as if Ferran's nakedness put her in any danger.

The heat in her cheeks, the pounding of her heart, said otherwise. It felt a lot like fear. She knew fear well. Much more intimately than most.

Though, there were subtle differences to this feeling.

Such as the not entirely unpleasant feeling between her thighs.

She wasn't that innocent. She knew what that was. Why was this happening to her now? With him?

You are marrying him....

Yes, but she'd intended to deny sex as part of the equation for as long as possible and then submit to it when she had no other option. Her plan, thus far, hazy as it was, had been to just lie there and think of Jahar, so to speak. As far ahead as she'd thought in the past hour, when she'd finally decided that yes, she would be his wife. Really. Not just as a reprieve to a sentence or until she could kill him.

Even so, she wasn't ready to contend with the idea that she might…desire him.

No. This was just garden variety, biologically inspired arousal that had nothing to do with desire. It was the first time she'd been exposed to a man, an attractive man, and not been worried about him being something of a threat in the back of her mind.

So that was all it was.

She frowned as she shut the door to the dwelling. When had she stopped perceiving Ferran as a threat? She was certain he wouldn't harm her. Certain he would never force himself on her. And she wasn't sure what he'd done to earn that measure of trust, when only two weeks ago she'd cowered in the middle of his bed, her own weapon in his hands, fearing he would kill her or use her body.

She didn't now. Not in the least.

Strange how things had changed. How they were changing.

Now, that made her feel afraid. Because without all the anger at Ferran, she wasn't sure what she had left. It had insulated her, consumed her, for so long, she felt almost bereft without it.

"I apologize that my body offended you."

She turned and saw Ferran in the doorway, tugging his shirt over his head. His pants were already on, riding low on his lean hips. Not that any of it helped now, since she could so clearly visualize how he looked without the clothes on. Problematic.

"It was not…offensive," she said. "I just am not accustomed to having conversations with nude men. Out in the open."

"You only have conversations with them in the enclosed?"

"Well, where else would I have them?" she asked.

"Outside, it turns out."

"No. That's why I came in."

"Stubborn creature. Since you're in an enclosed space now, I could always take my clothes off again as I know you find this preferable."

She held up her hands, her heart scurrying into her throat. "No!"

"Then perhaps you might like to come outside and have dinner."

"Clothed?"

"Only if you want. I have no such rules about women and nudity."

She narrowed her eyes. "But you aren't naked with women at all, if what you say is true."

"Come back outside, Samarah."

"I will require we both remain clothed." She walked out the door and followed the rising smoke, back down to the pond where he'd been swimming only a few moments earlier. The ground was damp here, but there were blankets and pillows spread out already. There was a pan over the fire, resting on a grate.

"You've cooked?"

"I come here alone often, as I said. I could cook inside, but I quite like to eat out here." He took the pan from the grate and moved it to a small, low table that was next to his seat.

"Obviously."

There was rice and meat in the pan, and he handed her a bowl filled to the top. It was much simpler than the way they ate at the palace. She liked it. It reminded her of who she was apart from all the comforts. Of the way she'd grown up.

But this was a piece of that memory with the absence of that wary feeling. The fear. The anger. This was different. This felt like they were totally set apart from the world. From reality.

It was nice, because she'd had far too much reality in her life.

Something about this felt much more like a fantasy. Strange, because never in all her life away from the palace had she imagined spending time with Ferran being part of a fantasy. In her life at the palace, perhaps. She'd been fascinated by him then. The handsome prince who was always in trouble. Always up to mischief.

He lifted his head, and the disappearing sunlight cast a glow on his face. She remembered then. An image pulled from deep in her mind. Standing in the palace in Khadra, watching him stride into the room. The way he'd smiled. He'd reached out his hand on her head and ruffled her hair.

And she'd been certain he was the most beautiful person she'd ever seen.

She didn't know why she was only remembering this now.

Or maybe she did. Maybe because her anger, her determination for revenge, wouldn't let her have a memory of him that was so…precious.

It was precious because it was a part of where she'd started, and she had so few memories of that time in her life. The time where things had been right. Before it had all gone to hell.

"I remember you," she said, allowing real memories to mingle with her words. Allowing herself, for the first time, to really remember the people they had been. Before their parents had destroyed everything.

"You should. I've been sitting here with you the whole time."

"From before," she said. "I remember you." It made her feel so strange. To connect him, suddenly, much more strongly with that boy than with the monster she'd made in her mind.

"And what do you remember?"

"I thought…I thought you were beautiful." They were true words, forgotten thoughts that rose up in her mind and poured from her lips, filled her chest with a strange warmth.

"Did you?" he asked. "That is…not the description one might hope for."

"I was a little girl. I thought you were fascinating." She looked down into her bowl. "And you were very nice to me." Little wonder she hadn't let herself remember that. Because it did not fit with the stories she'd told herself about Ferran the monster. But here and now, those legends were being overridden with something more powerful. With memory.

"It was impossible not to be. You would not be ignored, and being unkind would have been like kicking a puppy."

In this moment, she decided she would pretend there was nothing away from this fire. She would allow them to have nothing but these good, shared memories. A truce.

"Well, I appreciate it, anyway. I had a…nice memory just now. I'm short on those. I don't remember very much about my life before my father died. And I think a lot of that isn't so much because I was too young—I was six. I feel I should remember some things—but because I forced myself to stop trying to remember. Because it hurt so bad. Because it…made me hate where I was even more. Those memories didn't serve a purpose, so I didn't let myself have them." She looked up. "I'd like to have them again. I'd like to have…something normal."

"I'm afraid I'm not the man for that," he said.

Of course he wasn't. How could he be? Given the way things were all tangled up, he couldn't be. And still, she pressed. "Why?"

"I'm not sure I know what normal is. Though, I'm not sure either version of our lives, on this side of the tragedy or the other, were normal."

"Maybe not. But one was happy. In one, I did smile."

"And you're looking for your smile."

"I am. Currently seeking any emotion other than anger

or fear, actually. That's basically been my life for the past sixteen years."

His expression changed, hardened. "I cannot imagine all that you've been through."

"It's okay. I mean, it's not okay. But it's what is. And there is nothing that can be done about it now."

"I wish there was more I could do."

She laughed suddenly. So suddenly not even she expected it. "It's so strange. I never thought I would sit across from a campfire with you while you offered to try and fix things for me. Not so long ago, I would have cried death before dishonor but…I feel like I was wrong about you."

"Samarah…"

"I don't see how either of us could have won in the situations we were put in, Ferran. You were a new ruler and you had to act as a king. And that day my father did not act as a king. He was simply a jealous man. Ruled by emotion." She took a breath and tried to loosen the tightness in her chest. "He was tried fairly, and found guilty of a crime he absolutely committed. What happened to my mother and I was less just, but it wasn't by your hand."

It nearly pained her to say it. But there was no honor in misdirected rage. She knew that better than most. And yet she had spent sixteen years clinging to it.

It didn't make her friends with Ferran, but…but it made her feel as though a truce that extended beyond the moment might be possible.

"Samarah," he said again, "there are things… I am not a hero."

"Neither am I. I'm a victim. And I think you are, too. But isn't it time to stop?"

"You're not a victim now," he said, the words coming slowly. "You will never be again. You're a sheikha. And you have power in this country. You have power now."

"I think I've proven that I've always had power. Though,

it's nice to have that power backed up by…the law. And the army."

"Don't get too power mad."

"I can make no guarantees." She looked out across the water, dark blue now with the sun gone behind the horizon line. "Do you know, these past weeks with you…before them, I can't remember the last time I sat and just had a conversation with someone. I can't remember when I had the time for something so casual. Master Ahn was very good to me. The closest thing I ever had to a friend, but we didn't have many conversations. He instilled in me the will to survive, the sense to think with my head and to act with honor in all things. To know what was right, so deeply that it would be an instinct to act upon what's right when the time comes…." She paused. "Maybe…maybe that's why I hesitated in your room that night. Because something in me knew it was wrong. Because something in me knew I couldn't possibly be serving justice if I hurt you."

"A bold statement, Samarah."

"I realized something today. I was allowing rage to dictate my action. And in that, I was no better than my father. For all that I wished to avenge his death, I have never condoned his actions. My anger was for me. For my mother and our country. But revenge was never going to make that right. Rage would never do anything but lead to more devastation. I'm ready to let go. Even if that makes me weak." She looked down at her food, then back up at him. "Does it make me weak?"

"You have never been weak," he said. "Never."

"You say that with such confidence. But I've always been scared."

"Is that a weakness?"

"Not when it keeps you alive, I suppose."

He set his food down, then stood. "I'm going to bed,"

he said. "Tomorrow we'll stay for breakfast and then head back to the bedouin camp."

For some reason, the thought of leaving made her feel sad. "Okay."

"See you tomorrow, Samarah."

Another chance to simply sit. To be with another person. To live. She found she was looking forward to it.

CHAPTER NINE

SAMARAH WOKE UP to the sound of rain on the canvas rooftop. She slipped out of bed and looked outside. It was gray out, the sun trying to pierce through the heavy blanket of clouds that had rolled in overnight.

She ran her fingers through her hair and leaned forward, the silken strands sliding over her shoulders.

She looked out the window, at the rain pelting down, hitting the parched earth, large droplets creating ripples on the surface of the lake. And she had the sudden urge to go out in it.

She'd hated the rainy season when she'd lived in Jahar. Hated having to hide in rooms that were muddy and flooded. Hated looking for shelter during the day wherever she could find it, or more often, just spending most of the afternoon feeling like a drowned rat.

But it was different now. She wasn't forced to stand out in the rain. She had a choice. She could stay in here where it was dry, or she could dance in the water drops. It was up to her. Because she had a home now. She had shelter.

Everything had changed. There was more than survival. There was...enjoyment. Happiness. Something about yesterday's realization, yesterday's acceptance, had allowed her to capture these things. Or at the very least the possibility of them.

She stood and walked to the window, pressing her palm

against the glass. Then she turned and walked out into the living area. It was still hazy, and the house was dark. She hadn't checked the time but it had to be early.

She padded to the front door and pressed down on the handle before going out onto the deck. She was wearing only a nightgown, a soft, silken one with very little in the way of adornment. It had been provided for her at the palace and she'd packed it for the trip. It wasn't designed to be flashy, just to be comfortable.

Normally, she wouldn't go walking outside in it. And she wouldn't go walking out with her hair down, simply because there was too much of it, and letting it free was much more trouble than it was worth.

But right now she didn't care.

She stepped down onto the wet sand; it stuck to her feet while the raindrops poured down over her body, making her nightgown stick to her skin. She looked up and let the rain drop onto her face, sliding down her cheeks and her neck.

How different it was to stand in the rain when it was your choice. When you knew you could go back inside and get dry.

She spun in a circle, her arms held out wide. She felt like the child she had been. As if she was free. As if rain was just rain, and she didn't have to worry about the cold, or the discomfort, the mold or the damp. All of the cares she normally carried were washed away.

She walked along the path they'd taken last night, to the ashes of the fire from the night before, and to the edge of the water. She looked out across the surface, continually being shattered by heavy drops of rain and tilted her face upward again.

"You'll catch your death."

She turned and saw Ferran, and immediately the child-like joy, the simplicity of it, faded. And she realized she was standing there with nothing but a thin nightshirt clinging to her body, and her hair wet and stringy down her back.

"You're out here, too," she said.

And in nothing but a pair of jeans. He was wearing jeans. And no shirt. But he hadn't worn jeans to bed so that must have meant he'd been…well, he'd likely slipped the jeans on before coming outside.

"Yes, but you're…you're beautiful," he said.

"I'm wet."

"Yes." He took a step toward her and she looked behind herself, her heel at the edge of the water. There was no backing away from him. And she didn't feel very inclined toward punching him in the face, either. Which was new. He extended his hand and took a strand of her hair between his thumb and forefinger, twisting it lightly. "I wondered what your hair looked like down."

"It is also wet. Therefore not the most flattering representation."

"I disagree," he said, leaning in closer. "Do you know how much of your body I can see through that nightshirt?"

She looked down at the fabric, which had shaped itself to her figure. She could clearly see her nipples, hardened from the cold. The nightgown provided no coverage there.

"I have an idea," she said, looking back up.

"And do you know what it does to me?"

She started to speak, then closed her mouth. Then she blinked and shook her head. "No."

"I have not touched a woman in sixteen years. I… Right now I feel like the ground here. Like I've been too long without water, and it's finally here in front of me."

"Oh…Ferran…I don't…I…" She didn't know what to do. She wasn't sure what he wanted. She wasn't sure she could give it.

He hadn't touched a woman in sixteen years, and now he was here, his hands on her hair. Touching her. So much pressure on her, when she had no idea what might happen next.

"I'm going to ask you again, Samarah." His dark eyes were level with hers. "Have you ever been kissed?"

She felt as if the breath had been pulled from her lungs. "Not exactly," she said.

"And by that you mean?"

Samarah hesitated, her heart fluttering in her chest. She knew this admission would change things. That in a few moments, the answer to the question *have you ever been kissed*, would not be the same. Even with no experience, she knew it. In her bones. In her blood. And she wanted it. "Not by anyone other than my family. Never by a man. Never in the way you mean."

He put his hands on her cheeks and brushed the water drops away. Was she really going to let him kiss her?

He's going to be your husband.

He was your enemy.

He'll be your lover.

Her brain was fighting with itself. And she had no idea which voice to listen to. But she felt her lips parting, her eyes slipping closed as she tilted her face upward.

To know what was right, so deeply, that it would be an instinct to act upon what's right when the time comes...

"I have waited for this," he said, his voice a growl, "for longer than you can imagine."

And then his lips met with hers. They were hot beneath the sheen of rain that covered them. Slick from the water. And firm. But more so than she'd imagined they might be. He held her face steady, then tilted his head, opening his mouth and touching the center of her upper lip with the tip of his tongue.

A simple, delicate touch that sent a flash of heat, like lightning, through her body.

He pulled back slightly, his hands still on her face, holding her. "Kiss me back, Samarah."

"I don't know…how. I don't know…" Desperation grew wings and fluttered in her chest, fear and need gripping her tight.

"What do you want to do?"

"I…" She looked at his chest, at his stomach, and she put her hands on him, one palm resting against the hard ridge of his abs, the other just above his heart. She wanted to touch him. To feel those muscles with no clothing between them. She'd known that for a while now, even though she hadn't quite understood it.

Or, more to the point, she hadn't wanted to understand it.

Now she did. Now she wanted to understand it all. All this depth and nuance of being human, of being alive. This rich tapestry that existed beyond mere survival.

There was so much more than just drawing breath. There was the feel of Ferran's skin beneath hers. The rough hair, the heat of his body, the hard definition of his muscles. And there was the need it created in her. Reckless and heady. A high like nothing else she'd ever experienced. The adrenaline rush that accompanied fear coupled with a much more pleasant emotion.

So this was lust. Real, raw lust, so much more potent than she'd ever imagined it could be. Even though she'd known it must be something so very strong, there was a difference from knowing that and having lived it. She was living it now.

She leaned in and kissed him, freezing when her mouth touched his, a raindrop rolling between their lips and sliding onto her tongue. She laughed, then pulled back. "Sorry, I don't think you're supposed to laugh when you kiss."

He moved his hands from her face and wrapped them around her waist, pulling her against his body. "Why not?" he asked. "I like that you're finally smiling."

He closed the distance between them, his kiss harder this time. His lips moved over hers, his tongue sliding against the seam of her mouth before she opened and gave him entry. Then he took her deep, long. The sensual friction sending a deep, sharp pang of longing through her. An arrow of pleasure that shot straight to her core and left a hollow pain in its wake.

She fought to free her hands from where they were trapped between their bodies and wrapped her arms around his neck, holding him to her. She tried to match his movements, to make her lips fit against his. He adjusted some of what he was doing, and she adjusted, too. And then they found a way to make their lips fit together just right.

He moved his hands down over her back, her butt, and down to her thighs. Then he gripped her tight, tugging her up into his arms, the blunt tips of his fingers digging into her flesh, the points of pressure adding pain into the mix with the pleasure.

She clung to him, wrapped her legs around his waist so that she didn't fall back down to the ground, and the motion brought the heart of her into contact with his hard stomach. A short, shocked moan climbed her throat and escaped.

He growled and angled his head, biting the side of her neck, harder even than he'd done back in the gym.

She whimpered, and he slid his tongue over the spot, soothing the sting, ramping up her arousal. She kissed him back, feeling confident now. Maybe because he seemed as if he was on the edge of control, too. She certainly was. Because this wasn't necessary, or useful. And yet it felt essential. And she wanted it. More than she could ever remember wanting anything.

He cupped her bottom and pulled her hard against him. At the same time he bit her lip, then soothed it away. Pleasure rocketed through her. She curled her fingers tightly into his shoulders, understanding perfectly now why some people actually enjoyed biting.

There was so much more to this than she'd ever thought possible. To wanting a man. To sexual desire. It wasn't just nice feelings, or pleasure, or whatever it was she'd imagined it might be.

It was need, so deep and intense it made you burn. It was pain. Pain because there was too much pleasure, pain because you wanted more.

Kissing Ferran was both the best and the worst kind of torture.

It was everything. It filled up the moment. It filled her up. And yet, it wasn't enough. It hinted at things she didn't know about, made her desire things she didn't understand. Made her body crave something she wasn't certain existed. Tipped her beliefs on right and wrong onto their heads and twisted her into a stranger she didn't know, and wasn't certain she liked.

But she didn't care.

She rocked her hips against him and a low, feral growl rumbled in his chest. He moved quickly, decisively, lowering them both down to the ground. To the sand. And she didn't care that she was going to get dirty. That she would get wetter. It didn't matter as long as he kept kissing her.

He adjusted their positions, forking his hands through her hair, tilting her head back, tugging slightly. He slid one hand down her back, cupping her rear and lifting her up against him. And she wasn't pressed against his stomach anymore, but the hard line of his shaft. She'd seen him naked yesterday, but it hadn't prepared her for this. He hadn't been aroused yesterday in the lake.

Instinct, and need, had her flexing her hips against him, each movement making the ache inside her build, grow, until she thought she was going to die.

She was sure no one could withstand this kind of sensual assault. The rough sand beneath her; Ferran, hot and hard above her; the rain, cold against her skin.

He moved his hand to cup her breast, drawing his thumb slowly across her nipple, before pinching her lightly. She was still covered by the damp fabric of her gown. He lowered his head and sucked her deep into his mouth.

He pushed against her, the hard ridge of his arousal hitting her just where she needed it.

And the dam burst inside of her. A hoarse cry escaped her lips, much like the sound she made when she fought. Raw, passionate, bold.

Pleasure poured through every part of her. She arched against him, holding tight to his shoulders as the waves crashed over her, her eyes squeezed shut, her fingernails digging into his shoulders.

She just lay there for a moment, feeling spent, the fog slowly clearing. And then she started to feel other things. Shame. Embarrassment.

He moved against her again, kissing her neck, his hands firm on her breasts.

She shoved at his chest.

"What?" he asked. "Samarah, did I hurt you?"

"No…I…no…"

She couldn't tell him. She couldn't tell him that she'd had what she suspected was an orgasm from kissing him. That was…it was terrifying and way past the point of embarrassing straight into humiliating. Because how could that be? How? With him…with anyone, but especially with him.

This was not lying back and thinking of Jahar. This was not a truce. It was somewhere far over that line, and it was one she couldn't believe she had crossed.

He moved away from her and she scrabbled to her feet, her nightgown sticking to her legs, tugging upward, the sand caked over her skin, in her hair. "I just…I have to go back inside now."

"You do?" he asked, still on the ground, breathing hard. He looked nearly as shocked as he had the night she'd tried to kill him.

"Yes. I do. I…thank you. For the kiss. I have to go. I'm cold."

She turned away from him, her arms wrapped around her waist, and she ran back toward the house, then into the bathroom. She locked the door behind her and turned the water on, stepping inside fully clothed and watching the sand wash down the drain.

Then she started to shiver.

She'd never felt anything like this before. And it was much too big for her to deal with. Too big for her to process.

There was a whole new depth to life, and she'd just discovered it. And now she was terrified by what might come next. By what it meant about who she was.

Because once upon a time, Ferran might have been able to have lovers without feeling connection. But in that moment she knew for certain that *she* couldn't.

She thought of her mother, the author of her own destruction, and everyone else's, so desperately in love with two men that she couldn't give either of them up.

As much as she didn't want to be her father, she didn't want to be her mother. And God help her, she would not be a fool over Ferran Bashar.. And until she figured out how to get a handle on her emotions, she couldn't allow Ferran to touch her again. It was as simple as that.

Ferran called himself every kind of bastard as he kicked over the cooking grate that was still set up over the dead coals from last night's fire.

He was an animal. Of the worst kind. He'd known she was a virgin, hell, he knew she'd never been kissed. She'd been badly handled all of her life. Thrown out onto the streets when she was a child so that she could escape a grisly death.

He was responsible for every bad thing that had happened in her life. And now he'd added another thing to the incredibly long list.

He'd allowed himself to be ruled by passion. Had let the floodgates open after keeping them firmly closed for so many years.

No.

He was not that man. Not anymore. He would not allow it. Not again.

He had been rough with her. He'd been ready to take her, take her virginity, in the sand, in the rain. Without talking to her. Without making sure she was ready.

You're using your need for control to hold her captive.

He shrugged the thought off, turning his self-disgust to the more specific events at hand.

He'd led with his own desire, and had given no thought to anything else. He'd thought he was better than that now. He had to be. The alternative was unthinkable.

He stalked into the water, in spite of the fact that he was already wet, and submerged himself. It was much colder today, with the sun behind the clouds and the rain pouring down.

It didn't do anything to assuage his arousal. He was still so hard it hurt, need coursing through him like a current. He ground his teeth together and walked back out of the water, his jeans heavy and tugging downward, chafing against his erection.

That had been a stupid, damn idea. And it hadn't even worked.

He walked back toward the house and shrugged his jeans off at the door. Hopefully Samarah wasn't around because he didn't really want to ambush her with his body like this.

He could hear the shower running and he said a prayer of thanks for small mercies.

He went into his bedroom and started digging for dry clothes. They needed to get back to the palace. Back to civilization and back to sanity.

There, he would be reminded to keep his distance. He would be reminded of all the indignity she'd already suffered without him adding to it.

His weakness had caused her suffering.

He paused at that thought. She deserved to know. Because if there was one thing Samarah truly cared about it was honor. It was doing right.

Though, there was a limit to what he could say without adding to her pain. Without uncovering himself completely.

One thing was certain. Before he tied her to him for the rest of her life, before he jailed her in a whole different way than she'd originally threatened, she had to know at least in part, what sort of man it was she was tying herself to.

CHAPTER TEN

THEY ARRIVED AT the palace late that evening. The ride back had been torturous. Samarah had spent so much of her life without human interaction, she'd never fully understood just how awkward it could be to sit in an enclosed space with another person when you had nothing to say.

And when you had something obvious and tense hanging between you.

That morning seemed like a lifetime ago, and yet it had only been about fifteen hours since Ferran had held her in his arms. Since he'd pulled her against him and kissed her. Since he'd brought her to the peak of pleasure on the ground outside in the rain.

She could hardly believe that had been her. And that it had been him.

In the cold of the night, she could not understand what had possessed her to go outside in a rainstorm. What had possessed her to fall into his arms and kiss him as if he was the only source of water in the desert.

She moved through her chambers and stopped cold when she saw Ferran in the doorway. "What are you doing here?" she asked.

"I came to speak to you about tomorrow. We're to have lunch with the palace event planner. To speak to her about the upcoming engagement party and the wedding."

"Oh," she said. "I had forgotten about the party."

"As had I. Since I'm not particularly interested in parties, it was easy to let it slip my mind."

"I can't say I'm a real party animal, either," she said, her tone dry.

"I imagine not. I have brought you something."

"Oh?" She really had to try and find something more intelligent to say than that.

"I feel we got off track today."

"Oh." Well, dammit. That was not more intelligent.

"I should not have touched you like that. Not knowing how innocent you are. And I regret that I frightened you."

It was on the tip of her tongue to say he hadn't frightened her at all. She'd frightened herself. But honestly, his assumption was so much less revealing that she felt like letting him have it.

Coward.

Yes. But so what? He was about to apologize and since he owed her many, in reality, she would take one for this. Even though he didn't owe her one for that incident in particular. She bore the full weight of the consequences for the foolishness of her body.

"I lost sight of what it is we are doing. This marriage is to benefit our nations. And to heal the past. What I did accomplished neither of those things."

"Well…no I suppose not."

"This is to remind you, to remind me, of what this is about." He reached into his pocket and pulled out a small black box. "I spoke to the palace jeweler, and he managed to come up with something very quickly. It is not my mother's ring. All things considered I felt no monuments needed to be built to that marriage." He opened the lid of the box and revealed an ornate, sparkling piece of art. Gold with diamonds set into an intricately carved band. "But this is from the crown jewels, as it were. And it has been in my family for many generations. It's lasted longer than a marriage. Than the rule of any one sheikh or shcikha. And I hope what we build forges a bond between our countries that is the same. I hope that what we build transcends a simple marriage, and becomes something lasting that benefits both of our people."

"Oh that's…that's perfect," she said, banishing images of them kissing, of the heat she'd felt in his arms, and bringing to the front pictures of their country. Of their people. Of all that could be built between the nations if they followed through with this union.

"I am prepared to ask you to wear it."

"Of course," she said.

She waited for him to do something. To get on one knee or put the ring on her finger. She wasn't sure if she wanted him to do that.

He did neither. He simply stood there with the box held out in front of him until she reached inside and took the ring, putting it on her own finger.

"You may not want to do that just yet, princess," he said.

"Why not?"

"I am prepared to ask you to wear it. But only after this. I want to talk to you about what happened at the oasis."

"Oh," she said, looking down, heat bleeding into her face. "You know what? I'd rather not."

He took her chin between his thumb and forefinger and tilted her face up so that she met his gaze. "Did I hurt you?"

"What? No." She shook her head and took a step back. "No, you didn't hurt me."

"Did I frighten you?"

"I…I…no." It wasn't him that scared her. It was herself. The way he'd made her feel. The fact that he'd commanded a response from her, with such ease that she hadn't even realized she was capable of feeling.

"Then why did you run?"

"I didn't…run. I was cold and I went back in the house."

"You were right to be afraid," he said.

"I wasn't afraid."

"Then you should have been."

"I'm sorry—I should be afraid of you? I beat you in hand-to-hand combat, lest we forget."

"I believe I beat you," he said. "Both times."

She scowled. "You cheated. You bit me."

"It was not cheating. But that's beside the point. I have something to tell you about that day. And you won't like it. But I have to tell you before you concede to marrying me. Because it will change things. I owe you this explanation. Though I'm certain I will regret giving it."

"Then why give it?" she asked. She suddenly felt afraid. Because she was starting to feel at ease with this man. With this situation. With the fact that she was to be his wife.

More than finding ease…she was starting to want things. From him. From life. And she was afraid that whatever he said next might take it all away.

"Because you have to know. Because if you aren't afraid, then you need to understand that you should be. You need to understand why I can never be allowed to lose control. Why I have spent sixteen years doing nothing more than ruling my country. Why I despise passion so very much."

"The same reason we both have to distrust it," she said. "Because it led our parents to a horrible end. The only innocent party involved was your mother, and yet, she suffered just as badly for having been there as any of them."

"It is true," he said. "She was the only innocent party. She was true to her marriage vows. She didn't attack anyone. She was simply there when your father and his band of men decided to make my father pay for what he'd done."

"It was wrong, Ferran. All of it. And I'm willing to put it behind us." And she meant it. This time, she meant it for real. "Because…it has to be. It can't keep being my present and my future. I can't allow it. Not anymore. I want something different. For the first time I just want to move on from it and please…please don't take that from me."

"It is not my intent to take anything from you. But to inform you of the manner of man you're to marry."

"Does it matter what manner of man?" she asked. "If I have to marry you either way, does it matter?"

"You spoke to me of honor when we first met, Samarah. You were willing to die for it, so yes, I think it matters. I feel I have to tell you. For my honor at least. What little there is."

"And I have no choice?"

"This is giving you a choice. So that you know who you let into your body at night once you're my wife. I owe you that. Or I at least owe it to my sense of honor."

Her face heated. "That was unnecessary."

"It hardly was. I nearly took you this morning at the oasis. I nearly took your virginity on the ground. Do you understand that? Do you understand that I am capable of letting things go much too far when…when I am not in control."

"You didn't."

"You stand there and blush when I talk about being inside of you. It would have been a crime for me to do that there. In that manner."

It wouldn't have been. And part of her wanted to tell him that. That she was blushing because she was inexperienced. Because she was embarrassed by her response to him. Confused by the fact that she felt desire when she'd expected to endure his touch. Not because she found the idea of being with him in that way appalling.

"I don't…I don't think I would have stopped you. And if you say I couldn't have, I'm going to do my best to remind you that I, in fact, could have. Don't ever forget what I can do, Ferran. Who I am. I am not delicate. I am not a wilting flower that you've brought out to the desert. I survived that day. I survived every day after. You don't need to protect me, and I refuse to fear you."

"I killed your father," he said, his dark eyes boring into hers.

"I know," she said.

"No, Samarah, you don't. I did not have your father arrested. I did not send him to trial. I was hiding. In a closet. I heard everything happening out in the corridor and I hid. That is when your father burst into the family quarters. And he attacked my father with a knife. I stayed hidden. I did nothing. I was afraid. I watched through the partly open door as he ended my father's life. My mother was in the corner. A woman, unarmed, uninvolved in any of it. And then he went for her and…I didn't hide anymore. She begged, Samarah. For her life. She begged him to spare her. For me. For my sake and the sake of our people. For the sake of his soul. But he didn't. I opened the closet door and I took a vase off of one of the sideboards and I hit him in the back of the head with it. I was too late to save my mother. She was already gone. And I…disarmed him."

"Like you did me," she said, feeling dizzy. Feeling sick.

"Yes. Exactly like I did you. But unlike you…he ran. And I went after him."

She tried not to picture it, but it was far too easy. Because she'd been there that day. Because she'd heard the screams. Because she knew just how violent and horrible a day it had been. It was so easy to add visual to the sounds that already echoed in her head.

"Ferran…"

"I was faster than he was. Because of age or adrenaline, I'm not sure. But I want you to know that I didn't even give him the chance to beg for his life. Because he never knew I had caught him. I ended him the moment I overtook him. I stabbed him in the back."

Samarah took a step back from him, her eyes filling

with tears before she could even process what he was saying. She shook her head. “No…Ferran don’t…don’t…” She didn’t know what she wanted to say. Don’t say it. Don’t let it be true. *Don’t tell me.*

“It is the truth, Samarah. You should know what kind of man you’re going to marry. You should know that I am capable of acting with no honor. There was no trial. He was not given a chance. I acted out of emotion. Out of rage. And it is one thing I refuse to regret. You need to know that before you agree to bind yourself to me. I killed your father and I will not regret it.”

She growled and ran forward, shoving his chest with both hands. “Why must you do this now?” she asked, her voice breaking. “Why did you make me care and then try and rip it away?”

“I’m being honest,” he said, gripping her arms and holding her so that she couldn’t hit him again. “You have to know. Am I the man you want in your bed? Then you must know the man I am.”

She fought against him, not to break free, but just because it felt good to fight against something. Because it was easier than standing there passively while all these emotions coursed through her. Grief, rage, anguish, panic. All of it was boiling in her, threatening to overflow. And she didn’t know how to handle it. She didn’t know how to feel all of this.

This wasn’t simply breathe in, breathe out. This wasn’t a calculated plan for revenge and satisfaction of honor. This wasn’t even the low hum of sixteen years of anger. This was all new, and shocking and fresh.

And horrible.

Because she hurt. For what she’d lost. For her father. For the man he truly was. A man who killed an innocent woman because he was scorned. A man who was not the one she’d loved so much as a child.

And she hurt for Ferran. As horrible as it was to imagine him being involved as he had been, she hurt for him. The boy whose mother had died before his eyes. The boy who had avenged her.

As she would have done.

Oh, as she would have done to him if he'd allowed it. And then what? Would she be the one standing there with nothing but a scorched soul? With haunted eyes and the feeling that she had no honor left because in her rage she'd allowed herself to justify taking the life of someone else?

"You see now," he said, "who I am. And why I cannot permit myself to be led by my emotions? I am no better than they are, Samarah. I am no better. I am not stronger."

And neither was she. Not really. Because she'd been prepared to act as he had, but not in the heat of rage. Not in the midst of the fight. With years to gain perspective, she'd been ready to behave as her father had done.

As she looked at Ferran, at the blank, emotionless void behind his eyes, she felt she could see the scars that he'd been left with that day. It had been so easy for her to imagine him as the one who'd come out of it whole. He'd had his country. He'd had his palace. Hadn't that meant in some way, that he had won? That she had lost and therefore was owed something?

But when she looked at him now, she didn't just understand, she felt, deep down in her soul, that he'd lost, too. That there had been nothing gained for him that day. Yes, he'd ascended the throne, a boy forced to become a man. Yes, he had a palace, and he had power. But he had lost all of himself.

That was why he looked so different than the boy she'd known. It wasn't simply age.

She struggled against him, and he held her tight, his eyes burning into hers. "How dare you make me understand you?" she asked, the words coming out a choked sob.

"How dare you make me feel sorry for you?" Tears rolled down her cheeks, anger and pain warring for equal place in her chest. And with it, desire. Darker now, more desperate than what she'd felt at the oasis.

And she knew it now. There was no question. It was what she'd felt that first moment, in his bedchamber when their eyes had met. What she'd felt watching him shirtless in the gym, fighting him, getting bitten by him.

It was what she'd felt every time she'd looked at him since returning to the palace. It had just been so expertly mixed with a cocktail of anger and shame that it had been impossible to identify.

But now that she'd tasted him, she knew. Now that she'd gone to heaven and back in his arms, she knew.

Now that she understood how you could long for a man's teeth to dig into your flesh, she knew.

"How dare you?" she asked again, the words broken. "How dare you make me want you? I should hate you. I should kill you."

She leaned in and claimed his lips with hers, even as he tried to hold her back. He released one arm and reached around to cup the back of her head, digging his fingers deep into her hair, squeezing tight and tugging back, wrenching her mouth from his.

"Why are you doing this, Samarah?" he growled.

"Because I don't know what else to do," she said. "What else am I supposed to do?"

"You're supposed to run from me, little girl," he said, his expression fierce. He was not disconnected now—that was certain. He wasn't hollow. Her kiss had changed that. It had called up something else in him.

Passion.

Passion that he thought she should fear, and yet she didn't. She found she didn't fear him at all.

"I don't run," she said, her eyes steady on his. "I stand

and meet every challenge I face. I thought you knew that about me."

"You should run from this challenge," he said. "You should protect yourself from me."

She pushed against him, and he pushed in return, propelling her backward until she butted up against the wall. "You don't scare me, Ferran Bashar," she said.

"As far as your family is concerned," he said, "I am death himself. If you had any sense at all, you would run from this room. From this palace. And you would not wear my ring."

Her heart was raging, each beat tearing off a piece and leaving searing pain in its place. And she couldn't turn from him. It would be easy to get out of his hold if she really wanted to. A well-placed blow would have him at her feet. But she didn't want to break free of him. Even now.

"You need me to run, coward?" she asked. "Because you fear me so? Because I am such a temptation?"

That was the moment she crossed the line.

His lips crashed down on hers, his hold on her wrists and hair tightening. It wasn't a nice kiss. It was a kiss that was meant to frighten her. A show of his dangerous passion, and yet, she found it didn't frighten her at all.

She kissed him back. Fueled by all of the emotions that were rioting through her, fueled by the desire that had been building in her from the first moment she'd seen him again. From the moment she'd walked into the palace, with vengeance on her mind.

She had wanted him then, but she'd been too innocent to know it. And desire had been too deeply tangled in other things. But she knew now. The veil had been ripped from her eyes. And all the protection that surrounded her heart seemed to have crumbled.

Because she couldn't hate him now. Not even with the newest revelation. All she could see was what they'd both lost. All she could do was feel the pain of losing her father over again. The man who'd been a god in her mind transforming into a monster who would kill an unarmed woman. And all she could do was let it all come out in a storm of emotion that seemed to manifest itself in this.

At least a kiss was action. At least a kiss wouldn't end with one of them dead.

Though now, with all of the need, all of the deep, painful desire that had possessed her like a living thing, like a beast set on devouring her insides if she didn't feed it with what it wanted, she wondered if either of them would survive.

He pulled his mouth from hers, his hands bracing her wrists against the wall behind her head, dark eyes glaring, assessing her. "Why do you not run from me?"

"Because I am owed a debt," she said, her breath coming in short, sharp bursts. "You stole my life from me. You stole this," she said, speaking of the need she felt now. "I had never even kissed a man because I could afford to feel nothing for men but distrust and fear. I had to guard my own safety above all else because I had no one to protect me. I could never want, not things beyond food and drink. So you owe me this, Sheikh. I will collect it. I will have you, because I want you," she said. "It is your debt. And you will pay it with your body."

"So you want my passion, Samarah? After all I have told you?"

"Is it not my right to have it? If it has been used so badly against me? Should I not be able to take it now, when I want it, and use it as it would satisfy me?" Anger, desire, anguish curled around her heart like grasping vines. Tangled together into a knot that choked out everything except a dark, intense need.

"You want satisfaction?" he asked, his voice a low growl, his hips rolling against hers, his erection thick and hard against her stomach.

"I demand it," she said.

He leaned in, his breath hot on her neck, his lips brushing against her ear. "Do you know what you ask for, little viper?"

"You," she said. "Inside my body. As discussed. You seem to think I don't know what I want, but I will not have you disrespect me so."

"No, Samarah, I am of the opinion that you likely always know what you want, at the moment you want it." That was not entirely true, because she hadn't realized how badly she wanted him until today, when she knew it had gone on much longer than that. "But what I am also sure of, is that sometimes you don't always want what is good for you."

"Who does?" she asked.

"No one, I suppose."

"We all want things that will harm us in the end. Cake, for example. Revenge for another."

"Sex," he said.

"Yes," she said. "Sex."

"That's what you want? You want sixteen years of my unspent desire unleashed on you?"

"That's what I demand," she said.

He tugged her away from the wall and scooped her into his arms in one fluid movement, carrying her across the room. She put her hand on his chest, his heart pounding so hard she could feel it pressing into her palm.

"Then you shall have what you demand," he said, depositing her onto the mattress before tugging his shirt over his head and revealing his body to her. So perfect. So beautiful. Not a refined, graceful beauty. His was raw, masculine and terrifying. So incredible she ached when she looked at him. "But know this, my darling, your command stops here. For now you are mine." He let his finger trail over her cheek, his dark eyes boring into hers. "If you want this, I will give it you. But the terms will be mine."

"This is my repayment," she said. "I agreed to nothing else."

"And that is where you miscalculated, my little warrior. For in this, I am nothing short of a conquerer."

"And I no less a warrior."

"I would expect nothing else. But in the end, I will stake my claim. Run from me now, if you do not want that."

She could hardly breathe. Could hardly think. But she didn't want to think. She wanted to focus on what he made her body feel. Because this, this release that she was chasing with him, overpowered the feelings in her chest.

This desire won out above all else, and she so desperately needed for it to continue to do so. And she did not want to run.

His hands went to the waistband of his pants and he pushed them down his legs. She did gasp, virginal shock coursing through her, when she saw him naked and erect.

This was different than when she'd seen him in the lake, but she hadn't been prepared for just how different. Just how much larger he would be.

Neither had she been prepared for her body's response. She might not know exactly what she wanted, but her body did. Her internal muscles pulsed, the ache between her legs intensifying.

"Let me see you," he said. "I am at a disadvantage, for you have seen me twice, and I have only ever been teased by promises of your body."

She just sat there, staring at him, feeling too dazed to follow instruction.

He approached the bed, his hands going to the front of her dress, where it was fastened together with hooks and eyes. "Consider this *my* payment," he said. "For all that was stolen from me. For I have not touched a woman since that day. And it is fitting that you are the one who has returned desire to me."

"A fair exchange then," she said. "And in the end, perhaps neither will owe the other anything?"

"Perhaps," he said, his tone raw.

He pushed the little metal clasps apart at the front of her dress and started to part the silken fabric, slowly and deliberately. Her breasts were bare beneath the heavy material. She wasn't generously endowed there, so unless she was engaging in physical combat, there was little need for her to wear undergarments.

She wished for one now. For one additional buffer between her skin, the cool air of the room, and Ferran's hot gaze.

He pushed the dress from her shoulders, leaving her in the light pants she'd been wearing beneath them, and nothing more. He looked at her breasts, his admiration open. "You are truly beautiful. Let your hair down for me."

She pulled her braid from behind her and took the band from around the bottom, sifting her fingers through the black silk and letting it loose to fall around her shoulders, all the way down to her waist. She let the loose strands cover her breasts.

"That's a tease," he said. "Giving me only one thing that I want at a time. I want it all. I have waited long enough. Stand."

She obeyed the command, because she was more than willing to follow orders now. She was not the expert here. She had nothing but a deep, primal instinct pushing her forward, and if she stopped to think too hard, nerves were waiting in the background to take hold. They had no place here. They were not allowed to overshadow her desire.

He remained sitting at her feet on the mattress, and he reached up and tugged her pants down, along with her underwear, leaving her completely bare before him, with him on his knees, right at eye level with the most secret part of her.

"Ferran…"

He leaned forward and pressed a kiss to her thigh, then to her hip bone, his lips perilously close to…to…her. To places on her she didn't know men might want to kiss.

"You want my passion used for your pleasure, Samarah? You demand it? Then you must submit to it."

"I…I will," she said.

"Do not fight me."

"I won't."

He tightened his hold on her. "Do not fight what we both want. I feel that you're about to flee from me."

"I'm not," she said, her throat tightening, her heart fluttering.

"Liar," he said, his lips skimming the sensitive skin on her inner thigh. "Spread your legs for me," he said.

She obeyed. Because he would know the best way to do this. That she did trust. And he was right, if she wanted his passion, demanded it, then she had to accept it. Not try to control it.

He leaned in again, his tongue sliding through her inner folds, across the sensitive bud there before delving in deep.

"Ferran." She grabbed hold of his shoulders to keep herself from falling, her legs shaking, the mattress wobbling beneath her feet. He anchored her with his hands, holding tightly to her hips as he pressed in deeper, increasing the pressure and speed of his strokes over her wet flesh.

Her stomach tightened, pleasure a deep, unceasing pressure building deep inside of her until she thought she might not be able to catch her breath. Everything in her tightened so much she feared she was turning to glass, so fragile and brittle she would shatter if he pushed against her too hard.

He kept going, adding his hands, pushing a finger deep inside of her, the sensation completely new and entirely different to anything that had come before.

He established a steady rhythm, pushing in and out of

her, the friction so beautiful, so perfect, she very nearly did break. She held back, rooted herself to earth by biting her tongue, by gritting her teeth so hard she feared they'd crack.

Because she was afraid to let herself go over the edge again. Afraid of what her release would bring this time.

"Give it to me, Samarah," he said. "Give me your pleasure."

"I can't…I can't."

"You can," he said, adding a second finger as he continue to lick and suck her. He stretched her, a slight pain hitting as he did, and she used that to help pull her back again.

"I'm afraid," she said.

"Don't be. I will catch you."

He leaned in again, the hot swipe of his tongue hitting just the right timing with his fingers, and then, she couldn't fight it anymore. She let go. Her hands moved away from his shoulders as her orgasm crashed over her. Only Ferran kept her on her feet. Only Ferran kept her there. And she trusted him to do it.

She didn't try to keep herself standing, because she knew he would. Because he'd promised her.

He laid her down on the mattress afterward, rising up to kiss her lips, deep and long. She could taste her own desire there, mingled with his. His shaft was hard and hot against her hip, evidence of the fact that he'd given, again, while taking nothing for himself.

Evidence also, of the fact that he'd enjoyed what he'd done for her. A sweep of heat, of pride, pure feminine power, rolled through her. He had enjoyed doing that to her. Had relished the taste of her. He wanted her, even as he told her to run.

She didn't know why it made her feel the way it did. Didn't know why it made her feel so powerful. Only that it did. Only that it spurred her on. And this time, she didn't want to run after her climax. She wanted to stay. She wanted more. Because she couldn't be embarrassed by what he'd made her feel.

Not when he was feeling it, too.

She shifted their position and parted her thighs, the blunt head of his erection coming up against the slick entrance to her body.

"I tried to prepare you," he said, his voice strangled. 'But it will still hurt."

"I am not afraid of pain, Ferran," she said, sliding her hands down his back, feeling his muscles shift and tense beneath her fingertips. "I am not afraid of you."

"I do not wish to hurt you."

"But in order for us to join, you have to. So don't worry. Please, Ferran, I want you. I want this."

He started to push inside of her, slowly, gently. He stretched her, filled her. It did hurt, but not as much as she'd expected. It was only foreign, and new. But wonderful. Like every other pain he'd caused her physically, it was good.

He started to pull back and she locked her ankles over his, their eyes meeting. "Ferran, don't stop."

"I won't," he said, thrusting back inside of her, deep and hard, filling her completely.

She held on to him, getting adjusted to having him inside of her. She tilted her head and looked at him. His eyes were closed, the veins in his neck standing out, his jaw clenched tight. He looked as if he was in terrible pain. She kissed his cheek and a rough sound rumbled in his chest.

"Don't hold back now," she said.

"I am trying not to hurt you," he said, kissing her hard and deep.

When he separated from her lips, she was breathless. "You aren't."

He seemed to take that as permission. He started to move inside of her, slowly at first. Achingly so. Building all of that lovely, orgasmic tension in her again. Starting from the beginning, and this time, he brought her even higher. Further. Faster.

His rhythm grew fractured, his breath shortening. She shifted her legs, wrapped them higher around his waist and moved with him. He braced one hand on the mattress, by her head, and wrapped the other around her, pulling her against him, his movements hard and fast.

His eyes met hers, and she slowly watched his control break. She could see it, in the dark depths. Could see as he started to lose his grip. Sweat beaded on his forehead, his teeth ground together.

Watching him, seeing him like this, so handsome, so on edge, pushed her closer, too. Then he thrust inside her, hard, his body hitting against the part of her that cried out for release. As it washed over her in waves, she leaned in and bit him on the neck.

A harsh, feral sound escaped his lips, and he stiffened above her, his shaft pulsing deep inside of her. And she relished it. Reveled in his utter loss of control.

He moved away from her as if he'd been shocked, his chest heaving, his muscles shaking. He got off the bed and started collecting his clothes.

"Ferran…"

"That should not have happened."

"But it did," she said, the words sounding thick and stupid. She sat up and pushed her hair out of her face. "It did." A strange surge of panic took hold as Samarah tried to process what had happened. As she tried to deal with the fact that he was regretting what had passed between them.

She had given him, the man who had been her enemy all her life, her body, and now he was telling her what a mistake it had been. Shame lashed at her as she remembered the first night she'd met him.

I would sooner die.

And I would sooner kill you.

Oh, how she had fallen.

You did not fall. You jumped.

"You don't know what you want," he said. "You're an innocent." He tugged his pants on and turned away from her.

Even as she battled with the shame inside of her, his words ignited her anger. "Hardly. I was a virgin, but that does not equate to innocence."

"Well, I am a murderer." He pulled his shirt over his head, concealing his body from her view. "Compared to me, everyone is an innocent. Good night, Samarah. In the morning, if you are still here, and if I am still here, we will speak."

"Are you afraid I'll kill you?"

He lifted a shoulder. "I trust you to act in an honorable manner."

He walked out of her bedroom and closed the door behind him. Leaving her naked. And very, very confused.

She had slept with her father's murderer. She had wanted him.

She had laid herself bare to her enemy and joined herself to him. The man she had sworn to kill. The man she had agreed to marry. The man who heated her blood and showed her desire she'd never known possible.

Why could things never be simple? This future he had offered had seemed such a miraculous thing in many ways, but the strings attached were different, unexpected. The war, the one she had sought to wage in a physical manner, had moved inside of her body.

What she wanted, right now, was to forget everything. To process what it meant to be intimate with another person for the first time. But her lover was gone. And even if he were here, it wouldn't be that simple.

He would still be Ferran. She would still be Samarah.

She had never felt more alone than she did in that moment. She had spent years in near isolation, with no friends and no family, and here, with the imprint of his fingertips still burning on her skin, she felt completely abandoned.

She rolled over onto her stomach and curled up into a ball.

She felt utterly changed. By Ferran. By his confession. By his touch. And she would have to figure out what to do about both.

One thing she knew for certain, she would not allow his touch to transform her into a quivering mass. She had survived all manner of things; she would not allow herself to implode now.

She repeated the words she'd said to Ferran, just before he had touched her. Before he'd altered her entirely.

"I am still a warrior."

CHAPTER ELEVEN

FERRAN SUPPOSED HE shouldn't be too surprised by Samarah storming into the dining room early the next morning in her workout gear, her long dark hair restrained in a braid.

He also supposed he shouldn't be too surprised by the feral, tearing lust that gripped him the moment he saw her. Sixteen years of celibacy, burned away by this fearsome, beautiful creature.

"You're not exactly dressed for our meeting with the event planner," he said, gritting his teeth, trying to get a handle on himself.

"And you're not exactly dead, so perhaps you should just be grateful."

"It's true," he said, lifting his mug to his lips, "I suppose after last night, I should be happy that you allowed that."

"Again, I find myself merciful."

"I have no doubt. And are you here to tell me you're leaving, Sheikha? Though, I must warn you, I will not allow it."

"A change in tune from last night."

"After what happened, there is no way you can go."

She held up her hand and showed him the ring on her finger. "As it is, I've decided to stay."

"How is this possible?"

"I have nowhere else to go. I get thrown in your dungeon, I get sent back to the streets of Jahar, and neither option is entirely palatable to me. So I'm staying here. I find sheikhahood much preferred to street urchinhood. Imagine that."

"I would ensure you were cared for."

"And I would live on your terms. This way I have my own source of power and visibility in the public eye. I have my rightful position. It is the only way."

"Why are you not angry with me?"

"Perhaps I am," she said, her expression cool, impassive. "Perhaps this is simply me lying in wait."

There was something about the way she said it that sent a slug of heat through him, hitting him hard in the gut. Because it made him think of last night. Of her soft hair sifting through his fingers, of her softer skin beneath his palms.

It made him think of what it had been like to be inside her. A storm of rage and fire, of all the passion she'd asked for.

And in that passion, he had dishonored her. At least, he had not done what his mother would have expected from him with the daughter of their neighboring country. A virgin princess. He would have been expected to honor her. To never touch her until marriage vows had been spoken, until she was protected.

Now, he could not send her away. It was impossible. A bigger sin than the one he'd already committed.

More weakness. How he despised it. How he despised himself. A jailer now, by necessity, because he had ensured now that they must marry.

"If so, then I suppose it's no less than I deserve," he said. "Although, marriage is a life sentence, and some might argue a life sentence is more of a punishment."

"Glad to be your punishment," she said. "I always knew I would be your reckoning. Why did you leave me alone last night?"

"What?"

"You heard me. Why did you leave me alone last night?"

"Because, it was a shameless loss of control on my part."

"You made me feel ashamed," she said.

"That was not my intention."

"Regardless," she said, her voice trembling. "You did. We have a history thick with death and hatred. But in that moment, I was just a woman. And seeing your disgust—"

"At myself. One moment I confessed to stabbing your father in the back, the next you begged me to have sex with you. It was, without a doubt, the strangest encounter I've ever had with a woman."

She frowned, her cheeks turning a dark rose. "I'm not sure how I feel about my only experience with a man being called strange."

"Do you think it's common to go from death threats to making love?"

"Does it matter what's common?"

"I handled you too roughly."

"You handled me in exactly the right way," she said. "During sex. Not after. After…I find you in much fault on the way you behaved after."

"How would you know I treated you in the right way?"

"Because. I know what feels good to me. I know what creates…release."

"Orgasms," he said, not feeling in the mood to be considerate of her inexperience. If she thought she could handle it, then she'd have to be able to handle the discussion of it in frank terms.

"Yes," she said, the color in her cheeks deepening. "Obviously I know what gives me orgasms, and clearly, it is something you know how to accomplish. So you handled me correctly. I think we can both agree on that."

"Do you know what virgins deserve?"

"Do you even remember being one? How would you know?"

"This isn't about me," he said.

"Like hell it's not," she grumbled.

"Virgins deserve candles, and lovemaking and marriage vows."

"Do they? Did your first time come complete with those things? If so, I feel I should tell you, I've no interest in sharing you with another wife. And I find candlelight overrated."

"I'm a man. It's different."

"Oh? Really? Because I'm a woman and therefore must be coddled? Because for some reason my body is your responsibility and not mine?" Her face wasn't smooth now, not unreadable. She was angry. Finally. "If that's the case, where were you when I shivered in the cold? Where were you when I was alone and starving? Where the hell were you when men approached me and offered me shelter for sex? Or just demanded that I lie down and submit to them? Or perhaps, I should have taken them up on it? Since I clearly don't know what I need, perhaps they did?"

"That is not what I'm saying, Samarah," he said. "Hell. I didn't know.... I didn't..."

"Because in so many ways, you are the innocent here, Ferran. I have lived in the dark. You only played in it for the afternoon."

"The thing about something like that is that it never leaves you," he said. "On that you can trust me. You know, even if you've cleaned blood it shows beneath fluorescent lights. That's how I feel. That no matter how many years pass, no matter how clean I think I am, how far removed... it doesn't ever really go away. The evidence is there. And all I can do is make sure I never become the man I was in that moment ever again."

"This is one of the many things about my association with you that troubles me, Ferran," she said, grabbing her braid and twisting it over her shoulder.

"Only one? Do you have a list?"

She lifted her brows. "It's quite long. I made it last night. About what I want. About what all this means for me. And about what I find problematic about you."

"Is it a physical list?"

She nodded. "But this is just one of the things. Before you, everything was black-and-white to me. I hated you for what you did. I didn't have to know your side. I didn't have to see multiple angles. I just had to know you were responsible for the death of my father. But now I know you. Now I've heard your side. I should hate you more, knowing you ended my father's life, and yet I find it only makes me feel worse for you. Because coupled with it, comes the revelation that my father killed your mother. That you saw it. That…in your position, I would have acted the same, and that in many ways, had you not made him pay for what he'd done, I would have judged you a coward."

"I should have had him go to trial, Samarah. That would have been the right thing to do in the black-and-white world. In the one I aspire to live in."

"I think of that day like being in the middle of a war zone. It's how I remember it. I was just a child, and I saw very little. I was so lucky to be protected. My mother ensured that I was protected though…have you ever considered my father would have come for us next? For her? Would he have come for me too, Ferran, ultimate vengeance on my mother, if you hadn't acted as you did?

"Samarah…you're assigning heroism to me, and that is one thing you should never do. It's conjecture. Who knows what would have happened?"

"Yes, who knows? I only know what did. But now I know it from more angles. I miss my blinding conviction. The less I knew, the easier it all was. I could just…focus on one thing in particular."

"Your rage for me."

"Yes. And I could move forward, using that as my target. And now? Now everything has expanded and there are so many more possibilities. For what my life could be. For what I could do with myself and my purpose. But it's scarier, too."

"Scarier than gaining access to my palace? Being thrown in a dungeon? Facing possible trial?"

"Yes. Because when I was in that state I didn't want anything. I had accepted that I would probably die carrying out my mission, and that meant an end to… Life has been so hard. I've had no great love for it. But you came in and you offered me more, and the moment you did…things started to change. Now…now I don't want to turn away. I don't want to go back to how it was. And yet…and yet in some ways I do. It makes no sense to me, either."

He laughed. It was an absurd thing to do under the circumstances. Neither he nor Samarah had anything to laugh about. And yet, he couldn't help it. It was as if she was discovering emotions for the first time. Discovering how contrary it could be to be human.

"Is this your first experience with such confusion?" he asked.

"Yes," she said. "Emotions are wobbly. Conviction isn't."

"I'm very sorry to have caused you…feelings."

"Thank you," she said. "I'm…sorry in many ways to be experiencing them. Though not in others. Really, is it always like this?"

"Not for me," he said. "I'm not overly given to emotion."

"I suppose you aren't. Though, passion seems to be a strong suit of yours."

"No, it's a weakness."

She let out a long breath. "You're getting off topic. I have my list." She reached into the pocket of her athletic shorts and pulled out a folded piece of paper. "Now that I'm not merely surviving, there are some things I would like. I would like to be comfortable," she said, unfolding the paper and looking at it. "I would like to be part of something. Something constructive. Something that isn't all about breaking a legacy, but building a new one."

"Lofty," he said, standing, his stomach tightening as he looked at her, his beautiful, brave fiancée, who didn't seem to be afraid of anything, least of all him. She should be. She should have run. He'd given her the chance and she had not.

Why had she not run? Any normal woman would have turned away from him. From the blood on his hands.

She should be afraid.

He moved nearer to her, fire burning through his blood. A flame to alcohol, impossibly hot and bright. She should be afraid. He wanted to make her afraid. Almost as badly as he wanted her to turn to him and lean in, press her lush body against his chest.

"Is that your entire list?" he asked.

"No," she said, her voice steady. "I want to feel like I have a life. Like I have…"

"Sex," he said, leaning in, running his thumb over the ridge of her high cheekbone. "Is sex on your list?"

He let his hand drift down the elegant line of her neck, resting his palm at the base of her throat. He knew that she wouldn't fear his wrath. She would fight him to the death if need be. Here was where he had the undisputed upper hand. Here was where his experience trumped hers.

He felt her pulse quicken beneath his thumb. "I don't know."

"If you stay, there is no option, do you understand?" He slid his thumb along her tender skin. "You are my prisoner in many ways."

And it was true. A hard truth that settled poorly.

"It is better than the streets," she said, arching a brow.

"A high compliment," he said.

"It is," she said. "For in the beginning, I would have said death was better than this."

"Oh, my little viper." He moved his hand upward and cupped her jaw. "You are so honest."

"I am not," she said.

"Your eyes. They tell me too much." Liquid, beautiful and dark as night, they shone with emotion. Deep. Unfathomable. But the presence of that emotion twisted at his gut. Convicted him.

"Do not trust me, Samarah," he said, his voice rough. "I don't trust me."

"I don't trust anyone."

"See that you don't. You may be a warrior. You may be a strong fighter. You may not hesitate to cut my throat… now. But in the bedroom, I have the experience."

"Sixteen years celibate," she said.

He wrapped one arm around her waist and drew her to him, holding her chin tight, pressing her breasts tight to his chest. "And yet," he said. "I had the power over your body. Do you deny it?"

Dark eyes shimmered, her cheeks turning pink. She caught her breath, pressing her breasts more firmly against him. "No," she said, her voice choked.

Oh, Samarah. She revealed too much to him.

He wanted to press her back against the wall, wanted to take her. To show her that he was not a man to toy with. To prove he wasn't a man to trust.

He released her, moved away from her. The distance easing his breath. "Now, unless you're planning on wearing workout clothes to meet with the event coordinator, you may want to go change."

"Yes, I may. Thank you. How thoughtful." She turned away from him, head down, and walked out of the room.

The twisting sensation in his gut intensified. He was her jailer. Not her fiancé. Being with her…it was akin to force.

He gritted his teeth as pain lashed through his chest. No. He would not force her. He had not. What had happened last night could not be changed, but the future could. At the very least, he would begin showing her the respect a sheikha was due.

CHAPTER TWELVE

SAMARAH HUNG OUT in the corridor, listening to the sounds of people inside the grand ballroom of the palace. She was still a little bit nervous in large gatherings like this. More so now that she was a focal point for attention. And she felt as if there was nowhere to hide.

As palace staff, no one had noticed her. As the sheikh's fiancée? Yes, she was certainly going to be noticed. Especially in the green-and-gold gown that had been sent for her. It had yards of fabric, the skirt all layered, billowing folds. The sleeves went to her elbows, sheer and beaded, with matching details on the bodice, disappearing beneath the wide, gold belt that made her waist look impossibly small. It also kept her posture unreasonably straight, since it was metal.

A matching chain had been sent for her hair, an emerald in the centerpiece that rested on her forehead. She *did* like the clothes, but less now when she felt so conspicuous. And without Ferran.

She relied on his presence much more than she'd realized until this moment. Of course, after she'd gone and read him her list she felt more than a little embarrassed to see him again.

Though, really, she'd been naked with him, so nothing should embarrass her with him now. It did, though, because he'd run afterward. Because, when they'd spoken earlier, his intensity had unsettled her.

He was right. In this, this need, he was the master. And he could easily use it against her.

How sobering to realize that if the sheikh of Khadra were to defeat her, it wouldn't end in screams of terror, but in pleasure.

Just then, she saw him. Striding down the hall. He was wearing white linen pants and a tunic, his concession to traditional dress. She'd noticed that he never seemed to bother with robes.

She didn't feel so conspicuous now. Because surely everyone's eyes would be on Ferran. He was taller than most men, so he always stood out for that reason. But he was also arrestingly handsome. She'd kissed his lips, touched his face, his body. And she was still struck to the point of speechlessness by his beauty.

Or maybe it was even more intense now. Because she'd been with him. Because she knew what wicked pleasure his perfect lips could provide. Because she knew what a heaven it was to be in his strong arms, to be held against his muscular chest.

"You're late," she said, clasping her hands in front of her.

He paused, his dark eyes assessing. "You're beautiful."

She blinked hard. He'd said that to her before. But for some reason it hit her now, how rarely she'd heard that in her life. Not when it was said in a nonthreatening tone. Men on the streets had called out to her, but they had frightened her. Her father and mother had called her beautiful, but when she was a child.

Ferran said it to her just because. Because he believed it. Because it was what he saw when he looked at her. And for some reason, just then, it meant the world to her.

"Thank you," she said. "I think you're beautiful, too."

"I'm not often called beautiful," he said, one corner of his mouth lifting.

"Well, neither am I."

"That will change."

"Have you accepted than I'm not leaving you?" she asked.

"I'm not sure," he said, holding his arm out to her.

She took a step forward and curled her fingers around his forearm. "You have my word," she said. "My word is good. I want you to know that, at first, I didn't intend to marry you."

"Is that so?"

"I intended to bide my time. And carry out my plan."

He tightened his hold on her, his other hand crossing his body and settling over hers. "I had a feeling that might be the case."

"But it's not the case now. I will marry you," she said. "I will be your wife. And I will not leave you. So don't try to scare me away. You'll only be disappointed."

"Is that so?"

"Yes. Because I do not scare. And just because I don't intend to kill you doesn't mean I won't punch you in the face."

"I'll endeavor to avoid that," he said. "Are you ready to go in?"

"What are we supposed to do?"

He lifted a shoulder. "Wave. Eat some canapés. Dance."

"I have never danced with anyone."

"I'll lead," he said. "You have nothing to worry about. You are strong, Samarah, I do know that. But there's no shame in letting someone else take control sometimes. It can even be helpful."

"All right. In the bedroom and on the dance floor, you may lead," she said, testing him. He had tried to prove his power over her earlier, and while he had done so, while he had left her quivering, aching and needing in a way she hadn't thought possible, she rebelled against it. She wanted to push back.

Because if there was one thing in life Samarah didn't understand, it was defeat. She had spent her life in a win or die battle, and as she was here, breathing, living, it was clear she had always won.

And that meant, in this moment, she was determined to keep fighting.

"We'll discuss the bedroom later," he said. "After our wedding."

"What?" It was such a stark contrast to what he'd said earlier. To the implied promise in his words.

"We have to go in now."

"Wait just a second. You said…"

"Did you think you were going to seize control back?" he said, dark eyes glittering. "You, and my body, no matter how it might ache for you, do not control me."

His words, the intensity in his eyes, stopped her voice, stole her breath.

"You do not want me out of control," he said, his face hard. "I remind you. Now, come with me."

He led her into the ballroom, and as they drew farther in, nearer to the crowd of people, panic clawed at her. How was she supposed to smile now? How was she supposed to deal with all those eyes on her after what Ferran had just said?

They were formally announced, and Ferran lifted their joined hands, then bowed. She followed suit and dipped into a curtsy, shocked she remembered how, everything in her on an autopilot setting she hadn't known she'd possessed. Her muscle memory seemed to be intact. Princess training obviously lurked in the back of her mind.

"Who are all these people?" she asked, still reeling from the change. From his uncivilized words in the hall to this venue that was all things tame and beautiful.

"Dignitaries, diplomats. From here and abroad. Anyone who feels they may have a political stake in our union."

"Including the Jaharan rulers, I imagine?"

"Yes," he said. "This is the first time they've been at a political event in Khadra since..."

"Yes. Obviously."

"Already, we have done some good."

"I guess that remains to be seen," she said. "Just because they're here doesn't mean... Well, I guess I'm pessimistic when it comes to politics."

"I can see how you would be."

"But I can see that people are happy to be here. I feel like...I feel like this is good."

They spent the next hour wandering through the party, making light conversation with everyone they came across. This wasn't the time for any heavy-hitting, political negotiation, but everyone seemed very aware that it was the time to get on Ferran's radar.

And people seemed to want to talk to her, as well. As if she carried influence. As if she mattered. It was so very different to the life she'd had before she'd come here. So very different to the life she'd ever imagined she might have.

"Now," Ferran said, "I think it's time for you to dance with me."

"I think I could skip the dancing," she said, looking out across the expanse of marble floor, to where gorgeous, graceful couples twirled in circles, in eddies of silk and color. She doubted very much she would be that graceful. Martial arts was one thing. She kept time to the beat of the fight. Of her body.

She wasn't sure if she could follow music.

"I will lead you," he said. "As I think I've established."

"So you have," she said, but in this instance she was grateful.

Sex and dancing were Ferran's domain, it seemed.

He led her through the crowd, and to the center of the floor. The other dancers cleared extra space for them, as if in deference to Ferran's royal personage.

He grasped her hand, his arm curling around her back as he tugged her against his chest. She lost her breath then, captivated wholly by the look in his eyes. So dark and intense. Simmering passion. The kind he'd unleashed last night. The sort she craved again.

And he was telling her now that they would wait. That he could control himself.

She didn't like it. It made her feel powerless. It…hurt her. And she would not have it.

She'd waited all of her life. She'd spent countless nights cold and alone, and she'd be damned if she'd spend any more that way, not now that she'd been with him.

"I think we need to discuss what you said in the hall," she said.

"Which thing?"

"About abstaining until the wedding," she said.

He looked around them. "Are we having this conversation now?"

"I take your point. However, you just said some very explicit things in the hall and then we were cut off. And I'm not done. I just thought I should tell you that I'm not doing that."

"Excuse me?"

"It might interest you to know that I have obtained some very brief underthings."

"Samarah…"

"They're intended to arouse you, and I have it on good authority they will."

He looked torn between anger, amusement and, yes, arousal. "Whose authority?"

"Lydia's. She provided them for me when I asked."

"And they are meant to…"

"Arouse you," she said, her face heating. "I had thought, seeing as I was to be your wife, I should set out to…behave like a wife. And then you told me…you told me no."

"Tell me about them," he said, his voice lowering, taking on that hard, feral tone he'd had in the hall, as he leaned nearer to her.

"The uh…the bra is…made of gems. Strung together. It shows…a lot of skin."

"Does it?"

"Yes," she said, swallowing hard, her face burning.

"And the rest?"

"I don't feel like you deserve to know," she said, lifting her head so she was looking in his eyes, so their noses nearly touched. "If you want abstinence, you don't want to know about my underwear."

"That isn't the case. And I never said I *wanted* to abstain. Only that it's the right thing."

"For who?"

"For you."

She growled. "Stop doing that. Stop trying to protect me. I don't want you to protect me I want you to…to…"

Love me.

Where had that come from? She did not need that thought. No, she didn't. And now she would forget she'd ever had it. And she would never have it again.

"I just need you to be with me," she said, which was much more acceptable. "I'm tired of being alone. Now that I don't have to sleep by myself anymore I would just… rather not."

He pulled her closer, his lips pressed against her ear. "Yes, *habibti*, but do you want me? Do you want my body? Do you want me to touch you, taste you. Be inside you. If all you want is companionship, I would just as soon buy you a puppy."

"I want your body," she said, leaning in and pressing a

kiss to his neck. "I want you. I don't want a puppy. I'm a woman, not a child. I know the difference between simple loneliness and desire."

"And you desire me?" he asked, his eyes growing darker.

"Yes."

"Tell me what you desire."

"Here?" she asked, looking around them.

"Yes. Here. Tell me what you want from me. What you want me to do to you. You said you wanted my passion. You said you weren't afraid. Now tell me. Remember, I have much more practice than you at abstaining when temptation is present. So if you intend to break my resolve, you'd better damn well shatter it. If you want to take my control, you prepare for what you will unleash."

"I…" She felt her cheeks get hotter, and she wanted to shrink away. To tell him nothing. To tell him something quick, and unexplicit. Something dishonest that had nothing to do with what she'd actually been thinking about doing with him.

But then she remembered her own words.

I do not run.

She tilted her head up and leaned in so that her lips were near his ear, her heart hammering hard.

"I want to take this dress off for you," she said. "While you sit and watch. I want to watch your face as your need for me takes you over." She swallowed hard. "Then…then I want to…I want to get onto the bed, on your lap, and kiss your lips."

"You want to do all of that?" he asked.

"I'm not finished."

"I may need to be," he said. "This doesn't sound very much like you're planning to let me lead."

"You were the one who said I should let you lead in the bedroom. I never agreed to it."

"We were not taking a vote," he said, his tone hard.

"I deserve to get what I want from this marriage, too."

"You aren't talking about marriage. You're talking about now."

She lifted a shoulder. "Don't I deserve to be certain of the manner of man I'm binding myself to? You said that yourself."

"And you think seducing me will reveal me to you more than my confessions already have?"

"It's the one thing you've held back for the past sixteen years. That makes me feel like it's important."

Ferran wanted to turn away from her, and yet, he found it impossible. She was too beautiful. Too powerful. It wasn't simply beauty. It never had been. She was a glittering flash of temptation that could easily be his undoing.

But she was also to be his wife. And that meant he had to get a handle on himself with her, didn't it? That meant that he had to be able to sleep with her, to make love with her, without losing himself.

Here before him was the challenge. If he turned her away now, then he proved that she held the power to take him back to where he'd been before.

She didn't. No matter how strongly she called to him. No matter how much he wanted her, he could control it. He could have her tonight, and feel nothing beyond release.

It didn't matter what she wore, what she did. He would prove to himself he had the control.

"All right, Samarah. You want me? You want my body? Tonight?"

"Yes."

"Now?" he asked.

"Now…we're…Ferran, not now."

He pulled her closer, staring down into her wide, dark eyes. "If you want me, *habibti*, you will have me on my terms."

He released her from the close hold they were in, then

laced his fingers through hers, drawing her through the crowd of people, out into the gardens. The night was cool, the grounds insulated from view by palm trees and flowering plants.

And no doubt his security detail had seen him exit with Samarah. If for no other reason, no one would be following them out here.

He tugged her to him and kissed her, hard and deep. If this was what she wanted, it was what she would have. But he wouldn't be at her mercy. He wouldn't be taking orders from her. If she wanted him, she could have him.

And he would make her understand what that meant.

He cupped her chin, his thumb drifting along the line of her jaw as he continued to kiss her. To taste her. He could drown in it. He very nearly had before. Both when they'd kissed in the rain, and last night.

There were things about kissing a woman he hadn't remembered. How soft feminine lips were, the sounds they made. How it felt to be so close to someone living. To feel their heartbeat against your own.

Or maybe he hadn't forgotten. Maybe he'd just never noticed before.

But he did now. It was like slowly having feeling return to frozen limbs. To places that had been numb for years. So much so, he'd forgotten they were even there.

In his quest to be the best sheikh, to choke out all of his weaknesses, he'd forgotten he was a man. And the touch of Samarah's lips in his brought it all back with blinding clarity.

And with the clarity came a host of other things he'd spent years trying to deny. Fear. Anger.

He backed her against one of the walls that enclosed the garden from the rest of the world, taking her mouth with all the ferocity he possessed.

"You want this?" he asked again, kissing her cheek, her

neck, moving his hand to her breast. His whole body was shaking. He could hardly breathe. He could barely stand. Touching her like this…

It had nothing to do with how long it had been since he'd touched a woman. If he was honest, he had to confess that.

It was more. She was more.

He slid his palm over her curves, to the indent of her waist, over the rounded flare of her hip. He gathered up the material of her dress, curling his fingers around the heavy, beaded fabric.

"Ferran…"

"Scared, *habibti*?"

"No," she said. "But we're in the garden and…"

"And you said you wanted me. You do not get to dictate all the terms. If you want me, you will have me now."

He moved his hand between her thighs, felt the thin silk that separated the heart of her from his touch. He pushed it aside and growled when his fingertips made contact with slick flesh. "You do want me," he said, moving his thumb over the source of her pleasure.

She arched against him, her breathing coming in short, sharp bursts. More evidence of her need for him. He suddenly felt that he might require her more than air.

"Samarah," he said, sliding his fingers through her folds.

She pushed her knees together, forcing his hand more tightly against her body, her head falling back against the wall, her lips parted, an expression of ecstasy.

If he took her now, it would be over quickly. It would be so easy to undo his pants and thrust deep inside her, take them both to release.

But then he couldn't see her body. He couldn't touch her as he wanted, taste her as he wanted.

"I want to take you to bed," he said.

"I thought you wanted me here?"

"I do," he said. "Here and now, but I also want to be able

to see you." He moved his hand from between her thighs. "I want to touch you. I want to take my time."

He tugged her dress back into place.

"You can't expect me to walk back through there. We look…well, we must look like we've been doing exactly what we've been doing."

"I am certain we do. But I have no issue with it."

"I cannot figure you out."

"I've made the decision," he said, looking at her eyes, which were glittering in the dim lighting. And he could feel the desperation within himself. Could sense his own biting need to justify his actions.

But he'd decided he would do this. So surely that made it okay. Surely that meant he had reasoned it out. She was to be his wife. He repeated that fact in his mind. She was to be his wife, and that meant that he could be with her. That meant he had to be. It was duty and honor, and it had nothing to do with the heat in his blood.

And making sure he took his time and enjoyed it was for her. For his wife.

"Come with me," he said, holding out his hand.

She took it, delicate fingers curling around his. He flashed back to the moment in his bedroom, when those hands had struck at him. When she'd looked at him with fear and loathing. It was gone now. All of it. Replaced by a desire he wasn't certain he deserved from her.

But he needed it. Because they were getting married.

That was the only reason. For his people.

Not for himself.

But either way, he needed it.

He led her back through the garden, and into the brightly lit, glittering ballroom. She was flushed, her eyes bright. She looked very much like a woman who was on the brink of release, and suddenly, he was afraid that everyone in the room would know.

Not for himself, but for her. He didn't want to humiliate Samarah. He didn't want to expose her or hurt her. And yet, he feared that was what he'd done. All he would ever do.

Not tonight. Tonight she would be his, and he would worry about the rest later.

He gritted his teeth and battled with himself. With his reasoning, his justifications.

Spare me. Spare us.

No. There was no place for that memory. Not in this. This wasn't the same. He could keep control, and have this.

He could keep her.

He led her out into the hall, then down the corridor, toward his chambers. Halfway through, he swept her up in his arms. "I have no patience," he said, striding onward.

"I doubt this is faster," she said, her arms looped around his neck.

"But you are near me," he said.

Why had he said that? Why was he feeling this. Why was he feeling anything? Why did it matter?

He kicked the door to his bedchamber open and Samarah jumped in his arms. "I found that arousing," she said, her eyes locked with his.

"Did you?" he asked.

"I like your intensity," she said. "I like that you want me. No one has wanted me in so long."

He set her down and she leaned into him, curling her fingers into the lapels of his shirt. "No one has wanted me in longer than I can remember. Until you. You want me. And that matters, Ferran..."

He bent and kissed her, slamming the bedroom door as he did, the sound echoing in the cavernous space. "My wanting you is not necessarily something to rejoice in," he said, dragging the edge of his thumb along her cheek. "I am broken, Samarah, in every way that counts."

And there was more honesty than he'd ever given even to himself.

"I don't care," she said. "I don't care."

"Samarah..."

She took a step away from him and reached behind her back before unclasping her belt and letting it fall to the ground. The top layer of her gown fell open and she shrugged it off, letting it slither to the floor, revealing the simple shift beneath.

The heavy silk conformed to her slender figure. It revealed very little skin, and yet he found the sight erotic. So sexy he could hardly breathe.

She started on the little buttons on the front of her garment. She let it fall away, revealing another layer beneath. A skirt with a heavy, beaded waistband that sat low on her hips, strips of gauzy, nearly translucent fabric covering her legs. Every movement parted the fabric, showed hints of tanned, shapely thighs.

The top was exactly as advertised, and yet, nothing she'd said had prepared him for the deep, visceral reaction he had to it. Glittering strings of beads strung across her golden skin, conformed to the curve of her breasts, hints of skin showing through.

It wasn't the gems that held him captive, not the sparkling. No, he was trying to look past that, beyond that, to her. Because she was more beautiful than any gem.

"Sit on the bed," she said.

"I told you this would be on my terms."

"And I did not agree. I have a fantasy that I wish to fulfill."

"You have a fantasy?" he asked, his heart rate ticking up.

"Yes. You know, Master Ahn rented out the studio several nights a week to a dance teacher. I never took lessons, but I did watch. Sit on the bed."

He obeyed, his eyes on her, a ferocious tug in his gut.

"Take your shirt off," she said.

He tugged at his tie, then worked the buttons on his shirt before shrugging it, and his jacket off onto the bed.

She shifted her hips to the side, slowly, then back the other way, the motion fluid, controlled. "I used to practice in my room sometimes," she said. "But there was no practical use for dancing in my life. Still, I know what my body can do. I know how to move it. How to control my muscles. Dancing came naturally in many ways."

She shifted her shoulders, then reached behind her head and released her hair, letting it fall in loose, glossy waves. She kept her hips moving in time with a rhythm that was all in her head. But he could feel it. He could feel it moving through her body and on into his.

She rolled her shoulders, down her arms, to her wrists, her fingertips curling upward, her head falling back. He shifted in his seat, desire rushing through his veins, beginning to push at the restraint that he prized so much.

That he depended on.

She met his eyes, then tipped her head back, her shoulders following, bending back until he was sure she would break herself if she went farther. She held the pose steady, no strain in her muscles, then she lifted herself back up slowly.

Such a fierce, wild creature she was.

A tiger pacing the bars...

"You did pay attention during the lessons."

"Yes," she said. "But I've never had anyone to dance for. I've never had any real reason to dance. But I did it anyway. Alone. Now...now I can do it for you. I don't understand this...how you've become the most essential person to me. But you have. I almost robbed myself of you."

"You almost robbed *myself* of me," he said, gritting his teeth, trying to keep from telling her to stop talking. Trying to keep himself from accepting what she was offering. From begging her for more.

"I did," she said, walking toward the bed, each movement a temptation. Another hit against the barricade. She put her hand on his cheek, her fingertips dragging across his skin, sending a sensual spark down into his gut that ignited, desire burning hot and hard, threatening to rage out of control.

She reached behind herself and released the hold on her top, the jewels sliding down to her waist before she managed to free herself of it entirely. She put one knee on the bed beside his thigh, her breasts so close one movement would allow him to suck a caramel nipple deep into his mouth.

But if he moved, he wouldn't be able to find out what she had planned next.

The temptation was torture. Sweet, perfect torture. He'd held himself back for years, but it had never felt like this. It had never been physical pain. To have so much beauty in front of him and to refuse to allow himself to touch it, to test himself in this way…it was intoxicating. A rush he couldn't define or deny.

She leaned in, putting her hand on his belt, her beasts so near his lips his mouth watered. She worked at his belt, her fingers deft, confident, like all of her movements.

She freed him from his slacks, her palm hot on his erection. He couldn't hold back the tortured sound that climbed his throat and escaped his lips.

"Do you like me touching you?" she asked. "No other woman has done this in a long time…" She squeezed him gently and he swore. "Did I hurt you?"

"No," he said. "And yes. You're right…it's been a long time. It makes it… No, I don't think it's the time. It's you. Because nothing ever felt like this before."

She smiled, her dark eyes glistening. She looked at him

as if he was a god. As if he was her hero, not her enemy. And he felt like the worst sort of bastard for stealing that moment. One he didn't deserve. One he could never hope to earn.

And for what? Because he had given her shelter when she had none? Because he had offered her prison or marriage? He should stop her. But he didn't. Instead he watched her face and soaked in the adoration. The need. He didn't deserve it. Dammit, he didn't deserve a moment of it and he was going to take it anyway.

Such was his weakness.

"I want to…could…" She slid down, her movements graceful, her knees on the floor, her body between his thighs. "I want to taste you."

"Samarah…" He should not allow this.

"Please." She looked up at him, and he knew he couldn't deny her. What man could deny a woman begging to allow her to take him in her mouth? Certainly not him. He had established that he was weak.

Maybe for the moment he would let his guard down fully. Maybe he would let her see it all. He forked his fingers through her silky hair, curling them inward, making a fist. Holding her steady.

She lowered her head and he allowed it, holding her back only slightly so he could catch his breath. So he could anticipate the moment she would touch him.

But when she did, it was nearly the end of it. Because there was no bracing himself for this. For the sheer, blinding pleasure of her hot, wet tongue on his skin. For the unpracticed movements she made, so sincere. Only for him.

She dipped her head and took him in deep. His hold tightened on her hair, his other hand holding tight to the bedspread. Trying to anchor himself to earth. To something.

"Samarah…" He said her name like a warning. A curse. A prayer. He needed her to stop. He needed her to keep going. He needed this because it made the past feel like less. Made it feel like maybe this need wasn't so wrong. Like maybe he wasn't so wrong.

Pleasure rushed up inside of him. Hot. Dangerous. Out of control.

He tugged her head upward and tried to catch his breath, tried to get a handle on the need that was coursing through his veins like fire.

"Not like that," he said, his words harsh in the stillness of the room. "I want to be inside you. Just like you said. You said you wanted that. Wanted me."

"I do."

"Show me, *habibti*. Show me."

She rose up slowly, her hands on the beaded band of her skirt. She pushed it down her hips slowly, then stepped out of the fabric, leaving her bare to him.

"You are water in the desert," he said, pulling her close, his face pressed against her stomach. He kissed her tender skin, tracing her belly button with the tip of his tongue. "You are perfection."

She put her arms around his neck, one knee pressed onto the mattress beside his thigh. Then she shifted and brought the other one up, too. "I want you, Ferran Bashar. You are not my enemy."

Words he didn't deserve. Words he would never deserve. And yet, he did not have the strength to turn her away.

She lowered herself onto his length, slowly, so slowly he thought his head might explode. And other parts of him. But if that happened, he wouldn't get to see this through to the end. And he desperately needed to. If only to watch her face while it happened. When she reached her peak. If he could see that again…maybe he would put up the walls after. And carry that with him.

He watched, transfixed as she took him in fully, her lips rounded, her eyes closed. The pleasure there was humbling.

More than he deserved. But he was of a mind to take it all, whether he deserved it or not.

He curved his arm around her waist, his palm resting on her hip. And he put his other hand on her chest bracing her as he thrust up inside her. She gasped, her eyes opening, locking with his.

"Yes," he said. "Look at me, Samarah. Look at me."

He shifted his hold, tightened the arm around her waist, cupped the back of her head with his other hand, his thumb drifting to her mouth. She turned her head and bit him. Lightly, just enough to send a short burst of pain through him, the sensation setting off a chain of sparks.

She moved over him, with him, and he held her tight, held her against him, tried to brace them both for what was coming.

He thrust up hard as he pulled her down against him and she cried out, his thumb braced against her lips as she shuddered out her release, her internal muscles tightening around him.

He moved his thumb and claimed her mouth in a searing kiss as he thrust inside her one last time and gave in to the need that was battering him, breaking him down. And he gave in to his own need. His own desire washing over him like a blinding wall of cleansing fire. Strong enough to burn away the past. Strong enough to burn away blood.

And when they were done, he pulled her onto the bed with him and held her close, their hearts beating together.

"Don't make me go," she said, burying her face in his chest.

"I doubt I could make you do anything you didn't want to do."

"I don't know about that," she said, moving against him, her breasts against his bare chest sending a fresh shock of desire through him. He couldn't blame the celibacy. This was all Samarah.

"Maybe someday we can go back to the palace by the ocean, Ferran," she said. He stiffened, dark memory pouring through him. Like black ink on white, it stained. It couldn't be stopped. "Maybe together we can make new memories there. Memories that aren't so sad. I remember loving it. I remember...almost loving you."

Her words choked him. Made his vision blur. He didn't deserve this. A man like him. She knew he'd killed her father but she didn't know how he'd felt. The rage. The decisive, brilliant rage that had made sinking his knife into the other man's back feel like a glorious triumph...

"I don't know that we should go back, Samarah."

"We won't let the past win, Ferran. You were the one who taught me that. You were the one who made me want more."

"I should not be the one who inspires you, little viper." He was her captor, nothing more. A man who went through life ruling with an iron fist and—he envisioned the past washed in a haze of red—when he had to, blood.

And that was the man who held her.

He had enslaved her, and she was thanking him. He had robbed her of her choice, and she gave him her body. He should go. He should leave her.

He started to roll away, but she held tight to him. He felt the hot press of her lips on his back. "Don't do that," she said. "Please don't."

He put his hand over hers, pinned it to his chest. Then he turned sharply, pulling her naked body against his as he kissed her, hard and deep. He didn't deserve this. He shouldn't take it. He had no right.

But he was going to take it anyway. He lowered her back down to the bed and settled between her thighs, kissing her neck, her shoulder, the curve of her breast. "I won't do it then," he said. "Why? When we can do this instead."

"Ferran, we should talk."

"I don't want to talk," he said, his voice rough. "I don't want to talk."

"Why not?"

"Because…" He kissed her again. "Because words are dangerous, and until I'm not feeling quite so dangerous… I don't think I should speak."

"Then we won't speak," she said.

And they didn't for the rest of the night.

CHAPTER THIRTEEN

THEIR WEDDING DAY was fast approaching and Samarah felt as if she was sleeping with a brick wall.

Ferran Bashar was nothing if not opaque. He didn't want to talk. He didn't want her to talk. He wanted to make love. Frequently. Constantly, some might say, and she was okay with that. But she wanted something else. Something more.

She wanted him to feel what she did, and she had no earthly way of knowing if he did. Because she felt as if she was butting up against a brick wall whenever she tried to find out.

She thought of the woman she'd been only a month ago, and she could scarcely remember her. Angry. Hopeless.

Now her whole life stretched before her, a life with Ferran. But she was afraid it would always be like this. He talked to her more before they'd started sleeping together. At least then they'd tried. Now it felt like he only wanted to see her at night.

It could not stand. Because when she'd chosen him, she'd done so with the intent of having a life. A real life. Everything she wanted. So she would damn well have it. She was tired of feeling nothing but hunger, cold and exhaustion. Tired of only seeing to the basics.

She wanted more. Whatever *more* might be. And she wanted it with him. If she could walk away now and do anything, *be* anything. Be with anyone, she wouldn't.

She would stay here. Because her home was with him. She felt as if her heart might even be with him. And that meant it was worth pushing for what she wanted, didn't it?

Yes, it did. She would not question herself. She adjusted the tape on her fists and strode into the gym, where she knew Ferran would be. He was probably hoping for a quiet workout. But she wasn't going to allow it.

Because she wasn't simply going to accept what he gave. She was going to break through the brick wall.

"Hello, *hayati*," she said. *My life.* Because that was what he was. He'd changed her life, given her new purpose. New hope. And she would do her best to give him the same.

Ferran turned, his broad chest glistening with sweat. Samarah licked her lips. She loved him like this. It made her think of pleasure. Of being in bed with him, because he often looked like this there. Out of breath, physically exhausted.

They were an athletic couple, and they were not only athletic in the gym. The thought made her face hot, even now.

"What are you doing here, Samarah?" he asked.

"I'm sorry, were you looking for an exclusive workout time?" she asked, approaching the punching bag and treating it to a crescent kick, sending it swinging.

Ferran caught it, holding it steady, a dark brow arched. "And if I were."

"Too bad. I'm not leaving." She crossed her arms beneath her breasts and cocked her head to the side. "I want to spar."

"Do you?" he asked.

"Yes. I feel like we're both getting complacent. But when I win, I expect something in return."

"Do you?"

"Yes. I'm going to ask a question, and you will answer truthfully."

He tilted his head back, his nostrils flaring. "You think so?"

"Are you afraid I'll win, Ferran? You know my moves. I have no size advantage. But I will make a rule about biting."

"What are we playing to?"

"First to five?" she asked.

"And what do I get if I win?" he asked. "You have not offered me incentive."

"What do you want?"

"If I win, you ask me no more questions."

His expression was hard, uncompromising.

"That is imbalanced," she said. "I'm only asking for one question, and you're asking for none, ever?"

"It is not my fault if you set your sights too low."

"I do not…"

"I do not have to answer any," he said. "So I suggest you fight if you have a hope of getting even one answer. I do not live on anyone else's terms."

"All right," she said, moving into position. "We have a deal."

He took his stance, his dark eyes meeting hers. "Ready?"

Yes. She was ready to fight for her life. For this new life she wanted, with this man.

"Ready," she said. And then without waiting, she advanced on him, landing a kick that was a more of a tap, to the side of his neck. "One!" she shouted.

He narrowed his eyes and sidestepped her next move, then grabbed her arm and pulled her toward him, tapping her cheek with his fist. "One," he said.

"Bastard," she hissed, rolling out of his hold and stepping away, backhanding him gently before turning and landing an uppercut to his chin. "Two, three."

He reached for her arm again and she hopped back, side-stepping and moving to his side, flicking a snap kick into his side. "Four," she said.

He turned and countered, but she blocked. He grabbed her around the waist and tugged her against him, her feet off the ground. She wiggled, pushing herself up higher into his arms and over his shoulder. Then she shouted and felt his arms loosen, the jolt from the noise offering her just enough give to use her weight to flip herself over his shoulder, land on her feet and plant her foot between his shoulder blades "Five," she said.

He turned, his chest heaving with the effort of breathing. She knew she looked the same, sweat running down her neck, her back. But she was fighting for her relationship with him. She was fighting for a break in his facade.

She bowed, a sign of respect for him, even in his defeat. He squared up to her and did the same.

"You owe me," she said. "One question. We're getting married in two days and I require this."

He said nothing, he just faced her, his dark eyes blank. "You have earned your question. Ask."

He looked more like a man facing the justice she'd promised just a month ago.

"What are you afraid of?"

"You think I am afraid, Samarah?"

"I know you are."

"Not of anything outside myself."

"What does that mean?"

"That is two questions," he said. "But I will indulge you. Here is your prize. I have to keep control. At all costs. Because that day taught me not just what manner of man your father was. But what manner of man I was. Do you know why I keep the tiger pacing the bars?" he asked, moving to her, resting his hand on her throat. "Because if I ever let him free, he will destroy everything in his path."

"Ferran you won't..."

"You can't say that, Samarah."

"Yes," she said, feeling desperate to combat the bleakness in his eyes.

"No, because it happened before. And you can never guarantee if won't again. Unless I keep control."

He lowered his hand and turned, leaving her there, bleeding inside, bleeding for him. For wounds that hadn't healed. For wounds in both of them she wasn't sure would ever heal.

Maybe that was the problem. Maybe when she'd looked ahead and saw a life she'd never thought possible she'd only been dreaming. Maybe a life like that could never really belong to her and Ferran.

Maybe they were simply too broken to be fixed.

The day of the wedding was bright and clear, like most other days in this part of the country. Ferran didn't believe in abstracts and signs, so he considered it neither a particularly good or bad omen.

He had kept himself from Samarah's bed as a necessity ever since they'd spoken in the gym. Ever since she'd forced him to confess the one thing he wanted most to erase from his past.

The wedding was to be small out of concession for Samarah's issues with crowds. And frankly, it suited him, as well. There would be dignitaries and approved members of the press.

It suited him because he still felt far too exposed, as if his defenses had been torn down. He'd confessed his deepest sin to her, his biggest weakness. And now he felt desperate to build everything back up so no one else could see.

So that he was strong again.

So that nothing could touch him.

He strode out of his room and walked down the corridor, toward the room where the marriage would take place. It was far too hot to marry outside. They could have done so if they were by the oasis, or the ocean, but he hadn't seen the point in taking the trip out to the oasis.

He walked inside the room and looked at the guests, seated and ready. He strode down the aisle, completely deaf to the music, the faces of everyone present blurring. He had no family, so there was no one of real importance.

He took his position, his hands clasped in front of his body and waited. Only a few moments later, Samarah appeared in the doorway. She had an ornate gold band over her head, a veil of white and embroidered gold covering her head. Her gown was white, a mix of Western and Eastern traditions.

She looked like a bride. She looked like a woman who deserved to have a man waiting for her who wasn't so terribly broken.

But she did not have that. She had him. And he wondered if he'd truly spared her anything when he'd offered her marriage to him instead of prison.

She approached the raised platform and took his hand, dark eyes never wavering. He was shaking to pieces inside, and she looked as smooth and steady as ever.

The ceremony passed in a blur. He had no memory of what he said. Of what she said. Only that they were married in the end. Only that Samarah was his wife, till death ended it, and he could feel nothing but guilt.

He could give her nothing. He wouldn't. Opening himself up like that could only end in destruction.

They walked through the crowd of guests together, and he didn't know if people clapped for them or not.

"I need to talk to you," Samarah said, as soon as they were in the hall.

And he knew there was no denying her when she'd set her mind to something. Not really. She was far too determined.

"We have a wedding feast to get to."

"It can wait."

"People are hungry," he said.

"It can start without us. I have a question for you."

"I didn't agree to more questions."

Samarah tugged him down the corridor and into a private sitting room, closing the doors behind them. "I don't care if you've agreed. Here is my question. Do you know why I married you?"

"To avoid prison. To secretly plot my death? To gain your position back as sheikha."

"The first moment I agreed, yes, it was to avoid prison. And after that? To plot your doom. Then when I let that go, to become a sheikha and have a future that wasn't so bleak. But that was all why I was planning on marrying you weeks ago. Do you know why I married you today?" she asked.

"I'm damn certain I don't," he said.

"I didn't, either. I thought…well, I used all of those reasons. Until this morning. I was getting ready and I realized how much I missed you. Not just the pleasure, and you do give me that, but you. You're…grumpy, and you're hard to talk to. But you also tried to make me smile. No one else ever has. I dance for you. For you and no one else, because you make me feel like I want to dance. You've given my life layers, a richness it never had before. And I figured out, as I was going to make vows to you, what that richness is."

"What is it?" he asked, his throat tight, his body tense.

"I love you," she said. "I do. I am…in love with you."

"Samarah, no."

"Yes. I am. And you can't tell me no because it doesn't make it less true."

"You don't know what you're saying," he said.

"I do. I married you today because you're the man I want to be with. Because if you opened the palace doors and told me I could go anywhere, I would stay with you."

"And I married you not knowing you were going to say such a ridiculous thing. Did you not hear what I told you? I could end you, Samarah. What if I did? What if I lose control…"

"My father is responsible for it. I'm not listening to this nonsense."

"You're wrong, Samarah."

"Why are you so desperate to believe this?"

"Because it is truth," he said. "And I will never…I will never take the chance on failing like that again."

"Well, what does that have to do with me loving you?"

"I don't want your love. I can't have it—do you understand?"

"Too late."

"This was a mistake," he said.

"And it is also too late for you to have those concerns. We are married. And you know there is every possibility I could have a child. We've never taken precautions in all of our time together."

"I'm not divorcing you. Don't be so dramatic."

"You're rejecting my love and I haven't threatened to kill you. Considering our past history I'm not being overdramatic. I'm not even being…dramatic."

He gritted his teeth, pain burning in his chest, a low, painful smolder. "I don't want your love. I don't love you, Samarah, and I won't."

"What?"

"I'm not loving anyone. Never again."

"But everything that we've… You wanted to see me smile."

"That's not love, *habibti*. That's a guilty conscience. I don't have love, but I do have guilt in spades."

"What about our children?"

Pain lanced at him, the smoldering ember catching fire and bursting into flame in his chest. "I don't have it in me.

What could I offer them? A father whose hands have stolen a life? A father who loses all humanity with his rage."

"Coward," she said. "You're right. You are weak, but not for the reasons you mean. You're just hiding. You're still just hiding."

"I stopped hiding. I took revenge, remember?"

She shook her head. "No. Part of you stayed back there. Hidden. You've been out here fighting ever since, but you left your soul behind."

"For good reason. It's too late for me. I'm sorry you want more than I can give." He stepped forward, cupping her cheek. He swept his thumb over her silken skin, pain shooting through him. He had a feeling this would be the last time he touched her for a very long time. "This is never going to be a real marriage."

Samarah stumbled back. "Say it again," she said.

"I don't love you."

A sob worked through her body, her hands shaking. "No. Of course not. No one ever has… Why should you be the first?"

"Samarah…you do not love me. You're a prisoner. You've had no one in your life, so you think you love me, but you've been fooled. I did put you in jail today. A life sentence. And because of the nature of things, going back now would be foolish."

"Do not tell me what I feel!"

"You need to be told. If you think you can love a man like me? If you think this is what love is, offering you a life of captivity behind bars or captivity in my bed, then you need to be told!"

"That isn't what you've done. You're just afraid. You're afraid of—"

"I do not fear you. I would have to care first."

She reeled back, her hands shaking. "I'm going to go," she said.

"We have a feast to get to."

"I don't care. I'm going to…I need to go."

She needed some space. She needed to catch her breath. She'd been right the other day. She and Ferran could never have normal. They could never have happy.

The blinding flash of joy she'd felt today when she'd realized she loved him was gone now. In that moment she'd believed that loving him would be enough. That if she loved him, regardless of what he thought about himself, it could work.

But she'd been naive. She'd never loved anyone before, and she'd felt so powerful in the moment that she'd been convinced it could conquer everything. But it hadn't. It wouldn't.

Looking back into Ferran's blank, flat black eyes she knew it.

He had chosen to hold on to the past. He had chosen to stay behind his walls. And as long as that was what he wanted, there would be no reaching him.

"I can't go to the wedding feast alone," he said, his voice raw.

"And I can't sit next to a man who's just rejected my love. I won't. Don't worry—I'm not going to kill you," she said, turning away from him and heading to the door. "I'll just leave you to wallow in your misery. And I do believe that eventually you'll feel misery, even if it's not now. We could have had something. We could have had a life. As it is, I'm going to try and have one. I'm not sure what you're going to do."

She turned away from him, not wanting him to see her break. Loving always involved loss, and right now was no exception.

She'd just spoken vows to stay with Ferran forever, and in almost the same moment, she'd lost any hope she had of forging a real bond with him.

She was a married woman now, in a palace. With servants and beautiful gowns and a man who would share her bed. And she felt more alone than she ever had in her life.

Ferran hadn't realized she'd meant she was leaving. Samarah wasn't anywhere in the palace. She wasn't in his chamber, she wasn't in hers.

Panic raged through him. Had she gone? She was his wife. She had nowhere else to go. He tore at the collar on his tunic, hardly able to breathe.

He'd gone to the feast and made excuses for her being sick, and when everyone had gone, he'd discovered this.

If she had gone, he should be pleased. He should not hold her to him. To a man who might destroy her. Not knowing she was here because of coercion, whatever she said now.

And yet the thought of losing her…

"Lydia!" He entered the servants' quarters, shouting.

Lydia appeared from the dining area, her eyes wide. "Yes, Your Highness?"

"Where is my wife?"

"You do not know?"

"I don't know or I would not have asked, obviously. Do not insult me," he growled. He was being cruel, and he knew it. But he was desperate. Panicked. For a woman he did not love.

Because of course he didn't love her. He couldn't love her.

He didn't deserve her.

It was his life. No matter what he thought, no matter how controlled he was, he hurt the people in it. He saw that now. With blinding clarity.

With all his prized control, he had held a woman captive. He had forced her into marriage.

"Where is my wife?" he repeated.

"She went to your oasis. I helped her pack. She said she

needed some time away." Lydia's eyes were serious and slightly judging.

He gritted his teeth. Damn that woman. "Thank you," he bit out, turning and walking away.

He paused in the doorway, his hand on his chest. He thought he might be dying. Or maybe that was just what it felt like when your heart tried to beat against a brick wall.

He wasn't sure what scared him more. That the wall would hold…or that it might finally break for good.

After two days away, Samarah's head didn't feel any clearer. She was just wandering through the tent, such as it was, thinking about Ferran. All he'd been through. The way her father had twisted his caring. The way he'd been made to feel responsible for an insane man's secrets.

She paused at the doorway of the bedroom, her fingers tracing the woodgrain on the door as she stared out the window at the water beyond.

Had she ever offered to make Ferran smile?

She didn't think she had. He'd given her so much, and in the end, he'd been too afraid to give it all, but she could understand why. She turned into the doorway and rested her face in her hand, stifling the sob that rose in her throat.

She hadn't cried in so long before Ferran. But he made her want more. The wanting was complicated. It wasn't all blind determination and a will to live. It was a deep, emotional need that she was sure at this point was overrated.

She wanted him so much.

She wanted him to love her.

She wanted to make him smile.

Samarah lifted her head. She shouldn't be here, hiding from him. Seeking refuge from reality. From him.

And she'd accused him of being a coward.

She'd held on to her anger toward him for years. With no contribution from him. With no action from him. No confirmation that he even deserved it, and yet she'd been willing to commit the ultimate sin for that anger.

Shouldn't she love him just as much? Shouldn't she love him no matter what he gave back? No matter if he loved her? Wasn't that real love?

Pain lanced her chest. Yes, she wanted him to love her back. But if she truly loved him—and she did—it didn't matter what he said. She was no prisoner. He was behaving as though she was weak, and she was not weak.

She had to tell him that.

She had to go back.

She pushed away from the door and turned around, immediately falling into a fighting stance when she saw the man in white standing there.

She relaxed when she was able to focus on his face. "Ferran?"

He took a step closer to her, the look on his face unsettled. "I came for you," he said, his voice unsteady.

"I'm sorry. I was about to come home."

"No. Do not apologize. I had to release the past's hold on me before I could come to you. I think…I think that this was the best place for me to do this."

"To do what?" she asked.

"I am afraid," he said. "I told myself it was because I had held you captive. Because I am a monster and if I do not keep control I could easily make the same mistakes I had made before."

"I don't believe it."

"I know," he said. "And…I do not deserve your confidence."

"You do."

"You can leave," he said. "I will release you from this marriage. From me. I will give you whatever you need to start a new life. All of your decisions are your own. You have options. Live life. Live it apart from me."

She stepped nearer to him, her heart pounding hard. "Don't you understand? You're the life I've chosen. You're the one I've chosen."

"I can't believe that," he said, his dark eyes haunted. "At my core, I am a murderer."

"No," she said, putting her hand on his face. "You're a survivor. I recognize it. Because it is what I am, too. We have survived the unimaginable. And you know what? It would have broken other people. We aren't broken."

"I am," he said.

"Only because you're too afraid to put yourself back together."

"I am," he said. "Because there is every chance it would reveal a monster."

"There are no monsters here," she said, looking around the room. "Not anymore. And we don't have to let them rule our life anymore. I am not my father. I am not my mother. I am Sheikha Samarah Bashar. My allegiance is to you."

"I don't feel I can accept your allegiance," he said.

"Do not insult me by rejecting it. Not when you already insulted me by rejecting my love."

"I don't seek to insult you. It is…this is the only way I know to love you," he said. "And I find that I do. But I want to be sure that you want to be with me. That you have chosen it. Not because you are a captive. I want… If you choose to stay, I want to be able to trust I can give you passion. That I can give you everything. And you will want it. Not just feel trapped into it."

"Oh, Ferran." She wrapped her arms around his neck and pulled him close, kissing him, deep and long. "I love you, too."

"I do not deserve it," he said, his voice rough.

"I tried to kill you. I don't exactly deserve your love, either."

"Samarah…I don't trust myself."

She stepped back, then reached down and took his hand in hers, lifting it to her throat. "I do," she said. "I have witnessed your character. The way you treated your would-be assassin. I have heard the story of how you avenged your mother. How much you must have loved her to be so enraged. You are a man of great and beautiful passion."

"I have never seen passion as beautiful."

"Neither did I. Before you." She pressed his hand more firmly against her neck. "Would you ever harm me?"

"Never," he said, his voice rough, his touch gentle. "Our children…"

"I know you wouldn't. And you will never harm our children. I know your hands have had blood on them. Blood from the avenging of those you love. Ferran, you would never harm your family. But you would kill for them if it ever came down to it. You would die for them. And there is no shame in that."

"I…I never saw it that way."

"I see it. Because I see you. You are a warrior. As am I. Together we can face whatever terrible things come."

"I've always been afraid that *I* was a terrible thing."

"There was a time when I thought you were, and I very nearly became terrible, too. But you saved me."

"We saved each other."

"There will always be ugliness in the world, Ferran, but loving you is the most beautiful thing that's ever happened in my life. We have something beautiful for the first time." A tear rolled down her cheek and splashed onto his hand. "Don't fear your passion. I want it. I crave it."

"You make me treasure it," he said. "Something I never imagined possible. You told me once that you found a passion for breathing when breathing was all you had. That your desire for revenge was a passion that kept you going. That's what it felt like when you left. I breathed for you. For the one thing that mattered. And then I knew. That this was love. That it was worth anything to claim. That you were worth anything. That I would have to give you the choice to leave even though I wanted you to stay. That I would have to expose myself even though I feared what was inside me. Every wall inside me is broken down, for you. I would rather stand here with you, exposed and vulnerable, than spend the rest of my life protected without you."

"Oh, Ferran…I'm so glad I chose you instead of prison."

He laughed and her heart lifted. "I'm glad, too. It's nice to be preferable to a dungeon."

"You smiled," she said.

"So did you," he said.

"You give me so many reasons to smile."

"And I promise to continue to, every day."

EPILOGUE

THERE WAS SOMETHING incredible about the fact that he and Samarah had created a life together. After so much loss, so much pain, they had brought something new into the world.

Ferran looked down at his son, cradled in his mother's arms, and he felt his heart expand. He reached down, running his fingers along Samarah's flushed cheek. "I will never take for granted that I have you here," he said. "Because I remember a moment when I thought I was touching you for the last time."

She looked up at him and smiled. "You have a lot of years of touching ahead of you," she said.

"And thank God for it. I would like to hold my son," he said, his throat tightening as he looked at the baby in her arms.

"Of course."

He bent down and took the swaddled bundle from her. He was so tiny, so fragile. And she was trusting him with him. Just as she trusted herself to him, and had done for the past year. "He is perfect," Ferran said.

"I know," she said, smiling.

"Who would have thought your revenge would end this way?" he asked. "The creation of a life, instead of the end of one."

"Two lives," she said, smiling. "I feel like my life became so much more that day. It became life instead of survival."

"Three then," he said, running his finger over his son's cheek. "Because I was frozen in time until you came back to me. And now…now my life has truly begun."

* * * * *

A FORBIDDEN AFFAIR

YVONNE LINDSAY

To the memory of Sandra Hyde (writing as Sandra Hyatt) and the legacy of her friendship.

One

Nicole's hands shook uncontrollably as she tried to fit her key into the ignition. Damn, she dropped it again. She swiped the key ring up off the floor of her classic Benz, and gave up driving as a bad joke. If she couldn't even get the key in the ignition, how on earth did she expect to drive?

She got out of the car, slammed the door hard and swiped her cell phone from her bag. Thank goodness she'd had the presence of mind to grab the designer leather pouch from the hall table after her grand exit from the family dinner to end all family dinners.

Her high heels clipped a staccato beat as she marched down the well-lit driveway of her family home to the street, calling a taxi service as she went. Fine tremors shook her body as she waited for the car to arrive. The chill air of the autumn night made her glad she hadn't had a chance to change out of her tailored wool suit when she'd arrived home from work earlier.

Her father had requested that she dress up for dinner in honor of a special announcement he'd planned to make, but by the time she'd gotten home, there just hadn't been enough time. She hadn't thought her father would mind that she'd chosen to put in the extra time at the office instead of rushing home to get ready. After all, if anyone should understand her drive to devote her time and energy to Wilson Wines then surely it would be Charles Wilson, founder and CEO. Her father had invested most of his life into the business he had built, and she'd always intended to follow in his footsteps.

Until tonight.

Another rush of anger infused her. How dare her father belittle her like that, and in front of a virtual stranger, as well? Who cared if that stranger was her long-lost brother, Judd. Two and a half decades after their parents' bitter divorce had split their family in half, what right did he have to come back and lay claim to the responsibilities that were supposed to be *hers?* She clenched her jaw tight and bit back the scream of frustration that threatened to claw its way out of her throat. She couldn't lose it now. Not when she had just discovered that she was the only person she had left to rely on.

Even her best friend, colleague and life-long confidante, Anna, had shown her true colors when she'd arrived home in New Zealand from Adelaide, Australia, late last week with Judd in tow. Sure, she'd tried to convince Nicole that she'd only been following Charles's orders to find Judd and bring about a reconciliation, but Nicole knew where Anna's loyalties lay, and they certainly weren't with her. If they were,

Anna wouldn't have kept the truth from her about what Charles planned to use as Judd's incentive.

A painful twist in her chest reminded her to draw in a breath but despite the fact she obeyed her body's demand to refill her lungs, the pain of betrayal by her best friend—the woman she loved like a sister—still lingered. How *could* Anna have known what was going to happen and not given her prior warning?

In her bag, her phone began to chirp insistently. Thinking it might be the taxi company calling back to confirm her details, she lifted it to her ear and answered it.

"Nicole, where are you? Are you okay?"

Anna. Who else? It certainly wouldn't be her father calling to see if she was all right.

"I'm fine," Nicole answered, her voice clipped.

"You're not fine, you're upset. I can hear it in your voice. Look, I'm sorry about tonight—"

"Just tonight, Anna? What about your trip to Adelaide? What about bringing my brother home for the first time in twenty-five years, so he could take everything that was ever mine away from me?" Even Anna's gasp of pain at Nicole's accusations didn't stop Nicole's tirade or do anything to lessen the hurt of betrayal that rocketed through her veins right now. "I thought we were friends, sisters by *choice,* remember?"

"I couldn't tell you what Charles had planned, Nicole. Please believe me. Your dad swore me to secrecy and I owe him so very much. Without his support of me and my mum…you know what he was like…even when she was dying—"

"His support, huh?" Nicole shut her eyes tight and squeezed back the fresh round of tears that fought to escape. "What about your support of me?"

"You always have that, Nic, you know that."

"Really? Then why didn't you give me a heads-up? Why didn't you tell me that he was going to bribe Judd to stay by giving him my home as well as the business?"

"Only half the business," Anna's voice came quietly over the line.

"A controlling share, Anna. That's the whole business as far as I'm concerned."

The shock of her father's announcement had been bad enough. Worse was the way he'd justified the decision to give everything to Judd instead of her. *Just you wait,* he had said, *you'll find some young man who'll sweep you off your feet and before I know it you will be married and raising a family. Wilson Wines will just be a hobby for you.* Years of hard work, of dedication and commitment to the business and to further her father's plans and dreams dismissed as just a *phase,* a passing fad. The thought of it made her blood boil.

"Dad made it quite clear where I stand in all this, and by aligning yourself with him, you've made it quite clear where you stand, too."

Nicole paced back and forth on the pavement at the end of the driveway, filled with a nervous energy that desperately needed an outlet. Anna's voice remained steady in her ear; the sound of her friend's voice was usually a calming influence but tonight it was anything but.

"He put me in an impossible position, Nic. I begged him to talk to you about this, to at least tell you that Judd would be coming home."

"Obviously you didn't beg hard enough. Or, here's something to consider, maybe you could have just told me, anyway. You could have picked up a phone or fired me an email in warning. It's not that hard to do. You had to know what this would mean to me, how much it would hurt me. And still you did nothing?"

"I'm so sorry, Nic. If I could do it over I'd do it differently, you have to know that."

"I don't know anything anymore, Anna. That's the trouble. Everything I've worked for, everything I've lived for, has just been handed to a man I don't even know. I don't even know if I have a roof over my head now that Dad's given the deed of the family house to Judd. How would that make *you* feel? Have you asked yourself that?"

A sweep of lights coming down the road heralded the taxi she'd summoned, and not a moment too soon. She had enough dander up right now to march back on up the driveway and give her father a piece of her mind all over again—for whatever good it would do.

"Look," she continued, "I've got to go. I need some space right now to think things over."

"Nicole, come back. Let's talk this out face-to-face."

"No," Nicole answered as the cab pulled up alongside the curb. "I'm done talking. Please don't call me again."

She disconnected the call and switched off her phone for good measure before throwing it into the bottom of her bag.

"Viaduct Basin," she instructed as she got into the taxi and settled in the darkened interior with her equally dark thoughts.

Hopefully the vibrant atmosphere at the array of bars and clubs in downtown Auckland would provide her with the distraction she needed. Nicole repaired her tear-stained makeup as well as she could with the limited cosmetics in her bag. It annoyed the heck out of her that anger, for her, usually resulted in tears, as well. It was an awkward combination that plagued her on the rare occasions she actually lost her temper, and it made it hard for her to be taken seriously.

She willed her hand to be steady as she applied a rich red lip gloss and gave herself a final check in her compact mirror.

Satisfied she'd done her best with her makeup, she sat back against the soft upholstery of the luxury taxi and tried to ignore the echo of her father's words, the faintly smug paternal tone that seemed to say that she'd soon get over her temper tantrum and realize he was right all along.

"Over my dead body," she muttered.

"Pardon, miss, what was that you said?" the neatly suited taxi driver asked over his shoulder.

"Nothing, sorry, just talking to myself."

She shook her head and blinked hard at the fresh tears that pricked in her eyes. In doing what her father had done he'd permanently damaged his relationship with her, fractured the trust between her and Anna, and virtually destroyed any chance of her and Judd building a sibling bond together. She had no family she could rely on anymore—not her father, her brother, her sister and certainly not her mother. Nicole had not seen or heard from her mother since Cynthia Masters-Wilson had taken Judd back to her native Australia when he was six and Nicole only one year old.

Nicole had long since convinced herself she'd never wanted to know her mother growing up. Her father had been everything and everyone she'd ever needed. But even as a child, she'd always been able to tell that she wasn't enough to make up for the wife and son that her father still missed. It had driven Nicole to work harder, to be a top student and to learn everything she could about the family business, in the hopes of winning her father's approval, making him proud. Goodness only knew running Wilson Wines was all she'd ever wanted to do from the moment she'd understood just what held the balance of her father's attention every day.

Now that Judd was back, it was as if she didn't exist anymore. As if she never had.

Nicole reached up to remove the hair tie that had held her hair in its no-nonsense, businesslike pony-tail all day, and shoved her fingers through her hair to tousle it out into party mode. She would not let her father's actions beat her. Once she'd worked this upset out of her system she'd figure out a way to fix things. Until then, she was going to enjoy herself.

She alighted from the taxi and paid the driver then undid the top button of her suit jacket, exposing a glimpse of the gold-and-black satin-and-lace bra she wore beneath it. There, she thought defiantly, from business woman to party girl in one easy step. Squaring her shoulders, Nicole headed into the first bar on the strip. Oblivion had never looked better.

Nate leaned against the bar and watched the pulsing throng of bodies on the dance floor with disinterest. He'd only agreed to come along tonight for Raoul's sake. Hosting the guy's stag party was small recompense for the work Raoul had done holding Jackson Importers together after Nate's father's sudden death last year. Knowing the running of the business was in Raoul's very capable hands until Nate could return to New Zealand to pick up the reins had been a massive relief. Extricating himself from Jackson Importers' European office and appointing a replacement there had taken time, and he owed the guy big for stepping up to the plate.

His philanthropy didn't assuage his boredom, however, and Nate was on the verge of saying his goodbyes and making his way home when she caught his eye. The woman moved on the dance floor with a sensuous grace that sent a spiraling swell of primal male interest through his body. She was dressed as if she'd come from the office, although he'd never seen any of his staff look that good in a suit. Her jacket was unbuttoned just enough to give a tantalizing view of creamy feminine swells of flesh supported by sexy black satin and gold lace, and while her skirt wasn't exactly short, her long legs and spiky heels certainly made it look that way.

He felt a familiar twinge in his groin. All of a sudden, heading out to his home on the ocean side of the Waitakere Ranges wasn't his top priority anymore—at least not immediately and, hopefully, not alone.

Nate cut through the throng of seething bodies to get nearer. There was something familiar about her but he couldn't place it immediately. Her long dark hair swung around her face as she moved to the beat of the music and he imagined it swinging in other areas, gliding over his body. Oh, yes, definitely gliding over his body—or even spread across the starkness of his Egyptian cotton sheets while he glided across hers. He clenched and unclenched his jaw as every cell in his body responded to the visual image.

He let the beat of the music infuse him and eased in beside her. "Hi, can I join in?" he asked with a smile.

"Sure," she replied, before flicking her hair from her face and exposing dark eyes a man could lose himself in, and a delectably red-painted mouth that was made for pure sin.

They danced awhile, their bodies moving in synchronicity—close, but not touching. The air between them was incendiary. Would they move in such unison alone together, too?

Another dancer jostled past, knocking her against his chest. His hands whipped up to steady her and she looked up into his eyes with a smile that started slowly before spreading wide.

"My hero," she said, with a wicked gleam in her dark eyes.

He found his mouth curving in response. "I can be whatever you want me to be," he said, bending his head slightly and putting his mouth to the shell of her ear.

She quivered in his arms. "Anything?"

"Anything."

"Thank you," she said, so softly he almost couldn't hear her over the noise around them. "I could do with a dose of *anything* right now."

She draped her arms over his shoulders, the fingers of one hand playing with his hair where it sat at the nape of his neck. Her touch did crazy things to him. Things that made him want to do nothing more than take her out of here and transport her to his home, his bed.

Nate wasn't into one-night stands. Aside from the fact his mother had drilled respect for women into him from an early age, he'd never been that kind of guy. Nate liked to plan, to calculate all the angles—spontaneity wasn't really his strong suit, especially in his private life. He knew how important it was to be cautious, to keep people at a distance until you were sure of their motives. But there was something about the girl in his arms that made him want to take a chance.

He looked down into her face and recognition began to dawn. Suddenly he knew why she'd seemed familiar. She was Nicole Wilson—none other than Charles Wilson's daughter, and the second in command at Wilson Wines. Her picture had been in the dossier of information he'd asked Raoul to gather on the competition's business—and most especially on the man who had once been his father, Thomas's, closest and oldest friend. Charles Wilson, who had—after an angry row, rife with false accusations—subsequently become Thomas's bitterest rival.

Once, when he'd been a turbulent teen, Nate had promised his father he'd seek revenge for what Charles Wilson had done. Thomas, ever the peacemaker, had told him he was to do no such thing while Thomas still drew breath. Sadly now, his father was dead—not so sadly, all bets, in relation to Charles Wilson, were off.

Nate wasn't normally one to deliver on the sins of the father, but tonight's potential now took on a whole other edge. He'd been biding his time with Charles Wilson. Accumulating information, and planning his strategy carefully. But even if it hadn't been part of his plans, he wasn't about to ignore the opportunity that had just dropped into his arms.

A waft of Nicole's fragrance drifted off her heated body and teased his nose. The scent was rich and spicy, very much, he suspected, like the woman he held—their bodies moving in unison, undulating to the beat of the music that thrummed around them.

Nate didn't hide the arousal he felt for her. What was the point? If this didn't work out, then there'd be no foul. His plans would carry on regardless. But if it did, if she was responding to him the same way he reacted to her, his plans for revenge against Charles Wilson would take a very interesting turn indeed.

Nicole knew she'd had too much to drink tonight, and she knew full well that she should call another taxi to take her home. After all, it was only Thursday and she still had work tomorrow. At least, she thought she still had work tomorrow.

Thinking about work made her head hurt and the idea of returning to the house tonight just tied her stomach in knots and reminded her again of her father's low opinion of her. Earlier, she'd blocked out that reminder with a shot, and then another, egged on by a group of acquaintances she'd barely seen since she'd graduated from university and whom she could hardly call friends. Still, their lively and undemanding company tonight had been just what she sought. No questions, no answers. Just being lost in the moment. And right at this moment she was feeling very lost indeed. Lost in the undeniable attraction between two healthy young people in their prime.

Very little separated her and her dance partner and as her lower body brushed against him again, a classic Mae West line ran through her alcohol-clouded mind. She couldn't stifle the giggle that bubbled up from inside.

"Care to share the joke?"

She pressed her lips together and shook her head. There was no way she was sharing that little snippet.

"Then you have to pay a forfeit—you know that, don't you?"

"A forfeit?" she asked, her lips spreading into a

smile once more. "Surely you can't punish a girl for being happy?"

"I wasn't thinking of a punishment," he said.

She should be laughing at the line he'd just uttered, she told herself, yet, for some reason, a wicked coil of lust tightened inside her.

"Oh?" she managed through lips that she suddenly felt the urge to moisten with the tip of her tongue. "What were you thinking of?"

"This," he said.

She didn't have time to think, or room to move had she even wanted to dodge him, as he lowered his lips to hers. Lips that were unexpectedly cool and firm. Lips that sampled, tasted and teased her own.

The tight sensation inside her spread, tingling through her body like a slow-building charge of electricity, sensitizing her hidden places, draining her mind of any awareness of her surroundings. All she could think of, all she *wanted* to think of, was the touch of his mouth on hers. Of the delicious pressure of his body as his hands on her hips gathered her closer.

They continued to move to the music—her pelvis rolling against his, her awareness of his arousal becoming a hunger for more than the illicit touch of bodies through clothing. A moan built deep in her throat, a moan she fought to keep inside as he lifted his mouth from hers.

She swallowed and opened her eyes. In this light it was difficult to tell what color his eyes were, but they were definitely unusual and their hooded stare captured her and held her mesmerized. Didn't certain beasts of prey do the same? Was she about to be devoured? The thought didn't upset her as much as it should. God, she had to pull herself together.

"So, that's a forfeit, huh?" she asked, her voice thick with desire.

"It's just one of many."

"Intriguing."

Intriguing wasn't the word. His kiss had totally fried her synapses. It was all she could do to prevent herself from dragging his face down to hers again and repeating the experience. Once more with feeling, she thought, although she certainly hadn't been devoid of feeling while he'd been kissing her. For that moment in time she'd forgotten everything. Who she was, why she was here, what she had left to look forward to.

She'd liked that. She'd liked it a whole lot. She wanted to do it again.

"Hey, Nic!"

One of her acquaintances, Amy, appeared at her side and her dance partner released her. She instantly rued the loss of contact.

Her friend shouted to be heard over the music. "We're off to another club, you coming?"

Nicole's usual prudence screamed "safety in numbers" at the back of her mind, but tonight she wasn't in the mood to be prudent at all.

"No, I'm fine. I'll get a taxi home later."

"Okay. Hey, it was cool catching up again. Let's not leave it so long next time."

And then Amy was gone with the crowd she'd been hanging with.

"Are you sure you didn't want to go with your friends?" her dance partner asked.

"No, I'm fine. I'm a big girl, I can look after myself," Nicole answered.

"I'm pleased to hear it. I'm Nate, by the way."

"Nicole," she answered shortly, happy to keep their

introductions brief as she threw herself back into the thrum and energy of the DJ's latest sound selection.

She was distracted by the flash of someone's camera, no doubt someone's shenanigans would be broadcast on some social networking site tomorrow, but before long her focus was solely on the man in front of her. Boy, but he could move. Some guys just looked as if they were trying too hard on the dance floor but for him, movement came very naturally. And he was so good to look at, too.

His hair was dark, but not as dark as her near-black tresses, and his face was both masculine and had a refined elegance at the same time. And those lips—she was very keen for a repeat of what they had to offer.

"Do I pass muster?" he asked, one corner of his mouth twisting upward.

She smiled in response. "You'll do."

He laughed and the sound went straight to her toes, making them curl in delight. Was there anything about him that wasn't gorgeous?

The crowd around them had begun to thin and Nicole started to become aware that eventually this night would have to end. At about that point she'd be feeling the pain of dancing in high heels for several hours, along with the aftereffects of too much to drink. She hated that reality had to intrude again, especially when she was having such a good time. Nate said something, but over the frenetic pulse of the music she didn't quite make it out.

"What was that you said?" Nicole asked, leaning closer.

Mmm, he even smelled great—like a cool ocean breeze.

"I said, would you like a drink?"

She'd probably had quite enough for one night but an imp of mischief prompted her to nod her head.

"Here? Or we could head back to my place if you'd rather."

She felt a frisson of excitement. Was he suggesting what she thought he was suggesting? She'd never done this before—gone back to some random guy's house for a drink, at least not without a posse of friends with her. But for some reason she felt as if she could trust Nate, and then there was that amazing energy between them. She deserved to find out if those sparks were real, didn't she? Wouldn't it be some solace for the night she'd put up with?

"Your place is fine."

Actually, anywhere but home was fine.

"Great." He smiled, the action sending a sizzle of anticipation thrilling through her veins.

Sore feet and the prospect of a hangover were the furthest things from her mind as Nate took her hand and led her toward the exit. And if thoughts of "danger" or "risk" occurred to her, she brushed them aside. Tonight was a night for taking chances.

And besides, what was the worst that could happen?

Two

Nate caught Raoul's eye as he led Nicole away, giving his friend a nod. He briefly saw Raoul's answering wink before the expression on the other man's face changed to one of shocked recognition. Nate fought back the smug smile that pulled at his lips.

In all the years he'd spent imagining how he would bring Charles Wilson to his knees, he'd never once imagined this scenario. But then, he'd never imagined taking Charles Wilson's daughter in his arms and feeling such a searing sense of attraction, either. With such a ripe opportunity before him, he'd be a fool not to make the most of it—in every way possible. Still, he had to be careful. It wouldn't do to put the cart before the horse. He could just as easily be calling a taxi to take Nicole home after their drink, but something inside him told him that was very unlikely.

He reached in his pocket and pressed the remote to

the low-slung silver Maserati that waited for them at the curb.

"Very pretty car," Nicole commented as he held open the passenger door for her and she folded her delicious long legs into the passenger bay.

"I like to travel in style," he answered with a smile.

"I like that in a man," she answered, her lips curving in response.

He just bet she did. She'd never wanted for anything and every part of her life had been to the highest standard. It stood to reason that Nicole Wilson's demands of her men would be high. It was a gauntlet he relished picking up.

Unlike Nicole, Nate knew what it was like to struggle—his father had been a living example of the concept for most of Nate's childhood. After Charles Wilson had kicked him out of the business they'd built together, it had taken years for Thomas to reestablish his credibility and build a company of his own. Nate had watched as his father poured his everything into his fledgling business in an attempt to provide something, anything, to the woman he'd accidentally gotten pregnant and the son their liaison had borne. And while Thomas had done his best to shield his only child, the experience had left its mark, resulting in two rules that Nate had lived his life by ever since. Rule one: be very careful who you trust.

Rule two: all's fair in love and war.

Nate slid into the driver's seat and started the car, maneuvering it smoothly toward Hobson Street and the entrance to the North Western motorway.

"You're a Westie?" Nicole asked.

"After a fashion," he answered. "I have a couple of

places. Karekare is where I call home. You still want that drink at my place?"

His challenge hung between them in the dark interior of the car. He shot her a glance and saw her press her lips together and swallow before answering.

"I'm all good. I haven't been out to Karekare in ages."

"It's still pretty much the same. Wild and beautiful."

"Like you?" she asked, her eyes gleaming as she shot him a glance.

"I was thinking more along the lines of you."

She laughed, the sound filling the cabin of his car and making his gut tighten in anticipation.

"Oh, you're good. You know all the right things to say to salve a wounded soul."

"Wounded?" he probed.

"Just family stuff. Too complicated and too boring to bring up now," she hedged.

Was all no longer well in the Wilson household? Nate wondered. He'd made it his business to know what happened within Wilson Wines and he'd heard of the return of the prodigal son. Had Judd Wilson's arrival served to uplift the mantel of golden child off Nicole's shoulders?

"We have a long drive," Nate pointed out as they entered the motorway and his car picked up speed. "I'm willing to listen if you want to talk about it."

"Just the usual," she said with an attempt at flippancy. An attempt that failed judging by the tone of her voice.

"Sounds serious," he commented, keeping his eyes looking forward out the windscreen.

She sighed, the sound coming from somewhere deep

down inside her. “I had a fight with my dad. At the risk of sounding clichéd, he doesn’t understand me.”

“Isn’t that a parental prerogative?”

She laughed, a short, sharp sound in total contrast to the last time she’d done so. “I suppose so. I just feel so used, you know? I have spent my whole life trying to measure up, to be the best daughter, the best workmate, the best—well, everything. And he thinks I should settle down and have *babies!* As if. You know, I think he values a paper clip on his desk more highly than he does me. I’ve spent the past five years helping him to keep our family business thriving and he tells me it’s a nice *hobby* for me.”

“I suppose this argument is what led you to the club tonight?”

“Too right it is. I couldn’t stay under his roof another second. Oh, no, wait. It’s not *his* roof anymore, nor mine. He’s gone and given it all to my dear long-lost brother.” She expelled an angry huff of air. “I’m sorry, I’m always letting my mouth run away with me. I shouldn’t have said that. Just pretend you didn’t hear that last bit, okay? I think we should change the subject. Talking about my family is just going to spoil my mood.”

“Whatever the lady wants, the lady gets,” Nate replied smoothly, even though his curiosity burned to know more about the Wilson family home situation.

“Now that’s more like it.” Nicole laughed in response. “A girl could get used to that attitude.”

“What, you mean that isn’t always the case?”

Nicole swiveled slightly in her seat and stared at him. “You say that as if you think you know me.”

“You misunderstand me,” he said smoothly. “I just

would have thought that a woman like you would have no trouble getting what she wanted."

She gave an inelegant snort, then change the subject. "Tell me about your home. Are you overlooking the beach?"

He nodded. Partly in concession to her change of subject and partly in answer to her question. "I'm on a slight rise looking out onto Union Bay."

"I've always loved the West Coast. The black sand beaches, the crazy surf. There's something so, I dunno, untamed, unpredictable about it all."

"You surf?"

She shook her head. "No, always been too chicken."

Somehow she didn't strike him as the type of woman to be afraid of anything, and he said as much.

"Some boundaries I just never pushed. I grew up as an only child with a parent who could be pretty strict. Sometimes my dad took overprotectiveness a little far."

"Only child? You mentioned a brother?"

"He lived with our mother up until recently. And how on earth did we get back on that awful topic again?"

She pushed a hand through her tangled long hair, exposing the sweep of her high cheekbones and the determined set of her jaw. His fingers itched to trace the fine bone structure, to taste the smooth skin that stretched over it. Nate tightened his grip once more, dragging his eyes back to the road and his mind back to the goal at hand. Yes, he wanted her. And yes, he had every intention of having her. But he couldn't let himself lose control. He had to keep the endgame in mind.

"What about you?" she asked, turning in her seat to look at him. "What's your family like?"

"Both my parents are gone. My mother while I was

in university, my dad more recently. I never had any brothers or sisters."

"So you're all alone? Lucky you." She gasped as if she realized the potentially pain-filled minefield she'd just trodden into. "I'm sorry, that was insensitive."

"No, it's okay. I miss them but I still count myself lucky to have had them both in my life. And my dad was a great role model. He worked his heart out, literally, to provide for us, and I got to repay that once I graduated and started working in the family firm."

Nate deliberately kept things vague. He wouldn't, for a moment, begin to elaborate on exactly why his father's health took such a beating as he strived to build a new business from the ground up. Or who was responsible for that.

"So, surfing?" he asked, very deliberately changing the subject as he took the exit he needed that would eventually lead them out toward the beach.

"What about it?"

"Want to try it over the weekend?"

"This weekend?"

"Sure, why not stay. I have spare boards, spare wetsuits."

"Spare clothes, underwear?" She gestured to her voluminous bag on the car floor. "It might be a big bag but it's hardly *Doctor Who's* TARDIS, you know."

Nate laughed. Her sharp wit was refreshing and appealing at the same time.

"Let's play it by ear then, hmm? Trust me?"

"Sure. If I didn't think I could trust you, I wouldn't be here."

He reached across and took her hand, caressing the soft skin of her inner wrist with his thumb.

"Good."

He let go and placed his fingers firmly back on the steering wheel. From the corner of his eye he saw that she stroked her wrist with the fingertips of her other hand. He allowed himself a small smile of satisfaction. This night was going perfectly.

So why *did* she trust him, she wondered as she lapsed into silence and looked idly out the passenger window. It's not as if she knew him. She'd acted purely on instinct, a fact that—despite her earlier assertion about being a chicken—had gotten her in trouble many a time before.

She gave herself a mental shake. She deserved this night. She had it coming to her after the crap she'd put up with at dinner on top of everything else this week. And everything in her body told her that this was the man to take all her problems away—at least for the night.

Her skin still tingled where he'd touched her, the sensation a delicious buzz of promise hovering just beneath the surface. Did he expect to make love to her tonight? Just the thought of it sent a thrill of longing through her body, making her womb clench tight on a swell of need that all but knocked the air from her lungs. She'd never had this intense a reaction to anyone before. Just sneaking a glance at his hands on the steering wheel, at the way his long fingers curled around the leather, made her want those fingers on her, in her. She pressed her thighs together and felt the swollen heated flesh at her core respond. Just thinking about him touching her was nearly enough to make her go off. What would it be like when he did?

She cleared her throat against the sudden anticipatory lump that lodged there.

"Everything okay?" Nate asked.

"Sure. It's quite a drive from the city to your place. Do you work in town?"

"Yeah. I keep an apartment there for the nights I'm too tired to make it back out to Karekare, or if I have an early run to the airport or early meetings. I sleep better with the sounds of the sea and the rainforest around me, though."

"Sounds idyllic."

"You'll see soon enough for yourself."

She fell silent as they entered Scenic Drive, letting her body sway with the roll of the car as they wound on the narrow ribbon of road higher into the ranges, before winding back down again on the other side. She must have dozed off a little because the next thing she knew the Maserati was driving up a steep incline and pulling into a well-lit garage. A glance at her watch said it was almost 2:00 a.m. The drive had taken nearly an hour. She was miles from anyone she knew, miles from home. She should find the fact daunting—she didn't. In fact, she welcomed it. Knew that with her choice to come home with Nate that she'd thrown her cares to the wind.

"Home sweet home," Nate said, coming around to her side of the car and opening the door for her.

Nicole accepted his hand as he helped her out the car, her senses purring at his touch. To her surprise he didn't let go, instead leading her to a doorway which, when opened, revealed a short set of stairs leading down into a massive open-plan living/dining and kitchen area.

The furnishings were comfortable but spoke plainly of their price in the elegantly simple designs and top-quality fabrics. A large, open fireplace, bordered with gray slate, occupied space on one wall. Even the artworks on the walls and small sculptures on the occasional shelving were beautiful and no doubt expensive. What he surrounded himself with said a lot about him and, so far, she liked it.

"Still feel like that drink?" Nate asked, lifting her hand to his lips and pressing a kiss against her knuckles.

"Sure, what are we having?"

"There's champagne in the fridge, or we could have a liqueur."

"A liqueur, I think."

Something potent and heady, just like him, she thought privately. Nate let her hand go and moved toward a built-in sideboard on the other side of the room. She gravitated toward the wall of glass that faced the inky darkness outside. Beyond the floor-to-ceiling windows she could hear the sound of waves rolling heavily into shore.

In the reflection of the glass she saw Nate come to stand behind her, one arm coming around to offer her a small glass of golden liquid.

"A toast, I think," he said, his breath warm in her hair and making her scalp prickle in awareness.

"To what in particular?" Nicole asked, accepting her glass and raising it toward Nate's pale facsimile mirrored before her.

"To wounded souls, and the healing of them."

She nodded and raised her glass to her lips, her taste buds reacting instantly to the smooth, sweet tang of aged malt whiskey. She allowed the liquid to stay on her tongue for a moment before swallowing.

"Now that is pretty fine," she said, turning to face Nate.

Her breath caught in her chest as she saw the look

in his eyes. Eyes that were only a shade darker than the deep gold fluid in their glasses.

"Only the best," he answered before closing the distance between their faces.

Nicole felt her heart race in her chest. If this kiss was to be anything like the one at the club she couldn't wait to experience it. Her lips parted expectantly, her gaze focused solely on the shape of his mouth, on the sheen left there by the liqueur. Her eyelids slid closed as she felt the warmth of him, as his lips took hers, as his tongue swept gently across the soft fullness of her lower lip.

He made a sound of appreciation. "Now that's what I call the best."

His lips pressed against hers once more and she curved into his body as one arm slid around her back and drew her closer to him. He was already aroused, a fact that triggered an insistent throb in her veins—a throb that went deeper into her center. She pressed her hips against him, feeling his length, his hardness. Feeling her body respond with heat and moisture and need.

She could taste the liqueur on his lips, on his tongue—its fusion of flavors intrinsically blended with his own. When he withdrew she felt herself move with him, toward him. Drawn as if by some magnetic force.

Nate put his liqueur glass on a shelf nearby before also taking hers and doing the same again. He then lifted his hands to her hair, pushing his fingers through the long mass until his fingertips massaged the back of her scalp, gently tilting her face to his once more. This time his kiss held a stronger taste of hunger, a promise of things to come.

Nicole tugged his shirt free of his waistband and

shoved her hands underneath, her nails gently scoring his back as she traced the line of his spine, up, then down. Logic tickled at the back of her mind a final time, telling her she shouldn't be here, shouldn't be doing this, but need and desire overcame logic with the same inexorable surge and release of the waves that echoed on the darkened shore outside.

He wanted her. She wanted him. It was basic and primal and it was all she needed for now. That, and a whole lot of satisfaction.

Nate's hand shifted to the buttons on her jacket, swiftly loosening them from their button holes and pushing aside the fabric, exposing her to him. His hands were broad and warm as they swept around the curve of her waist before skimming her rib cage and moving up toward her bra.

He rcleased her lips, bending his head lower, along her jaw line, down the sensitive cord of her neck and across her collarbone. She felt her breasts grow heavy. Her nipples beading tight, almost painfully so, behind her expensive lace-covered satin bra. When the tip of his tongue swept across one creamy swell she shuddered in response, the sensation of the point of his tongue electric as it traced a fine line across the curve of one breast. He awarded the same attention to her other breast, this time sending a sharp spear straight to her core.

His tongue followed the edge of her bra before dipping in the valley between. Her breath came in quick pants, her heart continuing to race in her chest. She felt his hand at her back, felt the freedom of the clasp of her bra being released, the weight of her breasts falling free as he slid her jacket off her shoulders and pushed her bra straps down to follow. With scant regard for the designer labels of both garments, Nate let them drop to the polished timber floor.

Nicole was beyond caring as his mouth captured one extended nipple, pulling it gently between his teeth, laving it with the heat of his tongue. Her legs began to tremble and she clung to him, near mindless with the pleasure his touch brought her. When his hands went to the waistband of her skirt she barely noticed, and then, with a slither of silk lining, her skirt joined her bra and jacket on the floor at her feet.

Dressed only in a scanty pair of black-and-gold panties and her high-heeled, black patent pumps she should have felt vulnerable, but as Nate pulled away, his eyes caressing every inch of her, she felt powerful. Needed. Wanted.

"Tell me what you want," he demanded, his voice a low demand that vibrated across the space between them.

"I want you to touch me," she replied softly.

"Show me where."

She lifted her hands to her bare breasts, her fingers cupping their smooth fullness, lifting them slightly before her fingertips abraded the distended tips, sending another shudder through her.

"Here," she said, her voice thicker now.

"And?"

One hand crept down, over her flat belly, and to the top band of her panties.

"Here." Her voice trembled as she felt the heat that pooled between her legs, felt the moisture that awaited his touch, his possession.

"Show me what you like," he said, his hand sliding over hers.

"This," she replied, letting their hands push beneath the scrap of fabric.

She led his fingers toward her opening, dipping them in her wetness before sliding them back up toward the budded bundle of nerves that screamed for his touch. She circled the sensitive spot first with her fingers then with his, increasing the pressure then slowing things down before repeating the cycle once more.

"Keep touching yourself," he commanded, even as he slid his fingers out from beneath her hand, dipping them lower until they played within the soft folds of her flesh.

He hooked his other arm around her, supporting her weight as he stepped in a little closer. She felt the fabric of his trousers against her bare legs—a fleeting awareness only before all concentration went when he stroked one finger inside her body, then another. Her muscles clenched against him as his fingertips glided in and out, caressing with careful and deliberate pressure against her inner walls.

Sensation swirled throughout her body, drenching her with heat and pleasure. The combination of both their touches filled her with an overpowering awareness of him, his strength, his power over her. She'd never felt anything this deep, this intense. Had never been this reckless.

Nate bent slightly, capturing one nipple with his mouth, drawing the sensitive bud into his heat, his wetness, and suckling hard. As he did so, she felt the pressure of his fingers inside her increase and with that subtle change, her body splintered apart on a wave of satisfaction so intense, so immeasurable, that her legs buckled beneath her and tiny pin pricks of light danced behind her eyelids.

Her whole body shook with the intensity of her orgasm as ripple after ripple of pleasure coursed through her. She felt Nate withdraw from inside her, even as her inner muscles continued to pull and tighten against him, heightening the sensations and sending her into another short, sharp paroxysm of bliss. He slid one hand behind her knees and, with his other arm still supporting her back, he swept her into his arms and strode across the open plan area toward a darkened room.

His bedroom, her shattered senses finally recognized as he placed her on the bedcovers. In the fractured blend of moon and starlight that shone through the massive picture window, she watched as he stripped away his clothing. Exposing every inch of his silver-gilded male beauty to her gaze. He reached for her feet, removing the shoes she only just now realized she still wore, then his hands slid up the length of her legs. When he reached her panties he slowly removed them from her before lowering himself to the bed and gently kneeing her legs apart, settling between them.

He leaned across her and ripped open a bedside cabinet drawer and removed a box of condoms. Extracting a packet he made short work of ripping away the wrapper and rolling the protection over his jutting erection. Her hands fluttered to the breadth of his shoulders, his skin burning beneath her touch. Despite his clear and evident arousal, his movements were smooth, controlled and deliberate as he positioned himself at her entrance and looked up to meet her eyes, even now giving her the chance to change her mind, to decide for herself what she wanted. In response, she instinctively tilted her pelvis to welcome his invasion.

Nate lowered his face to hers, his lips a heated seal against her own, his tongue gently probing her mouth even as he eased his length within her. She felt her body stretch to accommodate his size, felt an unmistakable quiver deep inside. Nicole lifted her hands to his head, her fingers lacing through his hair as she held him to her and kissed him back with all she had left in her.

Her body swept to aching life as he began to move, his thrusts powerful and deep, so deep it felt as if he touched her very soul before she plunged into the abyss of sensual gratification once more. In answer, his body stiffened, buried to the hilt, and a nearly stifled cry of release broke from him as he gave over to his own climax, shuddering as her body clenched rhythmically around him. His lips found hers again as he settled his weight on top of her, and she welcomed him. It was real, he was real. His heart thudded in his chest and hers beat a rapid tattoo in answer.

What they'd done together was something unsurpassed in her experience and finally, as she drifted to sleep, the cares and worries of her life wafted away into oblivion.

Three

As Nate woke, he slowly became aware that he'd fallen asleep not just on top of Nicole, but still inside her, as well. He silently castigated himself for his inconsiderate behavior as he carefully supported his weight without waking her.

He ignored the unfamiliar urge to settle closer to her rather than pulling away. After all, certain precautions had to be observed, he reminded himself. He reached between them, feeling for the edge of his condom and cursing when he couldn't find it. He pulled farther away from her, his body instantly lamenting the lack of contact with her lush warmth. The condom was still inside her. In a moment of panic he wondered if she was on the Pill but that fear was quickly assuaged. A woman like Nicole wasn't the type to leave things to chance. It was highly unlikely that pregnancy was something either of them needed to worry about just now.

No, now was a time to concentrate on pleasure. They'd had sex once and he couldn't wait to repeat the experience.

He eased his hand between her splayed legs and found the condom, removing it carefully before disposing of it in his bathroom. As he eased his body back onto the bed beside her he safeguarded them once more by rolling on another sheath and gathered her to him. She curled instinctively against his body, her softness pressing against the hard muscled planes of his chest, her inner heat already beckoning to him.

Her eyes flickered open, a slow smile spreading across her face. He cupped one cheek in his hand. It was one thing to know from Raoul's report that Nicole Wilson was an attractive woman with an incredibly sharp business mind, but it was quite another to discover that she was also a warm and generous lover. The knowledge skewed his vision of how this would ultimately play out.

Sending Nicole back to her father was no longer an option. With a little luck, her anger against her father and her brother just might be deep enough and strong enough to make her willingly defect to Jackson Importers…and to Nate's bed. With Nicole at his side he could take Jackson Importers to the ultimate heights of success, while ensuring his nights were equally, if not more, satisfying.

Of course, there was always the possibility that loyalty to her family would win out. Nate would be a fool not to plan for that contingency. If that happened, he'd have to be more…creative in the methods he used to keep Nicole. He didn't want to hurt her—Charles was his only target—but if upsetting her a little was the price to get his revenge *and* keep Nicole in the bargain, then that was a price he was willing to pay.

Sooner or later, she'd thank him for it. He'd already known her father hadn't utilized her intelligence to his best advantage. But Nate would. And she'd know she was appreciated while he did it. Every glorious inch of her.

"You're so beautiful," he said, meaning every syllable.

"It's dark," she replied, a teasing note in her voice. "Everyone is beautiful in the dark. You can't see their bad side."

"You don't have a bad side," he said, leaning forward to kiss her.

"Everyone has a bad side, Nate. We just don't always show it."

There was a painful truth in her words. A truth he knew related directly to him and his intentions but he didn't want to think about that right now. More pressing matters were most definitely at hand.

"Sometimes it's better not to see, then, isn't it?" he asked before leaning across the short distance between them and kissing her.

Their lips touched in a burst of heat and desire, his every nerve striving to attain the heights of fulfillment he knew he would reach in her arms. This time the fire inside him burned steadily, not threatening to overwhelm him as it had before, but his hunger for her had not lessened despite the change in his appetite. This was to be savored, slowly, completely.

Time faded into obscurity and nothing mattered right now except the giving and receiving of pleasure. Each touch destined to bring a sigh or a moan from its recipient, each kiss a seal of the promise of what was yet to come. And when she positioned herself over his body and lowered herself over his straining flesh he gave himself over totally to her demands.

Their peak was no less intense than that first time together, and this time, when Nicole fell into his arms lost in the aftermath and falling rapidly into sleep, he made certain the same accident with the condom didn't occur a second time.

The next time he woke, sunlight was filtering through the native bush outside and into his bedroom window. He reached across the bed. Empty. Where was his quarry now, he wondered as he swung his legs over the side of the bed and stood, stretching as he did so.

"Nice view," a voice said from behind him.

He turned slowly, a smile on his face. A smile that widened when he saw that Nicole had found the camcorder he kept for filming some of the more wild surfing antics on the beach.

"Do you have a license to drive that thing?" he asked.

"I'm the kind of girl who likes to learn as she goes along," Nicole answered in response.

She was wearing just the shirt he'd worn last night, the fine cotton covering her body but leaving her long legs exposed to his hungry gaze.

"So you're more of the hands-on kind?" he said, feeling his body stir and his blood pump just a little faster.

"Oh, yes, definitely hands-on," she said, her voice a little rough around the edges.

"I've always thought practical experience to be vastly underrated, haven't you?" He was fully hard now. Every cell in his body attuned to her, to the camcorder she held, to the idea that now blossomed in his mind.

"Definitely underrated. And the value of visual aids, too."

Oh, God, he thought. She had just read his mind. "I have a tripod for that thing, you know."

She laughed, a deep throaty chuckle that made him clench his hands at his sides to stop himself from reaching for her.

"More than one, I'd say," she said, dropping the lens of the camera down, then slowly back up again to his face.

She was wicked. He liked that in a woman. He liked that a whole lot. "I'll go get the other one," he said with a slow wink.

Before she could say another word he brushed past her, dropping a kiss on the curve of her lips as he went by. "Why don't you get yourself comfortable on the bed? I'll be back in just a minute."

It took less than a minute before he was back in the bedroom and setting up the stand diagonal to the bed. She passed him the camera, her cheeks flushed with color, her eyes bright with anticipation. Beneath the fabric of his shirt he could see the sway of her breasts as she moved on the bed, not to mention the sharp peaks of her nipples that told of her excitement. She passed the camera to him and he carefully positioned it on its mount, ensuring the whole bed was square in the frame.

"You're sure about this?" he asked.

"Oh, very sure. And later, when we review it, we can see where we can improve."

He didn't think it was possible to get any harder but at that moment he did. It was one thing to know they were videoing themselves, another to know she wanted to watch it later.

"Where do you suggest we begin?" he asked, fighting to keep a lid on the carnal urge to simply have at her, to let her have at him and to hell with finesse.

"I think I need to get to know you better, don't you?" She patted the edge of the bed beside her. "Why don't you sit down?"

He sat and watched her as she slid off the tumbled linens and knelt between his legs on the rug beside the bed, placing her hands on the outside edges of his thighs, scratching lightly with her fingernails.

"It seems to me," she continued, "that last night was all about me. So this time, it's going to be all about you."

A fine tremor ran through his body and he watched as her hands stroked up his thighs and down again, each time working a little closer to the inside.

"Do you like that?" she asked.

He was beyond words and merely nodded.

"How about this?"

His mind nearly exploded as she bent her head and flicked the tip of her tongue over the aching head of his arousal. His penis jumped in response to her touch, a bead of moisture appearing only to be licked away just as quickly. Nicole's hair brushed against his inner thighs, obscuring her face. He reached down and pushed her hair aside, holding it against the back of her head with each fisted hand. He wanted to see this, all of it. And, just in case, he wanted the camera to see it, too.

Nicole felt an unaccustomed sense of possession as she lightly stroked her tongue along the length of

Nate's erection, painstakingly following the line of each vein from tip to base and back again. Heat rolled off him in waves as she did so and she felt him tremble as he fought to maintain control. But that control shattered the instant she took him fully in her mouth. He groaned, a guttural sound that came from deep in his belly, and she knew the exact moment he was going to climax. She increased the pressure of her mouth, her tongue, increased the rhythm of her movements until he spent himself. She slowed her pace, taking the last drop of his essence as he groaned again, his hands falling to his sides and his body falling back onto the bed behind him.

She pushed herself up onto the bed and lay propped on one elbow alongside him, letting her fingers trail up and down across his belly and chest as he caught his breath once more. His recovery said a whole lot about his fitness and stamina, she thought as he reached one arm up to her and dragged her down to kiss him. Already he was stirring again, and the knowledge gave her a wonderful feeling. It was all because of her.

"Mmm," she said, her lips bare centimeters from his. "Must be time for breakfast."

"Not yet," he said. "I think we should work up a bit more of an appetite first. And I think you should take that shirt off, too."

He deftly flicked open each button and slid one hand inside, cupping one breast and flicking his thumb across its hardened crest.

"I'm very hungry already," she purred. "I may take some convincing."

"You want convincing? I can be convincing," he said, pushing the shirt off her shoulders and then pressing her onto the bed.

What followed was an education in how someone could deliver a lifetime of hedonistic delight in very short order. Nate applied himself to her with assiduous intent, showing her just how artful he could be with the merest accessories—the tip of a tongue, a feather of breath, the stroke of a fingertip.

She was on the verge of begging, no, screaming for release when he finally sheathed himself with a condom and took them both over the edge of sanity and into a realm where only blithe elation resided.

The camera caught it all.

Their morning set the tone for the next three days. From time to time they would rise, bathe or eat—once taking a long stroll along the beach, Nicole wearing ill-fitting borrowed clothes—before the draw of their fascination with one another would take them back to bed again. By Monday morning Nicole was spent. Physically and emotionally, happy just to curl up against the hard male body beside her and revel in the intimacies they'd shared. Last night Nate had burned a DVD of their video and they'd viewed it while attempting to eat a civilized meal in the main room of the house.

The clothing they'd only recently donned—him in a pair of jeans and T-shirt, her in a sweatshirt of his with the sleeves rolled up and its length skimming the back of her thighs—had soon hit the floor. Their food cooling on their plates as the on-screen activity had incited a new hunger for one another all over again.

Nate still slept beside her and she watched his chest rise and fall on each breath. She was amazed at how natural it felt to be with him, especially considering how little they actually knew about one another. She'd heard the girls at work talk and giggle over their occasional one-night stands—guys they never expected, or in some cases even wanted, to see again—but she'd never believed she'd indulge in something quite so illicit herself. She felt as if the past few days had been a vacation, not just from work and responsibility, but from herself—her own fears and anxieties. On Friday she hadn't even given a care to the fact she had probably still been expected at the office, nor that over the course of the whole weekend she hadn't so much as told anyone where she was, nor checked her cell phone for messages.

It wasn't as if they cared, anyway, a little voice said from deep down inside. Her father didn't believe she had a valid contribution to make to the company, her best friend had turned on her and her brother? Well, he didn't even know her, nor she him. So what difference would it make if she walked away from all of them for good?

A whole lot of difference, she realized. She'd been angry on Thursday night. Really angry. And she'd acted completely out of character. Deep down she knew her family, including Anna, loved her and had to be worried about her having been out of touch for so long.

This person in the bed with a stranger, that wasn't her. Sure, it had been a great time, but all good things had to come to an end sometime, didn't they? Nothing this good ever lasted for long.

A wave of guilt for her behavior swamped her, driving her from the bed and into the bathroom where she gave in to the sudden well of tears in her eyes. She'd behaved irrationally. Stupidly. She had no idea of who she was really with. Everything that had anchored her these past twenty-six years lay on the other side of town—with her family, in her home. So what if her father had signed the property over to Judd? Her brother wasn't about to summarily eject her from the only home she'd ever known, surely. Judd was as much a victim of her father's shenanigans as she. So was Anna, who was far too grateful for all that Charles had done for her and her mother to ever tell him no.

And as for her father… It would be difficult for her to forgive or forget his words on Thursday night. But she couldn't forget twenty-six years of him sheltering and protecting her, either. For better or for worse, he was still her father. They'd just have to find a way to reach an accord. She was willing to take the first step, and come back home.

Nicole dashed her face with water and dried it before quietly letting herself out of the master bathroom and padding quietly across the bedroom floor. As she closed the door behind her she let go the breath she hadn't realized she'd been holding. She gave herself a mental shake. For goodness sake, she was an adult. Her decisions were her own, her choices were her own. The weekend had been great, just what she'd needed, there was no need to sneak around like a thief in the night.

She squared her shoulders and made her way to the laundry room where she'd hand washed and hung her underwear to dry during the course of the weekend. Her suit was on a hanger and had been brushed and steamed to get the creases out after being summarily left on the living room floor for several hours after Thursday night. She slid into her underwear and put on her suit. It felt strange to be dressed so formally after a weekend where clothing had been minimal.

She picked up her bag from in the living room and brushed out her hair before heading back to the bedroom to retrieve her shoes. She'd have to call a cab to get herself into work, she thought as she twisted her hair up into a knot and secured it with a clip she'd found in the bottom of her bag.

Nate was awake when she pushed open the door.

"Going somewhere?" he asked, his eyes unreadable as he watched her slide her feet into her shoes.

"Yeah, time to get back to reality." She sighed. "This weekend has been great. Better than great, thanks."

"That's it?"

"What—" she laughed nervously "—you want more?"

"I always want more, especially of what we've had."

"I never said I didn't want to see you again."

"But you implied it."

Nicole shot him a nervous glance. Was he going to get all weird on her now?

"Look, I need to get home and then head into work."

"No."

She shot him another look, this time the curl of fear in her stomach unfurled to bigger proportions.

"What do you mean, no?"

"What I mean is, you're coming to work with me."

Nate pushed aside the bed sheets and rose to his feet, calmly picking up the jeans he'd discarded last night and sliding them on. Nicole struggled to avert her gaze from the fine arrow of hair that angled down from his belly button to behind the waistband of his pants. She'd followed that path, and more, several times this weekend. A hot flush of color rushed to her cheeks. She couldn't let herself get distracted by sexual attraction. What on earth did he mean when he said she'd be working with him? She didn't even know what he did for a living. And he didn't know anything about her…did he?

"You've got it wrong, I have a job. A job I love, with a family I—"

"Don't tell me you love them, Nicole. Not after what they've done to you."

Instantly she rued the way she'd mouthed off in the car when he'd brought her here, and the truths she'd shared over a bottle of red wine as they'd curled naked beneath a blanket on the couch in front of a burning fire, late on Saturday night.

"They're still family. At the very least I need to clear the air with them."

"Oh, I think that's a bit more than they deserve. Besides, the air will clear soon enough."

Nicole crossed her arms across her stomach. "What on earth are you talking about?"

"When they learn who you've just spent this past weekend with, I very much doubt they'll be welcoming you home with open arms. I'm pretty much persona non grata with your father."

Nate's lips lifted in a half smile, as if he was laughing at a private joke.

"You're speaking in riddles. Why should they care who I spent the weekend with?" she snapped.

Nate came to stand in front of her. "Because I'm Nate Hunter—Nate Hunter Jackson."

Nicole's mind reeled on his words. Nate Hunter? *The* Nate Hunter? The reclusive billionaire who was the new head of Jackson Importers, her family firm's arch nemesis? Her father had never had a kind word to say about Thomas Jackson, or his staff.

Hang on a minute. Nicole replayed his words in her mind. Had he said Nate Hunter *Jackson?*

"I see you've made the connection," Nate said coolly. "And, yes, I am Thomas Jackson's son. Sweet, isn't it? All that time your father accused my dad of screwing around with your mother, he was actually with mine."

Nicole looked at him in horror as his words slowly sank in, leaving her mind reeling. She hadn't just been sleeping with a stranger over the entire weekend—she'd literally been sleeping with the enemy!

Four

Nate watched the shock and dismay play across Nicole's features as understanding clouded her beautiful brown eyes.

"So you knew who I was all along? This weekend has all been about you getting some twisted revenge on my family?" she asked. Her voice shook, betraying just how much his words had upset her.

It might have started that way, Nate admitted to himself, but now he'd been with Nicole so intimately he knew that for the better part of their time together, revenge had been the last thing on his mind. At least, revenge on *her*. Her father, of course, was another matter entirely.

"Did you hunt me out?" she demanded, her voice stronger now.

"Our meeting was by chance," he said smoothly. "A happy chance from my point of view." He stepped forward and reached one finger to her cheekbone, tracing the smooth feminine contour to the corner of her lips. "And I don't regret a second of it, Nicole."

She jerked her head away. "Of course you don't," she said angrily. "Well, your little game is over now. I'm heading back into the city to my family and my job."

"I don't think so," Nate responded smoothly, crossing his arms in front of him.

"You can't possibly be serious about me working for you."

"I'm serious, all right."

"No." Nicole took a step back from him, putting one hand out as if she could physically prevent his words from holding any truth. "There's no way in this lifetime that I'd do such a thing, even if my father didn't want me at Wilson Wines. It would destroy every last vestige of our relationship together. He may not understand me as well as I'd hoped for, but he's still my father. I won't do that to him. I just won't."

Why couldn't she have stayed angry at her family? That would have made this so much easier, Nate thought to himself. Was there any way he could stoke that anger again?

"You *are* talking about the man who said that Wilson Wines was a nice hobby for you, aren't you?"

She shook her head, more in frustration, he imagined, than to negate what he'd just said. Nate pursued his advantage in the face of her silence.

"And you're talking about the man who, without a word of discussion with you—his right hand at Wilson Wines—gave away a controlling interest in his business to someone who is essentially a complete and utter stranger to both of you."

"Stop," she moaned, wrapping her arms about herself and holding them tight. "I know that's what he's done, you don't need to repeat it. He's my father. No matter what, he'll always be my dad. I'll always be loyal to him."

"Really? Why? He's even given away your family home, Nicole. Again, without any prior warning to you, nor any assurance for you that you will have a roof over your head anymore. Haven't you asked yourself yet what kind of man would do that to his daughter?"

Nate was angry, furiously angry. Not at Nicole, who seemed determined to forgive her father anything, but at the man who was at the root of all Nate's unhappiness. The man whose brutal rejection of his best friend had crushed Thomas Jackson's spirit and had forced him into dire financial straits. And the man who had withheld his encouragement and support from his daughter for so long that she'd forgive any insult for the chance to earn his approval.

He pressed on as she stood there silent and pale.

"You deserve more, Nicole. You deserve so much more. You're a strong, intelligent and incredibly capable woman. You should work somewhere where you're valued and appreciated. Think about the team we'll make. We'll be the best the business has ever seen."

She raised tear-washed eyes to his face and he fought to ignore the spear of regret that penetrated somewhere in the region of his chest. He knew his words hurt her but he couldn't afford to be soft, not now. If she didn't give in soon, he'd have to hurt her a lot more. He didn't want to, but he would, if it came to that. All was fair in love and war. And this was war.

"Nicole, your loyalty to Charles Wilson is commendable, but sadly misplaced. Work with me. Help me grow Jackson Importers to its fullest potential. Be a part of something special."

She swallowed before speaking. "And what's in it for you? You can't expect me to believe you're doing this out of the goodness of your heart."

He laughed, a short humorless sound that hung in the air between them for only a second or two. "No, I'm not doing it out of the goodness of my heart. I'm a businessman. I play to win, at all times and," he hesitated a moment for effect, "at all costs."

She shook her head again. "I won't work for you and I'm leaving right now. You're not the man I thought you were, Nate. I can't do what you're asking of me."

"Nicole, I'm not asking."

"I still have some say in this, don't I?" she demanded, turning and heading for the front door.

"Sure, you still have a say," he said, his words halting her in her tracks. "But so do I, and there's still a card left for me to play."

"I wasn't aware this was a game," she said coolly.

"Not a game at all," Nate said, smiling, even though his voice held no warmth anymore. "But all the same, I *will* win." He gestured toward the video camera still on the tripod in the corner of the room. "Ask yourself this, how would your father feel if he saw our amateur movie? What would hurt him more? Seeing you work for me, or knowing that you'd spent this past weekend in my bed?"

"Th—that's not fair," Nicole stammered, struggling to keep her balance. It felt as if the floor had been knocked out from under her. "I didn't know who you were then."

"I never said I play fair, Nicole. Your father already

hates the Jackson name. Already believes your mother slept with my father—it's what tore Charles and Thomas's friendship apart, what divided your family and what destroyed mine. I'll be sure to include a note with the DVD, explaining my parentage. How do you think he'd feel about seeing his daughter intimately engaged with Thomas Jackson's son?"

"You wouldn't!" Nicole uttered the words even though her throat felt as if it had constricted with shock and fear.

"Oh, believe me. I very much would. I want you, Nicole. I want you in my boardroom, in my office, in the field as well as here—in my home and in my bed."

Her skin tautened as his words fell upon her ears. Her nipples hardening even as a rush of warmth spread through her lower belly and her inner muscles clenched involuntarily in reaction to his words. Stop it, she told herself. He wasn't simply talking about sex. He was talking about her betraying her father. About her walking away from the company she'd hoped all her life that she would eventually take over. The job that was so much more than a job. It had been her way of life—her dream. It had been everything to her father and, ergo, everything to her, as well.

What Nate was suggesting was appalling. If she quit her job at Wilson Wines to work for Nate, her father would never understand, never forgive her. But could she take the risk that Nate would follow through on his threat and send her father a copy of their illicit weekend? Even as the thought presented itself in her mind, she knew without a shadow of a doubt that Nate would do exactly what he said. Men like him didn't always play fair or clean—and they rarely bluffed. It would hurt her father if she worked for Nate but it would probably kill him if he saw that video.

"You're a bastard," she said quietly.

"Oh, yes, no question about that," Nate answered, a thread of bitterness in his voice that she hadn't heard before.

She racked her memory. Her father had rarely spoken about the man who had been his best friend from school, but when he did it had been in scathing terms. Thomas Jackson had never married. Never even publicly acknowledged he had a son. Was Nate even telling the truth about his relationship with the man?

She was hit with a sudden wave of hopelessness. Did any of her conjecture even matter when right now Nate held all the cards very firmly in those dexterous hands of his? Hands that had done wickedly delicious things to her over the past seventy-two hours. She clamped down on the thought before it took her over again. She had to forget the man she thought she'd grown to know a little these past few days. Had to remember, instead, the hardheaded businessman who had so mercilessly embarked on their time together knowing full well who she was and what being with him would mean to her family.

Her family. They were what had gotten her into this mess. Them and her blasted impulsiveness. She could see the lines of disappointment carved into her father's face even now.

"So, Nicole, what's it to be?"

Nate stood opposite her, his hands loosely on his lean jean-clad hips, his chest still bare, his shoulders still showing evidence of their passion where she'd clutched him tightly—her nails imbedding in his skin, lost in the throes of yet more pleasure. Even now, with his intentions out in the open, she still had to fight her desire for him. What did that say about her? She didn't even want to begin to examine that question.

She couldn't do it. She couldn't let her father see her wanton behavior, especially with the man who epitomized everything her father had fought against in the past twenty-five years. She had no other choice. She had to do as he said.

"You win."

"There, that wasn't too difficult, was it?"

She flung a fulminating look at him. "You have no idea."

She was damned if she did as he'd demanded, and she was damned if she didn't. At least this way she could protect her father from seeing the full extent of her own stupid behavior. Her face burned with shame as she remembered that she had been the one to pull out the camcorder in the first place. Furious and embarrassed, she pushed the thought away.

Nate Hunter Jackson might have won this round but he wouldn't win them all, she silently vowed. One way or another, she'd get her own back on him.

"This doesn't have to be a bad thing. At least with me you won't be taken for granted, Nicole," he said.

She ignored him. Being taken for granted was the least of her immediate worries. "I need to go home and get my things, and pick up my car," she said with as much control as she could muster.

"That won't be necessary."

She gestured to the suit she'd put back on this morning. Despite her attentions to it, the garment still looked a little the worse for wear and in need of a professional dry clean.

"Sorry to disappoint you, but I need my clothes. I can't wear this forever."

"Personally, I kind of like the idea of you not wearing it."

"Personally, I don't care what you like," she retaliated. She may have been forced into agreeing to his terms but she'd take a long walk off a short pier before she'd take her clothes off again at his behest. "I need my things—my car, my cell phone charger, everything. And I'll need to tell my father and brother that I won't be working for them anymore."

"I'll arrange for your car to be collected. As to your clothes, we can take care of that on the way into work. And, as to your father and brother, I'll take care of letting them know. There's no way to break it to them gently, and being blunt would be a miserable experience for you, but will be quite a lot of fun for me. Now, give me five minutes to shower and change. We can have breakfast in the city before we shop."

He turned and headed for the bathroom.

"I'm not hungry," she said to his retreating back.

Nate stopped and turned around, his hands already at the button fly of his jeans and exposing his lower abdomen to her gaze. "Not hungry? That's a shame. I'll have to have enough appetite for the both of us, then, won't I?"

Nicole dragged her eyes from the half open fly of his jeans and up to his face. His eyes burned with a heat that sent an answering response coursing through her body.

"Yes, you will," she said through teeth clenched so tight her jaw ached. She forced herself to relax the tiniest bit before continuing. "Because I have absolutely no appetite at all."

There, she thought, take that. She spun on one high heel and stomped through to the massive picture window facing the sea in the living room. Even there she was destined for disappointment, she thought. Instead of the rough roiling ocean she'd come to expect from the wild west coast beach ahead of her, there was nothing but a clear-blue autumn sky, rolling deep green water and foaming white crests of waves caressing the sparkling black sand shoreline. It was a complete contrast to the storm of emotion that tossed around inside her.

She was going to work for the son of her father's biggest business rival. He'd never forgive her this. Not in a million years. She shouldn't care, she told herself. He was the one who had summarily dismissed all her years of hard work for Wilson Wines and along with that dismissal had put aside her business and marketing degrees, not to mention the years of after-school and school holiday work experience she'd doggedly labored through so she could understand his business from the ground up. He'd never realized how important the business was to her because he'd never grasped how important *he* was to her.

Somewhere along the line, and from a very early age, Nicole had understood that her father's business was his everything. It was what he poured his heart and soul into every waking hour of every day. She'd thought that if she did exactly what he did, she'd earn his respect. And still he thought it was no more than a dalliance for her. Something to fill in her time before the more important matters of marriage and making babies filled her life.

Her hands tightened into fists, her perfectly manicured nails biting into the skin of her palms, as all her latent frustration built deep inside her. Getting angry at her father all over again would make it easier to walk away from Wilson Wines…but deep down, she knew the anger wouldn't last. She loved her father, and she knew that he loved her, even if they'd both fallen short on finding a way to connect. But even now, she refused to believe that it was too late. She closed her eyes to the perfection of the view outside and forced herself to draw in a steadying breath, and then another. Somehow she'd work her way through this. Somehow she'd work her way back to her family again.

"You ready?"

Nate's voice came from behind her. She opened her eyes and turned around. In a tailored charcoal-gray suit, with a crisp white shirt and flame-colored silk tie, he was a world away from the sensual creature who'd filled her weekend with sybaritic delight. A world away, but no less appealing. She ruthlessly pushed aside the admission.

"I was waiting for you, remember?" she said, scathingly.

He smiled, the action making something inside her tug hard. She silently cursed him for having this effect on her.

"Let's go, then."

The drive into the city was interminable. Nicole checked her cell phone for about the sixteenth time since they'd started out on the road. She hadn't had her phone on all weekend but even now the thing was down to only one bar of battery left. One bar and no blasted reception. Just as they crested a hill, she saw she finally had a signal and, with that, her phone began to vibrate in her hand as one message after the other poured in. By the time it settled down she saw she had six missed calls, an equal number of voice messages and more texts than she cared to count. Before she could do anything about them, though, her phone died—all the beeping and vibrating having drained the last of its charge.

"Argh!" she growled in frustration.

"Problem?" Nate asked, infuriatingly calm.

"My phone just died."

"No problem, I'll get you a new one. It'll be better that way—start over fresh."

"I like this one," she said doggedly. "It already has everything I need in it."

"It has what you needed for your old life—not for your new one. You've got a whole new list of people you'll be working with, communicating with. Besides, that was probably a company-subsidized phone—and you're not with that company anymore."

To her surprise, Nate took one hand off the steering wheel and reached across to take the phone from her hand.

"Needs updating, too," he said, giving the technology a cursory glance. "The one I get you will have better programming—and better access, too. I can't have you out of range whenever you're at the house."

"There's noth— Wait! What the hell are you doing?"

His driver's window rolled down smoothly and he lobbed the phone out onto the road where, to her horror, it was promptly run over by a truck coming in the opposite direction.

"How dare you? That was mine."

"I told you, I'll get you a new one. That one's no good anymore, anyway."

"No thanks to you."

She fought back the tears that suddenly came into

her eyes. This was a complete nightmare. Did he have to control everything? Maybe it would have been better to bite the bullet, after all, and suffer the consequences of her father seeing the DVD. Even as she thought it, Nicole pushed the thought from her mind. Her father's health had been declining in recent years. He'd ignored his diabetes for too long and the damage it had wrought on his system was beginning to tell on him, making him look much older than his sixty-six years. She didn't even want to imagine the impact a major shock to his system would have on his health.

No, she was in this for the long haul. No matter what it took, no matter the toll on her.

"The replacement had better be top of the line," she said, putting as much steel into her voice as she could.

"Of course. Nothing but the best for you, I promise."

"That's quite a promise. Do you really think you can meet it?"

Nate flicked a glance in her direction before returning his gaze to the traffic ahead.

"I'm a man of my word."

"That remains to be seen," she muttered, focusing her attention out the passenger window.

The way he'd said it, it held more threat than promise, and for some reason that, more than anything, chilled her to the bone.

Nate watched as Nicole was taken through to the fitting room of the third designer store they'd been to so far this morning. She'd insisted on getting a new wardrobe before eating, which now left him starving—but not for any food. He was hungry for her. For the feel of the texture of her skin beneath his touch, for the taste of her on his lips, for all the little sighs and moans she made while they explored one another's bodies with intimate precision.

Part of him wanted to say to hell with work—and clothes—and just head back to the house for another day in bed. Only two things stopped him.

The first was the office. Jackson Importers was his father's legacy in so many ways, and when Nate had taken up the mantle as CEO, he'd promised himself that he would invest every energy, every effort, into making the company the absolute best it could be. He didn't balk at long hours or working weekends, and even when he'd been stuck at home with a stomach bug, he'd still checked in through email all day long. Calling in sick on Friday had undoubtedly raised a few eyebrows. If he missed work on Monday, too, his staff would probably send an ambulance out to his house.

The second reason was Nicole, herself. Yes, he wanted her badly—both in bed and out of it. She was more than he'd ever dreamed of. He already knew she had a very smart mind—the dossier Raoul had prepared on the Wilson family had been thorough. If Nate could have found a way to headhunt Nicole Wilson for Jackson Importers after his father's death, he probably wouldn't have even needed to come home from Europe to take over the business. Her misplaced loyalty to her father was well documented, however, and he hadn't even bothered trying to steal her away.

That loyalty was the problem he was dealing with now. He supposed it had been too much to hope that her frustration with her family would lead her to welcome the chance to enact a little revenge along with him.

But her dedication to her father wouldn't be an obstacle forever, he rationalized. Sooner or later, she'd have to realize that Nate treated her better, and appreciated her more, than her father ever could. When she accepted that—and when she realized that the passion between them was impossible to ignore or deny—she'd turn her loyalty to him. She didn't know it yet, but he would be the best thing that had ever happened in her life. He just had to be patient until she came to terms with that—and watch her closely.

Yes, watch her *very* closely, because if the glares she kept giving him were any indication, any hand he reached out to touch her would come back to him bleeding. She was furious with him for forcing her into this position—and a smart, capable woman with a grudge was a dangerous creature, indeed.

So he'd have to be on his guard. Nothing new there—he was always on his guard. And he knew, far better than his father ever had, to be very careful before giving a Wilson his trust.

"Miss Wilson is finished now, Mr. Hunter," the store manager said, coming through with an armful of clothing and a smile that told of the sizeable commission she'd no doubt be earning today.

"So soon?"

"She has very specific tastes and was quick to decide on what she needed."

Nate gave the delivery address of his inner-city apartment for the clothing and handed over his platinum card, then looked back toward the changing rooms. Nicole was walking toward him in a new outfit, one that made his breath still in his lungs and all the blood in his body race to a very specific part of his anatomy. The ruby-red dress, while probably perfectly acceptable office wear on anyone else, skimmed every curve of her graceful figure. The scooped neckline offering a tantalizing hint of the swell of her full breasts. The three-quarter-length sleeves exposing her slender forearms. Forearms that led to delicate wrists and elegant hands. Hands that had gripped him and teased him and delivered all kinds of pleasure.

"All done now?" he asked as she drew alongside him.

"I just need some underwear and sleepwear."

"Sure. Do you want to eat first or keep shopping?"

"Still got that appetite?" she said, with a hint of an acerbic humor.

He looked her up and down very deliberately before meeting the unspoken challenge in her dark-eyed stare. "Always."

His reward came in the sudden flush of color that suffused her cheeks.

"We'd better get some food, then," she said sharply, breaking eye contact and giving her attention to the store manager—thanking the other woman for her assistance.

They stopped at a café in Vulcan Lane where he consumed Eggs Benedict while she played with a mixed berry muffin on her plate. While lingering over his coffee, Nate picked up the complimentary newspaper the café provided. He flicked through the pages, emitting a long slow whistle when he reached the society page.

"Looks like I might not have to make that call to your father's office, after all," he said, folding back the page and showing it to Nicole.

Five

They danced together, right there in black and white. Caught in time forever. Their intense absorption in one another as clear as day on their faces. Opposite him, Nicole paled and drew in a sharp breath.

"Did you orchestrate this?" she demanded.

Nate laughed. "I'm flattered you think I have that much power but, no, I didn't."

She looked at him as if she didn't believe a word that came from his mouth.

"Obviously you want to hurt my dad, but why go to all this trouble with me over something that happened so long ago? Our fathers fell out. Their friendship broke up. It happens."

Nate looked at her over the rim of his coffee cup. Did she really think it was that simple?

"Your father accused mine of something he didn't do. He wouldn't listen to reason nor would he ever accept he was wrong. He broke my father's heart, broke the man inside him, destroyed his honor. And thanks to your father's actions, my father had to work himself to the bone just to make ends meet as he got Jackson Importers off the ground, ruining his health and making him die before his time. My father deserved better than that and so did my mother."

"And will hurting mine bring them back? Will it make it all better again?"

"No, but it will give me the utmost satisfaction when Charles Wilson is finally forced to admit he was wrong."

Nicole shook her head. "You're the one who is wrong, Nate. Let this go. Let *me* go."

Let her go? Before her father had learned his lesson? Before Nicole had accepted how good they could be together? Oh, no.

"Not going to happen." He picked up his cup and drained the last of his coffee. "If you're finished playing with your food, we should get the last of your shopping done before heading into the office."

They walked together up Queen Street toward Auckland's oldest department store. It amused Nate that Nicole maintained a clear foot of distance between them at all times. Not easy to do in the throng of business people, shoppers and tourists who congested the footpaths. When they reached the department store, Nicole lingered awhile at the cosmetics counters on the ground floor leaving Nate to hand his card over again as she purchased skin care, fragrance and cosmetics.

"You don't need to do this," she objected, her own credit card in her hand already.

"Humor me," he said, taking her card and examining it. "This in your name or under your father?"

"It's all mine, paid for by my very own wages. Is that okay?" She snatched it back from him and pushed it back into her wallet before gathering up her bags from the shop girl and heading toward women's wear upstairs.

"I'll get you another one."

"This one is perfectly fine."

No it wasn't, he thought. Anything that led back to Charles Wilson in any way was, in his book, tainted—and her previous earnings definitely led back to Charles Wilson. Nate had every intention of paying her a generous salary, and until that began, he intended to take care of things. Take care of *her.* Nothing but the best for her—he'd promised her that, and he'd meant it.

Upstairs in the lingerie department he was again relegated to a chair while Nicole browsed rack after frothy rack of underwear. When she'd finally made her selection and gone through to the changing rooms he got up from his chair and paced the floor. As he did so, his eye latched onto a stunning ensemble on a floor mannequin. The ivory lace-and-chiffon nightgown and matching peignoir was both innocence and pure sin in one simple package.

Attracting the eye of the sales clerk he gestured to the ensemble.

"Include one of these in Miss Wilson's size with her purchases, thank you. And, please, keep it as a surprise."

He flashed the woman a wink and a smile and the blushing clerk hastened to fulfill his request before Nicole returned from the changing rooms. Already he could imagine peeling the diaphanous garment from Nicole's lithe body, but not before he'd tormented both her, and himself, with touching her through its silken texture first.

It would be torment enough for him waiting for her to come back to his bed. But the waiting would pay off sooner or later. It would all pay off in the end.

It was well past lunchtime before they made it into Nate's offices in a high-rise overlooking Auckland's Waitemata Harbor. He settled his hand on the small of her back as they exited the elevator and directed her toward a set of glass doors emblazoned in gold leaf with "Jackson Importers" and its stylized logo of a bunch of grapes.

He reached forward and opened the door, holding it for Nicole as she walked through and into the reception area. His receptionist looked up and smiled. He introduced Nicole immediately.

"April, this is Miss Wilson, she'll be working with us from now on. I'd like you to call all the staff into the boardroom to meet her in about fifteen minutes."

"Surely that won't be necessary," Nicole protested. "I can just—"

"I want everyone to know who you are and why you're here," he said in a voice that brooked no argument. "Tomorrow I'll introduce you to the staff at our warehouse and distribution center."

She pressed her lips together, clearly biting back whatever it was that she wanted to say. He guided her down the corridor and pushed open the door that led into the boardroom. Seeing her there, in his offices, in that stunning dress, his self-control cracked. The instant the door closed behind him, he couldn't stop himself from sweeping her into his arms, drawing her against his body and lowering his head to capture her mouth. The second their lips touched he felt electrified, the charge of energy he got from her sizzling a slow burn all the way to the pit of his stomach.

"I needed that," he groaned against her lips when he'd sated his need, however temporarily.

"Well, I didn't. I'd appreciate it if you kept your hands, and all your other body parts, to yourself," Nicole answered, moving out of his reach and smoothing her dress in a gesture that spoke more of nervousness than any real desire to stay out of reach.

Well, he couldn't say he hadn't expected that. But still… "You can't deny you enjoyed it," Nate said, observing the brightness of her eyes, the rapid rise and fall of her chest.

"How I might respond to you physically is one thing. Whether I actually want to, is another. Don't touch me again."

"Ever?" he asked, narrowing his eyes.

"Ever," she adamantly replied.

"So you're telling me that if I did this," he touched a fingertip to the slight swell of her breasts visible above the neckline of her dress, "that you don't *want* more?"

Nicole fought to control the wave of need that trembled through her body. She couldn't show him any weakness, not for a minute. Men like Nate Jackson capitalized on weakness and she could not afford for him to get any more leverage on her than he already had.

"There's a name for what you're doing," she managed to finally say. "I believe it's called harassment."

To her surprise, Nate laughed. Genuine pleasure at her words making his eyes lighten and shine.

"You're priceless," he said through his good humor.

"Harassment. Would you have said it was harassment at about 3:00 a.m. this morning, when I—"

Nicole was saved from the torture of hearing him repeat what they'd been doing in the small hours of this morning, and saved, thank God, from giving him an answer when the door behind them opened.

"Ah, Raoul, please meet our newest addition to the team, Nicole Wilson. Nicole, this is Raoul Benoit. Don't be fooled by his name, he's just as much a Kiwi as you or I."

Raoul inclined his head in acknowledgement of Nate's introduction and gave Nicole a shy smile.

"Miss Wilson, it's a pleasure to meet you, and even more of a pleasure to have you on our team."

"I..." What on earth could she say? She couldn't exactly tell Raoul she was here under duress. That she'd virtually been kidnapped and forced to come here. "Thank you."

Raoul looked at Nate and she didn't miss the question in Raoul's eyes as he did so. The expression of supreme satisfaction on Nate's face told her everything she needed to know. Raoul Benoit knew exactly who she was and exactly what Nate was up to. It made her feel alienated, as if she was completely alone in this horrible situation.

Nate's voice broke into her thoughts. "I've asked April to get the staff in here to meet Nicole. I think it's a good idea to let everyone know she's going to be with us from now on."

His words made her feel like nothing more than a trophy, but before she could utter a word of protest, the door opened again. A steady stream of people came into the boardroom, sitting where they could and standing, lining the wall, when all the seats were taken. She was surprised Jackson Importers carried such a large staff in their Auckland offices, and Nate had spoken of a warehouse and distribution staff, as well. It rammed home the reality of what he'd coerced her into doing—working with the thriving and very competitive enemy. The next quarter hour passed in a blur.

By the time Nate showed Nicole to his office, her head was spinning and she was beginning to regret not having eaten that berry muffin at breakfast.

"And this is where you'll be working," he said as he closed the office door behind them.

Nicole looked around the sumptuously appointed office, at the amazing view of the harbor beyond and then back at him.

"This is your office. I can't work here."

He shrugged. "I'm prepared to share my space with you. All my space, Nicole. Together we're going to head up the most successful wine importation business in the country. Why would I want you anywhere else but at my side?"

That all sounded very impressive—but what did it really mean? "Is that a fancy way of saying that you want to keep an eye on me?"

He smirked. "I'll always enjoy having my eyes—or anything else—on you." Nicole huffed in frustration, and Nate continued, "If you're asking if I'll be watching your work, then the answer is yes. I know that right now, you don't want to be here and you're angry with me for forcing your hand. I think that'll change. I think that once you understand the opportunities for you here, you'll see that this is where you belong. When that day comes, you can have any office you want. Until then, you'll understand if I prefer to keep you where I can see you. After all, I'll certainly enjoy the view."

"What about privacy for phone calls and things like that?"

"Worried I might overhear your conversations?"

"Do you plan to follow me to the bathroom, as well?" she demanded, her temper finally fraying. Since his very unwelcome revelation this morning, he'd been controlling everything about her except for how she drew breath—and even that was under deliberation. Every time he brushed past her she got a tightness in her chest that was all his fault.

"Do you need me to?"

"I don't *need* you for anything," she said mutinously.

"Like your father doesn't need you?"

He knew exactly how to cut to precisely where it hurt. Nicole turned from him and tossed her handbag onto his desk.

"Well, if this is where I'm supposed to be, I'd better get to work, then, hadn't I?"

He smiled and gestured to the laptop and cell phone on the desk that he'd arranged to have delivered while waiting outside her dressing rooms. "They're all yours, have at it."

"Mine. Already?"

"I told you I'd take care of you, Nicole. I meant every word I said."

She swallowed against the lump that suddenly filled her throat. He said it like he meant it. As if she was something—no, some*one*—important to him. She didn't want to believe it. Couldn't believe it. They'd had a weekend of great sex. Okay, it was off the scale great sex. But that was all. There couldn't be anything more between them, especially not now he'd made his intentions toward her father explicitly clear.

"Where do you want me to start?" she asked, crossing behind the desk and opening the laptop, determined to keep this on a professional level even if it was likely to destroy her.

"How about you spend some time on coming to grips with our new internet-only business? It's taken off far quicker than we anticipated and reaches beyond our existing New Zealand market and allows us to trade overseas, as well. It cuts overheads considerably as, in many cases, we've been able to coordinate shipping direct between the vineyard and the buyer, thus cutting freight and storage costs to a minimum."

Nicole felt the thrill of excitement at learning a new business model ripple through her. For years, she'd been urging her father to consider an online ordering system rather than solely relying on hands-on distribution. True, hand selling often gave wine-store customers a chance to try something new that they might not have considered before, but to hope that would continue to buoy the market forever was professional suicide. The world changed at an incredibly fast pace. The wine distribution industry no less so.

Another thought occurred to her. Nate's approach to supervision had thrown a spanner in her initial plans to use her access to sabotage some of Jackson Importers' business, but there was still a chance to come out ahead here. Deep down she knew this situation couldn't last. Eventually she'd find a way to return to Wilson Wines, and Nate was giving her the perfect opportunity to learn as much as she could of their successful business practices and think about how Wilson Wines could implement them, or use them to create something even better.

Remaining focused on business was easier said than done as Nate pulled up a chair next to hers and brushed against her as he keyed in the URL that would take her computer onto the Jackson Importers portal.

"You'll need your own password. I'll get IT onto that immediately. While I go and sort that out, why don't you cruise around the website and make a list of questions you want to ask me?"

She merely nodded as he stood again, sucking in a deep breath of relief when he left the office. She'd thought her anger and resentment toward him would allow her to cope better with his close presence here in the office. The opposite couldn't have been more true. She'd found her eyes riveted on his long fingers as they'd flown over the keyboard of her new laptop, and had been forced to quell the memory of what those fingers had felt like as they'd flown over her body.

Nicole leaned back in the high-backed, leather office chair and swung around to face the view out over the Waitemata Harbour. Even on a workday the water was scattered with yachts making the most of the autumn sunshine and the strong breeze. How she wished she could emulate their freedom. But freedom was something that would remain in limited supply for her until she could work a way out of this mess. Somehow, someway, she'd find a way to get her own back on Nate Jackson, and, like his father before him, he'd be sorry he'd ever tangled with a Wilson.

Six

Nate spent the rest of the afternoon with Nicole, discussing the wines they imported and the systems that Jackson Importers had in place both in New Zealand and overseas for distribution to their worldwide network of buyers. By the time the sun was dipping below the Waitakere Ranges in the distance, they were both looking pretty exhausted.

"I think it's best if we stay in town tonight, at my apartment," Nate said as he stood and stretched out the kinks he'd gathered in his back from sitting at his desk so long.

"Whatever you say," Nicole muttered.

"Would you rather head out to Karekare? We'll have to swing by the apartment and collect your new things first."

"I'd rather go home—to my home—but since that's

not going to happen, I don't really care one way or the other where I sleep tonight."

Her dark brown eyes met his in a silent challenge—as if she was daring him to contradict her. Nate knew full well when to pick his battles and she'd be disappointed if she thought he was going to rise to her bait this time around.

"Good then, it's settled. The apartment it is."

A flush rose in her cheeks. Annoyance, perhaps? Irritated or not, she gathered her bag and followed him out the office. She remained silent until they reached the undercover parking below the apartment complex.

"Is that my car?"

While she'd been interested and had plied him with questions about Jackson Importers all afternoon, this was the first sign of genuine animation he'd seen in her face since the weekend.

"Sure is. I have two spaces here. It makes sense for you to have your own wheels easily available, but we'll probably commute together most of the time."

She hastened out of the Maserati and he watched as she checked over her vehicle, examining every panel.

"It's a Roadster, right?" he asked.

"Yeah," she replied, finally satisfied the vehicle had come to no harm. "A '58 300 SL, to be precise. Good to see your people didn't do any damage."

"I only use the best," he replied.

Nicole eyed him over the soft top of her car. What would he do, she wondered, if she just jumped in, started it up and gunned it out of here? The instant the thought blossomed in her mind she knew she'd never carry it through. Not when he held such damning evidence over her and especially not now that the photo of the two of them last Thursday night had probably been brought to her father's attention.

"I'm pleased to hear it," she finally managed.

"Come on up to the apartment. You must be starving by now."

Now that he mentioned it, she was pretty hungry. She'd only had a nibble of the muffin at breakfast and had refused to stop and eat lunch.

"Sure, it's not like there's anything else to do," she said with a touch of defiance.

For some reason he gave her a look that she could only describe as approving. What? She'd subtly insulted him and he beamed back at her? The man was a conundrum, all right. A very powerful and sexy conundrum with an inordinate amount of control over her life right now. She may not like it, but she would just have to get used to it, she told herself. Even so, she didn't have to make him positively happy about the situation.

The trip in the elevator was smooth and swift and the doors opened to a corridor lined with expensive artwork. Her heels sank into the thick carpet as they walked to the end of the corridor where Nate swiped a key card and then pushed open one of two massive double doors and gestured her inside. Her breath caught in her throat as she took in the vista in front of her. She'd thought the view from his office was stunning, but this was something else. She could see over North Head and Mt. Victoria, out to Rangitoto Island and beyond.

"You certainly like your sea views," she said, dropping her bag on one of the wide and comfortable-looking leather sofas that faced out to the balcony.

"I do."

His answer was short and succinct and came from

right behind her. Suddenly she was aware of him. Painfully aware. Every nerve in her body attuned to the knowledge that right now very little space separated them. After that one kiss in the boardroom, he'd kept his distance. She hadn't realized up until now just how much she'd craved his touch. But she wouldn't give in. Couldn't. She had some pride left.

Before he could do anything, she stepped away, creating a void between them as she turned and faced him. A void that left her body silently screaming but which she refused to acknowledge, because that would only have her fall very firmly exactly where he so obviously wanted her, again. She might not be able to control much else in her world right now, but she could have some mastery over herself—however hard fought for.

"Where is my bedroom?" she asked.

"The master suite is right through there," he said, pointing down a wide hallway.

"No, not your bedroom," she said pointedly, "mine. I agreed to work for you. I never said anything about anything else."

"Anything else being?"

"You know exactly what I mean."

"Oh, you mean this?"

Nate traced the neckline of her dress with the knuckle of his forefinger, smiling approvingly when her skin reacted with a scatter of goose bumps. Nicole didn't move, she could barely breathe. One touch from him was about enough to send her up in flames. Already her entire body was invested in that tiny point of contact. She steeled herself for more, knowing she daren't so much as betray another measure of reaction.

"Are you going to force me, Nate?" she asked, her

voicc deadly calm and at total odds with the swirl of desire that fought for dominance.

"Force you? No, I don't think so."

"Believe me, I don't want you."

"You don't want me—or you don't *want* to want me?"

She held her ground, refusing to answer, still not moving so much as a muscle. Eventually Nate let his hand drop.

"There's a guest bedroom and en suite second on the right. I'll move your things in there."

"Thank you."

Nicole allowed herself to breathe again. It was a small victory but an important one. She felt as if she'd conquered Everest.

It was Thursday evening, a week since they'd met, yet it felt as if it had been a lifetime. Nicole shut down her laptop and grabbed the overseas market reports she planned on using as her bedtime reading tonight. Sleep had been elusive these past few days. Knowing Nate was only meters down the hall from where she slept each night was unnerving. *It was your own choice,* she reminded herself sternly.

She'd been surprised to find Nate appeared unperturbed by her insistence on separate rooms, and it made her wonder whether she was alone in believing their lovemaking had been way outside the usual realm of experience. Maybe he was like that with all his women. She was surprised at the bitter taste that formed in the back of her mouth at the thought. How many other women lay in their bed each night reliving, caress by caress, the exquisite beauty of his touch against their skin, the possession of his body as it filled theirs?

She closed her eyes as a surge of need billowed through her body. It was just sex, for goodness' sake, she reminded herself as she shook her head slightly and opened her eyes. She could live without it. *Liar,* an insidious voice in the back of her mind whispered.

The office door swung open and the object of her thoughts filled the doorway. Her eyes roamed his body, taking in every aspect of his perfection from the hand-tooled leather of his Italian shoes to the sharp line of his tailored suit jacket. Slowly she raised her eyes to meet his, cursing the flush she knew colored her cheeks.

"I'm glad I caught you," Nate said, dispensing with any social pleasantries.

He was like that, she'd noticed. Charming as all get out when necessary, but straight to the point when it wasn't. Clearly she fell into the "not necessary to be charmed" pile now, Nicole thought with an internal grimace. *Or maybe,* that little inner voice whispered again, *he's just as frustrated as you are and this is how he shows it.*

"What's up?" Nicole answered, forcing a nonchalance into her voice she was far from feeling.

"Your brother and Anna Garrick headed down to the Marlborough region today."

"Judd and Anna? Why?"

"I was hoping you'd be in the position to answer that. We all know it's one of New Zealand's major wine producing areas but Wilson Wines has only ever sold imported product for distribution before."

"Oh, no!" Nicole lifted a hand to her mouth.

"You know why they're there?"

She shook her head. "I can't be certain. Dad pretty

much dismissed my study as being a waste of time and energy."

"Study?" Nate's expression became intent, every muscle in his body drawn tight.

"With the rising cost of international freight and the fluctuation of the New Zealand dollar, I thought it would be a good time to explore the internal distribution of a solid range of New Zealand wines. Wines not already being sold through major liquor retailers and supermarkets. The kinds of wines people might find in upmarket restaurants, bars and hotels. But make those wines a bit more accessible to the average consumer," she explained.

"Makes sense." Nate nodded. "Why did your father dismiss the study? Was it not feasible?"

Nicole laughed. "You think my father explained his decision to me? You don't know him as well as you think. No, he just told me we weren't pursuing it any further and not to waste any more of my time on it. So I didn't. Judd or Anna must have found my reports and somehow persuaded him the idea had merit."

"They've gone down to solicit new suppliers?"

"I'd say so."

Nicole fought to hide the hot rush of anger she felt toward her father for his about-face on her recommendations.

"You must have put a lot of work into this. It pisses you off, doesn't it, that your brother is getting to see through what you started?"

"That's a polite way of putting it," Nicole said. She was angry and hugely disappointed that she hadn't had the opportunity to see it all through. "I'd already approached several wineries whose management teams were very keen to come on board."

"Then I'd suggest you stop wasting time," Nate said, a half smile on his face.

"Time?" She felt like an idiot. What on earth was he talking about.

"Yeah, get down there and win back your business. Show me you can go at this with everything you've got."

Nicole looked at him in amazement. Carte blanche to progress her idea? Just like that? What if it failed? There were already so many wonderful and inexpensive New Zealand wines on the market, could it support more? Would there be a demand for the more exclusive vintages? And what about the upmarket imported wines they already sold? Would they be eating into their current business instead of growing new opportunities?

Her market analysis and research had borne out a definite niche of demand. Maybe she'd been too quick to let her father quash her idea. Maybe she just should have fought harder for what she believed in, what she knew to have great potential. Excitement began to bubble through her veins.

"Right, I'll get right on it," she said, reaching into her handbag for one of the backup memory sticks she always carried with her and powering her computer back up. She'd show Nate, all right. Success or fail, she'd show him, and maybe—just maybe—somewhere along the line she'd get to show her father her true worth to him, after all.

"Need any help?" Nate offered.

"No, I think I'll be okay. I'll start making calls first thing tomorrow and plan to head down on Sunday. I'd rather not bump into Judd and Anna while I'm down there so if I can work out who they're likely to be seeing first, and when, I can follow along behind and make an offer the wineries can't refuse."

"I like the way you think. I take it you have those reports on your drive?"

She nodded, automatically pulling up the files even as he spoke.

Inside, however, she alternated between disbelief that Nate believed in her ideas and the sheer joy of being told to implement them. She hesitated before sending the print command, waiting for him to reveal the catch or to shut her down, but, to her surprise, it didn't come.

"If you print me off a set we can go over them together. I'll order some dinner up for us while you do that."

Nicole nodded again, forcing her focus on the screen in front of her as Nate left the room. He was really going ahead with this. She'd reprinted her list of contacts and her feasibility study by the time Nate returned to the office.

"I've asked a few others to stay back in case you need them," he said as he grabbed a chair and pulled it next to her.

"Really?" she said, trying to control the sudden acceleration in her heart rate as his large body filled the space next to hers.

"We're a team here, Nicole. I wouldn't expect any of my staff to do this all alone. Besides, when it comes to you making an offer your clients can't refuse, I think it would be best if that offer came from a brainstorming session among us all so that it is completely unbeatable."

Nicole murmured her assent and concentrated on her computer screen as unexpected tears sprang to her eyes. A team. Even though she was here under duress, Nate still trusted her with all the resources of his company, backing her play and giving her room to develop her plan collaboratively, with all the help she needed. It was quite a change from Wilson Wines, where an idea of hers would have had to be fully formulated, presented and approved by her father before any backup was given.

It was a system that had probably worked well when the company first began, and it had been so crucial to have a clear chain of command to keep the business stable and the employees on track. But even when the company had grown past that stage, the management style had never changed. At Wilson Wines she'd had to fight for change tooth and nail, losing more often than not to her father's dictatorial management style. When she had her emotions in check she asked Nate a question.

"Has Jackson Importers always done everything by committee?"

She aimed to keep her tone light, teasing even, but she knew she'd come off as sounding critical when Nate shot her a dark glance.

"For the very important stuff, yes. When we succeed, and we do tend to do that a whole lot, we succeed together. When everyone has a hand in it, everyone works harder and feels far more satisfaction on an individual level. Why, don't you think that's important?"

"No, no, it's not that. I've just…not really come across that before."

"Well, you have only ever worked at Wilson Wines, right? Even on your school holidays? You never took any other kind of after-school job, did you?"

She was surprised he knew that information. He

seemed to know a terrible lot about her. Just how much? she wondered, feeling a little as if she was under a microscope—pinned, as she was, by his intent gaze.

"No, I didn't. All I ever wanted was to work with my father."

Nate's expression softened and, if she wasn't mistaken, his eyes gleamed now with something more akin to compassion.

"I know what you mean. From when I was very young and I knew that Dad was working all the hours that God sent so he could provide for me and my mother, I knew that I wanted to help him. I couldn't qualify soon enough. If he'd have let me, I'd have started with Jackson Importers straight from school, but he insisted that I complete university first, and that I take jobs and internships with other companies while I was a student, so I could be sure Jackson Importers was where I wanted to be. At the time, I was upset that he thought I didn't know what I wanted, but now I can appreciate the experience I gained. It helped me have more insight than I would've had if I'd only ever worked here."

"And then you went overseas?"

"Yeah, first of all for a bit of a holiday—again, at his insistence—then, while I was there I just saw so many opportunities for our company if they had a man on the ground right there in the heart of our major European suppliers."

"Your father just let you do that without any experience in the company? You must have been so young."

Nate shrugged. "What can I say? He liked my proposal and he felt we had nothing to lose by it. I worked my butt off on my own for the first few years and then, over time and as we continued to grow, we built up our staff."

Nicole fought back the pang of envy that struck her fair and square in the chest. What would it be like, she wondered, to be able to just pitch an idea and then have a free hand in following it through? Suddenly it occurred to her that that was exactly what Nate had done for her here and now. He'd heard her out, he was now examining her report and making notations on a pad of paper on the desk in front of him, and he'd assembled a team to support her in it.

Her mind reeled with confusion. He was forcing her to stay here—blackmailing her. Why, then, was he basically handing her the chance to see her idea through—an idea that her father had rejected—without any question?

There was a knock at the office door and it opened. Raoul stood there, his tie loosened at his throat and his shirtsleeves rolled up as if he meant business.

"Dinner has been delivered. We're setting up in the boardroom. You guys ready to join us?"

"We'll be through in a minute," Nate said. Once Raoul had gone, Nate stood and gathered up his notes and Nicole's papers. "Are you all set?"

"Sure," she said. "Just one thing."

"What's that?"

"Why are you doing this?"

"This?" he asked, holding her report up in one hand.

"Yeah. Why? It could just as easily fail and cost you a whole lot of money."

Nate shrugged, an eloquent movement of his broad shoulders beneath the fine wool of his suit. "I trust you, and I know you're onto a winner here. I can see it already in the work you've done to date. Why waste it? Besides, I can't wait to imagine the look on your father's face when we win."

"You think we will?"

"Don't doubt yourself or our team, Nicole. We're invincible when we put our minds to it." Nate crossed the room and held the door open. "Shall we?"

She nodded decisively and picked up her handbag and laptop and followed him through to the boardroom. Invincible. It should scare her that he was so supremely confident, but for some reason it gave her strength, instead. Strength and a belief that she could do this.

Hard on the heels of that thought she realized how much she was enjoying working with Nate. Too much, in fact. As an employer, he was the antithesis of Charles Wilson. She didn't have too much time to dwell on her thoughts, though, because once they entered the boardroom they were full-on. Nate invited her to explain her concept to the group in summarized format and then gave them his overview of her report. Over a selection of Chinese takeout they brainstormed ideas back and forth until Nicole barely recognized the idea as her own anymore. Even so, there was one thing she knew for certain. She was really excited about the direction this was taking and the fact that she'd been integral in instigating it.

By the time she and Nate went back to his apartment she was shattered, and yet incredibly buoyed up at the same time. They had a solid plan in place and she had all the ammunition she needed for when she went to win over any business that Judd and Anna might already have secured.

As she went to turn in for the night she paused in the hallway leading to the bedrooms.

"Nate?"

Nate was almost at his door and he stopped the instant she called to him. "Yeah?"

"Thank you for today."

He walked back up the hallway toward her. She couldn't read his expression in the dim lighting but as he drew nearer, she could see the half smile on his face.

"You're thanking me?" he asked.

She nodded. "For believing in me."

He shook his head slightly. "You're worth it, Nicole. I don't know why your father kept you under a bushel the way he did but, with your mind, the whole world should be at your feet. I'm just letting you use what is your own natural talent."

"I—I appreciate it," she answered, unused to receiving such direct praise. "I hate to admit this, but I really enjoyed this evening."

"Hey, there will be many more of those," Nate said.

"Well, like I said, thanks."

She hovered outside her door, her mind still humming with all the excitement of seeing her brainchild grow and expand into a working business plan. A plan she'd be implementing the moment her feet touched Marlborough soil.

It only seemed natural to brush her lips against Nate's cheeks and then, when that wasn't enough, to kiss him on the lips. He remained still for a moment but then his arms were around her and his mouth was hungry against hers. Her heart rate accelerated as she accepted the inevitable. They were going to make love. A part of her was glad of it, glad she no longer had to fight her instinctive and constant response to Nate's presence. But deep inside she knew she was, in part, surrendering to him. Giving a piece of herself that she'd held back. A piece she knew she'd be lucky to get back whole, ever again.

Seven

Nate backed Nicole against her bedroom door and relished the taste of her as they consumed one another with their kiss. He'd known it would only be a matter of time before Nicole capitulated to him again. With a passion as incendiary as theirs, it was bound to happen. Knowing that hadn't made the waiting any easier, but having that advantage over her—making her stay with him—had tempered his desire just enough to take the edge off. Just enough so that he could wait patiently and let her come to him as he'd planned. And now, at last, everything was falling into place.

It had been exhilarating seeing her in action today. There was nothing sexier than a woman with confidence and intelligence, and Nicole had both in spades. That she was perfectly assembled with features that could make even an angel weep was a welcome bonus, in his mind.

But now it was most definitely time to stop thinking and start doing. Doing and feeling. He reached behind Nicole and eased her bedroom door open, walking her slowly inside before closing the door behind them. Cocooning them in darkness only vaguely punctuated by the lights across the harbor that were visible through her bedroom window. He continued to guide her backward into the darkened room. At the edge of the bed he stopped, reaching for the zipper at the back of her dress and easing it down carefully before working the fabric away from her delectable body. For a split second he wished he'd taken the time to turn on a light, so he could feast his eyes upon her as he planned to feast with his mouth very shortly. But compulsion overcame his need to see what he was doing to her, to see her reaction to it. Instead, he would rely on his other senses.

His body craved urgency, but he held on to enough reason to know that he wanted to take his time, to stretch this out for as long as humanly possible. To give and to receive over and over again until neither of them could stand another second of the torment.

Nicole made a little humming sound in the back of her throat as he bent his head and traced a fine line from the edge of her jaw and down the cord of her neck with his tongue. Her hands gripped his shoulders as he moved lower, following the very top of the swell of her breasts inside the expensive lingerie he knew she wore. Lingerie he had paid for. Lingerie he'd tortured himself with all this week by picturing—wondering whether she was wearing the sapphire-blue ensemble, or the ruby red. Or maybe it was one of the other myriad feminine provocations he'd seen delicately wrapped in tissue before being placed in the store's shopping bag and handed over to her.

Here and now, in the darkness, he knew color didn't matter. All that mattered was sensation and, oh, God, she felt amazing in his arms, beneath his lips. He reached behind her, unsnapping the clasps of her bra.

He dispensed with the garment in an easy movement and reached with both his hands to cup the fullness of her breasts, testing their weight and lifting them slightly so he could bury his face in their softness before laving at the crease he'd created between them. He stroked the pads of his thumbs over her nipples, delighting in the straining peaks and the knowledge that his touch was making them harder, making her want him more.

Her hands let go their grip on his shoulders and moved to the collar of his shirt, unknotting his tie and sliding it free before her fingers were at his buttons, unsteady yet determined in their mission. He bit back a growl as her nails scraped across his chest, across his own sensitive nubs. Her hands shifted to the buckle of his belt and then, mercifully, eased down his zipper and pushed his trousers to pool at his feet. His erection strained at the restriction of his boxer briefs, strained for her silken touch, but instead, she scraped her nails softly along his length and he almost lost all control.

Nate eased her back onto the bed before bending to swiftly kick off his shoes and peel off his socks so he could step out of his trousers. He slid his briefs away, allowing his swollen flesh to spring free, and joined Nicole on the bed. Waves of heat rolled off her body, heat that intensified as his fingers roamed inside the fabric of her panties—sought, and found, the slick core of her. He played his fingers across her cleft, reveling in the heat and wetness of her body, knowing it was like this in readiness for him and him alone. She gasped when he brushed the tip of one finger across her clitoris, her gasp turning into a moan as he increased the pressure ever so slightly before easing it off again.

She pressed up into his hand, the movement making him smile. She'd been so controlled all week and now here she was. Her movements uninhibited. He gently slid her free of her underwear and then tugged it away from her body completely before settling himself between her legs. He felt her thighs tremble as he ran his palms across their silky smoothness. Tremble and then tighten as he lowered his mouth to her damp heat. He rolled his tongue across the bead of flesh hidden at her apex. Over and over until her body was so tense he knew she was seconds away from completion.

Completion he would give her. He closed his mouth around that special place and sucked hard, the action sending her over the edge.

Nate waited until the spasms that rocked her body eased off, then rose over her, reaching for the bedside cabinet where, as a good host, he knew there was a stock of condoms. He eased open the drawer and reached inside.

"They're not there," Nicole said from beneath him.

"They're not? Then—"

"I cut them up and threw them out. I didn't want to be tempted."

He'd have laughed if he wasn't so hard he was on the point of agony. Instead, he pressed a kiss to her lips.

"Don't move," he said, "I'll be straight back."

He covered the distance between their bedrooms in record time, then came back with a handful of condoms that he dumped into the still-open drawer, with the exception of the one that he ripped open and swiftly used to sheath himself.

"This time when you come," he continued, as he reached for the beside lamp and switched it on, "I want to see you."

She made a sound as if to protest but the noise cut off as he eased his length inside her. He gritted his teeth together, clenching his jaw tight as he fought to restrain the urge to take her hard and fast. To bring them both to a crashing climax within the shortest time possible. Instead, he moved slowly, painstakingly. She met his rhythm and he smiled down at her as she tried to hasten him in his movements.

"It'll be better this way," he said. "Trust me."

He knew it had been worth the wait as he felt her inner muscles begin to quiver and tighten around him. Nicole's eyes were glazed, her lips parted on a panting breath and her cheeks flushed. A fine dew of perspiration gathered at her temples. His own climax was only seconds away, and in the instant her body began to ripple around him he let go, letting her body wring his satisfaction from him. Giving himself over to the pulse that spent itself all the way from the soles of his feet.

Nicole lay beneath him, waiting for her heartbeat to return to normal, if such a thing were possible. It seemed that from the moment she'd laid eyes on Nate Jackson, she'd been in a constant state of hyperawareness. Colors were brighter, scents stronger and pleasure so much more intense than she'd ever known. She had no idea where this was all going to lead. She only knew, deep down inside, that she would probably never feel this much again with another man. The thought terrified her, because she knew this couldn't last.

She'd never been enough for anyone before. That's

why she hadn't been able to make her mother love her, or to make her father proud. And now she had Nate, who made her feel as if she could do anything…but she knew better than to rely on that. Because she wasn't enough for him, either—not on her own. He was only with her now to enact revenge on her father—once that was complete, she'd go back to being not enough.

Nate shifted above her, pulling from her body before rolling away. Despite the sternly chiding voice in her head telling her not to get too comfortable or too attached, she still made a sound of protest as his warmth left her—right before she froze at his next words.

"Let me get rid of this, we don't want another near miss like last weekend."

Every last vestige of afterglow fled her body as her blood ran cold. "What do you mean 'near miss?'"

"Didn't I mention it? We went to sleep like this that first night. The condom came off. But you're on the Pill, right?"

She wasn't. But that wasn't the issue. He should have told her straightaway so she could have gone to a pharmacy and gotten the morning-after pill. Being with Nate was bad enough but how on earth would she explain a baby to her father?

"Nicole? You *are* on the Pill, aren't you?"

"No, I'm not," she told him, a panicked flutter beginning in her chest. "Why didn't you tell me? What if—"

"I'll deal with it," he said firmly.

He'd deal with it? What about her? Didn't her thoughts or feelings on the matter count at all? And just how would he deal with it? Would he insist on a termination, or would he use a pregnancy as another tool to hurt her father? It occurred to Nicole that while

Nate had given her all the freedom in the world when it came to the workplace, he gave none in her personal space whatsoever. When Nate came back into the bed she had already rolled onto her side and was feigning sleep. She had a lot on her mind—and she knew she wouldn't be able to think if he was touching her.

By the time Wednesday morning rolled around Nicole had everything in the bag. Four out of the six wineries Judd and Anna had visited had jumped ship to Jackson Importers, due in part to the relationship she had already built with them during her feasibility study. And along with them she'd also picked up at least three additional contacts, who were excited about the prospect of widening their distribution.

Her days had been full-on. Judd had done a very good job of selling Wilson Wines to the contacts she'd had on her list, but she'd done a better one and it felt good to be on top. As she awaited her luggage at the baggage carousel at Auckland's domestic airport, she allowed herself a smile of satisfaction.

"Well, if you don't look like the cat that got the cream, hmm?"

Her pulse leaped in her veins as Nate's voice surrounded her in its velvet softness. She turned and faced him, willing her heart rate back under control. Willing her body to calm and cool down just a notch so he wouldn't know just how much she'd ached for him each night she'd been away.

"It went well," she said smoothly. "I didn't expect you to be here to pick me up. I could have taken a taxi."

"I wanted to see you," he said simply.

He bent and kissed her on the lips, a hard press of skin against skin and then he was gone again. She fought the urge to press her fingers to her lips, to hold him there for just a moment longer. Nate constantly surprised her. On the one hand he could be so overbearing and yet, on the other…

"Oh, there's my bag," she cried, seeing the distinctive iridescent red case coming through on the carousel.

She'd been delighted with the set of luggage when Nate had had it delivered to the apartment before her departure, even if it was a little brighter than anything she'd owned before. Still, it was distinctive and cheerful.

Nate moved to collect her bag, appearing nonplussed about carrying such a feminine item as he placed one hand at the small of Nicole's back and guided her out to the parking building.

"Are we heading straight into the office?" she asked as he directed the car up George Bolt Memorial Drive and toward the motorway interchange.

"No."

"Oh, I thought—"

"I told them we wouldn't be in until after midday."

Nicole was surprised. She'd thought he would have wanted her to debrief the team and keep the ball rolling. Losing momentum with this could be disastrous, as Judd and Anna would shortly find out, to their cost.

Judd and Anna—that was a combination she'd never considered before. And yet the representatives from the wineries had told her that her brother and her best friend had worked quite well together, and had, moreover, seemed…close.

She sighed. There was a time when she would have been the first to know if there was a new man in Anna's life. The two of them had shared everything, and there had never been any secrets between them, until now. They'd been friends from childhood, her father's new housekeeper bringing an inbuilt playmate when she'd taken on the role.

They'd even attended the same private schools, with Charles picking up the tab for Anna's fees so his daughter would never be without her best friend. Thinking about it, she could see why Anna was so fiercely devoted to her father. Charles Wilson had given her the world on a platter. A world her mother couldn't have provided alone on a housekeeper's salary. If Anna hadn't done what Charles had asked of her, it would be like saying she didn't appreciate everything the old man had done for her over the years, and Nicole knew without a shadow of doubt that he would have held his own loyalty to Anna over her head in some subtle way.

She desperately wanted to reach out to Anna again. To mend the breach that had been caused by the conflict of loyalties. To rebuild their friendship if they still had that chance.

And while she longed to talk to Anna about Judd, and the rumors she had heard about the two of them, she also wished for a chance to talk to someone about her relationship with Nate. Nicole snuck a glance over at the man beside her and had to resist the urge to squirm in her seat. Just looking at him drove her crazy—she needed a good dose of Anna's gentle practicality to get her thoughts and feelings in order.

Nicole knew she *wanted* Nate—that was impossible to deny. Yet she still resented what he was doing to her, the leverage he held over her head. And underneath it all, she worried about what would happen next. How long would she spend as a pawn between her father and her lover, and how would it all end?

Nate was surprisingly quiet as they journeyed into the city and he handled the car with very deliberate movements, staying at the upper limit of the speed restrictions. By the time they pulled into the covered car parking at the apartment building she could feel tension rippling off him in waves. What on earth was wrong?

He stayed silent as they traveled in the elevator to his floor but the instant they were inside the apartment, she got her answer.

Nate pulled her into his arms and kissed her, really kissed her this time. Hot, wet and hungry. Her body bloomed with heat, moisture gathering at her center in rapid-fire time. Barely breaking contact with one another, they shed their clothing in a heap on the tiled entrance floor and Nate lifted her onto the marble-topped hall table. She gasped at the cold surface against her bare buttocks, but the marble didn't feel cold for long. She was on fire for him, resenting the time it took him to sheath himself with a condom. And then, thankfully, he was sliding inside her, stretching her with his hard length and driving her to the point of distraction as his hips began to pump.

Her orgasm took her completely by surprise. One moment she was accepting him into her body, the next she was flying on a trajectory that led to starbursts of pleasure radiating throughout her body. She clutched at Nate's shoulders, her heels digging into his buttocks as wave after wave consumed her, barely hearing his cry of satisfaction as his own climax slammed through his body.

It took several minutes for her to come back to reality, to realize just what they'd done and where. Nate rested his forehead against hers.

"I told you I wanted to see you."

Nicole laughed. "Well, you're definitely seeing all of me now. I was beginning to think something was wrong. You were so quiet in the car."

"I wanted to concentrate on getting here as quickly as possible. Believe me, the airport hotels were looking mighty good there at one stage."

He withdrew from her and caught her mouth with another deep kiss. This time with the sharp edge of passion assuaged, and with a tenderness she hadn't sensed in him before. It confused her, but then he was constantly doing that. In some respects he seemed to want to dictate every part of her life, yet in others he let her have her head. She could never predict how he'd react. She wanted to push back at him, verbally and physically sometimes, just to get a bit of space and control back in her life, and then he'd go and literally sweep her off her feet and do something like this. Something that transcended reason and gave her an insight into just how she affected him on a personal level. Or did it? Was she still reading him wrong—seeing what she wanted to see? There was no way to know for sure. She doubted she'd ever have him figured out completely.

Nate lifted her from the tabletop, allowing her body to glide against his as her feet found her footing. She shuddered anew at the skin-against-skin contact. There was nothing she wanted more right now than to prolong the physical link they had between them. In that, at least, they were in perfect harmony.

In their earlier eagerness they hadn't noticed the enameled brass vase had toppled off the surface of the table—its fall to the floor leaving a sizable chip in one of the tiles. Nicole bent to lift the vase back into its place.

"That's a shame," she said, gesturing to the floor. "Will you be able to get it repaired?"

"I won't bother. I like the reminder of how it got there," Nate said with a smile that sent tingles through her body all over again. "Come on, let's go take a shower."

It was well after midday by the time they made it into the office and Nicole was feeling the effects of making her 6:45 a.m. flight and the vigorous lovemaking she and Nate had indulged in before going into work. She made it through her debrief without making any mistakes or leaving any glaring holes in her rundown of who had come on board with them and why, and what she had negotiated in their individual contracts.

The meeting was just tying up when she overheard Raoul mention her father's name to Nate.

"…he wasn't looking all that good. Are you sure you want to keep this up?" Raoul said in a voice that was meant for Nate's ears only.

Nate flicked her a glance before turning his back to her and saying something to Raoul that saw the other man glance her way also before giving Nate a slight nod. Raoul gathered his papers and left the room, signaling the exodus for the rest of the staff. Nicole waited until everyone else had left the boardroom before fronting up to Nate.

"What's wrong with my father?" she demanded.

"Nothing more than the usual," Nate responded flatly.

"So what were you and Raoul talking about?"

"Look, he just mentioned he saw your father at a function over the weekend and that he looked more tired than usual. He hasn't been well, has he?"

Nicole shook her head. No, he hadn't been well. And her leaving Wilson Wines and working for Jackson Importers would be exacerbating that. Responsibility struck her fair and square in her chest as she realized the further ramifications of the business she'd just secured and what it would mean to her father on a personal level. She'd been so focused on beating Judd to the finish line, on winning the business away from *him,* that she'd lost sight of her father's stake in all this. Wilson Wines had been holding on to its market share by the skin of its teeth in recent years. She knew that better than anyone. And yet, with her usual impulsiveness, she'd just made matters worse for them. In particular, worse for her father's already weakened health.

"Nicole, it's not your fault he's not well." Nate's voice broke through her fugue of guilt.

She raised her eyes to meet his. "No, but my being here won't be doing him any good, either, will it? Did you know about his health problems all along? Was that a part of your plan, to take a sick man and make him sicker?"

"What, you think I want your father dead?"

"An eye for an eye, a life for a life. Isn't that what revenge is all about?"

"Nicole, you misjudge me if you think I'm capable of something like that. I'm angry at your father, yes, I'm very angry for what he did to mine. I'm furious that he's never admitted, ever, that he made a mistake in treating his best friend the way he did. But it's not his state of health that I want to change—it's his state of mind. Your father needs to stop thinking of himself as the one on top who is always right, and who can never be questioned. Don't tell me you haven't realized that about him, or that his autocratic ways haven't hurt you, too. *That's* the revenge I want—for him to realize that the world doesn't run on his terms. That he's made mistakes, and people have suffered as a result. Then he can finally start to take responsibility for the damage that he's done."

"Can't you leave it in the past?" Nicole pleaded. "Yes, he made mistakes, but he's paid for them, too. For twenty-five years, he didn't even know if Judd was truly his son!"

"You think that's enough to make up for what he did?" Nate sneered. "He *destroyed* my father. Do you know what that means? He sucked every last bit of joy out of him, every last bit of pride. With his accusations he tainted my father for life. Dad lost more than a friend and a business partner over your father's twisted blame. He lost the respect of his peers, as well, not to mention his income. The roll-on effect to my mother and myself was huge. Don't ever underestimate that. Life became very hard for us all. While you were still in that gothic monstrosity you call home, eating hot meals every night and wearing your designer labels, my mother and I were reduced to being reliant on food parcels and hand-me-downs."

Nate's words rained down on her like hail from a black cloud and, through it, all she could hear was the hurt in his voice. The pain of a boy whose father had changed and withdrawn from him. A boy who'd spent his whole life driven by the dispute between two men.

"But do you see what you're doing to him now?" she asked softly, all her earlier anger and defensiveness having fled. "You're the one in the position of power this time," she reminded him, "and how much damage are *you* doing by refusing to forgive?"

"Look, we're never going to see eye to eye on this and I'm not prepared to discuss it any further."

"Well, that's a lovely cop-out," she pushed back, not ready to let things go just yet. She deserved answers. "You think you were the only one affected? I lost my mother and my brother over the whole situation. Isn't it enough for you, now, that my brother is back? That my father knows that *he* is Judd's father and your father isn't?"

Nate shook his head. "It's not as simple as that."

"Yes, Nate. It is," Nicole insisted. "Judd's DNA testing proved he is Dad's natural-born son. The argument between our fathers was just that. Between *them.* Why let that keep affecting us now?"

"Because he's never apologized. Charles Wilson has never admitted he was wrong," he said stubbornly.

"And if he did, would that make it all go away? Would that change the fact that you and your mother suffered while your father found his financial feet again?"

"You don't understand."

"No, you're right," she said sadly. "I'll never understand. Too many people were hurt back then, Nate. Don't carry on the feud. It's just not worth it."

"I'm not letting you go back to him, Nicole."

"I don't think you can stop me."

"Aren't you forgetting something?"

"No, Nate, I'm not forgetting that you can still hold that DVD over me. I'd just hope that you'd be man enough not to."

Eight

They went back to Karekare that night, their journey completed in silence, and once at the house Nicole said she was turning in early. She woke in the early hours of the morning to find the bed still empty beside her, a faint flicker of light coming from the main room down the hall. She got up from the bed and pulled on the peignoir that matched her ivory chiffon nightgown. The floor was cold against her bare feet, yet she made no sound as she padded along the polished wooden floor.

The room was in darkness, the only light coming from the massive LCD television screen mounted on the wall. Nate was sitting on the couch opposite the TV, a glass of red wine on the coffee table in front of him. Even though the sound was off on the television, he hadn't heard her enter the room, his attention fixed on the screen.

Nicole hazarded a look and instantly wished she'd

stayed in bed. There, in all their glory, were the two of them—making love. At the time she'd thought it would be a bit of fun. After all, she'd been the one to instigate it. Again, her rashness getting her into a situation she'd have done better to avoid. She closed her eyes for a moment, but behind her lids she could still see the images of their bodies entwined. Of the expression on her face as Nate did things to her she'd never allowed any other man to do. Of how she'd trusted him and loved every second of it, never for a moment thinking there could possibly be any consequences.

Opening her eyes, she turned and left the room before Nate could sense or hear her there. In the bedroom she yanked off her peignoir and threw herself back into the bed, closing her eyes tight once more—but not tight enough to stop the flow of tears that came from beneath them.

Nate sat alone in the dark, staring at the screen in front of him, at the evidence of the incredible connection he had with the flesh and blood, passionate woman sleeping in his bed down the hall.

He'd threatened her now twice with the DVD. The first time he'd meant it. The second? Well, he'd thought he'd meant it. Until now. Until he'd started to watch it again and had realized that he could never use this against her.

He still wanted his revenge against Charles Wilson. But he wouldn't—couldn't—hurt Nicole to achieve it. Her words today had struck deep inside him. Logically he knew she was right, but emotionally he was still that determined little boy who'd wanted to make his father's eyes smile again.

Nate had always understood his parents' relationship

was an anomaly amongst his friends' parents' bonds. Deborah Hunter and Thomas Jackson had never married. Never even lived together. Yet they were united as one on the upbringing of their son. He'd asked his mother once, when he was still small, why his daddy didn't live with them, and his mother had had such a sad expression in her eyes when she'd told him that Thomas simply wasn't like other daddies. Nate had never wanted to see that sorrow on his mother's face again, had never pushed for more answers.

It wasn't until he was older that he'd realized what it was that made his father different, and it was something that had made him even more determined to teach Charles Wilson a lesson. Thomas Jackson was gay. His sexual orientation had been misunderstood and even feared by others when he was a young man—if it had been public knowledge then he would have been touched by a stigma that might have seen him lose friends, not to mention business.

Nate himself was the result of a last-ditch attempt on his father's part to disprove the truth about himself. Thomas had explained it to Nate during his last visit to Europe before he'd died. How he'd met Deborah Hunter and, desperate to deny his own sexuality, had embarked upon an affair with her. It was a short-lived fling, but it had resulted in Nate's conception—a fact that had bound both Thomas and Deborah together as close friends for the rest of their lives. Nate didn't doubt that his mother had loved Thomas deeply, nor that he loved her in return. Just not in the way his mother needed.

The knowledge had explained a lot to Nate. Had answered so many questions he'd had but had never put into words. Nate knew his father could never have had the affair with Cynthia Masters-Wilson that Charles had accused Thomas of. It was something Charles Wilson should have known from the start—*would* have known, if he'd truly been a good friend to Thomas. But the man was known for his up-front, old-fashioned and often righteous attitude. In itself that was probably the reason why Thomas never confided his homosexuality to him. He had been afraid that he would lose Charles's friendship—and he had, even if it wasn't in the manner he'd anticipated. But Charles should have trusted Thomas, and the loss of that trust had decimated his father.

Yes, Nicole had been right when she'd said he couldn't change the past. But the little boy inside him still suffered. Charles Wilson had to pay. Nicole, on the other hand, had already paid more than enough, having to walk away from her home, her friends and her family.

Nate reached for the remote and snapped off the television. No, he wouldn't use the DVD against Nicole. The content of it was theirs, and theirs alone. But if he told her he had no intention of using it against her anymore, how could he ensure she would stay? Now that he had her, he didn't want to let her go.

Sure, knowing she was a pivotal member of the Wilson Wines hierarchy, he'd wanted to use her to hurt their business—and if her recent trip was any indication, he'd succeed quite well in that goal. And he'd relished the thought of staking his own claim on someone who Charles Wilson took for granted would always be there. But keeping Nicole with him was no longer just about pulling her away from her father. Now he just *wanted* her, for reasons that had nothing to do with anyone but him and her.

It was more than desire, he admitted, although that was in itself an itch he found he couldn't scratch hard enough, or often enough with her. No, he wanted Nicole in a way he didn't fully understand, and could never describe. A way that had nothing to do with his plans.

And the truth of that scared him.

She was still alone when she woke in the morning but through the bathroom door she could hear the shower running. She lay between the tangled sheets that were the evidence of her restless night and wondered what Nate had been thinking while he'd watched the DVD last night. Was he imagining her father's anger and disgust? Would he send it with a letter accompanying it, explaining that he, Nate, was Thomas Jackson's son? A son Thomas Jackson had raised while Charles had sent his own away in a fit of pride and anger?

The very thought of her father opening such a letter, or even beginning to watch the DVD, made her feel physically ill and she dashed from the bedroom to the guest facilities, heaving over the toilet bowl until her stomach ached with the effort. She flushed the toilet and leaned both hands against the basin, willing her body back under control. With a shaking hand she turned on the faucet, letting the cold water splash over her hands and wrists before rinsing out her mouth and vigorously scrubbing at her face.

She felt like death warmed over. In fact, when she thought about it, she hadn't felt physically fit in days. Was this all the toll of the days she'd spent in Nelson and Blenheim and the emotional demands of living and working with Nate every day, or was there something else she should be worried about? She didn't want to think about the night Nate had said his condom had come off inside her as they'd slept. She didn't want to believe that she could have been vulnerable to falling pregnant for even an instant.

Pregnant? Her stomach clenched on the very thought and she stared at herself in the mirror, noting the dark shadows under her eyes, the lankness of her hair, the pallor of her skin. It had to be the stress, it just had to be. She was worried about her father and under immense strain with Nate.

Nicole wondered again about Charles. It worried her to think that his health had worsened, and she wished she could get a fuller report. Short of visiting him, though, where she had no doubt she would be told in no uncertain terms of how unwelcome she was, she had only one other option. She had to ask Anna. Her friend would know the truth about Charles's health. She'd email Anna today when they got into the office, arrange to meet for lunch if the other woman was willing. And then maybe, just maybe, Nicole would begin to get her life back on track again.

Sharing an office with Nate hadn't bothered her before but today it most definitely did. She had to wait until almost lunchtime, when he headed out for a meeting, before she could compose the email she wanted to send to Anna. By now Wilson Wines would know that she'd wrested their new business from them. Would Anna even respond to her email? There was only one way to find out. She typed in the short missive and hit Send before she could change her mind.

She waited, drumming her fingers on the desk to see if Anna would respond. Maybe she was away from her desk, or maybe she was just ignoring the request to meet at Mission Bay for lunch. She couldn't stand it. She powered her computer down and grabbed her handbag. She'd wait at the restaurant. If Anna showed up, she showed up. If she didn't, well, then Nicole would just find out about her father some other way.

Nicole couldn't get over the relief that swamped her body as Anna made her way through the tables to where she was sitting at the back of the restaurant. Even so, the relief was tempered with a generous dose of apprehension as Anna sat in the chair opposite.

"I ordered for us already," Nicole said, hoping that Anna wouldn't mind she'd gone ahead and done so.

"Thank you, I think."

Dread clutched her heart. Was there to be no reconciliation between them, after all? If the look on Anna's face was anything to go by, twenty-odd years of friendship was about to go down the tubes.

"Oh, Anna, don't look at me like that, please."

"Like what?" her friend said, giving nothing away.

"Like you don't know whether I'm going to hit you or hug you."

Anna smiled, but it was a pale facsimile of her usual warmth. "Well, you weren't exactly happy with me the last time we talked to each other."

No, she hadn't been. She'd been feeling betrayed at the worst level possible, and she'd felt angry and trapped. A situation which she'd only made worse by yelling at her oldest friend, and running off. Nicole forced a smile to her lips and reached across the table to squeeze Anna's hand, the tension in her body easing just a little when the other woman didn't pull away. The waiter arrived at that moment with their Caesar salads and she let Anna's hand go. Once they were alone again, Anna asked her how she was doing. How she was really doing.

Nicole ached to tell her the truth, to tell her she'd gotten herself into an awful situation and that she couldn't see her way out of it, but she held it all inside, instead skating across the reality her life had become. But, she reminded herself, meeting with Anna today hadn't been about her. It was to find out how Charles was doing. She wasn't surprised when Anna told her he was less than impressed with her working for Nate. And, of course, Charles still had no idea that Nate was Thomas's son.

She asked about Charles's health, and was partially relieved when Anna told her he was okay. Anna wouldn't lie about something as important as that. What did hurt, though, was hearing about how easily Judd had picked up her side of things at Wilson Wines. She'd never been able to measure up to him, even though he'd grown up in another country. Always, she felt as if she'd been found lacking, and when Anna began to beg her to come back to Wilson Wines, to come home, she felt as if her heart would fracture into a million tiny pieces.

"I…I can't," she said, shaking her head, wishing the opposite was true.

"What do you mean, you can't? Of course you can. Your home is with us, your career was with us. Come back, please?"

If only it was that simple. Even if she told Anna about the blackmail, how could she admit the deeper truth—that she actually liked working for Jackson Importers? That she felt more valued and appreciated there than she had in her father's own company.

Nicole was ashamed of herself for even thinking it. She skirted around the issue and focused instead on the much-needed apology she had to deliver to the woman who had been her best friend for as long as she could remember. To her relief, Anna accepted the apology with her natural grace and they turned their discussion to anything and everything other than work, or men. How she felt about Nate was too raw and complicated for her to share with Anna just yet. She didn't even fully understand it herself, and until she did, talking about him was off limits. By the time their lunch was over, it almost felt as if everything was back to normal. As normal as it could be without them both returning to work in the same office.

"I'm so glad you emailed me," Anna said, standing and giving her an enveloping hug.

"I'm glad you're still talking to me. I don't deserve you, you know."

"Of course you do, and more," Anna replied. "I'll settle the bill, okay? Next time will be your turn."

"Are you sure?" Nicole had issued the invitation, lunch should have been on her.

"That there'll be a next time? Of course there will."

"Not that, silly." Nicole laughed, happy, on one level, that they were back to their usual banter.

But her joy was short-lived. Being with Anna had just reminded her of all she'd walked away from. All she'd thrown away with her reckless behavior. And now she had another problem to consider—that her impetuosity had possibly gotten her pregnant. That sense of fear and nausea she'd experienced this morning swirled around inside her again. Before Anna could notice she wasn't feeling well, or say another word that might see Nicole blurt out the whole ugly truth of what she'd gotten herself into, she gave her friend a farewell hug and left the restaurant.

The sunshine outside did little to dispel the coldness that dwelled deep inside her. Seeing Anna was an all-too-painful reminder of all Nicole was missing—her father, despite his recent behavior to her, her best friend. Even the opportunity to somehow carve a new relationship with the brother she'd never had a chance to know, and work with him to help stabilize and protect the family company. Instead, she was working against them all—and enjoying it. Shame swamped her. Somehow she had to make things right for what she'd done. Anna hadn't mentioned how the Nelson and Blenheim wineries business loss had been taken in the office, but Nicole knew it must have hurt. She had to find a way to make that up to them.

It was during the short drive back to the city that Nicole's mind began to work overtime. There was most definitely a way she could continue working with Nate and yet remain loyal to her father and Wilson Wines. It would be tricky, but hey, no one had made her sign a confidentiality agreement. She could feed information to Anna on Nate's current development plans. Not enough that it would immediately point a finger at her when it came to light—and it most definitely would come to light, she had no doubt about that at all—but hopefully enough to give Wilson Wines an edge against Jackson Importers. After all, in very many cases they were competing for the same business, anyway. It would only be natural to assume they'd continue to cross swords in the marketplace.

Satisfied she'd finally found a workable answer to her situation, Nicole continued to the office, steadfastly ignoring the conflicted sensation that what she was about to do would hurt the very people who'd welcomed her into Jackson Imports with open arms. She swallowed against the lump that formed in her throat. If she could make this work, Charles would have to see her in a different light. Would have to value her worth to him. Wouldn't he?

Nate came from the 7:00 a.m. Monday morning meeting with his head of IT undecided about whether he was furious with Nicole or filled with admiration for her audacity. Over the weekend, while he'd thought she was sulking in her room, she'd been emailing information to Anna Garrick at Wilson Wines. Information he could well do without them knowing. At least, thanks to the tracking software he'd had installed on her laptop right from the beginning, his team had been able to find out exactly what information she'd passed on. Between the software and the team he had tracking her laptop activity, keeping an eye on Nicole had been an expensive investment, but well worth it if it made him aware that this was the tack she was taking.

But why was she doing it? She'd seemed satisfied with her success with the Marlborough district wineries. Then they'd had that blasted discussion, which had turned them back into silent ships that passed in the office, and in the night. Even at the Karekare house, she'd moved into another bedroom. He couldn't understand it. She was just as strongly attracted to him as he was to her. He knew it to his very bones. Knew it in every accidental touch from the ache it created deep within him and in the clouded look of suppressed need he saw in Nicole's eyes immediately afterward.

And it wasn't just physical. He was making every effort to satisfy all of her needs—including her need to feel valued and appreciated for her work. He was giving her every opportunity to excel at what she did best and yet it still wasn't enough. What more could he possibly give her? And why was everything he'd already given her not enough to make her happy? Was it truly that necessary to her to please her father, to the point where she'd throw away everything else he'd given her for the chance to make Charles Wilson proud?

He could cope with the collateral damage this time, but what she was doing had to stop. For his sake, for the company's sake, and for *her* sake, too. If there was one thing Nate knew, it was that Charles Wilson was a stubborn bastard who never forgave. Not his best friend, or his daughter. Nicole couldn't buy her way back into her daddy's heart with Jackson Importers secrets—she could only sabotage her own chances of succeeding with them. And he wasn't about to let her do that.

He pushed open the door to his office and felt a jolt of satisfaction when she jumped in response to his presence.

"I thought you were in a meeting," she said, swiftly covering her discomfiture.

Rain battered at the office window behind her as autumn's weather finally did an about-face and delivered on its usual wet and windy promise. The weather suited his mood.

"I was," he replied, his voice short as he chose his next words very carefully. "A very interesting meeting, in fact. It seems someone from our office has been feeding information about our latest initiatives to Wilson Wines. I don't suppose you'd know who that was, would you?"

To his satisfaction, she paled visibly under the onslaught of his words.

"How…?"

"How I know isn't relevant. But it's going to stop right here and right now, Nicole."

"You can't stop me," she said defiantly, rising from her chair and lifting her chin. "If you're going to make me work here and I'm privy to certain information, you can't prevent me from sharing it. I haven't signed any confidentiality agreement."

"No? I would have thought that the DVD was enough of a substitute, wouldn't you?"

She wavered where she stood and he fought to control the urge to comfort her. To take her in his arms and assure her he would never dream of using the DVD against her anymore. But he had to stop her in her tracks. Had to keep her where she belonged, where she could be appreciated and valued—*with him.*

"Remember, Nicole. I can just as easily give you access to bad information as I can to good. Ask yourself this—how would you feel if what you were so merrily passing onto your friend at Wilson Wines was enough to turn very strongly to their *dis*advantage? What if it was the straw that broke their financial back?"

She sat back down in her seat, her face drawn into harsh lines of worry. "Have you?"

"Not this time, but don't be so sure I won't in the future. Now, let this be the first and last time you do this, or I will take punitive action, Nicole. Don't think I won't."

"I—"

She was interrupted in her response by the chirp of

her cell phone. He watched as she glanced at the screen and, if it were possible, paled even further.

"Your friend, I assume?" he sneered.

In response, Nicole snatched the phone up and dismissed the call, only to have it start ringing again a few seconds later.

"You'd better take it," Nate growled, "and while you're at it, tell Ms. Garrick that they can expect to have to do their own research and development in the future."

He turned and stalked out the office.

Nicole watched the door close behind him before answering the call. In the face of what she'd just been through with him she really didn't think her day could have gotten any worse, until she'd seen her home phone number come up on her screen. Try as she might, she couldn't fight back the feeling of dread that suffused her.

"Hello?"

"Nic, it's Anna. Charles collapsed this morning at breakfast. Judd's gone with him in the ambulance. You should meet us at Auckland City Hospital's emergency department as soon as you can. It doesn't look good."

"But you said he was doing okay," Nicole protested, at a complete loss for anything else to say.

"He has obviously been feeling worse than he let on. Look, I must get going. I'll see you at the hospital."

Anna severed the connection before Nicole could say another word. Shaking, Nicole grabbed her handbag and headed straight for the elevator bank. She slammed her hand against the call button several times waiting for the car to arrive at her floor.

Finally the elevator doors slid open and she dashed inside, punching the ground floor button as she did so.

The doors began to slide closed but suddenly an arm appeared between them, forcing them to bounce open again.

"Going somewhere?" Nate asked, entering the car and standing close beside her.

"It's my dad, he's collapsed. I need to see him. Please don't try and stop me."

Nate's expression changed rapidly. "How are you planning to get there?"

"I don't know, taxi, something!" A note of sheer panic pitched her voice high.

"I'll drive you."

"You don't n—"

"I said, I'll drive you. You're in no state to be left on your own." He reached forward and pressed the button for the level below ground.

"Thank you," she said shakily, watching as the car slid inexorably down to the basement parking floor.

She couldn't have said later on how long it took to get to Auckland City Hospital. The journey should only have taken about ten minutes but, as with everything since she'd received Anna's call, it seemed to take forever. The second Nate rolled his car to a halt outside the emergency department she shot out the door and headed inside, not even waiting to see if he followed her or not. Ahead of her she could see her brother and Anna. She strode across the floor, her high heels clicking on the polished surface.

"Where is he? I want to see him."

"He's with the doctors," Anna said quietly. "They're still assessing him."

"What happened?" Nicole demanded, turning to Judd, more than ready to lay blame for their father's current condition firmly at his feet. Life had been simple before he arrived. Not necessarily always happy but certainly less complicated.

"He collapsed at breakfast," Judd replied.

"I thought your being here was supposed to make him feel better, not worse," Nicole fired back before promptly bursting into tears.

God, what was it with her these days? So overemotional. She needed to hold it together, especially if she wanted them to let her in to see her father.

A nurse came toward them, "Mr. Wilson, you can see your father now."

Nicole didn't notice that Judd had reached for Anna until she heard her friend say, "No, take Nicole. She needs to be with him more than I do."

What was with that between the two of them? Were they a couple?

"Are you coming?" Judd asked with thinly veiled impatience.

Her tears dried instantly. How dare he act and speak to her as if she didn't belong. It wasn't her fault her father was in there, possibly fighting for his life. "Of course I'm coming. He's *my* father."

Nicole was horrified when she saw her father. Lines ran into his arms and monitors were beeping around him. He looked so ill, so frail. So very old. Guilt assailed her anew.

"What's she doing here?" he rasped, turning his head away from her.

But not before she saw the anger and rejection in his eyes. Nicole stiffened and halted in her tracks. The words of love and care that were on the tip of her tongue drying on her tongue like a bitter pill she'd been unable to swallow. She reached down deep and found what dignity she had left.

"I came to see if you were all right, but obviously you're just fine. You won't be needing me here."

She turned and pushed past Judd, desperate now to get out of the cubicle. Desperate to get anywhere where her father wasn't. He hated her. That much was all too clear. As far as he was concerned, she'd burned her bridges when she'd walked out on him and straight into Nate Hunter Jackson's arms. He'd never stopped to listen before, why should he start now? Well, two could play at that game, she decided, ignoring Anna who was still waiting outside, and kept her gaze fixed on the exit ahead of her.

Nate waited outside in the chilled morning air.

"How is he?" he asked, stepping forward as she came out through the main doors.

"He's about as much a bastard as he ever was. Take me home, please. I can't face going back to the office today."

Nate gave her a searching look before nodding. He wrapped one arm across her shoulders and gathered her to him.

"Sure, whatever you need."

The Maserati ate up the miles that led them back to the beach house and the instant they were inside she turned into his arms, wrenching away her clothing and then his, and pouring her energy into setting his soul on fire for her all over again.

She dragged him to the bedroom and pushed him onto the bed, sheathed him with a condom and then straddled his body. There was no finesse, no whispers of passion. Her movements were hard and fast and before he gave himself over to her frenetic love-making, he made her a silent promise. Charles Wilson would never hurt her again.

Nine

Nate watched Nicole as she slept beside him. She'd been like a madwoman exorcising a demon. As if she was desperate to fill all the loss and pain inside her with something else. While he didn't regret that whatever had happened at the hospital had driven her back into his bed, he hated that she was hurting so much inside. Throughout the day she hadn't said a word about her father's condition or whatever it was that he'd said or done that had upset her so deeply. Even as they'd walked along the beach during a break in the bad weather, wrapped up tight against the bracing wind that streamed across the sand, she'd adroitly steered their conversation away from work and anything associated with her family.

Throughout their talks he'd begun to get a clearer picture of what her life had been like growing up. It hadn't all been a bed of roses, as he'd assumed. For a start she'd only had her father, and while he'd lavished his extensive resources upon her and given her every childhood heart's desire, including a live-in friend in the shape of Anna Garrick, he hadn't been able to atone for the fact that her mother had essentially abandoned her. Mostly, he hadn't tried.

After the collapse of his marriage and his family life, Charles had dedicated himself to his work. When he'd spent time with Nicole, it had mostly been in the role of stern authoritarian, making sure she did her homework, got good grades, behaved well in school. She'd worked hard to excel, hoping to win his approval, but his praise was sparse and hard to gain. And when she fell short of his expectations, well…

Little wonder that right now, Nicole felt as if she'd been cast adrift by both her parents. He knew she was in pain but he didn't know how to make it any better. He also knew that he was responsible for some of the scars she bore right now, and the knowledge carved at his chest with relentless precision.

He could make this all go away. He could destroy the DVD and release her. Even as he thought of it, everything within him protested. She murmured in her sleep as he gathered her against his chest. No, there was one thing these past few days had taught him and that was he never wanted to let her go. Ever.

Charles Wilson didn't deserve her. In contrast, Nate would do everything in his power to make sure Nicole wanted for nothing while she was under his roof. Surely someday, that would be enough.

Nicole poured her energy into two things for the rest of the week, work and Nate. By Friday evening she was shattered. Lack of sleep and the concentration her work demanded as she finalized every last contract for the Marlborough wineries had culminated in a thumping headache by the time she and Nate drove back to the apartment. She wished they were heading out to Karekare. The sounds of the waves and the birds in the bush that surrounded the house were just the kind of tranquility she craved right now. They would drive out there late Saturday evening, though, and she was looking forward to the time-out. Perhaps she'd even take Nate up on that earlier offer to learn to surf, she thought, as they waited for yet another change of lights before they could get closer to their final destination.

Her cell phone chirped in her bag and she ignored it. She should have turned the damn thing off before they'd left the office. After all, any calls she got tended only to relate to work—or Anna, who had been giving her unwanted updates on her father's medical condition.

Things were looking pretty bad for Charles Wilson but Nicole refused to let herself think about that. Refused, point-blank, to acknowledge that the one biggest influence on her entire life could soon be gone if things didn't improve. He hadn't wanted her there at the hospital. He'd made it abundantly, and painfully clear on Monday morning.

Was she so unlovable? Her chest tightened on the thought. Her mother abandoned her, her father now hated her. Even Nate only wanted her because of what it would do to her father and her brother. Nicole had never felt more adrift in her entire life. The pounding in her head sharpened and she must have made a sound of discomfort because Nate reached across to take one of her hands in his.

"Are you okay? You're looking really pale."

"Just this darn headache. I can't shake it."

He shot her a look of concern, his hand lifting from hers and touching her cheek and forehead before returning to the steering wheel.

"I don't think you have a fever, but do you think you should see a doctor? You haven't been looking well all week."

"Look, it's been a stressful week, you know that. I'll be fine. I just need a couple of painkillers and then about a month's worth of sleep."

"Well, I can't promise a month but I have no objection if you want to stay in bed all weekend."

She gave him a weak smile. No, she had no doubt he'd be happy to spend that whole time in bed with her, too. It was about the only time she could dismiss everything else and just concentrate on the moment, on how he could play her body like a finely tuned instrument. But right now, forget-the-rest-of-the-world sex was the last thing she felt like.

"Hey, I can change my plans for tonight. I don't feel so good about leaving you alone if you're not well."

"No, no," she protested. "Raoul's wedding rehearsal is important. You must go."

"If you're sure?"

"Of course I'm sure," she told him. Right now the only thing she craved was maybe a warm bath, those painkillers she'd mentioned a moment ago and then sleep.

In the apartment, Nate went straight through to the master bedroom to get ready for the wedding rehearsal and subsequent dinner that was being hosted in one of Auckland's premier hotels. Raoul had extended both a dinner and wedding invitation to Nicole, as well, but she'd refused, saying she'd feel like a gate-crasher. The wedding was tomorrow at midday, and she'd planned to go into the office in an effort to get ahead for next week.

Half an hour later she was on her own. She roamed through to the master bathroom and ran a deep bath, treating the water with lavender-and-rose-scented bath salts. Already she could feel the tension in her head begin to ease. She took a couple of headache tablets just before she undressed and lowered herself into the soothing water.

In the living room, she heard her phone begin to chirp again. She sighed, and gave herself a mental reminder to check the thing before turning it off. There was no need to rush to check it right away. If Nate needed her, and couldn't get through, he would ring the apartment, and who else would need to reach her right away? She closed her eyes and leaned her head back against the edge, letting the water and the pain relief weave their magic.

The water was cooling by the time she dragged herself out and dried her body before wrapping in a luxuriously thick bathrobe. There was no point in putting on a nightgown. Nate would only remove it the minute he got home, she thought with an anticipatory smile. Besides, her headache was completely gone now and she was ravenous. Maybe she'd watch a movie on cable while she had something to eat, she thought, abandoning her earlier idea of having an early night. And then, by the time Nate got home, maybe she could meet him at the door, dressed in nothing but a smile. The idea began to sound better and better.

First, though, she had to check her phone. Two missed calls, both from the same caller, and one voice mail. Nicole immediately identified her old home number and her blood ran cold. Had Charles's condition deteriorated again?

She punched the numbers to listen to the voice mail, and was surprised when the well-modulated tones of an unfamiliar woman's voice sounded through the speaker.

"This is Cynthia Masters-Wilson and I'm calling for Nicole Wilson. I'd like to meet with you for lunch tomorrow, one o'clock if you're free." She mentioned the name of an inner-city restaurant before continuing, "I think it's time we got to know one another, don't you?"

The call disconnected but Nicole still stood there, staring at her phone. Her mother? After all this time? She sank to the sofa as her legs weakened. Why now?

All her life she'd told herself she never wanted to meet the woman who had so callously abandoned her one-year-old daughter, never to look back, never to contact her or attempt to see her ever again. While she was growing up she'd told herself it didn't matter. She had her father, she had Anna and Anna's mother who was more Charles's companion than housekeeper in the massive gothic mansion Nicole had grown up in. Yes, it had always been easy to dismiss Cynthia Masters-Wilson as entirely unnecessary in her life.

But what did she have now? Nothing. Absolutely nothing. All week she'd been frantically trying to fill the emptiness inside her—working hard and playing twice as much so. If she was completely honest with herself, neither activity had managed to assuage the hollow feeling her father's rejection had left her with.

Reason told her to be cautious, though. This was the first ever, active contact her mother had made in twenty-five long years. As far as Nicole was aware, the woman had never spared her a second thought.

But what if she wanted to make amends? What if her reasons for leaving Nicole motherless for all those years were justified, her remorse for her absence in her daughter's life genuine? Surely she had to have a reason for finally getting in touch with Nicole after all this time.

Curiosity won out over caution as Nicole made up her mind. She would meet with Cynthia—she couldn't ever imagine calling her Mum, or Mother—and she would be seeking a few answers of her own.

Butterflies battled in her stomach as she entered the restaurant located in the historic Auckland Ferry building. She'd chosen to walk the short distance from the Viaduct, but with each step she'd come to dread her decision to attend. What on earth could they possibly have to talk about? And if her mother wanted to offer an olive branch, maybe even try to establish some form of mother-daughter relationship, why do it in such a public place? Surely a private meeting would be more appropriate for a mother and daughter reuniting for the first time in a quarter century.

"You must be Miss Wilson," said the immaculately attired maître d' as she hovered in the entrance, in two minds about turning around and walking back to the apartment. "Your mother is already seated. Please, follow me."

Too late now, she realized. The restaurant hummed with activity and most of the tables were occupied. The sun shined through the windows that looked out over the water, casting a solitary figure seated at a table there in silhouette.

Nicole swallowed back the lump that formed in her throat and focused on placing one foot in front of the other. She smiled at the maître d' as he held out her chair, not wanting to immediately make eye contact with the woman who had summoned her there. She kept her eyes downcast, fiddling with her bag before setting it on the floor beside her chair. Then, with a steadying breath, she raised her eyes.

It was as if she was looking at herself in another twenty-five years. Same eyes, same hairline, although Cynthia's hair now bore wings of gray, and while her features mirrored Nicole's own, there were lines around her mouth. Regret? Bitterness? Would she ever know the truth about that?

"Well, my dear, this is going to be interesting, isn't it?" Cynthia said with a tight smile.

Of all the things she'd imagined her mother first saying to her, that was most definitely not on the list. Nicole bristled.

"Why now?"

"What? No, hello Mother, pleased to finally meet you?" Cynthia gave another of those artificial smiles. "I don't blame you for being angry, my dear, but you have to realize that I'm as much a victim of your father as you and your brother."

A victim? Somehow Nicole thought that was stretching the truth. Her brother had already been proven to be Charles's natural-born son. Why would he have thought otherwise? Charles had believed his wife had an affair with Thomas Jackson. She couldn't imagine Nate's father having been the one to put that idea in her father's head, which only left one other person in that particular triangle.

"Ah, I see you don't believe me." Cynthia sighed. "I feared as much. Come, let's order, and hopefully we can talk."

Even though she didn't feel in the least like eating, Nicole placed her order with the waiter who'd materialized at Cynthia's request. Once they were each settled with a glass of wine, Cynthia began again.

"You're quite the beauty, aren't you? I'm so sorry that I didn't get to see you grow up. It was the hardest thing I've ever done in my life, walking away from you, leaving you with your father. But I knew he loved you, would protect you. Judd deserved the same, with me."

"How could you leave me like that?" Nicole blurted out the question. Goodness only knew she'd waited all her life for the answer.

To her surprise, Cynthia's eyes swam with tears. "Oh, my darling girl. Do you really think I wanted to leave you? Your father wouldn't let me near you. Once he'd come to his ridiculous conclusions about Thomas and me he wouldn't even let me *see* you. He had Judd and me out of the country before I could so much as blink."

She sounded genuine enough, and the grief on her mother's face certainly appeared real. Nicole found herself wanting to believe her, but an inner caution still held her back. Without being able to talk to her father, or her brother about this, she had no way of knowing if her mother was telling the truth. The waiter interrupted them with their lunch order and Nicole picked up her fork, playing with the mushrooms in her salad while her mother daintily tasted a sliver of scallop that had come with her dish.

"You could have written," Nicole said, still not willing to give an inch.

"I did. I wrote to you so many times over the years, but all the letters came back. I can only assume that your father had given the staff orders to return any mail addressed from me."

It was the sort of thing her father would have done, Nicole conceded, but there were still means around such a thing. After all, twenty-five years was a very long time. Nicole was an adult now—approachable in ways that were outside of her father's control. To never have been successful was a bit of a stretch of the imagination. Cynthia could obviously sense her skepticism and waved her hand in the air between them.

"That's all in the past now. We can't change that. But surely we can get to know one another now? Tell me about where you're living. Judd tells me you moved out a few weeks ago. I have to say I was very sorry to hear that you two haven't had a chance to get to know one another. I'm staying at the house now. I was hoping we could all be together again, the way it should be."

"Judd didn't tell you why I left?"

Cynthia gave her a sharp look before shaking her head and placing her fork down on her plate. She took a sip of the mineral water in her glass before speaking.

"He did mention something, but I'd prefer to hear it from you."

Nicole gave an inelegant snort. She'd just bet Judd would prefer their mother hear it from her. No doubt he'd already fed Cynthia a sanitized version of what had happened that night.

"My father and I had a disagreement about his plans for Judd. I felt it better that I be away from them both for a while."

"So where are you staying?"

"I'm living with Nate Hunter." She didn't want to let on about Nate's relationship to Thomas Jackson. As far as she was aware, no one at Wilson Wines knew him by his father's surname. Even at the office he was known as Mr. Hunter. "He's the current head of Jackson Importers. I'm working with him, too."

She watched her mother pale beneath her carefully applied makeup, her pallor making the lines around her mouth stand out even more.

"Would Jackson Importers be connected to Thomas Jackson at all?"

"It was his company before he passed away," Nicole confirmed cautiously.

Cynthia's brow furrowed for a moment. "Hunter? Would Nate's mother have been Deborah Hunter?"

Nicole stiffened. Had Cynthia made the connection? "That might have been his mother's name, yes."

"So, it was true. There were rumors that Thomas and Deborah were an item, but nothing was ever substantiated. Charles, of course, pooh-poohed the notion. He said if Thomas was having an affair he'd be the first to know about it." She made a sound that almost approximated a laugh. "As if he paid attention to anything but Wilson Wines. Anyway, I heard that she had a son out of wedlock, but since she didn't move in the same circles as I did when I lived here, I never really gave her another thought."

Nicole didn't know what to say. It hadn't been her secret to divulge and yet Cynthia had put two and two together so simply. If that was the case, why then had her father never reached the same conclusion?

Cynthia suddenly reached across the table, her slender fingers wrapping around Nicole's wrist and gripping tight.

"My dear, you have to get out of there. No one associated with Thomas Jackson can possibly be trusted. Who do you think lied to your father about me, ruining our marriage? Think of the damage that man's lies have done to our family. You have to realize, there's a lot of bitterness between those men. If you're with Thomas's son there can only be one good reason behind it—he's trying to get at your father."

Her words rang too true, as Nicole knew to her cost. Hearing it from her mother's lips only made her situation worse. She knew full well what had been on Nate's mind when he'd taken her back to his home that first night. She had no reason to believe his vendetta against her father had altered in any way. She was still his greatest weapon, even if through her own distress at her father's treatment of her she'd recently become a more willing one.

"Nicole, tell me, is Nate Hunter holding something over you? Is he forcing you to be with him?"

Her mother's astuteness shocked her and she bit back. "Is it too hard to believe that I might actually want to be with him for no reason other than that he treats me well and appreciates me?" Even as she said the words she was sure her mother would see them for the lie they were.

Cynthia shook her head gently, a look of pity on her face. "You love him, don't you?"

"No!" The single word of protest fell from Nicole's lips even as she questioned the truth of her rapid denial. Did she love him? How could she? She was his lover, his captive, his colleague. His tool for vengeance against her father. How she felt about him was far too complicated to examine in front of her mother. Instead, she settled for a middle ground, saying, "Our relationship—it's convenient for us both."

"Well, I certainly hope that's true, because I'm sure, if he's anything like his father, he has an agenda and that would probably be having some kind of revenge against Charles for when he kicked Thomas to the curb."

"Can we change the subject, please? I'd rather not talk about my relationship with Nate, if you don't mind. Besides, I thought you wanted to get to know me."

"You're so right. I'm sorry." Cynthia smiled, one that almost reached her eyes this time, and skillfully shifted their conversation onto other matters.

By the time Nicole walked back to the apartment she was in a quandary. When they hadn't been talking about Nate, or her father, Cynthia had been excellent company. She'd talked a great deal about her family home—The Masters, a vineyard and accommodation on the outskirts of Adelaide—and Nicole's cousins who lived there. Cousins! She had an extended family. One she'd never had the chance to know. And Judd had enjoyed the benefit of that, as well, on top of her father's total attention, her home and the job she'd loved. While she, even now, had absolutely nothing.

Ten

Nate knew something was up the instant he let himself into the apartment. Nicole was nursing a frosty glass of white wine in one hand, her gaze fixed on the twinkling lights of the Viaduct Basin below, her body language shrieking a touch-me-not scream. Every part of her was tense, a far cry from the languorous woman he'd left in their bed this morning before heading out to Raoul's wedding.

He knew she saw his reflection in the massive window in front of her, yet she didn't so much as acknowledge his presence. A flare of concern lit deep inside him.

"What happened? Is it your father?" Surely he would have heard if Charles had passed away. That kind of information would still have filtered through to the guests from Jackson Importers who were at the wedding.

"No." she huffed a short sigh. "My mother, actually."

"Your mother? I thought she lived in Australia."

"Apparently not. Apparently she's moving back to my old family home. Seems like everyone has a place there—but me."

Despite her attempt at nonchalance, he could hear the pain in her voice.

"Did she contact you?"

"We did lunch together. Such a normal thing for a mother and daughter to do, don't you think? Except we're not a normal mother and daughter, are we?"

He was shocked when she turned to face him, her eyes awash with tears. Instinctively he reached for her, enveloping her in his arms and ruing the fact that he hadn't been here for her when she so clearly needed the support. His father had never said as much in words, but Nate had always suspected Cynthia of being behind the lies that had torn apart Thomas and Charles's friendship. Her poison had tainted the lives of so many people, and now she was here, poisoning Nicole, as well.

"You know," Nicole said, her voice muffled against his chest, "as soon as I was old enough to realize that I didn't have a mother, I wanted answers. Even after I convinced myself I didn't need her in my life. I still wanted to know why I didn't have unconditional love from her the same way all my friends had from their mothers. She wants us to get to know each other. Now. After twenty-five years. Can you believe that?"

Nate remained silent, knowing she wasn't looking for an answer. At least not from him.

"And underneath it all, I don't think I can believe it. I don't know that I can believe *her.* And in spite of that,

I still *want* to believe her, because what girl doesn't want to think that her mother loves her?"

Nate set her away from him a little, so he could see her face. "I don't think you should trust her motives, Nicole."

Nicole laughed. A sharp brittle sound that was nothing like the usual humor in her he'd come to know. "Funny. She said exactly the same thing about you."

He stiffened. "She did? Why?"

"Oh, she had you pegged from the start. Said you were probably just like your father. And she knew your mother apparently. Not well, of course." Nicole lowered her voice. "We didn't move in the same circles, you know," she said, in a parody of her mother's tone.

A chill went through him. "I mean it, Nicole. The way she's come here, after all this time and while your father is so ill—something's not right. She could have reached out to you any time in the past. I don't think you should have anything to do with her."

Nicole pulled free from his arms. "Well, that's my judgment call, isn't it?"

Nate knew he'd overstepped the mark with his last comment but he couldn't take it back now. He'd been speaking his mind and he knew he was right. Cynthia Masters-Wilson was not a woman to be trusted. And he didn't want to see Nicole hurt ever again. But he didn't want this to turn into a fight.

"Yes, it is," he finally agreed with Nicole. "Do you still want to head out to the beach?"

Nicole shrugged and took a long sip of her wine. "Whatever."

"I think we should go, it'll do us good to get out of the city."

"Sure," she agreed, but without any enthusiasm.

He watched as she finished her wine and took her glass through to the kitchen. She rinsed it and put it in the dishwasher and then went through to the bedroom they were sharing again. Her actions were wooden, automatic, as if she'd retreated somewhere in her mind. To a place he knew he couldn't reach. The knowledge chilled him to the bone.

Being at Raoul's wedding today had struck something home to him. It had been a happy, relaxed affair, full of people Nate liked and valued—and yet he'd spent the whole time counting down the minutes until he could leave, wanting to come home to Nicole. Being with her had long since stopped being about having his revenge on her father. What was past, was very definitely past. What he wanted now—Nicole—was very much in the present—and he wanted her to stay that way.

Nicole sat quietly in the car, mulling over her meeting with her mother. It certainly hadn't been the reunion she'd always imagined. Cynthia was a piece of work, all right. Coming back into her life after all this time and then thinking she could tell Nicole what to do. It seemed that all around her everyone was telling her what to do these days. And she was letting them. Everything in her life had become topsy-turvy. Even her period was late and she was never late.

Cold fingers of fear squeezed around her heart. Could she be pregnant? *Oh, please, no,* she thought fervently. *Please just let it be stress.* She wasn't ready for this on so many levels it wasn't even funny. She and Nate hardly had the kind of relationship that could sustain a nurturing environment for a child. Not to mention, she had no idea how to be a mother. She'd always been so professionally focused, so determined to excel in her work at Wilson Wines that she'd never given much thought to building a home and family. Even if she wanted such a thing, she didn't know if she could pull it off. And she couldn't bear the thought of proving her father's prophecy about becoming a mother and downsizing her responsibilities in the workplace.

Suddenly it was all the more important that she know, one way or another. With everything else in her life spiraling out of control, surely fate couldn't be so cruel as to throw her a curveball like that, as well?

"Could we stop at the shops in Titirangi on the way?" she asked. "There are a few things I forgot."

"Sure," Nate said.

When they got to the township he pulled in off the road.

"Do you want me to come with you?" he asked, shutting down the engine.

"Oh, no. I'll be fine. I won't be long," she said, getting out the car as hastily as she could. "Really, I'll only be a minute or two."

Please don't come, she chanted in the back of her mind. *Please don't come.* Thankfully, he stayed in the car and she walked briskly toward the bank of shops near where he'd parked. Where to go now? she wondered. If she went into the nearby pharmacy he'd probably see her and he'd no doubt ask her what she'd been in there for. He kept a full stock of over-the-counter medicinal products at both his homes so she couldn't say she'd needed any painkillers or anything like that. And if she said she was after sanitary products, and she didn't need them, that would just open up a whole new can of worms.

Think! she exhorted herself. The grocery store.

Sure, it was smallish, certainly not on the scale of a full supermarket, but surely they'd carry pregnancy tests, as well. She ducked inside the store and scanned the aisles, praying she'd find what she needed. Finally, there it was. She grabbed a test kit and made her way to the counter. On the way she also pulled some moisturizer and a lip balm off the shelf to add to her purchase. The kit, she'd ferret away in her bag. The other items would be camouflage in case Nate asked what she'd bought.

She was back at the car in under five minutes.

"Get everything you needed?" Nate asked her as she buckled her seatbelt.

"Yes, thanks. I'd just run out of a couple of things."

He gave her a studied look, one that made the hairs on the back of her neck prickle. She'd never been an effective liar. Never had to be. She felt as if the test kit in her bag was emitting some kind of beacon. As if any second now, Nate would be giving her the third degree.

"Right, we'll be on the way, then."

She sagged back into her seat with relief. She was overreacting. He had no reason to suspect her of anything, although he had to realize that she should perhaps have had a period by now. She counted back. It was just over three weeks since she'd met him. Only three weeks and they'd been through so very much. She felt as if she'd lived through a lifetime with him. Even so, it gave her a window of at least another week before he might start to ask questions. Questions to which she hoped to have the answer very soon.

The rest of the journey to the house seemed to take forever, even though it was only just over twenty minutes. Nate kept her attention occupied by talking about Raoul's wedding and the people who had been there, often drawing a quiet laugh from her as he mimicked some of Raoul's older and more eccentric family members. She detected a note in his voice, though, that she identified with.

Neither of them had grown up with a large family group supporting them. No uncles, aunts, curmudgeonly great-anythings. No cousins to play or fight with. Just a tight unit of parent and child.

"Some people are lucky, aren't they?" she said, as Nate's voice trailed off as they neared the driveway to the house.

"Lucky?"

"To have the richness of all those people in their family lives."

"I don't know whether Raoul thought it was particularly lucky when his great-uncle got up to make a toast to absent friends. Fifteen minutes he went on."

She laughed again. She should have gone to the wedding rather than have lunch with her mother. By the sounds of it she would have been in a much happier frame of mind right now if she had.

"Still, it would have been nice, growing up..." Her voice faded on the thought.

Nate's hand came across and grasped hers, squeezing tight. "Yeah, I know what you mean."

They were both silent as they went inside the house. Nicole made her way immediately to the bathroom, locking the door behind her and carefully removed the test kit from her bag. Her hand trembled just a little as she opened the box and withdrew the instructions. It seemed straightforward enough. She extracted the test stick and followed the instructions to the letter.

If she'd thought the trip in the car had taken forever, this felt as if she was aging threefold with every second. She counted silently in her head, refusing to look at the stick until she'd counted over the time the instructions said. She could hear Nate in the bedroom. She needed to get this over with before he decided to check on her.

Nicole forced herself to look at the stick. Stripe in one window...the other window clear. A negative result! A rush of exhilaration coursed through her. She shoved the test back into its packaging, and scrunched the whole thing up as small as she could make it before shoving it into the waste bin in the bathroom, and throwing some crumpled tissues on top of it. That would have to do until she could empty the waste bin into a trash bag later on.

She flushed the toilet and then washed her hands at the basin. Her hands were still shaking with the aftermath of the adrenaline surge she'd felt at the confirmation. She was relieved, immensely relieved, but hard on the heels of that sense of relief came a vastly contradictory spear of loss. Would it have been so very bad to have Nate's child? While they didn't have a normal relationship, maybe something good could have come from all of this. Something that could have healed the rift that had been driven between Thomas Jackson and her father all those years ago.

Babies brought with them their own very special brand of implicit trust and love. At least if she had a child, wouldn't she then have its unreserved love? A love that didn't come with tags and conditions. A love she could return wholeheartedly.

Nicole looked at herself in the mirror over the bathroom vanity and shook her head at her fanciful thoughts. She had worked damn hard to establish her career and she wasn't about to walk away from that now. Not even for some pipe dream of a perfect family life. A dream that would probably go horribly wrong if she ever tried it in reality, just like her long-anticipated meeting with her mother.

No, things were definitely better this way. She had no time or space in her life for a baby, not when everything was so horribly complicated—not now, maybe not ever.

Nate had begun to hate Sunday afternoons. In the past it had never been an issue. He loved his time here at the beach house, even more so since he'd been spending it with Nicole. But for some reason the coming week filled him with foreboding. Something was off with Nicole, too. She'd been different all weekend. He'd tried to put it down to her dealing with her feelings about the meeting she'd had with her mother, but he sensed there was far more to it than that.

Even when he'd reached for her in bed last night, he couldn't help feeling as if she was just going through the motions. He knew she'd climaxed, that wasn't the problem. No, what worried him was the mental distance she'd maintained from him. With the roller coaster they'd been through in these past few weeks, the only time the veils they'd held between them had fallen away was when they'd been intimate.

Now, they didn't even have that.

It worried him. Something had happened to change her and he had no idea what it was or how he could fix it. Talking to her elicited no more than a polite response and when he tried to probe deeper, she just shut him down by changing the subject. Short of holding her down and refusing to let her up until she admitted the truth about what bothered her, he had no idea of what to do next. What he did know was that he was losing her, and that was unacceptable.

He went through to the garage to double bag the trash sack to avoid any leakage, and put it in the trunk of his car. It was easier to transfer his waste to the massive trash bin at the apartment building in town than to leave it on the appointed day at the rubbish collection area here. Sometimes being remote from the city had its drawbacks but this was one he could live with.

Nate was picking up the bag and easing it into the second one when a tear suddenly appeared in the plastic and garbage spilled onto the garage floor. Cursing under his breath he scooped up the offending articles and pushed them back into the bag. As he did so, he noticed a small cardboard box that had been twisted up. The lettering on the box was not completely obscured, though, and he saw enough to pique his interest.

He separated it from the rest of the trash and unraveled the packaging. A pregnancy test? There was only one person here who could be responsible for this. He fished the used pregnancy test out of the package, but frustratingly, it was probably too long since it had been used to still show the result. But the fact that she'd taken a pregnancy test at all was enough to have his heart racing.

Every cell in his body demanded he march right up to her and insist she tell him the result of the test, but he forced himself to remain exactly where he was until he could recover some semblance of calm.

Nicole, pregnant? The very thought sent a wave of longing and warmth through his body. He couldn't think of anything he'd like better than watching her ripen with his child. Of sharing each special milestone along the way until they could hold their newborn son or daughter in their arms. Of having a family of his own, a family that included Nicole at its very center.

His heart pounded in his chest at the thought. A family, together, forever. It was everything he'd ever wanted and yet denied himself because he'd been unable to trust, unable to let anyone close enough to have the chance to hurt him since he'd been so twisted by the pain his father had undergone. And now he had the opportunity to put all that bitterness behind him. To forge forward with something new and right and special.

No wonder Nicole had been distant all weekend. She was probably worrying about how to break the news to him, about how he'd take it. He would have to take extra pains to reassure her he would take care of her and the baby, and that she had nothing to worry about, ever, while he had it in his power to take care of her.

Nate forced himself to put the pregnancy test box back in the trash bag and tied off the sack. A few minutes later, as he washed his hands, he thought about what he would say. There was no easy way to approach this. How did you tell the woman you had blackmailed into being with you that you wanted her to spend the rest of her life with you?

Back inside the house, he looked for Nicole. Through the windows he could see her out on the beach, her clothing buffeted by the wind. She was just standing there. Alone. Contemplating the life she carried within her, perhaps? How could he reassure her that everything was going to be okay? That she could trust him?

He reached a decision. He'd just come straight out and tell her. He'd learned a long time ago that occasionally you had to take risks—especially when something was as important as this.

Without taking another moment to think, he pushed open the massive sliding door and headed down the stairs that led to the beach. Nicole must have sensed him coming because she shifted her gaze from the seagulls wheeling on the air currents and turned to face him.

"Nicole, we need to talk."

"We do? What about?" she asked, her long hair whipping around her face in the stiff breeze.

Nate shoved his hands in his jeans pockets. "I know what's bothering you and I want you to know it'll all be okay. I'll take care of you. Once we're married, you won't have a single worry in the world, I promise."

"Married?"

"Of course. There's nothing stopping us. We know we're totally compatible. You can even keep working if you want to, I won't stand in your way. I know how important your career is to you."

To his surprise Nicole just laughed.

Nate frowned, somewhat less than pleased with her reaction. "What? What did I say?"

"Why on earth would I marry you?"

"Of course you'll marry me. We owe it to our baby to provide a united front. You, of all people, know as well as I do what it's like to grow up with two parents who aren't together. Our situation is not ideal, but we can make it work. I know we can. I swore an oath to myself that, no matter what, when I had children I'd be married to their mother, and that's what's going to happen now."

"What makes you think I'm pregnant?" Nicole asked him, taking a step back.

"You've been different these past couple of days and now I know why. I saw the box, Nicole. I know you've taken the test."

Nicole stared at him in horror. He'd found the test? What had he done? Trawled through the rubbish bins? Was he so determined to control every facet of her life? No, she pushed the idea aside. If she was being totally honest with herself, deep down she knew he wasn't like that.

"So, what? You think that if I'm pregnant that we must get married? That's being very old-fashioned of you, don't you think?"

She watched as his face changed, becoming harder, more determined.

"Old-fashioned or not, Nicole, my baby will not grow up illegitimate."

"Of course it won't," she flung back at him.

How dare he be so dictatorial? Didn't her thoughts or feelings factor into this equation at all? Just because he said something was a certain way, didn't mean it had to be so. Even if she was pregnant, marriage to a man who patently didn't love her would be the very last thing on her mind.

The fact that she was totally peripheral to his entire proposal was borne out by his assertion that his baby—*his,* not *theirs*—would not grow up illegitimate. Did he give her any consideration as an individual at all? There was no way she was marrying Nate Jackson. Absolutely no way.

"Good, then it's settled. We'll get married. It doesn't have to be anything big. I'm sure we can sort something out within the next few weeks."

"You can't treat me like some possession to be ordered about. I'm a human being. I've already had quite enough of that kind of treatment from my own father and I certainly won't put up with it from you." She drew up short as a new thought had occurred to her. "My father…is that what this is about? Do you want to get married to rub it in his face? Is this the next part of your revenge?"

"No!" His protest was immediate, and almost seemed instinctive, but how could she believe him? He'd been following his plan of payback right from the start. How was she to know this wasn't his next step?

"Really?" she drawled.

"Look, I know this wasn't the most romantic of proposals—"

"Romantic?" She laughed again, a harsh sound that came from a place deep inside her. A place that hurt with an ache that throbbed through her entire body. "Sort out what you like, Nate, but I'm not marrying you. There were two possible outcomes when I took that test. One, that I was pregnant, the other, that I wasn't. I'm not pregnant, and I'm not marrying you, so you can shove your proposal right back where it came from."

She pushed past him and strode on up the beach toward the house. She thought he couldn't hurt her any more than he already had done. She'd thought that perhaps they'd found a workable solution to their situation. She did enjoy her work at Jackson Importers. She had a freedom there that she didn't have at Wilson Wines and she loved the opportunity to spread her wings and to brainstorm her ideas with others who were on the same wavelength. And she couldn't argue that she and Nate were exquisitely compatible in the bedroom. It had been about the only thing that had kept her sane these past weeks. Knowing that she could seek, and find, oblivion in his arms at night.

But right now she was so angry she could barely see the steps in front of her. She went inside the house, sliding the glass door closed so hard the panes inside it wobbled. Through the window she saw Nate standing on the beach, his hands still in his pockets as he faced the house.

Childishly, she wanted nothing more right now than to flip him the bird, but she wouldn't lower herself to that level. Instead, she turned away from the glass and tried to bring her roiling emotions under control.

Damn him. Damn him for asking her to marry him that way. For asking her to marry him at all! She didn't want to marry, she just wanted to be able to do her job. A job was something she could measure herself by. It had no feelings and only relied on her showing up every single day and giving her very best. A job wouldn't hurt her when the going got rough.

And yet, she couldn't help wondering how she would have felt if the situation had been different. If she had been pregnant, after all—if Nate's proposal had come from a different angle where he'd expressed a desire to have a family with her, even expressed affection or maybe even love for her—would she have been so quick to turn down Nate's suggestion? Nicole knew in her heart her response would have been "yes." She felt the same way he did about raising a child in a unified relationship. In a stable and loving environment. It had been a dream of hers from when she was a little girl. She and Anna had played families, both of them pretending their respective man-about-the-house was at work while they cared for their doll-babies with infinite maternal care.

No, she had to be honest with herself. No matter her feelings for Nate—feelings she couldn't quite put into words—with no mention of love spoken between them, they would only have been setting themselves up for failure. It took a committed parent to raise a child and parents who were not committed to one another, and yet still lived under the same roof, only created a divisive and, in the long term, unhappy home.

And that, sadly, left her right back where she'd started. A pawn in a game where she held none of the moveable pieces. Waiting for the inevitable checkmate when Nate reached his goal against Wilson Wines.

She wanted out of this horrible situation. She wanted out, right now. But how?

Eleven

Nate lay in the bed listening to Nicole breathe, her back as firmly presented to him as it had been when they went to bed. She had barely spoken more than a handful of words to him since the beach and he could hardly blame her. He'd been careless and stupid—thinking only of himself and what he wanted.

He'd used her shamelessly for weeks and expected her to simply roll over and agree to his demand without a single consideration for what it meant to her.

One thing he'd learned from this was that his feelings for her went far deeper than those of revenge. Far deeper than he'd ever wanted to acknowledge. Understanding had struck when she'd accused him of proposing as part of his revenge. That's when he'd realized that her father hadn't even crossed his mind when he'd found the pregnancy test. All he'd thought of was Nicole, and the child they might be having together.

He knew, now, that everything that mattered in his life was tied to the woman who lay in the darkness beside him—beside him yet not touching him and not allowing him to touch her. The woman who'd rejected him most emphatically on the sandy shore outside.

Nate wasn't the type of person who took no for an answer, yet in this he had to. He had no other choice. He'd messed things up between them, well and truly, and he could see no clear way to fix them.

He still had her here in his life, would continue to do so while he could hold the DVD over her. But what did that prove? Nothing. It only proved that, given the choice, she wouldn't be with him and that truth was the most painful of all.

He knew now that he loved her. He didn't want to imagine a life without her. These past weeks had been an eye opener for him. From the start he'd been attracted to her, but that attraction had very rapidly gone far deeper than merely a face-to-face—or skin-to-skin—appreciation of one another. He hadn't wanted to admit it to himself but her rejection had forced him to be honest.

Nate didn't just want to marry her to provide for her and their unborn child—the child that had existed only in his imagination. He wanted the whole shebang. He wanted to love Nicole and spend the rest of his life loving her. And being loved by her in return. He wanted to marry her, for *her*.

Problem solving had always come naturally to him. It was one of the things that made him good at his job—being able to see solutions before anyone else even fully understood the problem. Yet in this he was helpless.

How on earth could he convince her that his intentions toward her came from his heart? He'd tried to lay it on the line on the beach, but he'd gone about it in entirely the wrong way. Had told her, rather than asking her, how things were going to be. With each syllable he'd destroyed every last chance of creating the reality he had really wanted all along.

This was his mess. And for the first time in his life he didn't have a plan for dealing with it.

He pushed back the bedcovers and rose, leaving the room on a silent tread. Streaks of moonlight lit the rest of the house, cold and gray, just like the future that stretched ahead of him without Nicole willingly by his side. It was no better than he deserved for the way he'd treated her, but he didn't want to accept that. Couldn't accept that this was all over. Somehow he would find a solution. It was what he did. And this time, his very happiness depended on it.

They'd remained civil to one another, at least that was something she could be grateful for, Nicole thought as she studied the distribution reports that had been sent for her perusal. Civility was one thing, but how on earth would they continue to live together? Already she could feel the strain between them. She'd had no appetite for anything all day and she knew that food would not ease the hollow that echoed inside her.

Nate had told her to bring her own car into work today as he would be working late entertaining overseas clients. She hadn't suggested she assist him as she was only too grateful for the excuse to put a little distance between them. Leaving the office was a relief.

At the apartment, she'd barely had time to put her laptop case down when the phone began to ring. She let the answering machine pick up but hastened to lift the receiver when her mother's voice could be heard through the speaker.

"Hello?"

"Nicole, darling, I was hoping to catch you at home. How was the rest of your weekend?"

"It was fine. We went out to the beach house."

"I see. Have you thought any more about what I said to you about the Jacksons? I really don't think it's a good idea for you to spend any more time under that man's roof. Seriously, my dear, nothing good will come of it. Surely you can see that."

Another person telling her what to do. Nicole fought back the sigh that built in her chest.

"I'm an adult, Cynthia, and I'm long used to making my own decisions."

"I know, but allow me a mother's care in this instance. I know I wasn't there for you growing up, but trust me when I say I do know better in this case."

"Was there anything else you rang me for?" Nicole asked, struggling with a desire to hang up before she was bossed around again.

"Yes, well, there is, actually."

Was it Nicole's imagination or did her mother sound a little upset? She waited, saying nothing, until Cynthia continued.

"Things haven't really worked out here the way I'd thought they would and I've decided to go back to Adelaide for now. I'd really love it if you could come with me. I'm leaving in the morning and I'll leave a ticket for you at the check-in desk."

"I really don't think—" Nicole started, only to be shut down by Cynthia's voice talking over her.

"No, please, don't make a decision right this minute. Take the evening to think it over. We really haven't had a chance to get to know one another, have we? After all, one lunch together does not a relationship make." She laughed at that, the sound ringing false to Nicole's ears. "At The Masters' we could just spend some time learning to understand one another a little better and you would have the chance to meet up with some of your cousins—get to know your extended family. After all, you're a Masters by blood, and you have every right to be there with me. It's your heritage, too."

Nicole felt a throbbing pain start behind one eye. Did Cynthia instinctively know all of Nicole's hot buttons? But to leave, now, just like that? With her father still direly ill in the hospital and with Nate still holding the DVD over her head?

"Okay, I'll think about it," she conceded.

"You will? Oh, that's marvelous." She gave Nicole the flight time and details. "I'll expect to see you in the departure lounge, then. I can't wait."

Cynthia hung up before Nicole could say another word and Nicole replaced the handset of the phone on its station, a sensation of numbness enveloping her body.

Her life was in tatters. Could her mother's offer be the new beginning she really, desperately, needed? Could she just walk away and say to hell with the consequences of what would happen when Nate gave her father the DVD? She had no doubt he would do it. If she'd learned anything about Nate in this time, it was just how far he was prepared to go to get what he wanted. He wouldn't rest until he'd pulled her family down from its pedestal. She'd already done her part—he didn't need her anymore. When you got right down to it, she was as disposable to him as she was to her father.

Was she prepared to let him hurt her father like that without even trying to interfere? Was she ready to end their affair, once and for all? Could she really, in all honesty, walk away?

Nate woke to an empty bed. Nicole had been sound asleep when he'd come in last night, a little the worse for wear after a few drinks with his hard-drinking clients. His head gave him a solid reminder that drinking on an empty stomach was not conducive to clear brain function the next day. He felt across the bed. Her side was stone cold. A glance at the bedside clock confirmed it was much later than they usually rose. Obviously she'd left him to it and gone into the office already.

He dragged himself from the bed and through to the kitchen where he downed the better part of the liter of orange juice that was in the fridge, then grabbed a banana from the fruit bowl. It was all he had time for. He'd have to make up for it later in the day.

Showering and dressing took more effort than he wanted to admit and, concerned he may still be over the safe driving limit, he caught a taxi to the office. Nicole had her car there so they could travel home together at the end of the day.

"Is Miss Wilson not with you this morning?" April asked as he entered the office.

Nate felt the first pang of warning. "Isn't she already in the office?"

"No, she left a note for me saying she wouldn't be in. I thought she would be arriving with you."

Nate felt his blood run cold in his veins. She'd been into the office already?

"Let me know if she calls, will you?" he directed as

he strode through to his office and rang the concierge of the apartment building.

Five minutes later he had confirmation that her car had left the parking garage a little after five this morning. Another call confirmed she'd swiped in at the office block parking floor shortly after, but that she'd left again within ten minutes. Which begged the question. Where the hell was she now?

He punched the redial on his office phone for the seventh time this morning, only to get the same automated message—that her phone was either switched off or outside of the calling area. He thought about his own cell phone, which had been damnably silent all morning, and reached into his pocket.

Sometime during the night he'd turned it off while he was out and hadn't turned it back on again. He must have been more intoxicated than he'd realized. Nate thumbed the on button and waited for the phone to power up. The instant it had connected to its service provider the screen flashed up—one missed call, one message. Cursing himself for all kinds of idiocy, he hit the numbers required to play the message. Nicole's shaking voice filled his ears.

"I can't stay with you anymore, Nate. It's slowly killing me inside. Do what you like with the DVD. I don't care anymore. I just know that if I don't get some distance, from you, from everyone, I'm going to go insane. All my life I've tried to be everything for everyone. I even had to do it with you, but I can't do it anymore, not now, not ever again. It's all too much. I need to take care of *me* and to learn to put myself first for a change. In fact, I need to find out who I really am, and what I want. I'm sick to death of being told.

My mother has asked me to go with her to Adelaide. Please don't bother trying to contact me again."

She'd left the message at about six o'clock this morning and it sounded as if she was crying toward the end, as if she was teetering on the edge of a breakdown. Nate felt every muscle in his body clench as the urge to protect her fired through him. He had to find her, needed to find her. As vulnerable as she was right now, she needed a champion. Someone to watch over her while she got her act back together. Someone like him. Certainly not someone like Cynthia Masters-Wilson.

Nate remembered the GPS device in her phone, the one that could track where she was at any given time. He called through to his IT guy, Max, who promised to get on it and let him know within the next few minutes where her phone was. In the meantime, Nate hit the search function on his desktop computer and keyed in Auckland International Airport's departures. Hopefully he wouldn't be too late to stop her from leaving on the flight for Adelaide.

Hope died a swift and sudden death when he saw the only direct flight to Adelaide that morning had departed at eight o'clock. The time she left the apartment, the time she'd left the message for him—it all fit with her being on that flight out of the country. The flight with her mother.

Anger and frustration vied for dominance as he weighed up the idea of booking the next available plane to Australia and making his way to Adelaide to get Nicole back. He wouldn't put it past Nicole to refuse to see him, though, nor her mother to prevent him from making any contact with her. Even if he could track her now it wouldn't be much use to him.

His phone rang on his desk and he swept the receiver up.

"Nate, the tracker shows this address for the phone. Are you sure she's not hiding in your office somewhere?"

Nate bit back the growl of frustration at his computer geek's humor. He reached across and opened a drawer where Nicole had often put her things during the day. There, in all its totally specced-up splendor, lay her cell phone. A sticky note on the screen said, *I won't be needing this anymore,* in Nicole's handwriting. Nate slowly slid the drawer closed and thanked Max for the information, then hung up the phone and, propping his elbows on the desk, rested his head in his hands.

The headache he'd woken with was nothing compared to how he felt now. He closed his eyes for a moment and thought hard about what he should do next. Flying to Adelaide was a definite option, but before he did that he needed some ammunition behind him and what better ammunition than her brother's support?

Nate went to grab his keys, then cursed anew as he remembered he'd left his car at the apartment. Not to worry, there was a taxi rank near the office block. The fare to Parnell and Wilson Wines would be a short one but he'd make it worth the driver's while.

"I want to see Judd Wilson," he demanded as he walked past the reception desk at Wilson Wines about fifteen minutes later.

"Mr. Wilson isn't taking appointments today," the girl behind the desk stated very primly, her expression changing to one of outrage as Nate totally ignored her and started to climb the stairs that led to the management offices of the two-storied building. "Wait, you can't go up there!"

"Just watch me," he said, ascending the stairs two at a time.

At the top of the stairs he caught sight of a woman he recognized as Anna Garrick. Raoul's reporting had been spot-on as usual. The woman was attractive, not unlike Nicole in coloring, but her hair was a little lighter and she was a bit shorter, too.

"Mr. Hunter?" she asked, a startled expression on her face before she pushed it back under a professional facade.

"Where is Wilson? I need to see him."

"Mr. Wilson is still in hospital and visitors are restricted to immediate family only."

"No," he huffed in frustration, "not Charles Wilson, I want to see Judd Wilson, right now."

"Well, then," she said, now appearing completely unruffled. "If you would like to take a seat I'll check if he can see you."

"I'm not waiting. Just show me where he is. This is important."

"Is that so?" Another male voice sounded across the carpeted foyer. "Don't worry, Anna, I'll see him in my office."

Nate couldn't help but intercept the look that passed between the two of them. Questioning his presence, for sure, but there was something more between them. Something that made him feel very much on the outside.

"Where's Nicole?" he demanded, not taking time for introductions or finesse.

"Why don't you come into my office and we'll talk, hmm?"

Judd Wilson gave him a cool blue stare, one that reminded him that he was on their turf right now and in no position to be making demands. With ill-concealed frustration he moved into the room Judd had gestured him into and seated himself in a chair opposite a large mahogany desk. If Jackson Importers was everything that was modern and current, Wilson Wines was the opposite. There was a sense of longevity about the fixtures and fittings, even about the building itself. As if they'd been here awhile and they would be here for quite a while still to come.

The sensation that filled him now was not unlike envy. This should have been part of his father's business, too, part of his legacy. But he didn't have time to dwell on old bitterness and recriminations. Right now he had one priority. Nicole, and her whereabouts.

"Now, how about you tell me what it is you want?" Judd said from the other side of the desk, his gaze still unfriendly.

"Nicole's gone. I need to find out where she went so I can get her back."

"My sister is a big girl now, Hunter. I think if she cannot be reached by you, then perhaps she simply doesn't want to be."

"She's not herself at the moment. She's been under immense pressure and I don't think she's capable of making a rational decision right now. Please, you must help me," Nate implored, shoving pride to one side for the sake of the woman he loved and cared for more than anyone else in the world.

"Must? I don't think so. Not under the circumstances. She left us to be with you. Now she's left you, too. What makes you think we'd do anything to help you get her back?"

"I think she's gone to Adelaide with your mother."

Judd leaned back in his chair, the lift of one brow his only expression of surprise at the news.

"No, she wouldn't have done that," Anna Garrick's voice came from the door.

"Why not?" Nate asked, confused. Nicole had made the point quite clear in her voice message that her mother had invited her to leave New Zealand with her.

"Because she couldn't, that's why. Her passport is still here in the office safe."

Nate felt all the fight drain out of him. Now he had no idea where Nicole could be. Searching for her would be like looking for a needle in a haystack. He had no rights to find out where she was. She'd left on her own accord, severing all ties with him.

"Thank you," he said brokenly, getting up from his seat and making for the door.

"Hunter, can I ask why you're so desperate to find her?" Judd asked from behind the desk.

"Because I love her, and I've done the most stupid thing in my life by letting her go."

Twelve

The look of shock on Judd's and Anna's faces had been little compensation for the empty days, and nights that stretched ahead. By Friday night Nate was a mess—his concentration shot to pieces, his temper frayed. He'd never been this helpless in his life. Well, at least not since his father's fallout with Charles Wilson, when his whole world had turned upside down.

It didn't help that everything around him reminded him of Nicole. From the lotions and perfume on his bathroom vanity, to the items of clothing that were mixed in with his laundry. Even in the office there was the constant reminder of her phone in his drawer, her laptop neatly sitting on the top of the desk.

Every day since she'd left he'd asked himself where she could be. He'd toyed with reporting her missing to the police, but he was quite certain he'd have been laughed out of the station. After all, she was an adult.

They'd had a fight. The separation that had come next was a natural progression. Except it felt unnatural in every way, shape and form.

Someone had to know where she was. She was a gregarious creature, one who got along with people. A pack animal rather than a loner. He wracked his brains to think of who she could have been in touch with. Only one name came to mind.

Anna Garrick. She'd said very little when he'd been at their office on Tuesday morning. Mind you, he'd been an over-reactive idiot—making demands and being belligerent. Hardly the way to garner respect or assistance. It was possible, too, that Nicole may not have even been in touch with her at that stage, but who was to say she hadn't been in touch since?

The time between making his decision to speak with Anna and arriving at the Wilson home became a blur. As he directed his car up the driveway he couldn't help but admire the enormous replica gothic mansion that loomed at the top. It had taken a hell of lot of hard work to build all of this and then to hold on to it, he knew, and he found himself experiencing a begrudging respect for the man who had held it all together.

He went to the door and lifted the old-fashioned knocker, letting it fall against the brass plate behind it.

A neatly suited man answered the door.

"I'd like to see Ms. Garrick, please," Nate said, after he gave his name.

"One moment please, sir. If you'll just take a seat in the salon, I'll see if she's free."

Nate didn't know if Anna was playing games with him or if she was simply genuinely busy, but he didn't like having to cool his heels for a good twenty minutes before she came into the salon to greet him. He had to remind himself more than once that he needed to keep his impatience in check if he was to find out if she knew where Nicole was.

When she finally deigned to see him she was composed and solicitous, probably more so than he deserved after the last time he'd seen her. She offered him a drink, obviously comfortable in her role as hostess. Nate declined her offer, too filled with nervous energy to do anything but pace the confines of the room. She composed herself on an elegantly covered antique two-seater sofa and eyed him carefully.

"What can I do for you, Mr. Hunter?"

"Nate, please call me Nate."

"Nate, then. What is it that you want?"

He swallowed and chose his words carefully. "Have you heard from Nicole?"

"If I had, do you really think she'd want me to tell you?"

He sighed. "I take it you have, then. Is she—"

"She's fine, but she doesn't want to see you or anyone else right now."

Nate lifted his eyes to Anna's, searching her calm hazel gaze for any sign that she was worried about her friend.

"I need to see her," he said, the words blunt and filled with an edge of pain he couldn't hide.

Anna shook her head. "Isn't it enough to know she's okay?"

"What do you think?" he asked her, letting every raw pain of loss show in his eyes. "I love her, Anna. I have to tell her I'm sorry, and I need to see if she'll give me another chance."

"I would be betraying her trust if I told you where she was. I've already done that once, recently, and I have to tell you that I'm not prepared to do that again. It nearly destroyed our friendship."

"Don't you think I know that? I'm begging you here."

"I can't. She needs to know she can trust me."

Nate felt as if a giant ball of lead had settled in his gut. Anna had been his only hope. "I want her to know she can trust me, too," he said brokenly as he rose to his feet and headed out the room. At the doorway he turned, "Thank you for seeing me. If you talk to her soon, please tell her…ah, hell, don't worry, it wouldn't make a difference, anyway."

The pity in Anna Garrick's eyes cut him straight to his heart. Nicole was lucky to have a friend like her, he told himself as he forced his feet toward the front door and headed down the stairs toward his car.

The heavy tread of rapid footsteps followed him down the stairs.

"Hunter, wait up."

It was Judd Wilson. Nate turned to face him.

"Yeah," he said, without even the will to fake a politeness he certainly didn't feel.

"I know where she is."

Nate felt something leap in his chest. "And you'll tell me?"

"Anna will kill me for this, but someone needs to cut you a break," the other man said. "Anyone can see you're hurting. The two of you need to work this out one way or another. You both deserve that much." He gave Nate an address about a two-hour drive north of Auckland. "Don't make me regret this, Hunter. If you hurt her again, you'll be answering to me."

Nate proffered his hand, and felt an overwhelming

sense of relief when Judd took it. Their shake was brisk and brief. "I owe you," he said solemnly.

"Yes, you do," Judd replied just as gravely. "We can talk about that later."

Nate gave him a nod of assent and headed for his car. He needed to swing by the apartment before driving up to see her. There was something he needed to collect. It was late, but maybe Nicole would still be awake by the time he made it to where she was staying. And if she wasn't, well, then he'd just wait until she was.

Nicole brushed the sand off her feet with an old towel she'd been keeping on the edge of the deck for just that purpose. Late-night walks along the sandy shoreline of Langs Beach had become a habit as she tried to do what she could to exhaust herself into sleep every night.

Since making the decision to leave Nate, and risk the consequences, she'd hardly slept a wink. So far Nate hadn't sent the DVD to her father, she knew that much. Anna had been keeping her up to date on her father's progress and it looked as if he'd turned a corner health-wise. Of course, that could all change if he viewed the thing. And while that preyed on her mind, when she was honest with herself, she knew she wasn't sleeping mostly because she missed Nate. Missed his strength, his solid presence beside her at night.

She sighed as she made her way across the deck, her feet frozen in the frigid night air. She could have worn shoes, probably should have, but she loved the feel of the squeaky white sand beneath her feet and, at this time of night, she could enjoy the sensation completely on her own with only the stars above her for company.

The aged French doors groaned as she opened them to let herself inside the rather decrepit holiday home she'd rented. After she'd left her laptop and the phone Nate had given her at the office, she'd just driven north—stopping only long enough to pay for the toll charge on the Northern Motorway and to pick up a cheap prepaid cell phone from a gas station on the way.

She didn't know what had drawn her to the area, aside from the fact it was near the sea and it was nothing like the west coast beach that Nate's house overlooked. Of course, if her goal had been to avoid reminders of Nate, then she'd failed. She hadn't been able to stop thinking about the man since she'd gotten here.

Nicole secured the door and went through to the kitchen to put on the kettle. Maybe a cup of chamomile tea would make the difference tonight and help her to sleep. She stiffened as she heard the sound of a car's tires rolling along the gravel driveway that led to the house. No one knew she was here but Anna, and she wouldn't have come without calling Nicole first.

The walls of the cottage were thin and she could hear a heavy measured tread come toward the house. A tread that seemed to hesitate on the wooden steps that led to the front door before she heard a solid one-two-three knock on the peeling painted surface.

Her heart hammering in her chest, she moved closer to the front door.

"Nicole, it's me, Nate."

How had he found her? More to the point, now that he had, what was she going to do?

"Nicole, please. I'm not here to hurt you or to argue with you. I just want to talk."

She hesitated a moment before reaching a trembling

hand to the lock at the door and swinging the door open. Shock hit her when she saw him illuminated beneath the bare bulb that lit the front porch. As much as she tried to harden her heart against him, she couldn't help but be concerned at his appearance. He looked as if he hadn't slept or eaten properly in days. Probably much as she looked herself. Except when she looked at him all she wanted to do was comfort him.

She fought against the urge to hold her arms out to him, to offer him respite from the demons that had obviously ridden him this week. Demons that might be similar to those she'd been wrestling with herself—unsuccessfully, too, if her instinctive reaction to him was any indicator. She took a deep breath and forced her hands to stay at her sides.

"You'd better come in," she said stiffly, standing aside and gesturing toward the open-plan living room/kitchen.

The place was basic. One bedroom, one bathroom and everything else all there for anyone to see. The property's saving graces had been its proximity to the beach and a modern lock-up garage where she'd stowed the Mercedes.

"Can I get you a warm drink?"

She didn't want to offer him any alcohol before sending him back on his way again, especially not looking the way he did right now. The last thing she wanted to be responsible for was him having an accident.

"No, thanks," he said, his voice ragged. "How are you, really?"

She poured boiling water over the tea bag in her cup and then took it over to one of the chairs in the lounge. Nate sat down on the sofa opposite.

"I'm okay. Look, I don't know why you're here but you won't change my mind. I meant what I said in my message."

Nate reached inside his jacket pocket and took out a flat case. A case she recognized with dread. He tried to hand it over to her and when she didn't take it—she couldn't risk touching him—he placed it on the scarred coffee table between them. She could see her refusal to take the case had surprised him, perhaps even hurt him.

She looked at the case, lying there, inert on the tabletop. So seemingly nondescript, yet so potentially damaging at the same time.

"It's yours," he said.

"What? A copy?"

"The only copy," he said, lifting his face so his eyes met hers. "I couldn't send it to your father—I couldn't do that to you, Nicole. I want you to know that. I could never hurt you like that. I know I threatened to, more than once. But even if I hadn't fallen in love with you I couldn't have abused your trust of me that way."

A fist clenched tight around her heart. Had she heard him right? Or was this just another ploy to get her back where he wanted her?

"You seemed pretty determined. Why should I believe you've changed your mind now?"

The voice that came from her mouth didn't sound like her at all. It was harsh, unforgiving.

He hung his head. "I don't deserve for you to believe me but I hope that you can find your way clear to understand where I'm coming from." He lifted his head again, his eyes filled with anguish. "I know I've been a total monster. I should have told you from the beginning who I was. I should have left you in the bar that night. But I couldn't. Even then I was compelled to be with you. I wanted you and I had to have you."

Nicole gripped her mug tight, mindless to the heat that stung her fingers. Just hearing him say the words about wanting her had her body beginning to light up in response. The old familiar coil of desire tightening deep inside her, craving his touch. Craving him.

"And once you had me, you used me," she said bitterly.

"I'm sorry. I know it sounds trite and empty and worthless, but please believe me. I am so sorry I treated you that way. If I had the chance again I would do everything differently."

And so would she, Nicole thought. For a start she wouldn't have left the house that night. Wouldn't have stormed away and wouldn't have lost herself in the one man who could hurt her more than any other. The man she'd fallen painfully in love with. Her heart beat faster in her chest as she acknowledged the painful truth for what it was. Hopeless. She couldn't trust him. He was a master at manipulation, he'd borne a grudge against her father for most of his life. How could she even begin to believe his words were anything more than another tool to control her?

"Is that everything?" she asked coolly. She held her body so rigid that she was afraid she'd shatter into a million pieces if he so much as reached across the table and touched her.

"No, it's not everything. I could spend the rest of my life telling you how much I regret treating you so badly and it would never be long enough. I love you, Nicole. I'm ashamed that I had to lose you to admit it to myself, but there you have it. On the beach that day I asked you to marry me. I'd fooled myself into thinking it was for the baby's sake, and hurt you by asking you for all the wrong reasons when I should have just asked you for you. Will you give me another chance? Let me make it up to you. Let me love you the way you deserve to be loved."

Nicole shook her head. It was a slight movement but Nate saw it and recognized it for what it was. He tried one more time.

"Please, don't make your mind up right now. Give it a few more days. Come back to the city, come back to me. Let's try again and this time I promise I'll get it right."

"No," she said, feeling as if her heart would break with verbalizing that one syllable. "I can't, Nate. I can't trust you not to hurt me like that again. Me or my family. I just can't." And she couldn't trust herself, either. She loved him too much. If she went back, if she let herself be with him again, she'd find herself falling back into his plans, for better or for worse. And she wasn't going to do that again.

Nate looked at her for a full minute, her words hanging in the air between them like an impenetrable shield. Then, slowly he nodded and rose from the sofa. She didn't move as he crossed the room and moved down the short hall toward the front door. It wasn't until she heard the snick of the lock as the door reseated in its frame behind him, that the shudders began to rack her body and the sobs rose from deep within.

He was gone. She'd sent him away. It was what she wanted, wasn't it?

Nate walked to his car wrapped in a blanket of numbness. She'd refused him. It was his worst-case scenario come to living, breathing, painful, life. He settled behind the wheel of the Maserati, and switched the wipers on only to turn them off again as they scraped across the dry windscreen. It was only then he realized the moisture he felt on his face had not been from any rain outside, but from his own tears.

He started the car and eased it up the driveway, away from the house, away from Nicole, swiping at his cheeks and eyes as he did so. He felt as if he was leaving his soul behind, as if he was just a shell now. An empty shell. She'd completed him and he hadn't even had the good sense to know it or appreciate it until it was too late.

At the top of the driveway he looked back, hoping against hope that she might be silhouetted in the doorway, that she might beckon to him to come back. If she did, then together they could find a way to work past the damage he'd wrought. Instead, he saw the outside light extinguish, and with it his last remaining hope.

He blinked hard. He'd lost her. He'd abused her trust, he'd threatened her family. He had gotten exactly what he deserved.

Nate turned the car onto the winding road that would eventually lead him back to State Highway One, back to Auckland. Back to a life lived alone with his grand, empty plans for revenge.

His eyes burned in their sockets by the time he crossed the Auckland Harbor Bridge and turned off toward the Viaduct Basin. Weariness dragged at his body as he let himself into the apartment, a place that felt empty without Nicole inside. As exhausted as he was, sleep was the last thing on his mind. Somehow he had to find a way to convince Nicole she could trust him and that his love for her was real. There had to be a way, there just had to be, because he couldn't imagine the rest of his life without her by his side.

It simply wasn't an option.

Thirteen

Nate straightened from his car outside the Wilson family home. He hadn't slept all night and was running on pure adrenaline right now. He hammered at the front door and stood back in the portico waiting for someone to respond.

It took a while but eventually the door swung open to reveal Judd Wilson dressed in pajama bottoms and a robe. His hair was rumpled, as if he'd run his fingers through it in an attempt to tidy it before answering the door.

"Good grief, man, have you any idea what time it is?" he grumbled at Nate.

"Look, I know it's early but I had to talk to you. This is too important to wait."

"You'd better come in, then." Judd gave him a hard look. "Have you seen yourself this morning?"

Nate grimaced in response. He knew he looked

about as rough as he felt. He hadn't shaved or combed his hair and he was still in the clothing he'd worn last night.

"Judd? Who is it?" Anna's voice came from the top of the staircase.

"It's Natc Hunter."

"And Nicole? Is she all right?"

Anna came down the stairs, a dressing gown wrapped about her and tied with a sash at her waist.

"Nicole was fine when I left her," Nate ground out. "She doesn't want a bar of me but I'm hoping that we can change that, together."

Judd and Anna exchanged a look before Judd spoke. "You need to fight your own battles, Hunter. My sister is responsible for her own choices."

"I know, but I have a proposal I think you might find worth listening to. Something that will benefit you and Wilson Wines, and that just might show Nicole how much I care."

"Sounds like something best done on a full stomach with a decent cup of coffee inside you," Anna said. "Judd?"

"Sure, come through to the kitchen," Judd agreed.

"We gave our house staff the weekend off, so I hope you don't mind if things are a little more basic than we can usually offer," Anna said as she pushed open the swing doors that led into the spacious modernized kitchen.

"Food is the least of my worries," Nate said, lowering himself into one of the kitchen chairs and pulling a sheaf of papers from his coat pocket. "Please don't go to any bother on my account."

As Anna began to make coffee, Nate started to outline his plan. Judd remained silent through most of it, only stopping Nate every now and then to ask him to clarify one point or another. By the time Anna slid plates of French toast and bacon in front of them both, and topped up their coffees, he was wrapping up.

"So, to sum it all up, I suggest that we amalgamate Jackson Importers and Wilson Wines and go forward as one powerful entity for the future, rather than two companies, which are absorbed in competing with one another. It's how it was meant to be all along, it's up to us to make it that way again."

"Why?" Judd asked. "I mean, the idea is definitely worth exploring, but why now?"

"Because I don't see why we should continue to be victims of our fathers' falling out."

"Your fathers?" Anna asked. "You're—?"

"Yes, I'm Thomas Jackson's son."

Judd leaned back in his chair and gave Nate a hard look. "You're certain you want to do this?"

"I've never been more certain of anything in my life," Nate said emphatically.

"You realize I can't do anything without discussing this with my father and with Nicole."

"I understand that. If possible, I'd like to be there when you talk to your father. I think it's time that the past be firmly put to bed. That all the bitterness be dissolved once and for all. It's hurt too many people for too long. It has to stop."

Nicole missed Nate with an ache that went painfully deep. Nights were fractured with dreams of him, days were filled with trying to forget him. But try as she might, she failed miserably. If only they could have met under normal circumstances, without the stupid feud between their families. If only she could trust that he loved her for herself and not out of some twisted sense of revenge. A person didn't let go of that much animosity easily.

She'd thought that getting away from him, getting away from the city would help. But it hadn't helped a bit. If anything it had only served to magnify her feelings for him. Without anything else to distract her, he was all she could think about. Especially after he told her he loved her—and she'd had to send him away.

Maybe she should get a dog, she pondered as she sat on the deck outside the cottage in the watery sunshine and watched a local resident throwing a stick for his dog on the beach. Even as she considered it she knew it couldn't replace the hole in her heart loving Nate had left. Loving him? How could she love him? He'd virtually kidnapped her, had held her against her will, had forced her to work with him instead of where she rightfully belonged. She made a mental note to look up Stockholm syndrome as soon as she could access a computer. She had to find some reason for this irrational attachment to the man.

But was it so irrational? Their attraction that night at the bar had been mutual and instant. Fierce. At least it had been on her side. His? Well, the jury was still out on that one. He'd been following an agenda, hadn't he?

Seeing him last night was tough. Had their circumstances been any different, had he not been so bent on revenge for what her father had done, she'd have dragged him to the tiny bedroom and laid him bare upon the covers of the double bed and taken her time in punishing him slowly for his behavior.

Her body flushed with heat at the thought. Heat that was rapidly diminished by the cool breeze coming in off the ocean. Exercise, she needed exercise. Anything to wear her out and distract her from her thoughts. She grabbed her puffy jacket from inside the cottage and pulled on a pair of sneakers before heading north up the beach. The wind had risen by the time she reached the end and started to walk back, bringing with it the scent of rain.

By the time she got to the cottage the rain was driving across the sand. She hastened inside, taking her jacket off in the tiny bathroom and hanging it over the shower rail to dry. Making her way to the kitchen, she put on the kettle for a warming cup of tea, as she did so she noticed her phone flashing that she had a message.

Not just one message. Several. And several missed calls, as well. All of them from Anna. What could be so important on a Saturday morning? she wondered. She knew it wasn't her father. He was making steady progress at the hospital and they were even talking about him coming home soon. Dialysis would be a major part of his future but at least he had a future. The messages were all the same—Anna asking Nicole to call her back right away. Her friend sounded excited, but not upset, Nicole noted. She poured her cup of tea and took the cup and her phone over to the sofa where Nate had sat last night, the stuffing so worn that the imprint of his body was still there.

Before she could stop herself, Nicole reached a hand to where he'd been sitting, as if she could somehow sense the man in the impression he'd left behind. A particularly strong gust of wind drove against the beachside windows of the house, making her jump and shaking her from her reverie. She had a call to make. She didn't need to be thinking about Nate. Not now, not ever.

Anna answered the phone on the first ring. "Nic, Judd needs to speak to you. Hold on and I'll put him on."

Judd's warm deep voice filled her ear. "How's it going?"

"It's okay. The weather's rubbish but aside from that I'm doing all right." Ironic, she thought, one of the few conversations she should have with her brother and it should be about the weather.

"Glad to hear it. Look, I'll cut to the chase. I have some important Wilson Wines business to discuss with you but I don't want to do it over the phone. Can you come into the office on Monday? I'd really rather do this face-to-face."

Monday? She could do that. It wasn't as if she had any other pressing social engagements on her calendar, she thought cynically.

"Sure, what time?"

"Let's say eleven. That should give you plenty of time to get down here, shouldn't it?"

"I'll be there."

Judd wasted no further time on any pleasantries, severing the call almost immediately after her confirmation. Well, it wasn't as if they had a normal brother-sister relationship. They hadn't ever had the chance. She wondered what it was he wanted to discuss. Hopefully it would have something to do with her coming back to Wilson Wines and reassuming her position there. Then, maybe, she could undo some of the damage she'd done with her work for Jackson Importers.

Monday morning rolled around slowly and Nicole was on the road earlier than she needed be. After another night plagued with dreams of Nate, she couldn't wait to have something else to distract her. The traffic heading into Auckland was that and then some.

Pulling into her usual car park at Wilson Wines felt strange, but that was nothing to what it felt like walking back into the building. Everything was still exactly the same. She didn't know why she'd expected it to have changed in any way, except that she had been through so much since the last time she'd been here that she felt that time should have marked its passage here somehow.

Their receptionist told her to go on upstairs and that Judd was waiting for her. Anna met her at the top of the stairs and gave her a quick hug.

"Do you know what this is about?" Nicole asked.

"It's better you hear it from Judd," she said with a smile. "He's waiting in your dad's old officc."

"Old office? So he's not coming back?"

"It's unlikely. Even though he's a lot better he's not up to the day-to-day demands of business anymore."

Nicole was shocked. Her father had always been invincible. A powerhouse. They'd butted heads over his unwillingness to accept her ideas for advancement but, that said, she couldn't imagine the company without her father at the helm.

"Is that what Judd wants to talk to me about?"

"Go and see him," was all Anna would say.

Squaring her shoulders, Nicole walked toward her father's office. Judd's office, now, she supposed. He got up from behind the desk when she knocked and pushed open the door.

"I'm glad you could come," he said, first holding out his hand and then drawing her into his arms for a swift embrace. "We haven't exactly been able to get off to a good start, have we?"

"No," Nicole said, a nervous smile on her face. Considering she'd pretty much been pouting like a spoiled brat when he'd arrived, followed a few days later by her storming out of the house, his comment was a mastery of understatement.

"Hopefully we can amend that, if you're willing?"

"Sure. Who knows, we might even like each other."

Judd flashed her a smile and in it she could see a hint of their father's humor. It made her instantly feel more comfortable with him. It was a comfort she clung to as he started to talk about what he'd asked her in to discuss.

"You mean this was Nate's idea? That he *wants* to amalgamate the businesses?"

She got up from her seat and walked over to the window that looked out over the city. Nate? Merge Jackson Importers with Wilson Wines? What ever happened to his passion for revenge? By his own admission it had driven him since he was a child. Why stop now? They both knew that the deal was to Wilson Wines's advantage. The company was in a weakened managerial position with Judd inexperienced with the firm and her father incapable of reassuming his role. If Jackson Importers wanted to put them out of business, now was the time. Why was Nate throwing them a lifeline, instead?

"It was his idea, and after discussing it with him and going over the figures, I'm inclined to accept. It makes sense. Not only that, but it closes a door that's been open too long. It gives both our families a chance to heal."

Nicole shook her head. She couldn't believe it. "Are

you sure he doesn't have some ulterior motive behind this?"

"We stand to gain far more than he does at the moment. I'm sure you're even more aware of that than he is. You've worked with him. You know how strong they are in the marketplace, here and overseas. He's done that. With him running the whole company, they're poised to grow even stronger. Of course, Wilson Wines brings a respected name and established reputation to the table—but unless we modernize and expand, our company will grow weaker while his grows stronger. This is just what we need to get back on track."

She sat back down in her seat. Could Nate have been telling the truth when he came to see her on Friday night? Was he really letting all that resentment and hostility toward her family go, just like that? Was this a chance to finally mend the gaping rifts in her family life and allow her to feel whole again?

Was this the chance for her and Nate, after all?

"And you want an opinion from me today? Really, I need some time to think about this," she said.

"Look, I know it's a lot to take in. Goodness only knows Anna and I have made the most of having the past couple of days to begin to get used to the idea. But it's not just my decision to make. It affects you, as well."

Nicole felt the old acrimony rise in her throat again. "No, it doesn't. You have the controlling share in Wilson Wines. Dad holds the balance. It's your decision, Judd, whether you want that or not."

Judd lifted an envelope from the top of the desk and handed it to her. "Here, maybe what's inside will help you make up your mind."

She took the envelope. "What is it?"

He laughed. "Nothing that'll hurt you, Nicole. Seriously, just open it."

She slid a nail under the flap and ripped the envelope open. Inside was a single sheet of paper. A company share transfer, to be exact. Her eyes widened as she read the terms of the transfer. Judd was giving her everything their father had given him. Not half, not less than half. All of it. If she signed this paper she would have the controlling share and the decision as to how Wilson Wines would go forward.

"Have you lost your mind?" she asked.

"No, if anything I've found it. I learned the hard way that a life bent on revenge is no life at all. I think that Nate has recently discovered much the same thing. I nearly lost Anna over my need to make our father pay for abandoning me and our mother. For denying me my birthright until it suited him to get Anna to bring me back. I don't want to lose out on anything else. Neither does Nate.

"We've all been hurt, Nicole. But we deserve to be happy—*really* happy. I know I'm doing the right thing in giving this to you and I know you'll do the right thing in return."

"And are you happy now, Judd?"

"With Anna, yes. I'm going to marry her, Nicole. I know you two are close and I want you to know I'm going to look after her."

Nicole sat back in her chair and looked at him, and smiled again. Her first genuine smile since she'd arrived today. Maybe her first genuine smile in a long, long time. "You'd better, or you'll answer to me."

"Noted," he said with a nod. "Now, how about you take the next day or so to think about things? Anna has a folder ready for you to take with you so you can analyze Nate's proposal in depth."

Nicole sat in her car in the car park still shocked by the news Judd had given her today, especially his intention to marry her best friend. When pressed, Anna had admitted her love for Judd in return, but said they weren't going to make a public announcement until Charles was home and settled again. They'd already sought his blessing, which had been rapidly forthcoming, apparently. Which left Nicole exactly where?

She had plenty to think about, she realized as she started the car and backed out of the car space. It wasn't until she'd headed for the motorway interchange that would lead her back up north that she made a sudden decision to turn around and drive back the way she'd come.

The Auckland City Hospital car park was pretty empty given the time of day, and it didn't take her long to find a space. In no time she was in an elevator, heading for her father's ward. She only hoped that he'd agree to see her. If, as Judd had said, they all deserved happiness, then it was time for some truths between her and her father, especially the truth about her more recent behavior. Only with everything out in the open could the wounds—both old and more recent—finally heal.

She fought to hide her shock when she saw him lying against his pillows, his eyes closed. The ravages of illness had made him lose a great deal of weight and his skin held an unhealthy pallor. She could have lost him. Would have never had the chance to make amends. And all for what?

"Dad?" she said tentatively as she closed the door to the private room behind her.

His eyes shot open and Nicole was relieved to see they were full of their usual fiery intelligence.

"You came back."

His tone of voice gave nothing away but she caught the telltale tremor around his mouth. And was that a hint of moisture in his eyes?

"Oh, Dad. Of course I came back. I miss you."

"Ah, my little girl. Come here," he said, his voice shaking as he parted the side of the bed and opened his arms.

Nicole shifted to his side and let herself be enveloped by his hug, mindful of the monitors and tubes he was still attached to. But all that was peripheral to the fact that she was here, that he hadn't sent her away again.

"I've missed you, too. I've had plenty of time to think, lately, and I know I owe you an apology. Several apologies, actually."

"No, Dad, it's okay," she protested. "I've always acted first, thought second. I should have stayed. We'd have worked it out."

"No, it's not okay. I never gave you a fair shot, did I? I was so angry with you for defecting to the enemy after Judd came home that the sight of you in the emergency department just made me see red. But I was wrong. When all is said and done, family comes first. I should never have pushed you away in the first place. I should have included you when I decided to approach Judd about coming back home. It was wrong of me to make those decisions, decisions that affected you, without any consultation as a family."

"It's okay, Dad, I understand. It hurt me, but I do

understand. You never got the chance to raise Judd the way you wanted to. All of that was stolen from you."

"Stolen with a single lie," he said sadly. "Did you know that? Your mother told me Judd wasn't my son. To my shame I believed her and when she named my best friend as Judd's father, I stupidly believed that, too. So many years lost, so much time wasted."

"But you can make up for that now," she urged, shocked at the way his body trembled and happier than ever that she had chosen not to run away from her problems to Australia with Cynthia. She did want to meet her family at some point—get to know her cousins and uncles and aunts, but cementing things with her family here took priority.

"For what time I have left," Charles replied. "You know, Nicole, pride is a terrible thing. Because of pride I lost my wife, my son, my best friend and my health. If I had my time over again, I'd do so much differently. Maybe then I could have been the husband Cynthia needed. I've made some bad decisions in my life, not least of which with you.

"I know you think I was holding you back at Wilson Wines and, yes, I suppose I was. But I could just see so much of myself in you. You were so driven, so determined to grow the business to the exception of everything else in your life. I've always wanted the best for you but when I saw you going down the same road that I went, I had to do something to hold you back. You deserve more than just a business. You deserve a life enriched with a husband and children and steadiness at home—not all your energy driven into work and serving the mighty dollar as I have done."

"But I love my work at Wilson Wines, Dad. I've missed it."

"I thought limiting your requirements at work would push you to invest more of your time and energy into relationships. I shouldn't have made that decision for you. I'll wager you had more freedom with that Nate Hunter than you had with me. Don't bother denying it. He saw a good thing and he took advantage of it."

"Dad, there's something you should know about him."

"Beyond the fact he's a fearsome business opponent? Can't help but admire him for that, if nothing else."

She didn't know how to phrase this carefully, so she just came out with it. "He's Thomas's son."

Her father closed his eyes briefly before giving a deep sigh. "That explains a lot," he said quietly. "Another life harmed. Clearly I owe him an apology, too. It can't have been easy for him growing up. Are the two of you an item?"

Nicole shook her head. "We were. But I ended it. He wanted me for all the wrong reasons."

"And what are those?" Charles urged.

"Revenge against you, for one thing," she admitted. It sounded so pathetic when she put it into words to the man it had been directed against. But that's pretty much what it all came down to in the end, wasn't it?

Charles chuckled. "A chip off the old block, hmm? Well, I can't say I blame him. He had just cause."

Nicole could barely believe her ears. All his life her father had spoken in derogatory terms about Thomas Jackson and now he laughed about Nate's vendetta?

"Aren't you angry?"

"Not anymore," he said with a deep sigh. "There's a lot to be said for facing your mortality. It makes you see things differently."

"Judd gave me his controlling share of the company," she blurted.

"Did he? Well, that was his choice to make. I should never have created such a divisive position between you two but it was so important to me to bring Judd home, and I really did want to force you to create some balance in your life."

By the time she left the hospital it was growing late. Despite a few dark looks from the nursing staff, she'd been allowed to stay at her father's side all afternoon and they'd talked to one another as they'd never talked before. As she clipped her seatbelt across her chest she recognized that the feeling inside her now was one of happiness and acceptance of her position in her father's heart. She held all the cards now. She was no longer a pawn, she was the player.

Which left her only one last thing to do.

Fourteen

Her headlights picked out the possum ahead of her on the winding curve of road. Thankfully she avoided it without incident and could focus her attention to the confrontation she had ahead. Nate hadn't been at the office when she'd called, nor had he been at the apartment when she'd stopped in there. Which only left the beach house.

How appropriate that this would end where it had begun.

She cruised through the bends in the dark ribbon of tarseal slowly, more familiar with being a passenger on the journey than the driver. It was an interesting analogy for her life. Despite her efforts to get ahead and to be noticed in her life, she'd always allowed herself to be acted upon rather than to take charge and be fully responsible for her own behavior.

The idea that she was free of her previous constraints, constraints she'd allowed even into adulthood, was intensely liberating. Even so, she felt as if hummingbirds danced in her stomach as she neared the driveway to Nate's house. She pulled up outside the garage door and walked around to the main entrance, pressing the door bell several times in quick succession.

The door opened.

"Nicole!"

Nate looked stunned to see her, but she felt his eyes roam her as if he were touching her. Her traitorous body responded in kind. She dropped her eyes from his, hoping he hadn't seen her reaction reflected in her gaze.

"We need to talk," she said brusquely. "May I come in?"

He stood aside and gestured for her to take a seat in the living room. "Can I get you anything?" he offered.

"This isn't a social visit," she said firmly. It was important to her that she set the parameters right from the start. "I need to know something."

"Ask me. I'll tell you whatever I can."

"Are you still playing some game with my family with your proposal to join the companies together?"

He looked surprised. "You know about that already?"

"Judd called me down from Langs Beach to discuss it. He's given me a written report, which I haven't read yet. I needed to talk to you first so I can decide whether to read it, or whether to use it to light a fire, instead."

He gave a disparaging laugh. "It's not a game—it's anything but."

"So this is really what you want?"

He looked her square in the eye and she could see

the truth burning there in those sherry-brown depths. "Yes."

"And you're not doing this to somehow undermine my family or to hurt them?"

"No, I'm not."

She took a deep breath. "Or to hurt me?"

"Never to hurt you, Nicole. That was *never* my intention. I wanted to give you every opportunity to succeed all along."

"Why are you doing this, then?"

Nate sighed and leaned forward, resting his elbows on his thighs and clasping his capable hands in front of him. His gaze was fixed on her face, as if he was willing her to believe him.

"I made the suggestion for three very good reasons. The first is that it makes sound business sense. If we stop competing with one another we'll be in a stronger position when it comes to securing new business—one less player in the market should give us an edge on pricing. It's all in the report, when you read it you'll see what I'm talking about."

Nicole nodded. "Okay, so that's one reason. What about the others?"

"It was time to stop the feud. It's hurt too many people for too long. One of us had to make the first move. I decided it was time for me to let go of my grudge. Sure, I had a tough upbringing, a lot of kids did. I still had more advantages than most. Even while my mother and I were living hand to mouth my father was ensuring that I still had the best education that he could provide for me. And having to struggle a little made me tough, it made me determined. It made me the man I am today. Flawed, sure, but I know what's right, and letting go of the anger, letting go of the pain—it all had to happen so we can move forward.

"Pride can be a killer. I didn't want it to destroy every last thing I held dear."

Nicole nodded. Hadn't her father spoken along the same lines? She said as much to Nate.

He nodded gently. "You know, I want to see him if he's agreeable. We have a lot to talk about."

"I think he'd like that. I told him today about you. I was sure he was going to tell me that he'd be quite happy to carry on the competition between Wilson Wines and Jackson Importers indefinitely, but this latest illness has changed him, too. It's altered his perspective on things."

She paused for a moment, reflecting on the things her father had said, then reminded herself she was here for a reason. "What's the third reason?" Nicole pushed.

"The third reason? You already know that one."

She looked at him, puzzled. She already knew? When she said nothing, Nate continued.

"I love you."

"That's it?" She felt her skepticism rise.

"Yeah, that's it," he said with a deprecating chuckle. "Although I never quite expected to get that response."

"That's not what I mean—" she started to protest, but he cut her off.

"Nicole, I knew that after what I'd put you through, for you to believe that I love you would take an action on my part to prove it, beyond any shadow of a doubt. And I was already working at a disadvantage, because of the mistakes I'd made in our relationship. When I asked you to marry me on the beach out here, when I thought you were carrying my baby, I was prepared to do whatever I could to protect you and provide for you and our child, but I know I went about it all wrong. You have to understand. I grew up illegitimate. Sure, I know that wasn't the worst thing that could happen to me and I certainly wasn't the only kid in class from a single-parent family—but I wanted more for my child than I had."

He got up and began to pace the room, shoving his hands through his hair and sending it into disarray before pushing them deep into the pockets of his trousers. Nicole could see the outlines of his fists through the fine wool of his pants, could sense the tension in every line of his body.

"Go on," she urged softly. "Tell me the rest."

He stood where he was, staring out the window toward the dark shoreline, to where the moon and stars lit the foam of the waves that curled and raced inexorably onto the sand.

"I wanted to ensure that my child never wanted for anything the way I wanted, but at the same time I wanted him or her to know they were loved. You see, even though we struggled, even though I had to put up with the bullying at school because I was different—because my mother was seen shopping at the local thrift store or because one of the boys' mothers delivered our food parcels while doing her bit for the community—through all that I always knew I was loved. Always. I will never be an absentee father to my children. I will be a part of their lives and I will be there when they need me."

Nate turned and faced Nicole again. "That's the way I love, Nicole. With everything I am. It's the way I love you. I asked you to marry me without even fully understanding just how much a man could love a woman, but I learned that, and more, when you left me. You're everything to me and I knew that I had to prove that to you, even if it meant letting go of everything I'd always believed while I was growing up.

"That's it. I love you. Pure and simple."

Nicole sat there, stunned. What he'd just told her was anything but pure and simple. It showed the depths of the man before her. The man she'd rejected and who hadn't given up.

This wasn't the same person who'd calculatedly brought her back here on that fateful night just over a month ago, a man who was prepared to blackmail her over an illicit weekend of wild pleasure just to hurt her father. He'd changed. The old Nate would never have dreamed of combining their two businesses together to form one perfectly strong whole.

This was a man who loved her. Truly loved her. And she'd changed, too, into someone who wasn't afraid to love him back. She pushed herself to her feet and moved to stand in front of him.

"I believe you," she whispered, her voice shaking with the depth of her own love for him. A love she could finally acknowledge to both herself and to Nate. She raised one hand and cupped his cheek. "I love you, too."

The sound he made was part human and part something else. He turned his face into her hand, pressing his lips against her palm.

"It's more than I deserve," he said brokenly.

"We deserve each other. We're neither of us perfect, but together, maybe we can cancel out the bad and be nothing but good. Love me, Nate. Love me forever."

"You can count on it."

He pulled his hands from his pockets and swooped her up into his arms, carrying her to the bedroom where they'd already created so many special memories. This time they undressed one another slowly, painstakingly—taking their time to kiss and caress every part of each other as they bared skin. As if it was their first time—a voyage of discovery.

When neither of them could wait any longer, Nate covered her body with his own, pausing only to reach for a condom. Nicole stayed his hand.

"No condom," she said. "I want whatever naturally comes next in our lives and I don't want any more barriers between us."

"Are you sure?" he asked, his body rigid beneath her hands as she stroked his buttocks with a featherlight touch and then traced her fingers up the muscles that bracketed his spine. She relished the strength of him, loved that he was all hers.

"Certain," she whispered as she lifted her mouth to his, claiming his lips in a kiss that imbued everything she felt at that moment, and when he slid inside her she knew she'd made the right decision. Nothing had ever felt as good as this contact between them, heat to heat, nothing but him and her.

Nate started to move and she met him, stroke for stroke, her cries of pleasure intensifying as he pushed them over the edge of sanity and into another realm where only the two of them existed.

Afterward, they lay still locked together as one. As their breathing slowed and returned to something approaching normal, Nicole lifted a hand and traced the outline of Nate's face. He had never been more precious to her than he was at this moment.

"Do you think we'd have ended up like this without our parents' falling out?"

Nate smiled. "Who knows? I'd like to think so. I

know there's no one out there in this world for me, but you."

She snuggled against him. "Why do you think she did it?"

"She?"

"My mother. Why do you think she lied to my father for all those years? She drove a wedge between everyone without a second thought."

"You know that for sure?"

"Dad didn't tell me all of it, but he did say that her lie was responsible for what happened."

Nate shifted onto his back, pulling Nicole with him. "I suspected she instigated it all. I couldn't imagine anyone else but her having that power over them. Maybe she resented the time Charles put into the business—who knows—but it's no wonder he reacted the way he did to what he perceived as the ultimate betrayal from his best friend."

"But for her to have let it go on this long…I just don't understand it. Why would she do that?"

Nate closed his arms around Nicole and held her tight against him, making a silent vow that nothing would ever separate them again. "She was obviously a very unhappy woman. I'm sorry she never got to have what we have, but we can't let her spoil it for us, either."

Nate pressed a kiss to the top of Nicole's head. "I'm so sorry for everything I did to you, Nicole. I kidded myself that if I gave you everything I thought you wanted that you'd be happy to stay with me. I should have realized you deserved so much more."

"Good thing you got it right this time, then, hmm?" Nicole murmured as she shifted and raised herself above him. "Because I'm going to expect a whole lot of this loving."

"I think I'm man enough for the job." He smiled from beneath her, his body hardening inside her as she rocked gently against him. He gripped her hips with his hands, stilling her motion and his eyes grew serious. "Nicole, I mean it, though. Can you forgive what I did to you?"

"Of course I can, Nate. I already have. We both did things we regret."

"There's one thing I'll never regret," he said, continuing to hold her still. "And that's meeting you. You taught me to open my eyes and to love with all my heart. No conditions, no strings. You will marry me, won't you?"

"Yes," she replied. "I love you, Nate Hunter Jackson, and I will marry you."

"That's good," he replied, "because I'd hate to have to kidnap you all over again."

She laughed, her inner muscles tightening around him as she did so. She'd never felt this happy, or this complete before in her life. She belonged with him, as he did with her. All the security, love and recognition she'd craved all her life lay here with this incredibly special man. Their road together hadn't been smooth so far, but nothing worthwhile in life came easily. She knew that to the very depths of her soul. She also knew she loved him, and that her future would be all the better for having him at her side.

* * * * *